WICKED BEAUTIFUL

WICKED GAMES BOOK 1

J.T. GEISSINGER

Published by J.T. Geissinger, Inc.

ISBN 978-1-7338243-2-3

Cover design by Letitia Hasser, RBA Designs

Editing by Linda Ingmanson

www.jtgeissinger.com

To Jay, for always being there.

Heaven has no rage like love to hatred turned,
nor hell no fury as a woman scorned.
— William Congreve, *The Mourning Bride*

VICTORIA

Bitch: *noun* a slang pejorative for a woman who is belligerent, unreasonable, malicious, a control freak, rudely intrusive, or aggressive.

From behind a Plexiglas podium on the vast, lighted stage in the Broadway Ballroom of the Marriott Marquis hotel in Times Square, I stand looking out, scanning the faces of the twenty-five-hundred women in the audience.

Pride suffuses me. Even after raising the price to two hundred dollars a ticket, I'm still packing these seminars to standing room only.

Man-hating is big business. I've built my entire empire on it.

I lean forward and speak into the microphone. "Ladies, a show of hands, please. How many of you have ever been called a bitch?"

Over two thousand hands shoot into the air.

"Well, congratulations. You're doing something right."

Scattered laughter from the crowd. Smiling, at ease because

I've given this particular speech dozens of times before, I unhook the mic and stroll out from behind the podium, smoothing a stray wrinkle from the perfectly tailored waist of my white Armani suit.

"Let's take a closer look at this definition of *bitch* for a moment." I turn to the large projection screen on the wall behind me. "*Belligerent.* A word meaning hostile, combative, warlike. We all know what *unreasonable* means: uncooperative, unhelpful, difficult."

Grinning, I turn back to the audience. "So far, so good."

More laughter.

"Then we have *malicious*. That's a real baddie. It means intending to do harm, cruel, or unkind. And how about *control freak*? A person who attempts to dictate how everything around her is done. Not so great. *Rudely intrusive* is self-explanatory, then we come to my favorite one. *Aggressive.*"

The smile fades from my face. For a silent beat, I examine the audience, enjoying watching them watching me. I get such a charge from being up in front of so many people, having them hang on my every word. It's almost better than sex.

"The word *aggressive* is commonly only used in reference to rabid dogs, savage dictators, or a woman with an opinion. If a man is aggressive, he'll be described as a go-getter, or ambitious, or even simply masculine. In fact, every word in the definition of *bitch* that you see here is a masculine attribute. Warlike? Difficult? Unkind? Controlling? Those are all the antithesis of what society tells a woman she should be, because they are inherently masculine traits. So when a man calls you a bitch, he's really saying *you're acting like a man.*"

I pause for effect and then say forcefully, "And I'm here to tell you that acting like a man is the only way you'll ever get what you want out of life."

In the ballroom, it's silent as a graveyard. Everyone stares at me, waiting.

2

"This is a man's world, ladies. It might be cliché, but it's the truth. Women are born at a disadvantage. We lack testosterone, the hormone responsible for the urge to build skyscrapers and fly to the moon and go to war. We are conciliators, peacemakers, nurturers. We are self-sacrificing, which is not only ridiculous, but also a ridiculous waste of potential. What we need to be in order to live truly fulfilled, productive lives is *powerful*. Can anyone tell me how a woman becomes powerful? Just shout it out. You don't have to raise your hands."

There are a few calls of "Education!" and "Self-knowledge!" and even "Weight lifting!" which brings on laughs. I laugh too, loving the energy of the room.

"Those are all good examples. But none of them get to the heart of the matter."

I always make sure to use the word *heart*. It's every woman's Kryptonite. Well, that and *love*. But that word is strictly verboten in my seminars.

And in every other part of my life.

"Here's a quote from Roseanne Barr. 'The thing women have yet to learn is that nobody gives you power. You just take it.' Sounds simple enough, right? The problem with that is that it assumes the source of power is outside you. *It isn't.* You already have all the power you need, but you've been giving it away. You've been trading it, bartering it, squandering it, because your need to be *liked* is stronger than your need to honor yourself. Every time you don't speak up if you're disrespected, every time you say 'yes' when you should say 'no,' every time you put someone else's needs or desires ahead of your own, you give away your power. And what do you get in return?"

I wait. The audience leans forward, a collective held in thrall.

"Frustration. Resentment. Anger."

Heads nod. I'm preaching to the choir. Picking up energy, I turn and stride stage right. Every eye in the auditorium follows me.

"Here's a fun statistic. Women are nearly twice as likely as men to suffer from depression. *Twice* as likely. Do you think that's fair?"

When I hold out the mic toward the audience, I get a blistering shout in return.

"No!"

"Of course it's not!" I pace back the way I came, my legs eating up the stage, my hair tumbling over my shoulders, a lioness going in for the kill. Agog, they watch me.

"And can you tell me who NEVER suffers from depression?"

Right on cue, hundreds of voices cry out. "Bitches!"

"That's RIGHT!" I roar. "Bitches *never* suffer from depression! They don't suffer from anything, in fact, because if it makes them unhappy, they *move on*! They don't try to change it, or whine about it, or spend hours with their girlfriends analyzing why. They simply open their hands and let it go!"

Clapping. Ah, how I adore the sound of clapping. It takes a great deal of effort not to break into another grin, but I manage it. I stand with my legs shoulder-width apart in the center of the stage and gaze lovingly at my audience.

Even in my thoughts, I'm careful not to call them my "minions," as my best friend Darcy does. The word is far too disrespectful for a group of people who are putting half a million dollars in my pocket for a few hours of listening to me talk.

"The bitch's motto is, 'After me, you come first.' Whether it's a man, or a job, or a family member, the priority is always her own happiness. In this way, and in this way only, a woman controls her own destiny, and realizes and safeguards her power. She's never at the mercy of anyone else." I pause briefly to let that all sink in. "What you need, ladies, is simply a new interpretation of that old insult for a strong woman. A definition you can truly embrace."

A new graphic flashes on the large projector screen on the wall behind me.

Bitch: *noun* a woman in control of herself, her life, and her destiny, who always gets what she wants.

Shouts of "Amen!" and raucous hoots of approval erupt from the audience. Now I can't help myself. My mouth breaks into a huge smile.

"That's right. A bitch always gets what she wants. A bitch isn't bossy. She's *the boss*. In life, in work, and in relationships, bitches *always* do better. Now let me ask you ladies…"

I throw my shoulders back, lift my hand to the sky, and raise my voice to the rafters.

"Are you ready to become a BITCH?"

The answering screams are deafening. Applause thunders. The audience leaps to its feet.

And I stand laughing on the stage, soaking in the adulation of over two thousand women, thinking there's no way life gets any better than this.

Seven hours later, after the seminar is finished, all the questions have been answered, all the books have been signed, and the last of the audience has finally filtered out the ballroom doors to wreak havoc on the men in their lives with their new, enthusiastically embraced titles of capital-*B* Bitches—and they have the lapel pins, mugs, and bumper stickers to prove it—I'm exhausted.

Unfortunately, I committed to dinner with Darcy tonight at Xengu, the new hot spot in Tribeca. There's no way she'll let me off the hook, no matter how tired I am. Darcy has turned dining out into an art form and a highly lucrative business. She's one of the most successful food bloggers in the States.

She's also the only woman I've ever met who can make a grown man soil his pants in fear at the mere sight of her. If a restaurant gets a thumbs-down review from her, its owner might as well close the doors and start over. She's utterly, unapologetically ruthless.

And brilliant. And hilarious. If there's anyone in my life I'd use the forbidden *L*-word for, it would be her.

I'm back in the lobby of my high-rise, awaiting the private elevator that will take me to the penthouse level, when my cell rings. My assistant, Tabby, is carrying it, along with my Hermès bag, my laptop bag, and my rolling travel bag.

Rule #1: Bitches don't carry their own luggage.

Tabby fishes the cell from her pocket, blows her fire-engine red bangs off her forehead, eyes the readout, and holds the cell out to me.

"It's Darcy."

I take the phone and say cheerfully into it, "Hey, babe!"

In response, I hear a sigh. "Can we please talk about how late you're running? Because I'm not walking into Xengu late. They won't hold the reservation, even for me."

The elevator doors slide open. Tabby and I step inside, and the doors close behind us.

"They wouldn't dare give away your reservation! Don't they know who you are?"

"Right?" agrees Darcy, reveling in her bulldozer reputation. Her voice turns sour. "But apparently the owner isn't fond of food critics, because I was told in no uncertain terms that if I were more than ten minutes late, my reservation would be given away, no matter who I am. This place is on fire right now, girl. They can afford a few bruised egos."

I snort. "Too bad neither of us have egos that can be bruised."

"Don't change the subject! When are you getting there?"

The elevator doors open again to reveal the elegant marble-and-glass foyer of my penthouse. Tabby and I walk inside. She leaves my handbag on the mirrored console against the wall. The rolling luggage bag she takes into my home office, where she'll spend the next several hours going through mail, answering emails, scheduling meetings, and generally making my life easier.

I pay her an ungodly sum of money, but she's worth every cent. I couldn't do what I do without her efficient support. More importantly, she's proven her loyalty time and again, guarding all my secrets, exercising total discretion in the running of my affairs. She's one of only two people on earth I can trust.

The ironclad nondisclosure contract she signed when she came to work for me doesn't hurt.

Still with my phone to my ear, I unbutton my jacket, toss it to the back of a white leather chair in the living room, and head to the master bedroom and my favorite thing in this six-thousand-square-foot ultramodern space I call home: the Jacuzzi bathtub.

"Give me half an hour. If you get there before me, order me a—"

"Filthy Grey Goose martini with three blue cheese olives," she interrupts. "I know. And lemme guess. You'll be wearing white Armani."

I pretend I'm offended. "Are you saying I'm predictable?"

"I'm saying you're anal, V. Why not break out some color once in a while? Maybe a floral print? Or, if you're in the mood to really go for broke, maybe try a drink other than a Grey Goose martini?"

Because, dear friend, there's safety in routine.

"I'll try something else when they make something better. See you soon," I say, and hang up.

I run a bath. When it's ready, I strip out of the rest of my clothes and sink into the steaming water, sighing in pleasure. The only thing that mars my contentment is that my legs are too short to reach the end of the tub, so I have to hold on to the edges so I don't sink.

I wish I had longer legs.

In my mind, I'm six feet tall. In my mind, I'm a Viking warrior. In my mind, I'm a goddess: irresistible, powerful, and—most of all—beautiful.

The reality, however, is that I'm of average height and weight with no particularly interesting features. I admit I do have a good head of thick, dark hair, and straight white teeth. Which, like my crooked nose, weak chin, thin lips, nearsightedness, and flat chest, I had fixed years ago.

Thank God for plastic surgery. Even if I don't look like a swimsuit model, I definitely look completely different from the country mouse I used to be—and that was the goal. There's nothing of my old life left in the new me, and I wouldn't have it any other way.

Rule #2: Fake it 'til you make it, bitch.

I soak in the hot water until the muscles in my shoulders and lower back release their knots. Then I get out, dry off, change into a cocktail dress, do my makeup, and fluff my hair. On my way out, I shout a goodbye to Tabby, who has her head buried in a stack of my mail. I head downstairs to the lobby, where my car and driver await. In eight minutes, I'm walking into the noisy, delicious-smelling entrance of Xengu.

Which is when I see him.

Him.

And the safe, carefully constructed world I've inhabited for the past fifteen years ends with a shock like a slap across the face.

PARKER

I notice her the instant she walks in my front door.

So does my cock. It practically sits up and begs.

"Oh no," says my number two, Bailey, following my gaze. "Not yet, Parker. We've got a million things to get done tonight before you go trolling for your next conquest. We're almost out of caviar *and* salmon, the burners on the second stove aren't working, and Kai is having a meltdown about the quality of the truffles. He says he didn't study at Le Cordon Bleu so he could come work for you and cook with shitty truffles. He's threatening to walk out. Which would be a *major* disaster, considering Darcy LaFontaine is supposed to show up any minute."

Gasping, Bailey grabs me. "Oh God, that's her!"

I would snap at Bailey to stop digging her acrylic talons into my arm, but I can't take my eyes off the woman who just walked into my restaurant.

She's an absolute stunner.

"The gorgeous brunette in white is Darcy LaFontaine? Hmm. Not what I pictured."

"Gorgeous?" With a sniff, Bailey releases me. "I wouldn't call her gorgeous."

I chuckle. "That's because you don't have a dick."

Bailey turns and glares at me. As it's one of her favorite things to do, I ignore it. She's been trying to get me to sleep with her for years, but she's too good an employee for me to take the bait. I don't shit where I eat, so to speak.

Also, she's clingy. I've seen how she is with some of her boyfriends, and I'd chew my arm off before I'd volunteer for that. No matter how pretty they are, needy women have always turned my stomach.

The brunette in white doesn't look needy. Though elegantly dressed, she somehow looks tough. Sharp, smart, and I'll-cut-you tough. In fact, the look she's just sent me seems to indicate she'd like to rip out my throat.

Interesting.

"Seriously, Parker, what's so gorgeous about that girl?" insists Bailey. "Aside from that killer Armani sheath she's wearing—okay, those Louboutins are pretty awesome too—she's just not that pretty."

Translation: I'm jealous of her in every way. I want to wear her skin.

Instead of calling Bailey on that, I say, "She looks like she loves to fuck."

Bailey's mouth drops open. Her head swivels around and she stares at me. "*What?*"

I'm still staring at the brunette. So is nearly every other male around her. Dressed in crisp, pristine white in a sea of dark suits and cocktail dresses, she stands out like a star. I know women, and I know that choice of dress is deliberate. She likes to draw the eye. Everything about her says *Look at me.*

And goddamn, I just can't stop.

"The way she stands, moves, holds herself. Her energy. I can tell she loves men, and she loves to fuck."

Executing a swift, one-hundred-eighty-degree turn in attitude, Bailey sticks up for the mystery woman. She snaps, "I don't think she looks slutty at all, Parker. She looks..." She searches for the word for a moment and then pronounces, "Classy."

"I never said she didn't. Now go tell Kai if he walks out on me, I'll break his kneecaps. Then call Le Cirque and ask Giovanni to send over some truffles and caviar. He owes me a favor. As for the salmon, get the word out to the waitstaff that we're out. Suggest the monkfish. And suggest we're almost out of that too."

Bailey frowns. "But we have plenty of monkfish."

"Yes, but if diners think we're almost out, they'll start ordering it."

People love first dibs on the last of anything.

"Fine. And by the way, the woman in white isn't Darcy LaFontaine. The woman who's hugging her is Darcy LaFontaine."

Across the restaurant, a tall Black woman in a dress with a splashy pattern of red flowers on it has grabbed the woman in white in a bear hug. They embrace for a moment before the woman in white throws her head back and laughs at something her friend said to her. It's a belly laugh, loud and unselfconscious. Startled by the volume, several people waiting for a table turn and stare.

The woman in white ignores them and keeps right on laughing.

It's obvious she doesn't care what anyone thinks of her. I admire a woman who isn't afraid to be herself.

Bailey turns to me. When she opens her mouth to speak, I cut her off. "Ass in gear," I say quietly, holding her gaze. "Don't make me repeat myself."

Her face reddens, but she doesn't argue. She knows me well enough to know that when I get quiet, it's best to clear out. Without another word, she turns and flounces off toward the kitchen. Heads turn in her wake.

I note all the admiring eyes trained on her swaying hips. *Careful what you wish for, boys. Even the shiniest apple can be worm-eaten inside.*

A lesson I've learned the hard way, one too many times.

I make my way toward the hostess stand at the front of the restaurant, nodding at people I know, shaking a few hands, schmoozing the crowd but never losing sight of the intriguing woman in white. She and Ms. LaFontaine are being led to an oval banquette against the far wall. It's the best table in the house, which makes me hot under the collar. I specifically told the hostess earlier tonight to place the LaFontaine party at table five near the front, a good table but not the best.

If she doesn't give us a good review unless we massage her ego, she can go fuck herself. I refuse to be one of those simpering restaurant owners who fawn all over food critics.

I reach the hostess stand just as Jenny, the hostess, returns.

"Mr. Maxwell! How are you, sir?"

Behind her glasses, her eyes are huge and blinking. I get the sense she'd like to curtsy. I don't enjoy terrifying the staff, but I admit it comes in handy sometimes. My commands are rarely questioned. Which makes this situation even more odd.

"I was doing well, Jenny, right up until I saw you lead Ms. LaFontaine to table thirty."

I stare at the hostess. She gulps.

"Oh...I...uh, yes, Mr. Maxwell." She starts blinking again, then speaks in a rush. "I know you said to put Ms. LaFontaine at table five, but Victoria Price asked if that was the best table, and I said it was a pretty good table, and then Ms. Price said she insisted on the *best* table or she'd tell Gloria Tartenberger there was a cockroach in her salad, and then we'd get shut down, and then you'd *really* be mad—"

"Stop."

Jenny's mouth snaps shut.

"Who is Victoria Price?"

Jenny swallows. "The lady with Darcy LaFontaine."

My gaze flashes to the banquette at back of the restaurant. There sits the woman in white, gazing steadily back at me, cool as ice. She turns her head and motions for the waiter, but not before I see her lips lift in a slight, derisive smile, there and quickly gone.

"You're telling me that woman threatened to call the head of the health department if you didn't give her the best table in the house?"

Glancing around, Jenny leans closer to me and whispers, "She said Gloria Tartenberger was a client of hers, Mr. Maxwell. That they were good friends."

My jaw flexes, and my molars grind together. "And you *believed* her?"

For a moment, Jenny looks confused. "Well…yes. I mean, she's Victoria Price."

She says the name as if it's self-explanatory, but I have no idea what she's talking about or who that woman is. What I do know is that *no one* throws their weight around in *my* place, with *my* staff, without blowback.

No matter how gorgeous and alluring that no one might be.

"I realize this is a new position for you, Jenny, but in the future, my instructions are to be followed to the letter, or you'll be out of a job. Am I understood?"

Paling, Jenny nods.

I leave her without another word and make my way back toward the kitchen, moving quickly now, cursing myself for putting someone so nice in the hostess position. It's becoming obvious that Jenny doesn't have the necessary level of ruthlessness it requires. If all it takes is a few words from some demanding socialite to throw her off plan—

I stop mid-stride as I see my chef, Kai, a man known to hate the human race as if every single one of us has personally offended him, bring a plate of amuse-bouches to Darcy

13

LaFontaine's table. He sets it on the linen cloth in front of her, then bows.

He *bows*. When he straightens, he's smiling like a clown.

What the hell is going on?

I catch the eye of the woman in white, Victoria Price, and the look she gives me pulls me up short.

Jesus. I never knew ice could burn with such heat.

"Sooo," drawls a voice in my ear. It's Bailey, materialized out of thin air like Dracula. She peers over my shoulder at the bizarre scene at table thirty. "It looks like you were wrong about your mystery woman."

I don't bother answering. She's obviously bursting to tell me, so I just keep my mouth shut and wait for it.

"Apparently she *doesn't* like to fuck, after all." She jerks her chin. "Your friend over there with the food critic is the biggest man-hater in the country. Maybe even the *world*." She grins. Her blue eyes twinkle. "Good luck with that, boss!"

She spins on her heel and is gone. When I look again at table thirty, Kai is bent over Darcy LaFontaine's outstretched hand, kissing it.

And Victoria Price is murdering me with her eyes.

Who the hell are these women?

3

VICTORIA

*T*he slender, tattooed chef with the wild thatch of blond hair who's bending over Darcy's hand is charming in an awkward, self-conscious sort of way, and is obviously going gaga over her, but I'm too busy chugging my martini and wrestling my personal demons to care.

I should leave. I should throw a drink in that bastard's face. I should call Gloria Tartenberger right this instant and tell her that there are not only cockroaches in the salad in this place but also a highly suspicious chemical odor in the air. A dangerous gas leak, perhaps? She'd be here with a shutdown order in five minutes flat.

After I coached her through her last divorce, she swore she'd throw herself in front of a train for me.

But I don't leave, or throw a drink, or make any calls. I sit beside my friend and listen to the chef prattle on about how *honored* he is and how *wonderful* it is to have Darcy dine with him and how he can't *wait* for her to try the hinoki-scented cod and the coconut-curried mussels, while I pretend to be something other than the pack of rabid wolves and chainsaw-wielding serial killers I suddenly am inside.

One look at the man who shattered my soul fifteen years ago and it all comes back with vivid, sickening clarity. The months of black depression. The feelings of utter worthlessness. The crying jags that wrung me dry and left my mother beside herself in a panic about what to do with her nearly comatose teenage daughter.

Parker Maxwell was my life. My first—and last—love. And he dumped me in the most cowardly way. With a letter.

That he *mailed*.

Two days later, I found out I was pregnant. I never saw him again.

Until this moment, that is. Standing at the far side of a noisy, bustling room, just as tall and strong as he ever was. Just as glamorous-rich-kid-quarterback-daydream as he ever was.

I'd like to gouge out his eyeballs with my soup spoon and set him on fire. Instead, I smile serenely at no one in particular and toss back the dregs of my martini.

"Well, aren't you sweet." Darcy bats her lashes coyly at the chef, who has introduced himself as Kai. She retrieves her hand from his grip and gives him a serious once-over. "You started your career at Pó with Batali, if I'm not mistaken?"

Kai nods vigorously and beams. "That's right. You know your chefs!"

He has a distinct German accent. One of his front teeth is slightly askew. Beneath his white chef's coat, he's wearing a pair of purple leopard-skin pants and orange Crocs. He's not one of the best-looking men I've ever seen, but he's adorable in his own way. I can tell Darcy thinks so too.

"I do know my chefs," purrs Darcy. She leans over her crossed arms, making her cleavage swell over the neckline of her dress. She lowers her voice and pins the chef in her seductive, long-lashed gaze. "And to be perfectly honest, Mr. Fürst, I've been really looking forward to having you feed me."

Poor Kai nearly swoons.

Darcy and Kai exchange pleasantries for a few more moments, and then he struts off, grinning from ear to ear.

Watching him go, Darcy makes an *mmm-mmm* noise and licks her lips, as if she's wishing it were he on the menu and not the hinoki-scented cod.

"I take it we like the chef?"

She picks up her glass of viognier and swirls it around, sniffing the bouquet. "He sure is cute. Did you see those dimples?" She makes the yummy noise again.

"I thought you swore off chefs?"

Smiling, she says, "I might have to reconsider."

Kai is probably a foot shorter than she is, but Darcy has never minded about things like that. I should probably change the subject before we get distracted from the reason we're here.

"So what do we know about this place? Aside from it being the hot new scene, that is."

Now that we're talking food, Darcy goes straight into business mode. "Opened three weeks ago to rave reviews. I'm highly suspicious of the necessity of yet another fusion restaurant, but the chef has an amazing pedigree, and the owner has been involved in the openings of some of my favorite places over the last ten years. Charleen at the James Beard Foundation was quoted as saying the truffle-dusted wagyu was perfection, so..."

With her fork, Darcy spears one of the wafer-thin slices of Japanese imported beef topped with shaved truffles that Kai has left us as his first offering. She pops it into her mouth and closes her eyes. She's silent for several moments.

I don't interrupt her. I've seen this ritual before. It will be repeated with each new morsel she eats for the entirety of the meal. We could be here for hours.

From the corner of my eye, I see Parker weaving through tables. He appears to be staring right at me.

Oh shit. Is he headed this way?

Darcy's brows knit. She purses her lips. As with Miranda

Priestly, Meryl Streep's character in *The Devil Wears Prada*, lip pursing is an unequivocal sign of disaster.

And yes—Parker is headed directly toward our table.

And yes—he is staring right at me.

The wolves snap and snarl. The chainsaws rev.

With a grimace, Darcy pronounces, "Funky truffles!" She spits out the piece of beef onto the plate in front of her. It lands with a distinctly unappetizing *plop*.

Parker stops beside our table. Looking amused as he eyes the piece of chewed meat on Darcy's plate, he says, "I see my chef was right. The truffles *are* shitty."

A punch in my gut, and all the air is sucked from my lungs. That voice. That voice I haven't heard for eons, deep and rich, calm and commanding, the voice that promised me a thousand whispered times, *"Bel, my sweet Isabel, I'll love you until I die."*

A wave of nausea hits me when I realize he said "my chef." Which means he's either the manager of this restaurant or the owner.

Which means he probably lives in the city. *My* city. And has for…how long? My God, how many months, possibly *years* have I lived near him? Breathing the same air he breathes, walking the same streets he walks, going about my life in blissful, pathetic ignorance?

Trying not to hyperventilate, I remain perfectly still, an icy smile plastered on my face, measuring each inhaled and exhaled breath as if it were my last.

One small mercy is that he doesn't seem to recognize me. He's stealing glances at me, but there's no recognition in his eyes. I thank the gods of time, money, and extensive plastic surgery for helping me morph from an ugly duckling into an anonymous swan, because if he said my real name aloud at this moment, there would be a violent incident involving my knife and his crotch.

Parker extends a hand to Darcy. It's tanned and elegant, like the rest of him.

"Parker Maxwell. It's a pleasure."

Darcy shakes his hand. "I would say the pleasure is all mine, Mr. Maxwell, but judging by that nightmare of an amuse-bouche I was just served, I'm afraid I'll be spending the rest of the night in search of a nearby vomitorium."

She smiles at him with all her teeth showing. I resist the urge to cackle like a witch.

Parker must sense my impending mental break because he glances at me again. I lift my chin and meet his gaze, concentrating on keeping my hands away from the cutlery. His eyes locked to mine, he says, "First impressions can be misleading, Ms. LaFontaine."

With withering disdain, I reply, "Or they can be incredibly accurate."

His eyes darken. I feel a distinct shift in his mood, from coolness to heat. Seemingly to himself, he murmurs, "I certainly hope so."

Then he blinks, straightens, and turns back to Darcy. "Not. Excuse me, I meant I hope *not*."

Darcy and I exchange a glance. Is he flustered? I sense an undercurrent here, but of what I'm not yet sure.

Parker turns to me again. "Victoria Price, is it?"

As his eyes hold mine, a terrible thought occurs to me: he *does* recognize me, and this is all a game.

No. It's not possible. You spent too much money, spent too much time in the hospital recovering, had too much work done. That country mouse is long gone.

Fortified by my little mental pep talk, I ignore his question and look over his shoulder, as if for assistance from some other, more interesting person. "Would you be so kind as to ask Kai to return to our table? I'd like to speak to him about—"

"You can speak to *me* about whatever you might need,"

Parker interrupts. His gaze drops to my chest. A fraction of a second later, his cheeks turn ruddy. Now I'm certain of the undercurrent I sensed moments before.

He wants me. The bastard wants me. *Me*, the girl he so callously kicked to the curb, once upon a million years ago.

Our gazes lock once again and hold. I say softly, "Can I now? Whatever I need. Hmm."

I look him slowly up and down, taking my time, relishing this, hating him, certain now from the subtle come-on that he has no inkling who I am, even more certain this is a once-in-a-lifetime opportunity for some bloody, take-no-prisoners, magnitude-of-Biblical-proportions revenge.

Rule #3: Bitches don't get mad. They get evil.

Everything that was thrashing and howling inside me turns to steel. My smile comes on slow and deadly. I can almost feel my canines elongate.

"I take it you're the maître d', Mr. Maxwell?"

His expression sours. "I'm the owner. And call me Parker. Mr. Maxwell is my father."

Don't I know it, you smug son of a bitch. And how is that bitter old bigot doing?

I relax back into the soft leather of the banquette, cross my legs, and shake my hair off my face. He watches all this with the focused intensity of a predator contemplating a meal.

"Well, *Mr. Maxwell*, as Darcy mentioned, your truffles are hideous. I can't imagine a chef so obviously dedicated as Kai—"

"Since we're being so formal, it's Chef Fürst—"

"—as our new friend *Kai* can be responsible for procuring them. Are they your doing?"

With a subtle smile, Parker repeats, "Hideous? Interesting choice of words."

My own smile widens. "Actually, that was just the one word. And you didn't answer the question."

"And you didn't answer mine."

I arch my brows. "Oh? Which question was that?"

A muscle in Parker's jaw flexes. He obviously knows I'm baiting him and obviously doesn't like it.

Good. Let him stew. A man as beautiful as this one is undoubtedly used to having women throw themselves at his feet. A challenge will pique his interest.

"It's Victoria," he says slowly. "Correct?"

I send him the sweetest smile I can conjure, which tastes about as sweet as a lemon wedge. "It's Victoria to my friends. To you, Mr. Maxwell, it's Ms. Price."

Slowly, Parker repeats, "Ms. Price." One corner of his mouth turns up. "Your reputation precedes you."

Score one for team Parker.

My lemon-wedge smile puckers even more. "Thank you," I say, brushing off the dig. "And since you're here, perhaps you could suggest something for our next course that wouldn't be quite so revolting?"

"Of course," he replies in the same smooth tone I used. "The salad is excellent this evening. Just the right amount of cockroach to flavor the dressing."

Darcy looks back and forth between us in fascination as if she's watching a Wimbledon match.

Kai appears at our tableside. "Here we are!" he says brightly.

He's holding two plates. He's about to set them in front of Darcy and me when he sees the piece of wagyu sitting in its sad state of mutilation on Darcy's appetizer plate. He recoils, horrified, then turns to Parker. Red-faced, he barks something in German.

It doesn't sound like a compliment.

Parker smiles. It's a lethal smile, not one I've ever seen him wear before, and definitely not one I'd like to be on the receiving end of.

He says, "Chef. Are you unwell? If so, Javier can stand in for you. He's perfectly capable of running the kitchen tonight. Or any other night, if necessary."

Kai's face turns purple at the threat. His eyes bulge. He begins to sputter, but Parker calmly removes the two plates from his hands and sets one in front of Darcy and the other in front of me. He takes Darcy's first plate and hands it to Kai, poking the edge aggressively into the shorter man's chest so he has to take a step back, clutching the plate with his hands.

With some growling and another few muttered words in German, Kai spins on his heel and stalks off.

Parker's dangerous smile still hardens his face. When he looks at me, there's danger in his eyes, too. It sends a swift, chilling tingle down my spine.

"Ladies. Forgive the outburst. My chef can be a little…temperamental."

Darcy says, "All the best ones are!" She looks at her plate and wiggles her fingers in glee. "Ooooh! Oysters with foie gras! If this is as good as it looks, Mr. Maxwell, all is forgiven."

Without further ado, she digs in. Parker and I stare at each other in silence.

Burning, cavernous silence.

Finally, he says, "I'll leave you to your meals, ladies. If you need anything, please let me know."

A final beat of silence pounds between us, and then he turns and walks away.

Around a mouthful of food, Darcy says, "Girl, don't be eye-fucking Brad Pitt's evil twin while I'm trying to concentrate on my oysters. That shit is distracting."

Because I've already killed my martini, I reach over and grab her glass of wine. I down it in one gulp.

Darcy sits back in her seat, swallows, and narrows her eyes. "Oh, it's like that, is it?"

I ask innocently, "Like what?"

"You know him? Pretty boy's an ex or something?"

Face, be stone. Be a slab of granite. "I've never seen him before in my life."

She snorts. "Really? You're gonna lie to your best friend?"

Instead of denying it, I deflect. "What makes you think I'm lying?"

"Because your poker face is as shitty as the truffles."

Sometimes I forget that underneath the Broadway show that is the fabulous Ms. Darcy LaFontaine, she's as sharp-eyed and cagey as a bounty hunter. I think she gets it from her mother, a Creole fortune-teller from New Orleans who reads palms and crystal balls and can tell you anything you want to know about yourself within two minutes of your meeting.

I exhale a long, unsteady breath. "Let's just say that our paths crossed once, in a former life."

Darcy studies my face. "And it didn't end well, I take it."

"No, it did not."

"And judging by his whole 'Ms. Victoria Price, I presume' spiel, he didn't recognize you, I take it."

"No, he did not."

There's a long, uncomfortable pause.

"And that's all you're going to tell me?"

I look away, to the wall of windows at the front of the restaurant. Outside in the cold New York evening, it's begun to softly rain.

I feel a touch on my arm. I turn to find Darcy gazing at me. After a moment, she murmurs, "Bob Marley said, 'You never know how strong you are until being strong is the only choice you have.' That sound about right?"

My voice wavering, I say, "You know, sometimes I think I'd like to marry you."

She laughs, squeezes my arm, and signals the waiter for another drink. "Honey, I'd like to marry myself. At least that way I'd know I'd be getting a hot piece of ass every night."

I can't help myself. I laugh.

When I happen to glance toward the kitchen, Parker Maxwell is standing half in shadow in a doorway, watching me with a look of grave intensity, as if he's trying to figure out where he's seen me before. Or perhaps he's contemplating whether or not to put a bullet in my head.

I shoot him my most insincere smile.

He doesn't smile back.

I can already tell this is going to get messy.

4

PARKER

"*A*ll right. Tell me what you know about Victoria Price."

I've got Bailey's arm in my grip. She just tried to brush past me on her way into the kitchen, but I need to know more. And I need to know *now*.

Bailey looks down at my hand. With quirked brows, she looks back up at my face. "Okay, Tarzan, I'll tell you. But get your fucking hand off my arm."

She's right. I'm out of line. Every once in a while, Bailey surprises me.

I release her and hold my palms up in surrender. "I'm sorry. Stupid move."

"Dick move." She emphasizes the first word.

I nod my head. "Agreed. Dick move. I apologize."

She looks at me closely for several seconds to see if I'm joking. I must not apologize as much as necessary. Oh shit, *am* I a dick?

Oh shit, am I turning into my father?

The thought drains all the blood from my face. I drop my hands to my sides and look Bailey directly in the eye. "I'm sorry, Bailey. I shouldn't have touched you like that. I wasn't thinking, but that's no excuse." Something new occurs to me, and I stare at her bare arm in horror. "Did I hurt you?"

Bailey rolls her eyes. "No, you didn't *hurt* me, for God's sake!" She pauses. "Though if you wanted to, something could definitely be arranged." She sticks out her hip, smartly smacks her behind, then winks at me.

That little gem makes me blink for a few seconds before I can compose myself. "I think we'll call it even on the inappropriate employer-employee behavior for the evening. But I'm flattered. Truly. If I were into beating women, I'm sure that would be an irresistible invitation."

"Spanking isn't the same as beating, boss. And you know, lots of women like a little rough play—"

"Bailey."

"Yeah, boss?"

"Stop talking now."

She mock pouts. "Oh, so you *don't* want to know about Victoria Price?"

I realize I'm being punished. Not for touching Bailey's arm, but for showing interest in Victoria Price in the first place. I'm irritated, not with Bailey but with myself. I should know better. Bailey has made her interest in me obvious, and even though I've made my non-interest perfectly clear, no one likes to have the competition rubbed in her face.

"Not if you don't want to tell me. And I have something else to apologize for."

Now it's Bailey's turn to blink. "What?"

"That comment I made when she walked in."

She makes a very unladylike sound and crosses her arms over her chest. "The one about her looking so fuckable, you mean? Gee, why would you think that would be annoying?"

Sighing, I run a hand through my hair. "You're right. It was rude, not to mention chauvinistic. I don't know what's wrong with me tonight. I'm being a complete idiot. I'm sorry."

Bailey takes pity on me. She gives me a friendly little shove with her elbow and chuckles. "Don't worry about it. You're a guy. You can't help being a complete idiot. Comes with the junk."

She flashes a look to my crotch, then grins.

I grin back. "I'll do better. I mean, I'll try. My junk might get in the way, but give me credit for the effort?"

I'll give her this, when Bailey really smiles, she does it with her whole body.

"Deal," she says, appeased. "And since you're being so nice, I *will* tell you about the ice queen in white. But prepare yourself. It isn't pretty."

She leans around me, peering out the doorway into the restaurant to where Victoria and Darcy sit. I follow her gaze. Victoria turns her head in our direction, and Bailey jumps out of sight behind the wall.

"Busted," she breathes, hand over her heart.

"Bailey, why are you hiding? It's not like we're plotting the woman's death back here."

"Ever heard of resting bitch face?"

I chuckle. "Yeah."

"Well, she's got resting bitch *everything*. I'm afraid she might turn me to stone with those iceberg eyes."

I glance at Victoria. Once again, she's glaring daggers at me. I say drily, "I'm familiar with the effect."

Bailey says, "She's known as the Queen B. And not bee like the insect, or Jay-Z's wife. The letter *B*, as in *beyotch*. She first made her money with a self-help book she wrote called *Bitches Do Better*, which became a number one *New York Times* bestseller when she was only twenty-one. Then she wrote half a dozen more *Bitch* books, started doing speaking engagements, and became a life coach for some über-swank clients. Teaching them her bitchy secrets for success, apparently. Which all must be pretty damn lucrative, because she lives in a penthouse in the Flatiron district that cost twenty-five million bucks."

Here Bailey pauses.

"What else?"

"Well...she has a bit of a reputation."

"Over and above being the reigning Queen B? I can hardly wait. Does she skin kittens alive?"

"More like she skins men alive. Or, more precisely, *eats* them alive. Loves 'em and leaves 'em, wham, bam, thank you, man, your money's on the dresser. Never sticks around for more than a few dates, never commits. She's never been married or engaged, never been in a long-term relationship as far as anyone knows." As an afterthought she adds, "Like you."

I ignore that. I know a minefield when I see one.

"Not to bring up a sore subject, but earlier you said she didn't like to fuck. And now you're telling me she's a man-eater? I don't see how those two lines ever cross."

Bailey rolls her eyes as if I'm the biggest idiot to ever walk the earth.

"What?"

"You really don't know anything about women, do you?"

"Of course I do. Don't expect them to be interested in sports, on time, or rational. What else is there to know?"

More eye rolling. "You're hopeless, Parker."

"Moving on—how do you know all this about her?"

In the following pause, two spots of color stain Bailey's cheeks. Her lashes sweep downward. "I may have googled her after she came in."

I look back to Victoria's table. She's ignoring me now, but I have the impression she knows I'm looking at her. The woman has the most smug, secretive smile I've ever seen.

A successful, intelligent, beautiful woman with a Mona Lisa smile, arctic laser beam eyes, and a reputation for being not only a ruthless bitch but also a voracious lover?

The way my mouth has begun to water, you'd think someone waved a meatball sandwich under my nose.

"Uh-oh." Bailey's tone is wry.

I glance at her. "What?"

"You've got that look."

"What look?"

She sighs and pushes away from the wall. "The same look you had when bitchface walked in the place. That hound-eyed, pricked-eared, nose-in-the-air-scenting prey look. That *it's on* look. Honestly, Parker, you're thirty-four. When are you going to get tired of the chase and find some nice girl to settle down with?"

No nice girl deserves a man like me. I turn my attention back to Victoria Price and her disdainful profile. A grim, determined smile curves my lips. *A Queen Bitch, however, is another story.*

An ear-splitting shriek emits from the kitchen, followed by a loud crash. Bailey and I share a look, then I stride into the kitchen to find out what's going on.

Chaos is what's going on.

Wild-eyed, Kai stands in front of one of the four large industrial stoves. Six pans with various steaming foods sizzle on the burners. Strewn all around him in a scattered mess on the floor are a variety of pots and pans, stainless steel bowls, and cooking implements. Flattened against the doors of the Sub-Zero refrigerator a few feet away are the sous chef and the pastry chef, both of whom are gaping in terror at Kai.

Who is brandishing a large cleaver.

"I cannot work under these conditions!" he screams, punctuating every other word with a shake of the gleaming knife. "I am Kai Fürst, not a *gottverdammte* line cook at a diner!"

I inquire, "Trouble, gentlemen?"

Two new cooks and a server who'd been trapped in a corner between Kai and the door take the opportunity of my appearance to make a run for it. They bolt from the kitchen. The rest of the kitchen staff, who are far more experienced than the three who just fled, simply watch with mild interest while continuing their duties.

The pastry chef, a twenty-year-old recent graduate of the Culinary Institute in Napa, looks a bit green. He's also shaking. Apparently he hasn't yet learned that executive chefs at top fine dining establishments are typically insane.

He stammers, "C-chef isn't h-happy with the crust on the ganache t-tart!"

The sous chef adds, "Or the crème fraîche for the egg caviar."

"I see." I look at Kai. "On a positive note, Darcy LaFontaine says the oysters are superb. And the foie gras was…" I purse my lips and gaze at the ceiling. "How did she put it?" I snap my fingers. "Ah, yes—orgasmic."

Kai drops the cleaver. It lands at his feet with a metallic clatter. "Really? She used that word, *orgasmic?*"

Now utterly calm as if a switch has been thrown, cutting off the conduit to his rage, he steps over the mess on the floor and comes to stand in front of me. His eyes are bright and hopeful. I wonder when he last ran a comb through his hair.

"She did indeed. In fact, Chef, I know she's very much looking forward to the next course." Frowning, I look over his shoulder. "Should I tell her it will be delayed?"

"No! No, no, everything is perfectly on schedule! The goddess will not wait!" He whirls around and sprints back to the stove, where he begins a frenzy of activity, shouting instructions to the staff.

I catch the eye of Julian, one of the busboys who's worked for me for years, and nod at the mess on the floor. With a smile, Julian gets to work. This isn't the first time he's cleaned up after Hurricane Kai blew through. I know it won't be the last.

One quick glance around tells me everything is back on track, so I leave them to it.

"I have to admit, you're pretty amazing at that," says Bailey when I walk back through the swinging doors to the kitchen. She's been listening just outside.

"At what, exactly?"

She smiles. "Handling people. Especially the crazy ones."

When I just shrug, she adds, "Did Darcy really say that? About the foie gras being orgasmic?"

"No. But judging by the way Kai was practically drooling over her, I thought a little sexual innuendo would go a long way."

Bailey chuckles. "Turns out you were right. And did I hear him call her a *goddess*? This from the man who thinks everyone except his mother and Julia Child are scum?"

We walk together to the doorway that leads from the kitchen to the main room of the restaurant, where we were standing before. When I look at Victoria and Darcy's table, I'm gratified to find Victoria glancing in my direction. Our eyes meet, but she quickly looks away. A waiter stops at their table, and they exchange a few words. Before he moves away, she bestows upon him a large, toothy smile.

The better to eat you with, my dear. I wonder if the poor waiter knows he's serving the Big Bad Wolf.

Just as I'm about to turn back to Bailey, Victoria lifts her hand to her face. She tilts her head and tucks a strand of her long, dark hair behind her ear in a gesture that is graceful and girlish, and also hauntingly familiar.

My heart skips a beat.

Where have I seen that gesture before?

5

VICTORIA

By the time Darcy and I reach the end of the meal, it's nearly midnight, the gentle evening rain has turned into an angry downpour, and my face is aching from hosting three hours of forced smiles.

And I'm more determined than ever that Parker Maxwell is going *down*.

He thinks he's being stealthy, but I know when I'm being watched. He and his blonde sidekick haven't stopped sending me furtive glances all night. More than once, I've caught them whispering together while looking my way.

I can't help but wonder what the deal is with the two of them. If I'm being honest with myself, they'd make a gorgeous couple. All-American Ken and Barbie, complete with golden tans and perfect hair. But I can detect no chemistry between them. There are no obvious flirtations or stray, admiring glances. If they're an item, they're being very discreet.

Chef Kai, however, is being anything but discreet about his blossoming obsession with Darcy. He's at our tableside—for the *n*th time—with a dazzling array of exotic desserts, proffering them to her with a deferential tilt to his head, like the court jester before the queen. I can almost see the stars glittering in his eyes.

"*Häschen*," he implores, "please try a sweet. Or four. You must!"

Darcy says, "Why don't you just leave the whole platter, Chef? I'll probably have more than four."

Kai's smile is blinding. After he's set the platter down on the table and bowed off, I turn to Darcy with a quizzical frown.

"What did he call you?"

"I dunno. Let's look it up." She digs her cell phone from her handbag and taps in a few words. After a moment she says, "According to Google translate, he called me 'little rabbit.'" She grimaces. "Is that supposed to be sexy? Rabbits aren't very sexy."

"I think it's cute, Darse. It's a pet name. Literally."

She laughs, shakes her head, selects an item from the platter, and pops it into her mouth. She chews for a moment and then moans in ecstasy.

"Watching you eat is almost pornographic." I sip my espresso while Darcy continues to moan. Then an amused voice says, "I hope I'm not interrupting."

Darcy looks at Parker, standing at our tableside. She smiles at him. A fine dusting of confectioner's sugar highlights the bow of her lips. "Mr. Maxwell. My compliments to the chef."

"He'll be thrilled to hear it. I think you've made his entire year tonight. I've never seen him so..." Parker glances at me. His voice drops. "Enamored."

I stare at him over the rim of my espresso cup. Neither of us looks away. All the little hairs on the back of my neck stand on end.

Darcy delicately pats her mouth with her napkin. "I have that effect on people. And if you came over to find out what I'm going to write about the food, I'm sorry, but you'll be disappointed. You'll have to wait for my article, just like everyone else."

"It isn't your article I'm interested in," Parker murmurs. He sends me a smile of such carnality, my stomach turns.

Or does it drop? Flip? I can't decide what exactly my stomach is doing. Whatever it is, it's strange, and I don't like it.

Parker isn't looking at Darcy, so he doesn't notice the outraged *Oh no you didn't!* glare she sends him. I know it's not because he's dissed her, it's that she's being protective of me.

She might have a point. Either Parker has figured out who I am and has some nefarious plan in mind, or he's a womanizing a-hole of epic proportions. Who would be more concerned with flirting than making a good impression on the food critic who could potentially write a highly unflattering piece on his restaurant and cost him money?

A womanizing a-hole of epic proportions, that's who.

I'm thankful I'm not one of those women who blush or giggle uncontrollably in uncomfortable situations. No. I am a woman who has turned eye contact into a contact sport.

I hold Parker's gaze. A violent smile hovers at the corners of my lips. Something bright and dangerous crackles between us.

I say, "We're ready for the check whenever you have a chance, Mr. Maxwell."

Parker lifts an eyebrow. "Leaving so soon?"

I don't have to look around the restaurant to know that Darcy and I are one of the last tables here. I simply widen my murderous smile and remain silent.

After a time, he says, "Well, it was my honor to have you. The meal's on the house."

"Oh, we couldn't possibly let you do that," I say.

Now Parker smiles. "Of course you could. It's my pleasure."

Darcy bats her lashes at him. "You're not trying to buy a good review, are you Parker?"

Parker's smile dies. Stiffly, he turns to her. "Pandering isn't my style, Ms. LaFontaine." Without another word, he stalks off.

Bemused, Darcy watches him go. "Proud much, Captain America?"

Yes, I want to say. *He's always been like that. Even when he was seventeen years old, he was proud, stubborn and easily insulted. If egos were animals, his would be a Siamese cat.*

He was never vain, though. Or pretentious or arrogant, even though he was the wealthiest and best-looking kid in town.

All this tripping down memory lane is giving me a headache.

"Well, if we don't need to wait for the check, I think I'll hit it, Darcy. I'm exhausted."

She examines me carefully from the corner of her eye while pretending to pick over the dessert platter. "Hmm."

I sigh. "I'm fine. Honestly. But the sooner I get out of here, the sooner I can forget about seeing him, and the sooner my headache will go away. Don't worry about me. You know I've got skin like stainless steel."

She sends me a pointed look. "Even stainless steel can rust."

I lean over and kiss her cheek, catching the sweet scent of the organic coconut oil she uses to soften her skin. "Good night, Grandma."

She cackles. "Good night. Don't let the bed bugs bite!"

I send my driver a text that I'm ready to be picked up, slide from the booth, gather my handbag and cashmere throw, then slowly walk through the restaurant toward the front door with my head held high and my behind swaying. I don't look back.

I'm unfamiliar with the man Parker has grown into in the past fifteen years, but knowing men the way I do, my hunch is that he isn't used to having women be indifferent to his advances. My other hunch is that his pride won't like it or let it slide. If I'm right, he'll do something to try to catch my attention before I get in the car.

I stand just inside the door, staring out into the driving rain, pretending to be lost in thought while I'm really counting down from ten.

Four. Three. Two—

"I hope you enjoyed your meal, Ms. Price."

One of the more difficult things I've done in my thirty-three years is not smirk at this moment.

I turn and look at Parker from over my shoulder. I'd forgotten how tall he is. I'm gazing quite a way up. "It was... interesting." Dismissively, I turn back to the window.

Parker moves a step closer. He stands beside me. His shoulder is almost touching mine. I'm hyperaware of the distance between us. It's breathtakingly difficult to stand still, even more difficult to keep my tongue and my fists in check.

He's still in as much unwitting danger as he has been all night. There's no guarantee that I won't snap at any moment, turn, and drive my thumbs into his eye sockets.

Beside me, he stares silently out into the rain. I'm startled when he says in a quiet, melancholy voice, "I've always loved the rain. Some of my best memories involve rainfall."

It hangs there between us. I can't tell if he's baiting me or just making conversation. I hardly know up from down right now.

Because I lost my virginity to this man during a thunderstorm when I was sixteen years old. In a barn, of all places. I can still smell the hay and the horses, hear the thunder, see the brief, brilliant flicker of lightning illuminate the night. I can still see him above me, staring down at me with wonder in his eyes.

I can still feel his mouth on my skin.

Some new emotion rises up inside me. It shaves a hair off my hostility and brings the hot prick of tears to my eyes. I don't recognize this emotion, but I hope never to feel it again.

I swallow around the rock that's formed in my throat. "I hate it. It's rained on all the worst nights of my life."

I feel his piercing sideways glance. I wish the earth would

experience an extinction-level event and I'd be conveniently rescued from the misery of this moment. A giant asteroid would do the trick.

Then—mercifully—a sleek black Mercedes pulls around the corner. It rolls to a stop in front of the curb.

"That's me." Grateful for the reprieve, I turn to Parker and extend my hand. "Thank you for dinner. I appreciate your generosity."

Another trait he's had since adolescence. And another thing I'd forgotten until now. How he was always so giving, always so thoughtful, always so concerned with everyone else.

Until he wasn't.

Parker takes my hand and holds it. His gaze burns into mine. "Ms. Price. It's been a singular pleasure meeting you."

His hand is big and warm. I like the feel of it entirely too much. Coolly, I withdraw.

"Mr. Maxwell. Good evening."

I turn for the door. Parker opens it for me before I can even reach for the handle. When he sees me exit the restaurant, my driver leaps from the car and opens the rear door.

Parker walks me from the restaurant to the car with an umbrella he's magically procured from somewhere, held over my head, protecting me from the rain. I step carefully over a puddle. Blocking the driver, Parker takes hold of my hand as I lower myself into the car.

He bends down to look at me. Rain pours off the umbrella, soaking his lower legs, trousers and shoes. He ignores it. Looking into my eyes, he says in a low voice, "I want to see you again. There's a charity gala I'm attending next Friday evening. Come with me."

I must be coming down with something. I haven't felt this fevered and shaky in years.

"How do you know I'm not married?"

A smile flickers over his mouth. His thumb brushes my

37

knuckles, leaving a trail of sparks in its wake. "You're not wearing a ring."

"I could be in a serious relationship."

"You're not."

"Oh no? And how would you know that?"

His smile deepens. In the low light, his eyes gleam as if he's running a fever, too. "Because if you were, Ms. Price, you wouldn't be looking at me like that."

The nerve. The self-absorbed, stuck-up, egomaniacal nerve of this man!

It doesn't help matters that I suspect he's right.

I say icily, "Perhaps you need your eyes examined, Mr. Maxwell. Or your head."

He chuckles. "Is that a yes or a no?"

I withdraw my hand from his grip and grant him my profile. "It's neither. Have a nice life, Mr. Maxwell."

I tell the driver I'm ready. Parker chuckles again, then straightens. "You do the same, Ms. Price."

He closes the door.

The car pulls away from the curb. I don't look back. But I do wait several moments before I open my handbag, pull out my compact mirror, and hold it up to my face. Through the rear window, I have a perfect view of the restaurant receding into the night, and of Parker Maxwell standing at the rain-swept curb under the shadow of an umbrella, watching me go.

For the first time in hours, I can breathe. I wait until the subtle tremble has left my hands, then I settle back into the seat and start to plot.

Let the games begin.

6

VICTORIA

$\mathscr{T}$he next day promptly at noon, Tabby knocks on my office door, then sticks her ponytailed head inside. When she sees me on the phone and starts to back out, I wave her in. I'm almost done with my weekly ten-thirty appointment, and I want to get started on the project I gave to Tabby last night after I returned from dinner.

"We've touched on this before, Katie. You know what to do when these thoughts paralyze you."

There follows a short silence. Then my client says, "You know, Victoria, just once I'd like you to just *tell* me what to do, instead of making me do all the thinking for myself."

"My aim as your life coach is to develop rather than impose. Remember how furious you used to get when Brokaw tried to tell you what to do at NBC?"

She sighs. "I wish I'd known you then. You'd have saved me fifteen years of ulcers."

"Just trust the process. Ask yourself the core questions and reevaluate the situation. Then decide what to do."

"You're not even going to give me a hint?"

I laugh. "Not even a little one. I have complete faith in your ability to work this out. And good luck with the Clinton interview. I know you'll be amazing."

"Thanks, Victoria. Same time next week?"

"Same time next week. Bye."

"Goodbye."

I set the phone in the cradle and look up to find Tabby gazing at me with a wry smile.

She says, "I'm sure Hillary Clinton will perform much better in her interview than Sarah Palin did back in '08."

I smile, leaning back in my chair. "A crowbar would've performed better than that. You're running for vice president and you don't prepare for an interview with America's Sweetheart?" I shake my head. "Palin should've hired me."

"You'd have agreed to work with her?"

Tabby seems surprised, which surprises me. "Of course. Why wouldn't I?"

"She's just so...Republican."

I raise my brows. "And?"

"And you're not."

"You know very well I'm not a member of *any* political party, Tabby. Or religious party, for that matter. All that divisiveness is bad for business. Plus it goes against rule number four."

Tabby smiles. "The only side a bitch takes is her own."

"Exactly. Now enough chatter. Sit down and tell me what you found."

Dutifully, Tabby flops into the chair across from my desk. She flips open the iPad she's carrying, taps the screen, then begins to read aloud.

"Parker Jameson Maxwell, age thirty-four. American restauranteur and philanthropist, owner of over twenty restaurants in the US, including his extravagant flagship in Las Vegas, Bel—"

"Philanthropist? Please don't tell me he founded a fair trade coffee organization called Maxwell House."

Tabby laughs, swiping at her bangs. "No. He founded The

Hunger Project, a charity that provides school meals for forty thousand underprivileged children in the South."

Sobering, she pauses. Then she looks up and meets my eyes. "He also gives millions every year to the Muscular Dystrophy Association."

A knot of pain appears beneath my sternum. Like a flower under the sun, it begins slowly to bloom.

Muscular Dystrophy. A group of diseases that cause progressive weakness and loss of muscle mass, eventually leading to the death of muscle tissue, and possibly to the loss of the ability to walk, breathing problems, heart problems, and, in severe cases, even death.

I can recall the medical definition by memory. I know MD like I know my own face in the mirror.

Unable to sit any longer or meet Tabby's sympathetic gaze, I stand and move to the windows that form the east wall of the room. In the glass, my reflection is as pale as a ghost.

Tabby continues reading. If she notices my sudden pallor, she's tactful enough not to mention it.

"Born in Laredo, Texas, to Bill Maxwell, the import-export mogul, and his wife, Dorothy, a homemaker, Parker was named after jazz great Charlie Parker, one of his mother's idols."

But not his father's.

Unlike Parker's father, his mother held no prejudice against anyone for the color of his skin. She had a generous, open heart, but also was as tough as nails. If she said her child would be named after a Black musician, that's what was going to happen, no matter how much her husband screamed.

And scream he did. And retaliate, in his own petty way. Bill Maxwell never once called his son by his given name. It was always "Boy."

I ruthlessly smother the memory of what Bill Maxwell always called me.

"Though the family was wealthy, his mother insisted that

Parker go to public schools, which he did until his senior year. He then moved to England and attended Oxford University. Did so well he finished his degree a year early."

The air takes on a distinct chill. I close my eyes and wrap my arms around myself.

England. So that's where you disappeared to.

Tabby muses, "That's a weird transition. The public school-educated son of a Texas business tycoon goes to college in England? Do Texans even know where Oxford is?"

Old Bastard Bill was a bigot, but he wasn't dumb.

"Excuse me?" Tabby says.

I realize that last thought was spoken aloud. I turn from the window and wave my hand. "Nothing. Sorry. Go on."

Tabby hesitates for a moment before continuing. "After graduation, Parker moved to France, where he met world-renowned chef Alain Gérard via a car accident. Parker was riding in a taxi that hit Gérard's car, and though he was injured himself in the crash, he came to the aid of the older man and administered CPR. They became extremely close friends, with Gérard even inviting Parker to live with him at his home in Paris, which he did for a year while nursing the chef back to health."

I roll my eyes at the window. "Barf."

"What?"

"Feeding impoverished children? Giving millions to fight muscular dystrophy? Saving the life of an elderly man while injured and then acting as nursemaid for said elderly man for another year?" I shake my head. "He's too perfect. That bio is obviously fake."

I hear an amused laugh. I turn to find Tabby grinning at me, her head cocked so her bangs fall to the side and her bright green eyes, for once, are clearly visible.

"So you two have something in common."

I say drily, "I didn't hire you for your sense of humor, Tabitha."

"No, you hired me because I'm a highly talented hacker who specializes in making inconvenient personal information disappear, because I'm an incredible girl Friday, and because I can keep my mouth shut tighter than a nun's snatch." She smiles. "Also probably because of my superior fashion sense."

I snort. "Oh, definitely that."

Tabby's fashion style defies categorization. Today she's sporting thigh-high electric-pink stockings paired with black gladiator platform boots, a miniscule plaid schoolgirl's skirt, and a tight, sleeveless Philadelphia Eagles T-shirt that bares her midriff and does nothing to conceal the fact that she isn't wearing a bra.

Let's not forget the black leather fingerless gloves.

She has multiple tattoos, piercings in unmentionable places, and a highly questionable fondness for Hello Kitty accessories. She's also the smartest human being I've ever met. She dropped out of MIT because it was too easy and she got bored.

She's the other capital *B* noun I most admire: *Badass*.

"Shall I go on?"

Sighing, I return to my chair. "Skip to the juicy parts. Any dirt? Arrests? Felony convictions?"

Her level green gaze bores into mine. "Don't you want to know about his wife?"

I blanch. "He's *married*?"

A satisfied smile spreads over Tabby's face. "Nope. But now I know for sure this isn't about you possibly investing in Xengu like you told me last night. There's something else about this guy you're interested in. This is personal, isn't it?"

Excited at the prospect, she leans forward, her eyes bright.

I stare back at her without blinking. "How long have I employed you, Tabitha?"

"Five years, six months, fourteen days," comes the immediate answer. She checks her watch, a pink plastic affair with the Hello Kitty logo splashed all over it. "And three hours."

"Five years," I repeat coolly. "And in all that time, have you ever known me to take a personal interest in a man?"

She hesitates, her smile fading. "No."

"There's your answer."

She turns the iPad to face me. Displayed above the list of facts she's compiled in her research are two pictures. One shows Parker in a formal business pose, in suit and tie, standing with his arms folded over his chest and his legs spread as he stares unsmiling into the camera. A team of uniformed chefs stands in a line behind him. It's obviously a publicity shot. He looks handsome but distant, the epitome of a focused, successful entrepreneur.

The other picture is a close-up of his face. Casual and unposed, it was taken outdoors. The sun gleams in his hair. His eyes are half-closed against the light. His head is tilted back a little, and he's wearing a boyish, unselfconscious grin, looking at whoever took the picture with a dreamy glint in his eyes.

His gorgeous, come-hither bedroom eyes.

Hazel. Such a lackluster word for the glory of gold, brown, and emerald mixed together in one ever-shifting canvas, like dappled sunlight on leaves.

Tabby says, "You're telling me this face does nothing for you? Holy mother of all vibrators! This face could make even the icicles in *your* vagina melt!"

I have to press my lips together so I don't smile. She knows many of my secrets, but the effect Parker Maxwell has on my vagina is one she'll never be privy to.

"Tabitha. Please. Continue before I reconsider that last raise I gave you."

She lifts one shoulder and says casually, "Okay. The icicles remain icy."

"That's the nature of icicles."

"No, the nature of icicles is to melt."

"Tabitha."

She twirls the end of her ponytail between her fingers and smiles at me. "It's sweet how you call me Tabitha when you're mad at me. Kind of like you're my mom or something."

"If I were your mother, I would have given birth to you when I was nine years old. Not everyone over thirty is ready for the retirement home, girl genius."

Tabby, not yet twenty-five, doesn't look convinced.

"Parker Maxwell," I prompt in a tone that leaves no room for argument.

She turns the iPad around with a dramatic sigh.

"Right. Parker Maxwell. Where was I? Oh, now *this* is interesting. When he returned to the States after his stint in France, he disappeared for two years. Just dropped off the face of the planet. No work history, no known address, no nothing. Then out of the blue one day, he opens his first restaurant, to huge acclaim. Then another. Then another, et cetera, repeat ad nauseam for ten-ish years. Which brings us to now. Twenty-three successful restaurants, over four hundred employees, a multimillion-dollar empire, homes in New York, Aspen and the Caribbean, a list of ex-girlfriends that reads like a Victoria's Swimsuit catalogue lineup, a charity foundation or two, and not a single friend in the world."

I'd been examining my manicure as she recited the list of his accomplishments, but now I look up, startled. "What do you mean, not a single friend in the world?"

"Just what I said. The guy's a total loner. You'd think a rich playboy would hang out with all the other rich playboys in his spare time, but the only thing your Mr. Maxwell does in his spare time is work."

My lips twist. "And date supermodels."

She gives me a look. "From what I can gather, his requirements of a 'date' are exactly what yours are: look pretty, be quiet, give me some head, get the hell out.'"

"I *do* enjoy these charming little observations of yours. Anything else?"

She consults the iPad again. "Hobbies include racing his collection of vintage Porsches, crashing his collection of vintage Porsches...and working."

I smile to myself. He never was a very good driver. He was always too easily distracted, most often by his hand on my leg, or my mouth on his neck—

Tabby clears her throat.

My head snaps up. "You? What?"

Tabby pauses for what feels like a long time. "Are you okay?"

"Of course. Why do you ask?"

"Because you look a little flushed. And you don't flush. Like, ever. I didn't think it was physically possible."

Smart people can be so inconvenient.

"I'm fine, Tabitha."

She mutters, "And we're back to Tabitha."

I check my Rolex. "I've got another call in five minutes. Is there anything else you found?"

Tabby gives me a look that says she knows I'm blowing her off, she knows I know she knows it, and she's going to let it go. She stands. "Nothing of real interest. Perfect credit, no criminal record, no bankruptcies, no litigation, no known tattoos, allergies, health problems, or kink fetishes."

When she sees my raised brows, she shrugs. "You did say everything."

"Okay. Thanks. Did you compile the list I asked for?"

"Of all the charity events in the city next Friday? Yeah, I did. Short list. I'll email it to you."

"Great. Thanks, Tabby."

She rises to leave. I flip through my Rolodex, searching for the number of my next appointment. Just before she's about to cross the threshold, my desk phone rings. The readout says it's the concierge downstairs. I hit the speaker button to answer.

"Hello?"

"Ms. Price, this is Carlton at the concierge. We have a delivery for you. May we send it up?"

"I wasn't expecting a delivery."

"It's flowers, ma'am."

I look up to find Tabby gazing at me from the doorway with an amused expression. For some reason, I feel as if I've been caught with my hand in the cookie jar.

"Send it up, Carlton. Thank you." I disconnect the call. Then I ignore the way Tabby is smirking.

Then, a few minutes later when the elevator doors open to reveal four of the front desk staff carrying huge bouquets of white roses, I ignore Tabby's cheerful, "Gee, I wonder if they're from Mr. It's Not Personal?"

"Put them on the dining table, please," I direct the guys.

"Sure thing, Ms. Price. Where do you want the rest of them?"

"The rest of them? There are more?"

The young man in the navy suit who is the manager of the front desk nods. "There are a lot more. Eleven more, I think."

"Wow," drawls Tabby, inspecting one of the extravagant bouquets. "This guy isn't kidding."

Once again, I ignore her. To the manager I say, "Fine, put the rest of them anywhere you can find a space in the living room and office. I'll move them later."

He nods and ushers the other three men out. One of the bouquets has a card attached, which Tabby removes and hands to me. It reads, "One dozen roses for every hour I've thought of you since we met." Then his initials and his phone number, and two final words. "Call me."

He's playing right into my hands...so why does that final instruction bother me so much?

Then it hits me: because it's an order he fully expects will be obeyed. He thinks *he's* in control.

"Bossy son of a bitch," I mutter, and tear the card into little pieces.

"Careful, Icicles!" says Tabby brightly on her way out of the room. "That looked suspiciously like an emotion."

I call after her, "You're fired!" She laughs, and then she's gone.

Of course she knows she's not fired.

Who would hide all my skeletons then?

7

VICTORIA

*S*ix days later and three hours late, I arrive at the New York chapter of the Muscular Dystrophy Association's annual gala, wearing ten thousand dollars of Bulgari diamonds and a long, skintight white Armani gown that exposes the entirety of my bare back, all the way down to the dimples above my tailbone.

The entry ticket cost more than my diamonds. That son of a bitch better be here tonight, or I'm anonymously mailing him a steaming bag of horse poop.

Tabby has assured me she has an Internet source for it.

My arrival is a calculated risk. Though Parker didn't specify which charity event he was attending tonight, the other possibilities that Tabby emailed me didn't seem nearly as probable as the one he gives millions to each year. I suppose I could have done some reconnaissance, maybe had Tabby call Parker's office and pretend to be an assistant from the charity confirming his reservation, but honestly, I felt like gambling.

Twelve thousand bucks seems like a good deal if it ends with me sending a bag of poop to my mortal enemy.

But, alas, the caca will have to wait for another time, because I spot him the moment I walk in the door.

The party is in full swing. This year the gala is taking place at the venerated Cipriani Wall Street, a luxurious event space sporting monolithic columns, Greek Revival architecture, and a seventy-foot ceiling with a spectacular Wedgwood dome. It's packed with elegantly dressed people who are eating, laughing, and drinking. A ten-piece band plays on a riser on one side of the dance floor, which is filled with couples. The party atmosphere is enhanced by dramatic violet lighting on the walls and enormous pink orchid arrangements, which are everywhere.

And there on the far side of the room, by an artfully arranged group of potted palms, is Parker. He's holding a drink, looking like a supermodel assassin in a perfectly cut black suit, with slicked-back hair.

Two young women flank him. One, a voluptuous blonde, is leaning so close, her breasts practically rest on his arm. The other, a brunette wearing a red skirt almost short enough to pass for a belt, bats her lashes suggestively at him while she sucks on the straw in her drink.

Parker happens to turn his head and look in my direction. Across the room, our eyes lock. His smile comes on slow and heated. I lift my chin and sniff as if I've just smelled something bad, then look away, mentally rubbing my hands together in glee.

"Victoria!"

I turn to the voice. My glee evaporates. With zero enthusiasm, I say to the man standing before me, "Hello, Miles."

Shit.

He's tall, good-looking, and a fabulous dresser. I'll give him that. But he's an absolute dud in bed. The man couldn't find a clitoris if you gave him a map. After a one-night hookup a while ago, I left him snoring in his bed without a backward glance and hoped I'd never see him again.

He steps closer, his eyes half-lidded. "You haven't returned my calls."

He smells like a brewery. I smile tightly, edging away. "Oh, I've just been busy. You know how it is. It's good to see you, though. Enjoy your evening."

I turn, but he grips my arm so suddenly, I'm caught off guard. He pulls me roughly against his chest and leans down to whisper in my ear. "Busy, were you? D'you know the last time I was blown off?"

I stiffen and snap, "Let go of me, Miles." I try to pull away but can't. He's too strong.

Ignoring my instruction, he answers his own question. "*Never*. Nobody blows me off. I'm the goddamn head of a billion-dollar corporation! Nobody fucks me and then leaves me in bed without a backward glance like I'm a fifty-dollar whore. Who the hell do you think you are?"

He laughs. It's an ugly, unstable sound that convinces me he's drunk. Then he snickers. "Oh, that's right. You're a *bitch*."

I want to yank my arm away and scratch his eyes out, but an older couple standing nearby is staring at us, and I don't want to make a scene. There are reporters here. Photographers. Speculation about my personal life is in the papers enough as it is.

I say in a voice meant only for him, "You have two seconds to let go of my arm before I knee you in your tiny, useless dick. Now *fuck. Off.*"

His fingers tighten so hard around my arm, I gasp in pain. He snarls, "You frigid cunt."

Then suddenly Miles is flat on his ass on the floor.

Bristling, hands curled to fists, Parker looms over him, glaring down. He says, "One more word and you'll be waking up in the hospital. Or hell."

His voice is calm. His face holds no expression. But oh God, his eyes. There's murder in his eyes. It sends a thrill straight down to my toes.

Not a thrill of fear. A thrill of exhilaration, as if I'm at the crest of an insanely tall roller coaster, about to plunge over the edge and throw my arms in the air.

Why? *Because he stood up for me.*

He thinks he just rescued a damsel in distress, but what he really did is prove that he's got a hero complex, a hair-trigger temper, and a disregard for social convention. He obviously couldn't care less that dozens of people are now standing around gaping at us, arrested by our little melodrama. He's too concerned with protecting my virtue.

And now I know exactly how I'm going to hook him.

Knights in shining armor are the biggest idiots of all.

I'm so excited by the thought of my pending victory that I'm physically aroused. I don't think my nipples have ever been this hard in my life.

Miles staggers to his feet and hurls another nasty insult my way before stumbling off through the crowd.

Watching him go, I lift a shaking hand to my mouth and stifle a manufactured cry of distress. Immediately, Parker turns to me, his hand extended.

"Come on."

Without waiting for an answer, he takes my hand and leads me away from the whispering crowd to the dance floor. I follow him, trying to arrange my face into a facsimile of trauma. I hope it's not the face I make when I've had too much vodka and too little sleep, because that face is deeply unattractive. Without a mirror, I can't really be sure.

Then we're dancing. I have no real awareness of how it happened because I've been concentrating so hard on plotting and trying to look distraught, but Parker has me against his body, his hand on my bare lower back. We move smoothly through a sea of other couples as if we've been dancing together our entire lives.

After a few silent turns, he says, "Ms. Price."

"Mr. Maxwell."

"Lovely to see you again. You look wonderful. That dress is stunning."

I sniffle but lift my chin, going for an I'm-traumatized-by-what-just-happened-but-don't-want-you-to-know-it vibe. "Thank you."

I feel his gaze on me. I look over his shoulder, acting like it's too difficult to meet his eyes.

"Was he your date?"

I shake my head.

"Good." Pause. "An ex, I take it?"

I whisper, "Just a mistake." I produce a shaky laugh. "In business, I never make those kinds of mistakes, but in my personal life…" I inhale a long, shuddering breath, then pause as if I'm struggling for words. "Never mind that. Thank you for coming to my rescue. And now let's never mention it again."

His arms tighten around me, as if for added protection. He murmurs, "Of course," then we both fall silent.

Well, outside I'm silent. Inside, there's some kind of rave party going on involving a lot of hallucinogenic drugs and death metal music.

I'm very certain of the path I'm about to go down, of my commitment to make him suffer for what he did to me, but it's difficult to reconcile my bloodlust for revenge with my hormonal response to Parker Maxwell's proximity. He's just so…mascu-line. Yes, he's *manly*, in that way that can't be learned or faked, or even really explained. The way he moves and speaks and holds himself, even his damn smell, all seem designed to make a woman's ovaries start producing eggs overtime.

Because I can't deny that I'm still profoundly physically attracted to him, that the electric connection I felt when I was a clueless little girl still remains, I hate him all the more.

I close my eyes. When I open them again, Parker is smiling down at me.

"What?" I ask.

"You're an enigma, Ms. Price. A puzzle."

"Oh?"

He nods but doesn't elaborate. I prompt, "In what way?"

His smile fades. The intensity in his eyes is breathtaking. "In every way. I can't seem to figure you out."

"There's nothing to figure out, Mr. Maxwell. What you see is what you get."

"No. You're a very good liar, Ms. Price, but what you see is definitely *not what you get*."

My breath catches. *What does he know about me? Has he discovered something, who I really am?*

But he couldn't. I've been too careful. I've covered all my tracks. Fifteen years, a new face, a new name, a biography scrubbed clean of any damning detail... I'm not that unsophisticated country girl anymore, that girl who loved with all her heart and soul.

That girl is dead. There's only this girl left, the one made of ice and vengeance.

"Do you like puzzles?" I ask quietly, holding his intense gaze.

Parker lowers his head. Into my ear, he whispers, "They're my favorite thing in the world."

The tip of his nose skims the rim of my ear. This time when I shudder, it isn't faked.

"Did you get my flowers?" he asks.

I have to take a steadying breath before answering. The way his hand is drifting down my spine is distracting. "Oh...were those from you?"

Chuckling, he lifts his head. "And she's back."

"Who?" I ask innocently.

"Xena, Warrior Princess."

In the most coquettish move I can manage without making myself vomit from the sheer sugar overload, I tilt my head back and peer up at him from beneath my fluttering lashes. This is far more difficult than romance novels make it sound. I worry he might think I'm about to suffer from a fainting spell. I'm sure I look utterly ridiculous, but I forge ahead anyway.

"Why Mr. Maxwell, I'm sure I have no *idea* what you're talking about."

He throws his head back and laughs, causing several couples nearby to look at us, startled. "That was terrible. You should never try to be coy. Xena is much better than Scarlett O'Hara."

I smack him on his tailored lapel. "It's rude to call a lady out."

"Then it's good you're not a lady, isn't it?" His grin is so dazzling, a woman gliding by with her partner trips over her own feet.

My mouth is in danger of breaking into a huge grin to match his, but I don't want him to know I'm having fun, so I scowl at him instead. "And you, Rhett Butler, are no gentleman."

He stares at me. I stare back at him. After a beat of silence, we both begin to laugh.

"All right, now that we've got that established, let's move on. What are you doing here?"

I shrug. "The same thing you are. Supporting a worthy cause."

"How disappointing. I thought you might be trying to run into me while giving the impression it was accidental."

Bye-bye Superman, hello cocky bastard. Making matters worse is that he nailed it. I say acidly, "Not even you are worth twelve thousand dollars a ticket, Mr. Maxwell."

He smirks. "Oh, but I assure you, I am."

"Ha! Egotistical much? Are you always this smug?"

He appears to give it serious thought. "No. Sometimes I'm just right."

I laugh again. He twirls me around, moving us neatly out of the path of a man weighing more than the two of us combined, and his wife, a sweating, red-faced dowager who looks in imminent need of a doctor. *Saved once again.*

"So tell me, Mr. Maxwell—"

"Please, call me Parker."

For some reason, he looks pained. I think of how he'd said at the restaurant that Mr. Maxwell was his father. I remember his face then. It's the same expression he's wearing now, almost... ashamed. I feel a brief flicker of pity for him, but strangle it.

"All right. Parker. Tell me, will your date be angry you're dancing with me and not her?"

His brows arch. "What makes you think I have a date?"

"Excuse me. *Dates*, plural."

"If I had any clue what you're talking about, I'd gladly answer, but unfortunately I don't."

"No? Because your brunette friend over there by the potted palms is staring at me like I'm her arch enemy from beauty school, and your other friend, the blonde with the alarmingly large boobs, has just sent me her third scalding voodoo glare. I think she's about to go to the ladies' room and make a wax figurine of me to stick some pins into."

Laughing, he spins me away and then pulls me back against his chest. He tightens his arm around my waist and flattens his big hand over the small of my back. That hand feels even more scalding than the blonde's glare. We whirl around and around, until I feel a little dizzy.

"I came here alone, Ms. Price. Those are just two mistakes I saw coming a mile away."

Heat rises in my cheeks. I'm embarrassed I told him Miles was a mistake. It was the truth, albeit calculated, aimed at trying to get him to feel sorry for me, but now I feel exposed by it. I feel the most awful, terrifying thing in the world, something I never thought I'd feel again.

Vulnerable.

His look sharpens when he sees my discomfort. "I'm not

judging you. I know it's harder for a woman than a man...especially one as famous as you, as successful... It can't be easy for you to have a relationship..."

When I blink, surprised in equal parts that he's being not only nonjudgmental but also understanding, he sighs and shakes his head.

"Jesus, I'm fucking this up. I'm sorry. It wasn't my intention to throw that in your face. Sometimes I open my mouth without thinking."

"Well, I envy you that. I can't remember the last time I spoke without thinking."

I pause, shocked. Actually, I can remember, because *I just did.*

Parker looks at me for a long, silent moment and then murmurs, "So she *can* tell the truth, after all."

A feeling starts in my stomach, slow to spread at first, then going everywhere at once. Part dread, part astonishment, part pure joy, it makes all my limbs feel weightless and my heart beat a million miles per hour.

I've just been seen. Not looked at, but *seen.*

I glance away, desperate to regain control of myself, desperate to hide. Parker slows and then stops, until we're standing still in the middle of a sea of dancing people. When he takes my face in his hands, it's so unexpected, I freeze.

In a voice unaccountably raw and dark, he says, "You don't have to hide from me." His gaze drops to my mouth. He bends his head toward mine.

Oh God. What's happening?

He's kissing me. I'm being kissed by the man I hate more than anyone else on the planet, and holy fuck does it feel good.

It feels so good, I break away, breathless, and tuck my face in the space between his neck and shoulder. I smell him, skin and musk and a hint of spicy cologne, the scent of memory.

The scent of a long-lost home.

One second or a hundred years later, I hear a flurry of fast mechanical clicking. Light flashes beneath my closed lids. When I open my eyes and look around, I'm staring at a group of photographers.

I come back to myself as if a bucket of ice water has been dumped over my head.

I jerk out of Parker's arms. He simply stares at me, his eyes shining. The cameras sound like gunfire. The photographers jostle and swarm. I do the only thing I can think of.

I slap his face. Hard.

Then I turn and walk stiffly off the dance floor, managing not to break into a flat-out run, but only just.

8

VICTORIA

Playboy and Ice Princess Take Off Gloves at Charity Gala

Friday evening at Cipriani, the Muscular Dystrophy Association's annual fundraising gala was held. In past years, the event has hosted some colorful entertainment, but nothing compares to this year's fireworks show provided by Victoria Price and Parker Maxwell. Guests were shocked when Mr. Maxwell shoved Miles Campbell, CEO of Global Oil, and sent him tumbling to the floor after apparently exchanging heated words with Ms. Price. They were even more shocked when Ms. Price later shared a passionate kiss with Mr. Maxwell in the middle of the dance floor and then slapped him across the face.

No word yet if Mr. Campbell will be filing charges for assault, but this unlikely love triangle has everyone's tongues wagging and our editors at the *Post* salivating for more.

a s it's been doing for the past several hours, the phone on my desk is ringing. As I've been doing for the past several hours, I ignore it. I toss the newspaper aside and lean back in my chair. The beginning of a monster headache pounds at the base of my skull.

It's Sunday morning, and the shit has just hit the fan.

Tabby hands me a much-needed mug of coffee. "I told you it was bad. I've already fielded calls from your literary agent, four of your clients, and TMZ."

I sip the hot liquid gratefully for a moment and then sigh. "It's not *really* bad until my mother calls."

Tabby perches on the edge of the desk, swinging one long leg back and forth. "Maybe she won't see it."

We both know that's wishful thinking. My mother religiously scours every newspaper, magazine, and trash-talking rag for any mention of my name. When she sees my name next to Parker's, it's going to be World War III.

I wouldn't be surprised if she hunted him down and put a bullet through his head.

"Well, you looked amazing, anyway. That dress was *kick ass*." Tabby pauses. "So are you going to see Mr. It's Not Personal again, or was the slap an actual fuck-you and not just your usual warm and fuzzy way of thanking a man for flowers?"

I massage my temples. "Can you please wait until after I've had my coffee to be clever? I can't deal with clever without caffeine."

"Sure." She checks her Hello Kitty watch. "I'll give you three minutes. That's as long as I can hold off the clever. There's so much of it, it tends to come bursting through."

I drink my coffee. The phone on my desk stops ringing. After a momentary pause, it begins to ring again.

Tabby waits until it stops to say, "You know, when I was doing my research on him, I thought it was really interesting that he's originally from Laredo, Texas. Like you. And he went to J.B. Alexander High School. Like you."

Shit.

You have to tell her. She has to know what to stay on top of. Your name has now been linked with his in the press, and if there's anything that could be unearthed—

"It's him."

Tabby blinks, asks innocently, "Him? Him who?"

I lower my head and look at her. "*Him.*"

There's a suspicious pause. "Oh."

I say incredulously, "You already know?"

She makes a face like she's afraid what I'll do if she admits the truth. "Um. Sort of?"

"Sort of? Are you kidding me? Wait—did you know he owned Xengu before I went in with Darcy?"

She pulls her lips between her teeth and stares at me.

I leap to my feet. "Oh my God, Tabby! How could you let me walk in there without warning me?"

"Are you saying you wouldn't have gone?"

"Of course I would've gone! This is *my* city!"

"So you're saying you would've handled yourself differently?"

"That's not the point!"

"Dressed differently? Worn your hair differently?"

"Stop trying to smart your way out of this! I pay you to stay on top of this kind of thing!"

She says bluntly, "Then you should have told me who he was sooner. I figured if you wanted me to know, you would've told me. But you didn't. And because I respect you, I think you're entitled to your privacy even if I do know where all the bodies are buried. Besides, he wasn't even supposed to be there that night. I checked."

I narrow my eyes and make a low, growling noise in my throat.

She sighs. "I know. I'm fired. Moving on. Does he know it's you? *You* you?"

When I flop into my chair and shake my head, she heaves a relieved sigh. "So then he doesn't know about—"

"No." It comes out hard and clipped, with an edge like a razor blade.

Tabby stands and slowly walks around the desk. Looking out the window to the bright morning light, she asks, "Are you going to tell him?"

"Don't be ridiculous."

She turns to look at me. "Then what's this about?"

I take a long swallow of my coffee. After a moment, I say softly, "Justice."

"In other words, revenge."

I remain silent, thinking. I wonder if, like me, Parker has things in his past he needs to make disappear. I wonder about that gap of his that Tabby told me about, the two mysterious years when it seemed he'd vanished from the earth.

And I suddenly realize that my prior plan of getting him to fall for me and dumping him has been entirely too simple. I need to up the ante.

I need to ruin his life.

An eye for an eye, darling bastard.

"Tabby, I need you to dig deeper on him. Find out everything. Go back as far as you can. There's got to be something there, something I can use. Look at his family, his father in particular. There's no way *he's* clean. Just get me anything I can use. Anything at all."

"Use to do what?"

"To get us square."

The phone starts to ring again. I glance at the caller ID and groan. "I need to take this."

I can tell Tabby wants to say more by how reluctant she is to rise from her chair. To avoid any further conversation, I pick up the phone.

"*Hola, mama. ¿Como estas?*"

The stream of curses that spews from the earpiece is so loud, I yank it away, wincing. Wisely, Tabby leaps up and hustles from the room, closing my office door behind her.

She's heard my mother's tirades before. She knows how bad it can get.

"Mother, please," I say in English. "Calm down."

"Calm down?" she cries, outraged. "You tell me to calm down when I see a picture in the newspaper of my daughter kissing *el diablo* himself?"

I sigh, close my eyes, and rub my forehead. *Here we go.*

She continues in English, punctuating every few words with a Spanish curse. "You see that *pendejo* after all these years and you don't chop off his pecker, you *kiss* him? *Que chingados?* Have you lost your mind? You should've shot that *puto!* Yours wasn't the only life the *hijo de puta* ruined, Isabel!"

Pain. Rage. Shame. How wonderful it is to be reminded that your own stupidity was the cause of so much chaos. Of so many shattered lives.

I whisper, "I know, *Mama.*"

"Your father, your brother, me, Eva... We all suffered because of him! Our whole family suffered! And you most of all! How many letters did you send him, *mija*, how many times did you try to tell him—"

I leap to my feet and slam my fist on the desk so hard, the computer monitor jumps. "*Mama!* I *know!*"

My mother falls silent. In the stillness of the room, all I hear is the sound of my own ragged breath.

She says quietly, "Then tell me what that kiss was, Isabel. Tell me what you think you're doing. Because from where I'm sitting, it looks like you're doing exactly the same thing you did when you were fifteen. Falling for a liar."

Slowly I lower myself to my chair. My voice comes out hollow. "By accident, I found out he owns a restaurant in New York. I went for dinner, and he was there. And he didn't recognize me." My voice breaks. I take a few shallow gulps of air before going on. "But he seemed...he's attracted to me. To Victoria. And I thought..."

I hear a sharp intake of breath. "You thought you could even the score."

I don't answer. It's a special kind of hell, having someone know you so well.

After a moment's pause, my mother speaks again. "Is he rich?"

"Disgustingly. He doesn't just own the one restaurant. He owns over twenty of them."

I can almost hear the wheels turning in her mind. "And he's famous, obviously. Or at least infamous. The papers called him a playboy."

My low laugh sounds ugly, even to my own ears. "Apparently he goes through women like water."

She mutters, "*Bastardo.*" Then: "A rich playboy with no morals—because we both know he has no morals—must have all kinds of things he doesn't want people to know. All kinds of things that would surely make him suffer if they came to light."

I hear the smile in her voice when she says the word *suffer*. My mother would have been an excellent mafia *doña*.

"Exactly."

She exhales. In my mind's eye, I see her standing at the kitchen sink in her drab housecoat, staring out into the front yard, the long pigtail phone cord wrapped around her wrist.

In the old days, when I was a kid, this time of year the grass would be dry and brown, as would the fields beyond the yard, but the sprinkler and irrigation systems I had installed after my first book hit it big ensure that everything is green now.

Beautiful, abundant green, the color of money.

"You must be careful, *mija*."

"He'll never know it's me, *Mama*. I'll get close to him, find out what I need to know, and then ruin him. In and out. Quick and deadly."

"No, *mija*. I don't mean that. You're smart. I know you can find out what you need to know. You must be careful of something else."

The quiet tone of warning in her voice alarms me. "What?"

"That you don't get hurt again."

Scalding heat flashes over me. "I'm not a child anymore, *Mama*," I reply indignantly. "And you just said I was smart. Why would you think I'd let myself get hurt by him again?"

There's a weighty pause. Finally, she says, "Look at the picture of the two of you, Isabel. Look at it long and hard. Look at your face. Then tell me why you think I might be worried."

Before I can say anything, she hangs up.

I put the phone back in its cradle. I pick up the newspaper and look closely at the picture of Parker and me. Specifically, I examine my face. Then I see exactly what my mother was talking about.

The woman in the picture isn't a ruthless businesswoman with years of professional bitchery under her belt. She isn't hard. She isn't calculating. She isn't, at the moment of the kiss, the mastermind of a wicked plot for revenge.

She's undone.

She's pressed against the man as if her life depends on it, clutching him, her arms flung around his shoulders, her fingers digging into his suit, his hair. She wears an expression any fool can see is one of utter pleasure, of utter abandon. As if the world itself no longer exists, as if there's only her mouth fused to his, her body pressed to his.

I mutter, "Damn," and toss the paper aside. I sit for a while, thinking, trying to decide on the best course of action.

Then I call Tabby back into the room and tell her to get me Parker's cell phone number.

It's good I talked to my mother. It was hard, but it was also a necessary reminder of everything that's at stake, of everything he needs to pay for. Now I'm even more determined than before.

Even if I have to burn the whole world to the ground to do it, that bastard is going down.

9

PARKER

*T*he call comes at exactly the right moment. If I have to endure Elliot Rosenthal droning on for one more minute about current margins versus historical sales data, I might throw myself out the window.

I pull my cell from my coat pocket. It's a number I don't recognize, which makes me frown. No one I didn't personally give it to has this number.

"This is Parker Maxwell."

"And this is your dance partner, with hat in hand."

The throaty voice takes me so thoroughly by surprise, I stand without thinking. My executive team, seated around the conference table at my corporate headquarters in Vegas, all look at me. Even Elliot Rosenthal pauses to see what's going on.

"Excuse me a moment," I say to Victoria Price and then put the phone to my chest. "Continue without me."

I bolt out of that boardroom so fast their heads must be spinning.

I stride down the hallway, find an empty office, and go inside, closing the door behind me. "Sorry about that. I'm back."

"Is this a good time? I can call back later."

"No, your timing's perfect. I was in the most boring meeting ever held. In fact, you've just saved me from taking a swan dive from the twentieth floor to escape."

Her husky laugh gives me chills. Jesus, this woman sounds sexy even when she's laughing.

"Well, good. We're even, then."

"How so?"

"You saved me from a gorilla attack, now I've saved you from suicide."

"I'd rather have you still owe me one."

"Why's that?"

"Because then I could negotiate how you might pay me back."

I'm a little surprised by how forcefully that came out. Judging by the short silence on the other end of the line, so is Victoria.

Finally, she says, "Oh, I'm more than willing to pay you back. In fact, technically I do still owe you one, since our last meeting ended on such a…strange note." Just to disarm me completely, she adds softly, "I'm so sorry about what I did. The slap. It's just that…well, that was probably the hottest kiss I've ever had in my life." Her voice turns flirtatious. "And I do have a reputation to protect, you know. The Queen Bitch can't be seen with her panties melted off by the kiss of a beautiful stranger, now can she?"

Two things happen in quick succession. The first is that I laugh. I can already tell she's going to give as good as she gets, and I love it. The second is that I picture her naked, standing in front of me with her panties melted in a puddle around her feet, and my cock acts as if it's just heard the call to arms and springs to attention.

I walk slowly to the office windows and gaze out at the hazy desert skyline, trying to ignore the throb beneath my zipper. By now, I give zero fucks about the board meeting I ideally won't be returning to, because I never want this call to end.

I match her flirty tone. "The hottest kiss you've ever had, hmm?"

She makes a girlish noise, part shy laugh and part embarrassed groan. It's so unexpectedly erotic, I almost groan myself.

What the hell is she doing to me?

She's getting under my skin, is what she's doing to me. I haven't been able to stop thinking about her, not since the moment I laid eyes on her. And then that kiss. Jesus. It's probably the hottest kiss I've ever had, too.

It was definitely worth the slap. In fact, if she said the only way I'd be able to kiss her again is if she tied me up and cracked a leather belt across my ass, I'd beg, *Yes, please. Now, please.*

I had such a raging hard-on for so long after she left me high and dry on the dance floor, I thought I might have to consult a doctor.

Victoria asks in a teasing voice, "Is someone fishing for a compliment?"

"Definitely. Hit me."

"Well... Okay." Her voice grows husky. "I really like the way you taste."

Fuuuck.

"You're not playing fair. I have to leave this empty office I'm in at some point and return to the real world, you know. I'd rather not do it with a conspicuous bulge in my pants."

"Speaking of bulges, was that a churro in your pocket last Friday night, or were you just happy to see me?"

"I don't know what a churro is. I hope it's something enormous."

She laughs. "Oh, it is. It's a delicious, thick, long, fried dough pastry covered in sugar." She pauses. "It's my favorite thing to eat."

I burst out laughing. Deep, belly-shaking laughs, the kind I can't remember the last time I had. "Ms. Price, are you trying to have phone sex with me?"

She giggles. "I don't know, Mr. Maxwell. Would you mind if I were?"

Instantly, my laughter dies. "No. I'd fucking love it."

The pause that follows is so filled with sexual tension, every nerve in my body starts to tingle.

She says, "I know your reputation with women."

Her voice has lost all its humor and lightness. It's gone totally dark. I recognize that we're done joking around. She's laying something out on the line now. She's testing me.

This is one test I'm determined not to fail.

"And I know your reputation with men. But I don't care about anyone else you've been with, or anything else that happened before we met. All I care about is getting to know you better. Getting to know *you*—the real you. I want to know the woman I saw on the dance floor, the one who comes out only when she thinks no one's looking. The one with the sad eyes, who hides and plays make-believe and kisses like it's her last two minutes on earth."

I hear her inhale a low, shaky breath. With crossed fingers and a pounding heart, I wait for her to speak.

"I don't do relationships, Parker. I don't do the connection thing. The getting-to-know-you thing. I don't know how."

"Me neither. I'm not asking for any guarantees. Just a chance."

Silence.

"How about a date?" I ask. "One date, nothing more. No thinking beyond that."

More silence.

"You said you still owed me one," I remind her. "Consider it payment. If you don't enjoy yourself, all bets are off. I promise I'm not a stalker." I pause. "Unless you like stalkers."

I'm gratified to hear her soft laugh.

"Not particularly."

"It's a deal, then?"

After a moment, she relents. "One date."

Though inside I'm cheering, I pretend to be hurt. "Don't sound so enthusiastic. It's not like you're being led to the gallows."

Her "hmm" doesn't sound convinced.

I check my watch. "I can be back in New York in four hours. What time should I pick you up?"

"Wait, you're not in New York? Where are you?"

"Vegas. Not that it matters. If I was on the moon, I'd find a way to make it back for our date tonight."

Now she laughs with a little more gusto. "Tonight? I never said anything about tonight! It's a Monday, pal. I've got work to do tomorrow!"

I grin. "Tomorrow night, then."

"No, no way. I'm booked this week. I *might* be open Saturday night, but I'll have to check my schedule and get back to you—"

"Don't say no to the man with the delicious churro in his pants," I interrupt.

Her answering laugh is so genuine and free, it makes my grin grow until my face hurts.

"Fine. I'll tell you what. There's a cocktail party I'm supposed to go to on Friday, but this person gives the worst parties, so I *suppose* I can blow it off. Just this once. For the man with the delicious churro in his pants."

The flirtatious tone is back. Along with it comes an overpowering feeling of triumph, like I've just scored the winning touchdown.

"Friday, then. I'll pick you up at seven."

She agrees, and we say our goodbyes.

I stand in the empty office for another few minutes, thinking of her, before I head back to the conference room with a big grin on my face.

Friday can't come soon enough.

VICTORIA

"How do I look?"

"The same as you always look."

"Which is how, exactly?"

Darcy, lounging barefoot on the tufted leather settee in my expansive walk-in closet, crunches into an apple and then chews thoughtfully for a moment. "A chick in a white outfit that cost more than my first car."

I turn from the mirror I've been fretfully examining myself in front of and rest my hands on my hips. "A confidence builder, you're not. Seriously, Darse, *how do I look?*"

I execute a slow turn. She purses her lips, eyeing me up and down.

"You look hot, girl. What do you want me to say, I'm in love with you? Please let me have sex with your vagina?"

I throw my hands in the air. "You're hopeless."

She stretches out her legs and examines her hot-pink pedicure. "Since when do you need me to tell you how you look, anyway?"

"Since I'm going on a date with *el diablo*," I mutter.

"What?"

I wave a hand at my reflection. "Nothing. Forget it. If this doesn't do the trick, nothing will."

Darcy cocks her head and pins me in a hard stare. "What trick is that?"

I don't answer.

It's Friday night. Parker is due at my house in twenty minutes. I've invited Darcy over for some moral support, but have told her only that I'm getting ready for a date. Not a date with whom.

I don't want her to try to talk me out of it.

Darcy rises from the settee, tosses the apple into a mirrored trashcan in the corner, saunters over, and stands beside me. She crosses her arms over her chest and gives me a really formidable stink eye, one even my mother would be proud of.

"What're you up to?"

I pretend innocence. "*Moi?*"

I slip into the pair of high-heeled, crystal-encrusted Alexander McQueen sandals I've chosen to go with my killer Balmain minidress. The dress is long-sleeved, high-necked, and otherwise demure, but so short my hoo-ha will make an unscheduled appearance if I need to bend over. I'm a little worried about getting into and out of Parker's car, but have decided to deal with that moment when it arrives.

"Yes, *vous*," says Darcy, still eyeballing me. "I know a setup when I see one. I grew up on the streets of N'awlins, remember, girl? If my mother taught me anything, it's what a woman looks like when she's about to take an unsuspecting mark for everything he's got."

I turn to my jewelry display, a column of velvet-lined rolling shelves that stretches to the ceiling. From one of the drawers I select a pair of drop earrings, but then put them back.

If Parker decides to nibble on my earlobes, I don't want anything getting in the way.

As nonchalantly as I can, I say, "I have no idea what you're talking about."

Darcy sighs. "You're lying again."

"Oh, just relax. You'll find out soon enough!"

As if on cue, the phone rings. I pick up the extension in the closet. "Yes?"

"Ms. Price, it's Carlton from downstairs. I have a Mr. Maxwell for you?"

I freeze. *He's here already? He's twenty minutes early!*

"I see. Send him up, Carlton." I put the phone down, my hand trembling from the chaos that has just exploded inside my body.

Darcy narrows her eyes at me. "You have two seconds to tell me what you're up to before I revoke your best friend card."

I chew a nonexistent hangnail on my thumb, buying time, but she doesn't release me from her laser beam gaze, so I finally relent.

"Remember Captain America from Xengu?"

She snorts. "You mean the one you were sucking face with in the middle of the dance floor at Cipriani?"

I cringe. "You saw that?"

"I don't live under a rock."

Right. The whole world probably saw that picture. I take a deep breath. "He's the one who's taking me on a date tonight."

Her brows shoot up. "Oh, *reeeallly*." Without blinking, she stares at me, waiting for me to say something else.

"And he's here. Like, now. I have to go get the door."

I turn and scurry away. Darcy follows hot on my heels.

"If I'm not mistaken, and I never am, this is the same Captain America you said you had a 'past' with?"

She's behind me, but I know she's making air quotes around the word *past*. I keep walking.

"A past that didn't end well? That he apparently didn't even remember because he didn't recognize you? And last week, you kissed him in front of four hundred people then slapped him silly, and now he's here to take you on a date and you're wearing a coochie-grazing dress, fuck-me heels, and a face like the wolf that ate Red Riding Hood's grandma, and you have no idea what I'm talking about?"

We're in the hallway now, headed past the sunken living room.

"You see why I didn't want to say anything? You're over-reacting."

She laughs. "Overreacting? Girl, I know you. If I thought you owned guns, I'd be calling the police right now to report a homicide."

The doorbell rings. I pull up short, my hand at my neck, my heart palpitating. Darcy walks around to face me, a wry twist on her lips. She jerks her chin.

"This is bad juju, V. I can see it a mile away. Do *not* answer that door. Tell the Captain you fell and broke your ankle, or choked on a chicken bone or something, but don't go on a date with him tonight. Or any other night. This won't end well."

I say grimly, "I know it won't. I'm counting on it."

"What the hell does that mean?"

"There are some people who deserve everything bad that happens to them…and he's one of them. You'll have to trust me on that."

She examines my face in silence for a moment, then sighs. "I believe you. But you know the old saying."

"Which old saying?"

"'Before you embark on a journey of revenge, dig two graves.'"

My smile is vicious. "One for the upper half of his dead body and one for the lower?"

She blinks. "You're planning on sawing him in half? Shit, girl, what did he do to you?"

After a moment, I say softly, "He broke me, Darcy. He not

only broke my heart, he broke my soul. And that was *before* all the other bad stuff he's responsible for."

The doorbell rings again. Darcy and I stand staring at each other in silence, until I begin to turn away.

"Wait." She rests a hand on my shoulder.

When I pause and look at her, she shakes her head as if she can't believe what she's about to say.

"Let me answer the door. If we're gonna roll this pigeon, we might as well do it right."

Excited to have her help, I clap. "I knew I could count on you! What do we do?"

She glances at the door. "You go back to your room. Let me have a few words with him before you come out. Give me five minutes. That's all I'll need."

"What're you going to say?"

She glances back at me with a dry smile. "There are only two things a man really needs from a woman, girl. One is affection. The other is admiration. But since you're not the simpering, flirty type, we're gonna have to make him think it's all a big show. That underneath the permafrost there's an actual human being. And that *he's* the only one who can melt all that ice."

Pleased, I say, "We're on the same page! That's exactly what I was doing Friday night!"

"Great minds think alike," she mutters.

It doesn't sound like a compliment.

When the doorbell rings a third time, Darcy snorts. "Well, whatever you're doing is working. Judging by his patience level with that damn doorbell, Captain America has a serious boner for you."

I give her a quick, hard hug, then head back down the hall and hide in the powder room with the door cracked an inch so I can hear. There's a short silence, the front door opens and the sound of low voices drifts to me.

Though I strain to hear, I can't make out the words.

Shit.

I look at my watch. *Five minutes. Ugh. I could have a stroke by then.*

I sit on the toilet, tapping my toe against the marble, feeling like a herd of wild stallions is thundering across an open plain inside my chest. When finally the time is up, my heart is beating so fast, I'm a little lightheaded when I stand.

What I see when I look in the mirror doesn't help me feel any better.

My face is red. My eyes are wild. I look as if I just shot something into a vein.

I insist to my reflection, "You're a badass bitch, and nobody fucks with you! Now get your shit together and focus!"

I square my shoulders, take a deep breath and blow it out, then open the door and walk slowly down the hallway with my head held high and a smile on my face.

When I get to the living room, Darcy and Parker are nowhere to be seen.

I stop, frowning, but then hear voices coming from the kitchen.

Why the hell are they in the kitchen?

Aside from my bedroom, the kitchen is my second-favorite part of my home. It's all white marble and glass, like the rest of the place, but there's a built-in fireplace that separates it from the dining room, which I have lit most every night of the year, lending it a warm, homey feeling. And it's usually a little messy. I often stand over the sink to eat and leave the dishes for the housekeeper. I read the morning paper with my coffee at the breakfast table, which is usually strewn with other papers and magazines, some mail, my vitamins, my medicine…

My medicine.

All the blood drains from my face.

I sprint toward the kitchen. My heels clatter against the

marble, and my pulse pounds. I round the corner and pull up short, because there they are.

Parker is seated at my breakfast table, in my chair, drinking a glass of what I know is my most expensive scotch, because the crystal decanter is sitting on the table in front of him. Leaning back in the chair with a satisfied grin as if he's king of the hill, he's looking up at Darcy, who stands over him with her hands on her hips and a look of maternal affection on her smiling face.

Her traitorous, backstabbing face.

Why the hell is she smiling at my enemy?

"Well, isn't this cozy." It comes out too loudly and without an ounce of warmth.

They both look over at me. Parker's smile dies. Slowly, he sets his glass of scotch on the table. His burning gaze rakes over me, head to toe.

Darcy says brightly, "Oh, there you are! I didn't think you'd be ready so soon. We were just talking about my review of Xengu." She laughs. "I told him it won't be published until Monday, but he can rest easy, because other than the truffles, he gets an A-plus."

An A-plus. She's giving the man who ruined my life an *A-fucking-plus*? What's going on here? Bristling, I take a step forward.

An open bottle of my medicine is not six inches away from Parker's hand, sitting on the lazy Susan in the middle of the table, plainly visible.

My voice controlled, I say, "Really? How interesting. I don't think you've ever given any restaurant such a great rating."

Her eyes flash. It's a warning or a message of some kind, but I'm too angry to try to decipher the meaning.

Parker rises. He's wearing a navy dress shirt with no tie, open at the throat, a pair of beautifully cut charcoal-gray slacks, and a chunky platinum watch I recognize as a Patek Philippe. It probably cost upward of a hundred thousand dollars. Countering the elegance of his clothing is his hair, which is a little tousled, as if he's been running his hands through it, and the glint of copper along his jaw. He hasn't shaved.

He looks like a Ralph Lauren ad.

Bastard.

In a gravelly voice, the bastard says, "Victoria."

He makes it sound as if he's just thrown me facedown across the table, hiked up my dress, yanked off my panties, and buried his stiff cock inside me.

All the blood that had left my face floods back into it. My ears go throbbing hot. Through clenched teeth, I say, "Parker."

Hearing my tone, Darcy's expression turns smug.

It's official. I'm going to kill her.

"Well, I gotta go! Great seeing you again, Parker. And I'll see you later, girl." Darcy sashays over to me and plants a kiss on my burning cheek. When she pulls away, she winks, leaving me completely confused. Then she's gone.

The devil stands on the other side of my breakfast table, staring at me as if all the mysteries of the universe can be found inside my eyes.

"You're angry."

I turn away, smoothing a hand over my hair. When he adds, "She said you would be," I spin around and stare at him.

"*What?*"

Has she told him our plan?

Parker moves out from behind the table and slowly approaches me. His gaze never leaves mine. When he's an arm's length away, he stops. A smile teases his lips.

"Because I was early. She said you hate it when people are early even more than you hate it when they're late. You don't like to be caught off guard. She also said that you'd freak out that I was in your kitchen—because you never allow men in your kitchen—and that she liked me and knew you did too, and the only way I was ever going to be able to climb that ivory tower you've constructed to keep out anything that hurts is with the help of your best friend."

A small, astonished breath slips past my lips.

She not only played him, she played *me*! She did something that would evoke a real emotion in me, which would be much more convincing than any act, then told him the truth about why I'd be angry, then tied it all up with the preplanned lie we'd agreed on.

It's brilliant. I'm so relieved, my knees are weak.

She's still got flack coming about that bullshit A-plus rating for his restaurant, though.

Parker says, "She also said I should kiss you as soon as I could," and moves a step closer.

My heartbeat accelerates. I nervously clear my throat. "She certainly said a lot, didn't she?"

Fire in his eyes, he moves even closer. "Yes," he murmurs, then reaches out and touches my cheek.

Like a deer pinned in headlights, I stand frozen as Parker leans close to me. He brushes his lips against my own, and I shiver.

Then, when he nips my lower lip with his teeth and I make a small sound of pleasure, he drags me against him and growls into my ear, "But I want you to ask me for it."

My hands are pressed flat against his chest. Beneath my palms, his heart throbs wildly. My own pulse keeps pace with his, hammering hard against my breastbone.

Keeping my tone light, I say, "And why would I do that?"

He noses my hair aside. Using his teeth again, he lightly tugs on my earlobe. Another involuntary shiver runs through me.

"Because you want me to."

I laugh breathlessly. "No, I don't. I'm angry, remember?"

He pulls away slightly and gazes into my eyes. "Because I want you to, then. Because I didn't give you an opportunity to say no last Friday night. Because I don't want to scare you away before I've even had a chance."

His mouth hovers inches from mine. The heat of his body warms me through my dress. I feel electrified. Electrocuted. As if I might at any moment burst into flames.

"A chance to do what?"

"Make you fall in love with me."

I can't look away. I don't want to. It's like a primal urge to witness the carnage, like driving by a fatal car wreck, craning your neck to see the bodies and blood.

"Parker—"

"Ask me."

"We agreed on just one date, remember?"

"Victoria. *Ask me.*"

Instead, I stall. "Are you always this stubborn?"

He ignores that. Staring deep into my eyes, he orders, "Ask me to kiss you, Victoria."

I make a sound of exasperation.

He leans so lose to my face, his lips brush mine when he speaks. "You like the way I taste, remember? Now ask me. Then, after I've kissed you, I want to see if there's anything else you'd like to ask me for."

Oh, the dark promise in that tone. The blatant sexuality of it. My nipples harden. My breath quickens. A tingle runs down my spine.

I hate you. I hate you. I hate you.

I lick my lips, take a fortifying breath, and whisper, "Parker, please ki—"

Before I can finish, he crushes his mouth to mine.

VICTORIA

*I*t's the first day of high school, and I'm sick with nerves. This is a new school for me. One much larger and farther from home than the middle school I left in the spring. I have to take the bus, which is stifling hot and smells like vomit.

I'm hopelessly lost as soon as I step off the bus. The campus seems endless. I have a map and my list of classes in my backpack, along with my books and my lunch in a brown paper bag.

Trembling with anxiety, I kneel on the grass of the quad and tear open my backpack. I'm going to be late. I pull the map out so fast, I tear it in two. Two senior girls walk by, look at my lunch bag and my glasses and my secondhand clothes, and snicker. They walk on. With shaking hands, I fit the map halves together, trying to locate Building B.

"You need help finding your class?"

Startled, I look up.

A boy stands over me. He's beautiful. He's also smiling, a smile more dazzling than the morning sun haloed around his golden head. I have the fleeting thought that he might be an angel. I'm so surprised, I can't speak.

"Here, let me help you." The golden boy kneels beside me on the dewy grass. I hope he doesn't get stains on the knees of his expensive-looking trousers.

"Where're you supposed to go?"

"B-Building B," I stammer, red-faced and sweating. I push my glasses farther up my nose.

The boy looks at me. Even his eyes are smiling. *"I'm going there too. C'mon, I'll walk you."* He stands. When I just stare at him stupidly, he laughs and holds out his hand. *"C'mon, we'll be late!"*

I put my hand in his. He gently pulls me to my feet. He says, *"I'm Parker. What's your name?"*

"Isabel," I whisper, looking at my shoes.

"Pretty name for a pretty girl."

When I look up at him sharply, already hurt, I'm shocked to realize he isn't teasing me, or just trying to be kind to the awkward mousy girl in the thrift store dress.

He means it. This boy named Parker just called me pretty. For real.

No one has ever called me pretty before in my life.

Gasping, I break the kiss and turn my head sharply, my vision blurred with memories. I try to push Parker away, but he holds me tighter, his muscular arms like a vise.

"Easy," he says. "Just sit with it for a minute. Don't run away yet."

His tone is the one my father used to quiet the horses during a storm. He'd go out to the barn to be with them when the weather was nasty, to stroke their sleek necks and murmur reassurances in a loving voice, crooning, *"Tranquilo, mi amor. Estoy aqui."*

My brother and I were left to cower alone in our beds in the dark.

I keep my eyes squeezed shut because I don't trust myself to look at Parker. I don't trust what he might see in my eyes.

He presses the softest of kisses to my cheek. "So I was thinking we'd get a bite to eat first, somewhere quiet and then see where the evening takes us. Maybe hear some music—I know a great jazz club—or take a walk in the park." He pauses. "Although those shoes you're wearing don't seem like good walk-in-the-park shoes, so maybe we'll skip that. What do you think? Sound good?"

He's being light, casual, letting me know he isn't going to say anything else about my near-meltdown. About how I just disappeared inside that kiss. How I drowned in it, and came back up for air shaking and gasping.

I nod.

"Great. Also, in the spirit of full disclosure, I should probably tell you that this dress of yours, which is really more like visual Viagra than a dress, is going to cause an ocean of drool among all the poor bastards you'll be passing tonight, so I'm going to have to stick very close to you in order to be ready to lend a gallant hand when you slip on said drool. Which is inevitable, considering the sheer amount of it we'll be dealing with. So."

I laugh a little shakily. "So be prepared to have a Parker barnacle?"

He nods seriously, though there's a gleam of laughter in his eyes. "Yes."

"Noted."

I take a deep breath, then release it slowly. Parker eases his arms from around me and takes a step back, eyeing me warily as if I might change my mind and sprint away. But I'm better now. More steady on my feet.

But I need to find a way to deal with kissing this man if I'm going to make him fall in love with me so I can dump him and then ruin his life. There will probably be a lot of kissing involved. I might even have to sleep with him.

Realization hits me with such force, I stop breathing.

I'm probably going to have to sleep with him!

How is this only occurring to you now? The howl of laughter inside my head is Darcy's.

"You have the most interesting internal conversations," says Parker, watching my face. "Someday I'd love to be in on one of them."

I blurt, "I was just thinking about sleeping with you."

He stares at me. I've never seen such a look of hunger. In a throaty voice, he says, "Go on."

My cheeks heating, I wince. "I can't believe I actually said that out loud."

Parker hasn't blinked. His pupils are dilated. I wonder if mine are, too.

"Seriously, let's just pretend I didn't say that, okay? Rewind. Erase."

We stand in silence, looking at each other, until Parker lifts his hand and brushes his thumb over my lower lip.

"Okay. We'll pretend you didn't say it. Please ignore the churro in my pants, because he's not quite as good at pretending as we are."

My gaze involuntarily drops to Parker's crotch. And there, in all its glory, is one large and determined-looking bulge.

"I just said ignore it, Victoria, not stare at it. Show some mercy, woman."

Mercy is the one thing you'll never get from me.

Gazing up at him, I flirtatiously flutter my lashes. "I can't help it. Remember I told you how much I love churros? Your churro looks especially big and yummy."

He exhales hard. "Jesus. I can't decide if I should laugh, kiss you, or bend you over the counter and have my way with you. That was just *evil*."

"Evil's my specialty. You've been warned."

He clasps my face in his hands and plants a firm, potent kiss on my mouth. In a husky voice, he says, "If we're going to dinner, we better get to it, because we've got only about thirty seconds left before Mr. Big Yummy Churro takes control of the rest of my body and I rip off your dress. With my teeth."

That's as blatant a proposition as I've ever heard. I'm thrilled he's so affected by me.

I'm far less thrilled by how affected I am by him.

But if there's anything life has taught me, it's that every worthy endeavor is challenging…and usually painful. Nothing truly valuable comes easy. A battle easily won is no battle at all.

And we are at war, he and I. Blood will be shed. By the end of it, we'll both bleed.

But he's the only one who'll be dead.

I stand on my tiptoes, brush my breasts against his chest, and whisper into his ear, "Let's go have dinner, then. I'm hungry. But maybe we'll save the dress-ripping for dessert."

I turn and walk away, leaving him standing in the kitchen, chuckling to himself and muttering, "*So* goddamn evil."

Oh Mr. Maxwell, you really have no idea.

"So, where are you taking me?"

Parker, who's spent more time with his gaze on my legs than the road, smiles. "You'll see. We're almost there."

We're in his sleek black Porsche Panamera. It smells like money. On the way down in the elevator in my building, he held my hand. He held it all the way through the lobby and out to the valet. He only let go in order to drive.

"Oh, a surprise. I love surprises."

He smiles. "I'll remember that."

We slow to a stop at a curb. When I look out the window, I really am surprised. We're at Xengu, which, by the looks of it, is deserted.

"It looks closed."

When I turn back to Parker, he's grinning. "I said we were going someplace quiet, didn't I?"

Now I'm really confused. "Your restaurant is closed on Friday nights? Isn't that the busiest night of the week for you?"

"No, we're open on Friday nights, just not this Friday night I canceled all the reservations. All seven hundred of them."

My mouth is open, but no sound comes out.

Parker's grin grows blinding. "Which was totally worth it just to see that look on your face."

"Parker...I'm...that's...wow."

He laughs. "And now the woman who gives extemporaneous speeches to thousands of people is speechless. I love it. You're good for my ego, you know that?"

I say drily, "As far as I can tell, your ego is doing just fine on its own, Mr. Maxwell."

He takes my hand and presses a kiss to the back of it. "Aren't you going to ask me why I canceled all those reservations, Ms. Price?"

"Let me guess. You didn't want an audience in case I decided to slap you again?"

He shakes his head. "No. Because I didn't want any distractions while I was getting to know you better, like I told you I wanted to."

The heat in his gaze makes me want to squirm in my seat. "We could have just ordered in if you were interested in my scintillating conversation."

"But then I wouldn't have been able to cook for you."

My brows shoot up. "Cook for me? Are you being literal? You're actually going to make our meal?"

He pretends to be offended. "What makes you think I can't cook?"

I almost say *Because you didn't even know how to boil water when we were together*, but catch myself in time. I smile sweetly at him and pull my hand from his. "Oh, nothing. I'm sure the can of SpaghettiOs will be delicious."

He chuckles. A valet opens my door and helps me from the car. He also politely averts his gaze from my crotch area, which I try to cover with my handbag, which is approximately the size of a postcard and therefore pretty useless at crotch-covering. But then Parker is beside me, leading me into the restaurant with his hand on the small of my back, and I forget all about my overexposed hoo-ha because I'm too busy gaping in shock.

"Well," I say after a moment. "Your florist must really be happy to know you."

The entire restaurant is filled with bouquets of white roses. Dozens and dozens spray from vases placed on every table, the hostess stand, the bar—every flat surface available. White rose petals are also scattered all over the carpet, a fine drizzle, as if the floor has been dusted with snow. The only light comes from the hundreds of candles flickering on tabletops and in niches on the walls.

It's over-the-top romantic.

It's not at all what I was expecting.

The son of a bitch has really outdone himself.

He moves slowly around me, watching my face. He murmurs, "Totally worth it."

I laugh, shaking my head. "You're quite the handful, aren't you?"

Smiling, he moves closer. "Are we talking about my churro again? You're really obsessed with it, aren't you, Ms. Price?"

"Not as obsessed as you are with my legs, Mr. Maxwell. I thought we were going to be involved in a traffic accident on the way over."

He's standing so close, I feel the heat of his body.

"It's actually not your legs I'm obsessed with."

"No?"

"No. It's your skin. Your skin is so beautiful, it makes me want to cry."

"Oh dear God. I know that's from a song. C'mon, you've got to have better material than that. I thought you were supposed to be this big playboy womanizer, and you hit me up with that? For shame."

His smile is amused. "You're inconveniently intelligent, Ms. Price."

I lift my chin and saunter past him, headed for the bar. "You'd better up your game, hotshot, or I'll send you back to your beauty school bimbos from the Muscular Dystrophy Association's party. Now make me a drink."

I try not to smile at the sound of his laughter, which I like far too much.

I take a seat at the long, polished oak bar. Parker strolls around to the other side. Without a word, he takes a bottle of Grey Goose from one of the shelves on the wall behind the bar, scoops ice into a stainless steel mixer, pours some vodka into the mixer, puts the cap on, and shakes the hell out of it. He then takes a bottle of vermouth and a martini glass, swirls the vermouth in the glass, dumps it out into the sink, adds the chilled vodka, and presents it to me.

"Oh," he says, holding up a finger. "Wait."

He retrieves a bottle from a refrigerator under the counter, opens it, spears three olives with a wooden cocktail skewer, and sets the garnish in my drink. Then he pours some of the juice in and stirs it with the skewer.

I say, "A filthy Grey Goose martini with three blue cheese olives. Have you been conducting surveillance on me, Mr. Maxwell?"

"It's my job to notice what the customers like."

"So I'm a customer now. Interesting."

"You're not a *paying* customer, if that makes you feel any better."

"Oddly enough, it does. I like knowing you haven't taken any of my hard-earned money."

His smile is knowing. "Of course you do."

I take a sip of the martini—which is ice-cold and delicious—and ignore the way he's looking at me, as if he knows all my secrets and is just waiting to see when I'm going to figure that out.

He opens a bottle of cabernet, grabs two wineglasses from a hanging rack, and motions toward the kitchen. "Shall we?"

"I hope you're not expecting me to play sous chef, because honestly, I couldn't cook to save my own life. The only thing I know how to make is a reservation."

"Then it's good you have a friend in the restaurant business."

I slip off the stool, careful not to spill a drop of my delicious martini. "Is that what we are, Mr. Maxwell? Friends?"

On opposite sides of the bar, maintaining eye contact, we slowly walk toward the kitchen. He says, "For the moment. Although if you keep calling me Mr. Maxwell, I might have to take you over my knee."

My laugh is low and husky. "Promises, promises."

I'm gratified to see a flush of color creep up his neck.

In the kitchen, a table for two awaits, complete with crisp white linens, a low centerpiece of roses, a breadbasket, and a pair of lit white taper candles. Parker sets the wine and glasses on the table and pulls out my chair.

I ease myself into it, pretending not to notice the way his gaze devours the sight of my bare thighs. "This must really go over."

"What do you mean?"

I gesture at the table, the kitchen. "This whole shut-down-the-restaurant-and-play-chef thing. I'm sure the women you do this for must really eat it up. No pun intended."

A muscle in his jaw flexes. His look turns dark. "I've never done this for a woman before," he says, and turns away.

Right. Because his back is to me, I roll my eyes.

Parker, stiff shouldered, goes to one of the large stainless steel refrigerators against the wall and brings out a rectangular wood tray, wrapped with plastic. He sets it on the table, along with a small plate containing a chunk of pale yellow butter dusted with black flakes.

He points at the tray. "Manchego, Saint-André, and Humboldt Fog cheeses, accompanied by a foie gras terrine, orange marmalade, Marcona almonds, and fresh figs." He points at the butter. "And salted truffle butter for the bread."

I would normally make a smart remark about shitty truffles at this point, but I'm too busy wondering if it's a coincidence that my three favorite cheeses, along with all my favorite accompaniments to those cheeses, are staring up at me from a bamboo tray. When I glance up at Parker, his face gives nothing away.

"Thank you," I say, equally straight-faced. "This looks lovely."

He inclines his head. Behind his stoic demeanor, I sense irritation mingled with mischief. It's an interesting mix, and my intuition tells me to sniff a little closer. I decide to probe.

"So what else is on the menu for this evening, if I may be so bold?"

He gazes down at me, his eyes unreadable. "Tuna tartar, Scottish salmon with mashed leeks and asparagus, sautéed cremini mushrooms, and tres leches."

He just recited a list of all my favorite foods.

I stare back at him, careful to keep my expression neutral. "I thought you said you hadn't been conducting surveillance on me."

His smile is enigmatic. "It turns out Google is an incredible source of information."

I scoff. "You're actually admitting you googled me?"

"You're saying you didn't google me?"

"Of course not."

I say it with convincing force, not only because I'm a good liar, but also because it happens to be true. I didn't google him.

Tabby did.

"Good," he says. "You can never believe what you read on the Internet, anyway."

That statement stops me cold, as does the pointed look he follows it with. We gaze at each other. I wonder if he can hear my heart jackhammering inside my chest.

He turns away again and begins to assemble food on the counter. He pulls items from the refrigerator and takes pans down from hanging racks, getting ready to begin cooking. I take a moment to compose myself, then pour two glasses of cabernet and join him at the stove.

I hold out a glass to Parker. "Do you mind if I watch?"

He takes the glass from me. That faint gleam of mischief returns to his eyes. "I'd love for you to watch."

He's not talking about cooking, that much I know.

Everything this man says carries a subtext within a subtext beneath a hazy veil of misdirection and innuendo. It's maddening.

"You should've been a politician." I sip my wine as he sets a skillet on the stovetop, pours in a dollop olive oil, and lights the burner beneath the pan.

"Funny you should say that. I've recently decided to run for Congress."

"You're joking."

"Dead serious, I'm afraid."

"Really? I wouldn't have pegged you for the political type."

He glances at me. *Damn, those eyes are gorgeous.*

"What type did you have me pegged for?"

Ruthless, lying, self-serving asshole. I smile my most innocent smile. "Why, the entrepreneurial type, of course."

Without taking his gaze from mine, he takes a long swallow of wine, lowers the glass, and licks his lips. "Is there anyone in your life you don't lie to?"

I look at the ceiling, pretending to think. "Hmm. Yes, actually there are several. My gynecologist. My accountant. And my mother." The vivid image of my mother's face sobers me, robbing the playful tone from my voice. "I could never hide anything from her, even if I wanted to."

He cocks his head, studying me. "So the Queen B has a mother. Somehow I imagined you brought yourself into being through sheer force of will."

I look at him sharply, all teasing gone. Now we're getting into more dangerous territory. *Truthful* territory. I have the horrifying thought that maybe Parker has his own Tabitha on payroll, someone who knows how to dig deep and uncover ancient, damaging lies.

If he does, and he or she is good at his or her job, this hide-and-seek game we're playing is already over. And Parker's won.

If he has, I'm going down swinging.

"That too," I say quietly, holding his gaze. "Because I was forced to. Because something terrible happened to me, and by extension to my whole family, and I had two choices: lie down and die, or stand up and fight. I decided to fight."

He examines my face, my stiff posture, my fingers white-knuckled around the stem of the wineglass, and says, "And you've been fighting ever since." When I don't respond, he says more softly, "And you're fighting right now. Why?"

I turn away, but he grasps my arm, sets his wine on the counter, takes my wine from my hand and sets it on the counter, and then takes me by the shoulders and forces me to face him. I look at my shoes instead.

In a low, urgent voice, he says, "I don't know you well. Hell, I don't really know you at all. But I do know I want to be one of the people you don't lie to."

Surprised, I glance up at him. His eyes are intensely focused on mine.

I decide to challenge him. "Why?"

His jaw works. There's a moment when I think he won't answer, but then he says, "Because every time you walk into a room, it's like déjà vu. Every time you laugh, it makes me happy. Every time I see you, I get this feeling... I don't know. I don't know." He stops, frustrated. "I can't describe it."

He doesn't know me. A tremor of relief runs through my body. His hands move from my arms to my shoulders, and he steps closer.

"You act like you can't stand me, but you kiss me like you're starving. You look at me like you want to carve out my heart, but when I touch you, you tremble."

"In anger."

"Bullshit," he snaps. "Don't lie to me!"

I turn my head. He takes my jaw in his hand and, with gentle pressure, turns my head back, forcing me to look at him. His eyes are angry but unguarded. I see how much he means what he's saying. I see exactly how much he wants me to be truthful with him, exactly how confused my mixed signals make him.

And—bitch that I am—I plot anew.

"Okay. I'll tell you the truth. But you go first."

"What do you mean?"

"Tell me something no one else on earth knows about you. Tell me a secret. Something you wouldn't want anyone to know. Something...bad. If you do that, then I won't lie to you anymore."

His eyes darken. He remains silent a long, tense moment, staring at me.

Though he's not saying anything, I feel great emotion

warring in him. I sense he's trying to decide whether or not to trust me, whether or not he wants me enough to give in to my demand. Finally, after several excruciating moments, he drops his hands to his sides, looks at his shoes, and inhales a deep breath.

Then he looks up. Staring straight into my eyes, he says, "I once killed someone."

1 2

VICTORIA

*T*hat's so far beyond anything I'm prepared for, I stand with my mouth open, staring at him blankly. Finally I manage a weak, "What?"

"I said I—"

"Yes, I got it. I just…don't get it. That can't possibly be true."

Parker runs a hand through his hair. He steps away, putting distance between us, his expression pained. I watch as he turns again to the stove, lowers the heat beneath the skillet, and tosses in a pinch of fresh garlic from a small jar on the counter top. It sizzles and pops in the oil. He takes a wooden spatula from a ceramic crock and begins to stir.

He just confessed to murder, and now he's browning garlic? Who the hell am I dealing with, Hannibal Lecter?

Parker says quietly to the pan, "That medicine you take, Coumadin. What's it for?"

He noticed the specific brand of my meds. Another bombshell, though not nearly as big as the first. I steady myself, careful to breathe normally. Careful not to bolt, because I won't get far in these shoes.

Besides, I'm not afraid of him. I should be—he's just told me he's a killer—but his demeanor suggests that whatever happened, he regrets it.

Plus, there's a butcher's block of cleavers on the counter within arm's reach. If he decides he's made a terrible mistake with his confession and the only way to remedy it is by bashing me upside the head with the skillet, chopping me into bits, and stashing my dissected corpse in the walk-in freezer, he'll get a belly full of steel before he's gone a single step.

"It's a blood thinner."

Parker stirs and stirs, his gaze focused on the pan. "For what?"

I struggle for a moment, hating this unspoken tug-of-war, hating how exposed and helpless I feel knowing that my mortal enemy now knows my greatest weakness. However, I know I won't get anything more from him unless I give him what he wants, which, at the moment, is more information about my medication.

So now it's tit for tat.

I *hate* this game. Why the hell did I even suggest it in the first place?

Oh yeah: I've sworn to bury him. I can't expect not to get a little scratched and bruised while I'm digging the grave.

Through gritted teeth, I admit, "I have a weak heart."

He stops stirring and looks at me. "The woman described by *Time* magazine as the 'Heartless Wonder' takes medication for a weak heart? That's probably the most ironic thing I've ever heard."

Anger rears up inside me, spitting fire. This bastard is calling *me* out? I feel my face do something strange. My stomach twists like a pretzel. I say coldly, "I might be a heartless wonder, but at least I haven't ended anyone's life."

Yet.

Parker stares at me silently for a moment, then refocuses his attention to the cheerfully sizzling garlic. "I suppose I deserve that."

He squeezes his hand around the back of his neck and closes his eyes, and it's all I can do not to reach out to him and apologize. Which isn't like me at all.

Which is why I decide to go with it.

If I'm going to convince this son of a bitch that I really do have a heart, I'm going to have to start acting like it.

I take a breath, put my game face on, and try my best to sound contrite. "I'm sorry. That was rude."

He stills, glancing at me.

"Very few people know about my heart condition. Three people, to be exact. I hate… I don't like admitting weakness. It's embarrassing. And what you said before… Well, it just doesn't seem like something that could be possible for a man like you. It doesn't fit with what I know of your character. I suppose I'm just shocked."

I look away, pretending to be confused and emotional, when what I really am is dying for a bottle of Listerine so I can wash the taste of all this hideous truth from my mouth.

Parker turns off the gas under the burner. His gaze fixed on nothing, he folds his arms across his chest and murmurs, "It was years ago. A lifetime."

I stand in silence with bated breath, waiting for more. Waiting for the helpless little fly to wriggle and flail and get himself stuck even deeper in my web.

"She was the only person I ever loved."

Which means he never loved me. Contrary to what he told me hundreds of times when we were young, he never loved me at all.

I hate myself for how much that hurts.

Swallowing down the acid bite of bile, I say, "What happened?"

After a tense pause, he says gruffly, "She shot herself."

Disappointment cascades over me as if a bucket of cold water has been dumped atop my head. I want to scream. I want to throw something. I want to rage and shout and put my hands around his throat, because he dangled such a tantalizing, ruinous skeleton in front of my face, and now it turns out he didn't kill anyone at all.

"But you said 'I once killed someone.'"

"I didn't pull the trigger, but it was my fault. If not for me, she'd still be alive."

Sick with defeat, I close my eyes.

This moron isn't a murderer. He's just riddled with guilt over failing to stop an ex from doing herself in! How the hell am I going to ruin his life with *that*?

I don't want to hear any of the ridiculous details, so I say, "This might sound terribly harsh, but you can't take credit for another person's suicide. She had to be very depressed in the first place, or at least mentally unstable, to even consider doing something like that. It isn't your fault, no matter what happened between you. People go through awful breakups all the time and don't do anything nearly as drastic."

He shakes his head stiffly. "That's kind of you to say. But it is my fault. She wasn't depressed. She wasn't unstable. She was perfect. We were perfect. And then I fucked it up. What she did is because of what I did. Cause and effect, simple as that. Her death is on me. And I have to live with that knowledge for the rest of my life."

I'm going to be sick.

Whatever Parker sees on my face causes him to unfold his arms and close the short distance between us. He reaches for me, but thinks better of it and lets his hand drop to his side.

He says, "I've never told anyone that story."

I look demurely at the buttons on the front of his shirt. "And I've never told anyone my story. So I guess we're even."

"That's technically not true."

I look up at him.

"Three other people besides me know about your heart condition, correct?"

My smile is wry. "Actually, if you want the complete truth, it's four. I wasn't counting my doctor before."

"Okay. But you know what that means, don't you?"

The faint lilt of humor in his voice makes me both wary about the direction he's headed and relieved that we might be past all this emotional bullshit. "What?"

"You have to tell me something no one else knows. Only then will we be even." He reaches up and strokes my cheek. His voice drops. "Make it good."

I lift my brows. "Better than the heart condition? How many secrets do you think I have, Mr. Maxwell?"

For the first time since we entered the kitchen, his smile is genuine. "I'd guess you need a closet the size of an airplane hangar to hide all your skeletons, Ms. Price."

I can't help myself. I smile back. "That's a very useful talent, to be so charming while you're insulting someone. I need to add that to my arsenal."

Now he laughs. The husky sound sends a rash of goose bumps up my arms. He takes my face in both his hands. His voice lowers. "I think your arsenal is plenty well stocked already."

"There you go again with the charming insults. Whatever shall I do with you?"

Parker's eyes are getting heated. His face is close to mine. I fight the urge to flatten my hands against his broad chest and instead leave them hanging loosely by my sides.

"And there you go again, channeling Scarlett O'Hara. What did I tell you about that, Ms. Price?"

"To the best of my recollection, Mr. Maxwell, you said that Xena, Warrior Princess, was far preferable to my transparent attempts at being coy. Perhaps I should run you through with a sword?"

He watches my lips with avid attention as I speak. One step closer, and his body is against mine. I can't retreat any farther. The kitchen counter is pressed against my bottom.

I'm trapped.

In an incredibly sexy, throaty voice, Parker says, "Tell me something no one else knows about you, Victoria. Not your doctor. Not your friend Darcy. Not even your mother. Give me something that's only for me. Then we'll be even. And then we can really begin."

"Begin what?"

He sweeps his thumb across my lips. "What we both want."

My mouth goes dry. My voice comes out sounding strangled. "Which is?"

Parker presses his pelvis to mine. His erection leaves little doubt as to what it wants, but just to underscore it, Parker growls, "Everything."

We're eye to eye, unmoving, breathing erratically. The tension between us crackles. He sees a flicker of doubt in my gaze or something else that makes him warn, "And don't you dare tell me anything but the whole fucking truth, or I *will* put you over my knee. And it won't be for fun."

Jesus, he's intense. For a moment, I close my eyes to escape him.

I might be getting more than a few scratches and bruises by the time I've reached the bottom of this six-foot hole I'm so merrily digging.

Then I look into his eyes, jump over the edge of the cliff, and confess.

I whisper, "I'm afraid of the dark. Clowns and snakes terrify me. And I'm pretty sure I'm going to die alone with one too many cats and it will be weeks before my body is discovered because no one in the whole world knows I'm dead because I push everyone away before they can hurt me."

A look of wonderment dawns over Parker's face. He breathes, "You're so goddamn beautiful."

For the second time tonight, he crushes his mouth to mine.

13

VICTORIA

*T*hese kisses of his, they're addictive. I bet he could sell them on the street and make millions.

This time, he breaks away first. We're both panting, hungry, clutching each other like a pair of horny teenagers.

I groan at the loss of his mouth. "Why'd you stop?"

His lids drift open. His voice comes out gruff and intense, more intense even than the look in his eyes. "Because I was about to do something so dirty to you on this counter, it would make your friend Gloria Tartenberger issue a permanent shutdown order. I'd have to tear down the entire restaurant and rebuild."

Delighted, I laugh. I maintained my control this time, and, inch by inch, he's losing his. "Now I'm intrigued. Give me a hint."

He lowers his mouth to my ear. "Do you know what tastes even better than a spoonful of four-thousand-dollar beluga caviar?"

"No, what?"

One of his hands drifts from my waist and cups my ass. He squeezes. When he speaks, his voice is hot and dark.

"A spoonful of four-thousand-dollar Beluga caviar eaten out of a freshly waxed pussy."

My breath catches in my throat. I dig my fingers into his shoulders. A shiver of desire runs through my body.

He chuckles. "I see you like the idea."

No—I capital *L*-word the idea. I'm veering dangerously close to coming right out and asking him for it, so I keep my tone light and playful to throw him off.

"It sounds a little unhygienic, actually. I don't think my gynecologist would approve. Besides, how do you know I'm not rocking some major seventies bush beneath my panties?"

In one swift, heart-stopping move, his hand slides lower, slips beneath the hem of my microscopic skirt, and pulls it up, exposing my naked bottom. Above my tailbone, he slides a finger between my thong and my skin.

"These panties, you mean?"

He jerks on the silk. It rubs against my clit. I jump, gasping, my eyes going wide.

His hot breath fans over my neck. His lips move against my earlobe when he speaks. "These wet panties I've been wanting to bury my face in since you walked into the kitchen at your house?"

He jerks on the fabric again, eliciting a low moan from me. I struggle to maintain my breathing, my sense of control. "They're not wet."

A deep, dangerous sound rumbles through Parker's chest. "No more lies, Victoria."

I close my eyes. Then I whisper, "It's not a lie. My panties aren't wet. They're *soaked*."

With that, I pull away.

He allows it, but I'm not convinced he won't lunge at me. The look in his eyes is nothing short of ravenous.

I turn and casually retrieve my glass of cabernet from the counter. Then I stroll back to the table, sit down, cross my legs and take a swallow of the wine. I look at him over the rim of the glass with big, innocent Bambi eyes.

His smile is carnal. "You like to play games, don't you?"

"Only games I can win."

Parker licks his lips and drags a hand through his hair. The vein in his neck throbs wildly.

He turns back to the pan of olive oil and garlic on the stove and relights the burner. I spread a chunk of triple crème Saint-André on a rosemary cracker and take a bite, all while trying to control my hormones.

It's about as effective as trying to herd cats.

The man is. *Smoking. Hot.*

I push away the whirlwind of memories crowding my mind. I push away the desire crashing through me, heating my blood, making it scald my veins. I push away all thoughts of how broad his back and shoulders are, how strong, how much I'd like to peel that shirt off him and sink my teeth into his flesh.

Instead I sit, poised, munching calmly on a cracker and sipping a fine cabernet, while inside I'm a boiling vat of noxious chemicals.

My talent for maintaining a false tranquility comes from years of practice. It's second nature now, as is my talent for deception.

Watching Parker calmly stirring his browning garlic, I'm beginning to realize he and I have much more in common than I thought.

The meal is exquisite.

Parker feeds it to me, forkful after forkful, an odd and completely sensual experience. I've never been hand-fed before and am not quite sure what to make of it, but after the first few awkward bites, I surrender to the sheer bliss of the food that's hitting my tongue and begin to enjoy it.

For every two bites I take, he takes one. For every few swallows of wine I take, he takes one. I doubt he's trying to get me drunk, but by the time the meal is over and we leave the restaurant, I'm feeling a little tipsy and tell him so.

"I know just what you need." He smiles and helps me into the Porsche. He closes the door behind me with a firm *thunk*, as if sealing my fate.

We go dancing.

It's a smoky jazz club right out of a noir movie set in Paris in the forties, the entrance unmarked, the music mingling with the smell of sweat and cigars in the air. I adore it. Parker commandeers a private table in a shadowed, elevated corner in the back of the room where we can see everything without being seen, where we can smile our secret smiles and play our secret games and act like none of it matters.

We order champagne. We hold hands. We dance, our bodies swaying to the beat, our eyes closed. As the night wears on, he looks at me often in silence, a strange light in his eyes, an intimate yearning I escape by averting my own eyes, taking a drink, forcing a laugh.

When the club closes at three, we're the last to leave.

Standing outside in the chill, Parker settles his jacket around my shoulders, and I'm wrapped in his warmth and scent. Neither one of us wants to go home, so we act like silly tourists and hire a horse-drawn carriage to take us on a meandering circuit of Central Park. Bundled beneath blankets, we talk in hushed voices about everything and nothing as the horse chuffs and shuffles, its breath steaming the air. Then there is birdsong, a lightening in the sky, and I realize with deep surprise we've stayed up all night.

With an even more profound sense of surprise, I realize I don't want the night to end.

When Parker pulls the Porsche into the valet drive at my building, I'm tense and unhappy, filled with regret. I didn't expect this night to be so...so...

Perfect.

"She was perfect. We were perfect."

Parker and his perfect, dead love. The memory of his sorrow-filled words about her is what finally snaps me out of my funk and gets me refocused on the goal.

His obliteration.

"Thank you," I say as the elevator doors open in the vestibule in the lobby. "I had a wonderful evening."

"You're not inviting me up."

He sounds resigned, though not particularly disappointed. He's the type of man who likes to chase things, after all. An easy victory would be a hollow one.

"Some other time, maybe. I'm tired. It's been a pleasure, though."

He touches my face. He enjoys doing that. Enjoys watching his fingers drift over my cheekbone toward my mouth, the same way he enjoyed it when we were young and he called me by another name.

I wonder how many other women he's enjoyed it with, too.

"So I've passed muster? There will be another time?"

I smile. Our gazes hold. "We'll see."

He steps closer. "That's not a no. I'll take it as progress. And Victoria..." He brushes his lips against my mouth. He murmurs, "The pleasure is all mine."

He embraces me abruptly in a hug so hard, it leaves me breathless. Then he's striding away through the lobby, his gait long and sure.

When he's gone, I enter the elevator and hit the button for the penthouse. As the doors close, I stare at myself in the mirrored panels.

My reflection mocks me.

Like the woman in the picture in the newspaper, I'm unrecognizable. My face is soft and unguarded. My eyes shine. I look like a woman stripped of all her armor, a woman standing naked in the middle of a battlefield as a thousand whistling arrows descend from the sky.

Once again, because of Parker, I'm weakened. Lessened. Vulnerable.

I turn my back on that vulnerable woman in the mirror.

Over my shoulder, I flip her the bird.

14

VICTORIA

I'm awakened by someone tapping me on the forehead. When I crack open an eye, Tabby stands beside my bed, holding a steaming mug of coffee. She's grinning.

Cheerfully, she says, "Here's a sight I never thought I'd see: Maleficent switched places with Sleeping Beauty!"

I grumble, "Go away."

"It's almost ten o'clock, boss."

"Maybe I need a day off."

"You don't take days off."

"Maybe I'm sick."

"Psh. You never get sick. Besides, I know what you were up to last night. Dinner, dancing, and a romantic turn around Central Park with the man you've sworn vengeance on?" She makes a hen-like clucking noise. "No wonder you're so tired. All that evil-doing must be exhausting."

Grouchy and grainy-eyed, I sit up in bed and take the coffee from her hands. It's strong and black, just how I like it. "Please tell me you didn't attach a GPS device to my shoes."

She wrinkles her nose. "I'm a hacker, boss, not Jason Bourne."

"Then how do you know what I was doing last night?"

"You had a tail from TMZ the entire time."

When I nearly choke on my coffee, she calmly adds, "But don't worry. When I got a ping on your name from their servers, I crashed their system and corrupted about fifty terabytes of data, so that story's toast. Along with a whole bunch of others."

"Oh. Good work. But the photographer still has his—"

"No, he doesn't." Her smile is sphinxlike.

I stare at her, blinking against the bright light streaming in through the bedroom windows. "How?"

She purses her lips. After a moment, she says, "You know how in *House of Cards* when President Underwood asks his minion Doug Stamper to do something unsavory, and he does, and then the president asks if it was done, and Stamper says yes, and the president wants details, and Stamper says something to the effect that it's better if he doesn't know in case, you know, there are some legal ramifications later on? Like so the president can claim he doesn't know anything, because he really doesn't?"

"Yeah?"

"It's like that. You really don't want to know."

I sip the coffee, collecting my thoughts. "That sounds rather ominous."

She shrugs. "Just another day at work under the Mistress of All Evil."

"Very funny." I take a closer look at what she's wearing. "Dear God, are those Hello Kitty boots?"

She sticks out a slender leg. It's clad in a bubble-gum-pink platform boot made of some kind of shiny manmade material, stamped all over with a white cartoon cat with a bow in its hair, holding a lunchbox.

"Aren't they adorable? I bought them for the Hello Kitty Con in November. I've totally got my whole outfit already planned."

I could have gone my entire life without knowing there's a convention devoted to all things Hello Kitty.

"They certainly pair wonderfully with the rainbow leggings and the sequined baby doll dress. You look like you're ready for the Electric Daisy Carnival."

The EDC is a giant outdoor concert and festival where twenty-something dance music fans dress in outrageous costumes, get high, and have sex in public. It's the annual Woodstock for Millennials.

Tabby laughs, tossing her long red ponytail over her shoulder. "That's not until June, silly!"

Undoubtedly, she already has tickets.

I swing my legs over the side of the bed, down the rest of the coffee, and hand the empty mug back to Tabby. "All right. I'm up. What's on deck?"

"Weekly phone conference with Katie Couric at ten thirty. Lunch with your editor at Per Se at one. Three-o'clock meeting with your PR firm to discuss the next book launch. Your trainer's coming at five, and Alyssa and Jenny are scheduled for six sharp. But you know they're always fifteen minutes late, so you'll have a chance to take a quick shower after Duke leaves. They should have you ready to go no later than seven-thirty, so you'll be on time at eight."

Alyssa and Jenny are the hair and makeup girls I have come over when I need to get glamorized for an event. "Remind me, what's at eight?"

"The mayor's cocktail party."

"Shit. I thought that was last night."

"Do you think I'd let you go tarting around the city last night with Mr. It's Not Personal if you were supposed to be at the mayor's?"

I mutter, "I *hate* his cocktail parties. Every time his wife gets drunk and tries to follow me into the bathroom to get advice about how to get him to have more sex with her. And his guest list sucks. And his house always smells like hot dogs."

"You won't hate this one."

The conviction in Tabby's voice makes me glance up at her. "Why not?"

Her sphinxlike smile returns. "This year your friend the mayor has invited a special guest."

I cock my head.

"Who may or may not be testing the waters to see how much local support he can drum up for his upcoming campaign." She pauses for dramatic effect. "For Congress."

We stare at each other. I say, "Seriously, does the universe love me or what?"

"And the new Armani you ordered with the pornographic side slit and the plunging neckline came in this morning."

I snort. "This is gonna be like shooting puppies in a barrel."

I stand, stretch, and smile broadly at Tabby, my feelings of weakness and vulnerability washed away with the morning sun.

I can do this. What I've been feeling around Parker is just nerves. It's perfectly normal to be unsettled by his reappearance in my life, but now I need to focus on the prize and put those nerves aside.

Reinvigorated, I head to the bathroom. Tabby follows closely behind.

"Can I make one tiny suggestion?"

"Not if it involves trying to talk me out of my plan."

Her sigh is loud and overly dramatic. "No. I know that's useless."

"Speak then, minion."

I squeeze a blob of toothpaste onto my toothbrush, run it under the tap, then stick it in my mouth and begin to brush my teeth.

"Well, I was just thinking that since it was pretty intense between you and Parker last night—"

"How do you know it was intense?" I interrupt.

Her lips twist into a wry pucker. "I saw the paparazzi pics, boss. Slow dancing? Snuggling under a pile of blankies in the carriage? Lots and lots of kissing while doing both? Pretty steamy stuff."

Oh. Right. I spit into the sink and wave my toothbrush, indicating she should continue.

"Anyway, since it was intense last night, maybe tonight you should throw him for a little loop. Just for shits and giggles. Mix things up."

Interested, I stop brushing and look at her.

She casually inspects her manicure. "Like for instance if you showed up at the mayor's with a date."

I spit the rest of the toothpaste into the sink and declare, "You, girl genius, are worth every penny I pay you. Who did you have in mind?"

Because of course she has someone in mind. She wouldn't have mentioned it otherwise.

She grins, green eyes flashing. "Luciano Mancari."

Thrilled, I gasp. "Oh my God. You're even more evil than I am!"

She giggles. "I thought you'd like that."

"Like it? I love it!" I run over to her and give her a hug. Suddenly we're giggling maniacally together like two despots plotting a nuclear war.

Luciano Mancari has been trying to get me to go on a date with him since I met him six months ago at a dinner party hosted by a mutual friend. He's extremely gorgeous, extremely Italian, and—best of all—extremely successful.

He even has his own television show. *Mangia with Mancari.* He's a celebrity chef.

He's also got an ego the size of Canada, an IQ the size of a flea, and an eye that could be called roving, only that would be like calling Godzilla a cute little lizard. No human person with a vagina is safe from his lascivious gaze.

He keeps his hands to himself, however. He just likes to look. And look.

And look.

No matter. I'm not in the market for a husband or even a lover. I just want to prance around with him on my arm for a few hours to piss off Parker.

Nothing motivates a man like a rival poaching his territory.

Tabby turns and leaves, saying over her shoulder, "I'll get him on the phone. Call you when I have him."

"Wait—one more thing."

She turns back.

"See if you can find out anything about a girl Parker dated who killed herself."

She grimaces. "What the hell?"

"Yeah, I don't know either. He mentioned it to me last night. Could be something I can use."

She shrugs. "Okay. I'll add it to my checklist of chaos."

"You're a doll."

After she leaves, I take off my pajamas, turn on the shower, and step into the hot spray, smiling to myself.

I'm really looking forward to tonight.

Nine and a half hours later, glossed and gussied, I step through the tall glass doors of the lobby of my building. Across the drive, Luciano leans against the back door of a ridiculously long stretch limo, smoking a cigarette. He looks me up and down, taking his time, his gaze clinging to my every curve, then he flicks his cigarette away. Smiling, he holds out his hand.

"*Buonasera, belíssima.*"

I walk slowly toward him, my hips swaying. The Armani fits like a glove. A five-thousand-dollar glove with a slit so high it's more like an open invitation to take a gander at my lady bits.

"*Buonasera,* Luciano," I purr. "How nice to see you again."

While ogling my cleavage with one eye and my legs with the other, he kisses my hand. When he straightens, his dark eyes are half lidded, as if he's already fucked me. He says something in Italian that sounds suspiciously dirty, but I don't speak the language, so I can't be sure. I just smile and allow him to help me into the limo.

Luciano sits next to me on the wide leather seat, the driver shuts his door, and we pull away. Then he turns to me and says in his formal, accented, slightly incorrect English that so many women find irresistible, "I am very pleased you have finally decided to accept my offers for a date, Miss Victoria. I am always finding you so very beautiful woman."

Aww. That was kind of sweet. Too bad I can't stand him.

"Thank you, Luciano."

"Please." He touches my arm. "Call me Lucky. This is more personal, no?"

Instead of rolling my eyes, I smile. "Of course."

His gaze drops to my arm, then drifts over to my crossed legs, on spectacular display courtesy of the giant side slit. He folds his hands in his lap but doesn't stop looking at my legs, which gives me ample time to study him.

He's a classically handsome man, with a straight nose, full lips, and a thick head of dark hair. His skin is flawless. His jaw is chiseled. He carries himself regally, wearing a beautiful bespoke black suit as if he were born in it.

All that beauty, yet he's entirely uninspiring.

I remember exactly this expression he wears. It's one of vague disinterest, even when he's paying close attention to something, like my legs. It's as if his mind is on the constant verge of sleep.

He's perfectly made for television. All bright and shiny on the outside, but empty when you look within. "All sizzle and no steak," as my father would have put it.

In comparison, Parker Maxwell is a goddamn filet mignon.

The thought makes me chuckle. Luciano glances up at me. A furrow appears between his sculpted brows.

"Are you finding me funny, Miss Victoria?"

"Oh no, Lucky, not at all! I was just thinking about your show last week. That woman you brought up from the audience to help you with the Bolognese sauce was so sweet. I thought she was going to faint from standing so close to you!"

He's surprised and pleased. I can tell by his expression. "You watch my show?"

"I never miss it! It's my favorite!" I lean closer and add in a confidential whisper, "It's *so* much better than Emeril's."

I bat my lashes at him. He beams back at me. *And we're off.*

I've never watched his show. Tabby gave me the Cliffs-Notes version while I was getting my hair done so I'd have something to talk to him about. I knew this would be a winning topic.

Luciano says with confidence, "*Certo.* This is because he is an American, no? From the South—a racist." He makes a dismissive hand gesture. "Cooking these disgusting crawfish creatures from the swamps. How anyone thinks this is real food, I cannot know. *Estúpido.*"

A wave of heat rises from my chest to my face, where it settles and burns.

Number one: I love crawfish. I grew up eating them. My mother, bless her heart, isn't a great cook, but she made do with what was available and we could afford. We had wire funnel traps in the pond on our property and had crawfish boils nearly every weekend in the summer.

Number two: The assumption that being from the South equals being a racist is idiotic. Racism isn't about where you were born. It's about how small your heart is.

Number three: He has no idea—nor has it occurred to him to ask—whether I'm from the South or enjoy crawfish. On top of that, he's insulted my country. Or my nationality. Certainly my national pride, at the very least.

If I get the chance tonight, I'm going to trip him and make him fall flat on his beautiful face.

I give him my most winning smile. "Oh, Lucky, you're so interesting. I could listen to you talk all night!"

He gazes at me for a beat, then says solemnly, "You are very intelligent for a woman."

I make a noise that was meant to be a casual laugh, but sounds instead as if I'm retching. Concerned, Luciano pours me a glass of champagne from the chilled bottle in the built-in bar along one side of the limo. He hands it to me, and I guzzle it.

It's going to be a long fucking night.

When I'm finished, I hand the glass back to him.

"More?" he inquires.

I nod. "I love champagne. The only thing I love more than champagne is limoncello."

I really don't like champagne or limoncello, but every single thing I've said so far to Luciano has been a lie, starting with, "How nice to see you again," so I'm just going with the flow. I can't remember if I'm on lie number eight or nine now. It might be fun to try to keep track.

Luciano snaps his fingers. "Ah! *Fantastico*! I make my own limoncello! You will come to my restaurant after this cocktail party and try it."

He pronounces that last part as if it's a kingly decree. Obviously, I have no say in the matter. How does this man ever get a real date?

I spend the remainder of the ride listening to Luciano drone on at great length about the process of making limoncello, which is as thrilling as watching paint dry. By the time we arrive at the mayor's house, my eyes are nearly crossed with boredom. I smile gratefully at the driver, who helps me from the car with a smirk that hints he has the same opinion of his employer as I do.

Then I take Luciano's arm and walk up the grand marble staircase that leads to the mayor's front door.

And who is standing at the front door but *el diablo* himself, Parker Maxwell.

He's got his arm draped possessively around the shoulders of a gorgeous young woman.

15

VICTORIA

*A*s if I've been kicked in the stomach, my breath leaves my body with a grunt.

Naturally, Luciano doesn't notice my sudden distress.

"Ah! My dear friend!" he exclaims.

He raises charges toward the mayor, who is welcoming people as they arrive. Luciano drags me along by my elbow. He strides through the small, well-dressed crowd standing on the wide patio, knocking people aside.

When we reach the threshold, Luciano releases me long enough to pump the mayor's hand enthusiastically. Then he throws his arms around him and gives him a dramatic hug, followed by an even more dramatic Italian male greeting that involves a lot of cheek-kissing and back-slapping. The mayor—a small, balding man with owly eyes—looks stunned by all the attention.

Then Luciano remembers me. "May I please present to you the *belíssima* Miss Victoria Price, a woman who has very much smart ideas!"

Luciano yanks me forward by the wrist. In my heels, I nearly stumble, but catch myself in time. I wrench my wrist from his grip, pull myself to my full height, shoot Luciano a deadly glance, then smile sweetly at the mayor.

"David. So wonderful to see you. Thank you for inviting me. I always look forward to your parties."

The mayor warmly clasps my extended hand and smiles back. "Victoria, thank you for coming! Christine will be so pleased you've arrived. She says you're her favorite guest. She was just asking for you, as a matter of fact."

Wonderful. I've got another drunken bathroom hijack from the mayor's wife in my immediate future.

Beside me, Luciano blinks. "Oh, you know the mayor?"

No, my entire life didn't start until you drove up tonight in your stupid limo.

"We've known each other for years," I reply cheerfully and am happy to see a flicker of disappointment cross Luciano's perfect features.

The mayor says, "Victoria, Luciano, have you met Parker Maxwell? He's my special guest this evening."

When he turns to Parker with a smile, I'm finally forced to look at him.

He stares back at me with hard eyes, a hard jaw, and thinned lips. Obviously, he wasn't expecting to see me. Even more obviously, he isn't pleased. His gaze cuts to Luciano, who immediately plasters himself to my side.

For the first time tonight, Luciano and I have something in common: the look of disgust we both give Parker.

So the pleasure is all yours, is it? You'd like to be one of the people I don't lie to, would you? Every time I laugh it makes you happy, does it, you lousy, lying louse?

And here he is the very next day with his arm wrapped around a hot little piece he's probably said the exact same shit to. I wonder if they had sex right before they came to the party.

Everything inside me vibrates at a high, dangerous frequency, like some kind of unstable Dr. Frankenstein electrical experiment, ready to blow all the fuses in the house before birthing a monster. These genteel partygoers are lucky there aren't any sharp objects within easy reach, or they'd be witnesses to a bloodbath.

With acidic disdain, Luciano says, "I know him."

I'd like to kiss his cheek. Instead I clasp his hand in mine and pull him closer. He gladly obliges, but then becomes distracted by my cleavage, which he stares at, all else instantly forgotten.

I say brightly, "We've actually never met. Though your reputation precedes you, Mr. Maxwell." I glance at the beautiful young brunette beside him. My laugh is low, throaty, and full of malice.

In a voice so terse the word is almost spat, he says, "Victoria."

He doesn't acknowledge Luciano or introduce his date, who has lifted her chin and squared her narrow shoulders. I look at her and show all my teeth, like a shark.

She blanches and shrinks closer to Parker.

The mayor looks back and forth among the four of us, confused by the odd tension.

"Ahem. Well, won't you all please come inside?"

He stands aside, arm held out, all polite smiles and warmth. I jerk on Luciano's hand to rouse him from his breast-induced coma and stride forward into the mayor's home without looking back, dragging him behind me.

The house is crowded with waiters passing hors d'oeuvres and guests milling around the rooms in chatting groups. Warmth hits me along with a confusion of scents, perfume and food and cigarettes, and above it all, the din of voices and music. I spot two bars on opposite sides of the grand, vaulted living room and head for one. With his long legs, Luciano easily keeps up with me.

I arrive at the bar slightly winded and bark my order to a bartender who looks all of twelve years old.

"*Belíssima*, are you all right?" Luciano touches my cheek. "Your face is like the ripe tomato."

From the corner of my eye, I see Parker. He's a head taller than everyone else, looking around the room as if searching for something. I turn away.

"If you must know, Lucky, I thought the way that Parker person looked at you was *very* disrespectful. It really made me mad. I mean, you're Luciano Mancari!"

He puffs out his chest. "Do not let him anger you, Miss Victoria. This man has very much jealousy of me. It has always been so."

"Oh? You know each other?"

The teenage bartender hands me my martini. I take a sip. It's not nearly as good as the one Parker made me, dammit.

Luciano shrugs. His gaze drifts over to a woman standing nearby who has quite impressive cleavage. As he speaks, he continues to stare at her breasts.

"He owns restaurants. But he is not a chef, an artist, you see? He is like a merchant. Only concerned with money. No talent is there, just this want for the money. He is very American in this way."

Another jab at Americans. I'm not just going to trip this idiot tonight. I'm probably going to push him into the mayor's Olympic-sized swimming pool.

"Well, he obviously wishes he could be you."

Luciano's smile oozes self-importance. "This is one of the great challenges for me, *belíssima*. For every gift, there is a price, no? And for me, with all my gifts, the price is this constant jealously from lesser men."

I stare at him. "You poor thing."

Luciano's dark eyes warm with something that looks suspiciously like admiration. He leans close to my ear and says, "You are different kind of woman than I maybe think before. Not so strong American hustler woman. More traditional. Understanding of the man. This job you have, this bitches thing, I guess this is funny thing for you, no? Like job you have until later, when you find right man and can be married?"

He pulls back and looks at me, smug, his brow cocked, smiling an *I've got you pegged, don't I?* smile, and I just about lose my shit and toss my martini in his face.

I don't, however. I simply say with total honesty, "Lucky, I have never met a man like you in my entire life."

For this, I'm rewarded with a dazzling grin. He shakes a finger in my face. "Aha! She is seeing so clearly! She cannot hide from Luciano Mancari!"

Anyone that insults my country, my intelligence, my feminist ideals, all women in general, and a favorite childhood food, *and* refers to both himself and me in the third person in one sentence automatically gets an honorary spot on my shit list. Now if he'd just kick a small animal, he'd earn himself top billing.

"I wouldn't be so sure about that if I were you," says a deep voice. When Luciano and I turn, Parker stands there, staring at us. The brunette is nowhere to be seen.

"Ah. It is you." Luciano sneers, then drapes his arm over my shoulders. "Have you come to see how a real man treats a woman?"

Parker's cheeks grow ruddy. I allow myself a toxic smirk.

He looks at me. With soft, dangerous intensity, he asks, "May I have a word?"

"I'm so sorry, but as you can see, I'm busy at the moment."

We stare at each other. Luciano clears his throat. Parker and I continue to stare at each other.

Luciano says, "Maxwell, why don't you go look for pennies people have dropped on the ground?"

"And why don't you go look for your manhood, Mancari."

Confused, Luciano blinks. "What?"

Eyes blazing, Parker steps closer. "Because I'm about to turn you from a rooster to a hen, you preening little prick."

I laugh, and Luciano looks at me in shocked betrayal. I squeeze his arm reassuringly.

"These American men are so vulgar, aren't they, Lucky? I'll bet in Italy, no gentleman would say anything like that in front of a lady."

From the pride in Lucky's eyes, I can see I've been redeemed. He says, "Of course not. Vulgarity is the sign of the lower classes." He sneers again at Parker, then says something in Italian.

Parker answers right back—in Italian.

Whatever he said makes Luciano go apeshit. He stiffens, drops his arm from my shoulders, and shrieks, "You *dare!*"

He lunges at Parker.

I jump out of the way with a yelp. Parker steps swiftly aside as Luciano dives for him. Momentum carries Luciano past Parker. He slams into a waiter holding a tray of food, and they both crash to the floor. Luciano hits his head on the marble with a *crack* and falls still.

A crowd gathers. The waiter struggles to rise, bits of deviled egg smeared all over his jacket. Facedown, Luciano moans.

I take the opportunity to down my martini and ask the bartender for a refill.

Parker comes up beside me. Tall and imposing, he faces me as I give him the cold shoulder. "This is a dangerous game you're playing, Victoria."

His voice is unexpectedly rough. Without looking at him, I say, "Don't you dare talk to me about games, Parker."

"What's that supposed to mean?"

Two men are trying to help Luciano to his feet, without success. He keeps falling down, his feet unwilling to stay put beneath him. The gathered crowd is whispering. Giggling.

"Please don't insult my intelligence. I've had enough of that already tonight."

"Oh, are you referring to your date? The one with the room-temperature IQ?"

I turn and glare at him. "You're insulting *my* date? Is yours even of legal voting age?"

He looks at me with such fire in his eyes, I'm surprised I don't ignite. He takes me firmly by the upper arm and turns away from the bar.

"I haven't gotten my drink yet!"

"You'll get it later. There's something else you need first."

When I hiss at him, he pulls me against his hard body and growls into my ear, "That spanking you've had coming since we met. You're getting it. *Now*."

16

VICTORIA

*P*arker leads me away from the crowd and up a staircase to the second floor. He pulls me into the first room at the top.

It's a dimly lit library, packed floor to ceiling with books. Two overstuffed armchairs flank an occasional table. A burgundy velvet sofa faces an unlit fireplace.

I don't have time to see more, because as soon as we're inside, Parker turns, grasps me by my upper arms, pushes me against a wall of books, and kisses me.

God, I love the way he tastes.

He breaks away, breathing hard. "Luciano Mancari? Is that your idea of a joke?"

"It's my idea of a gentleman. You don't see *him* dragging me off by my hair like a caveman!"

He snaps, "When I go caveman on you, Victoria, you'll know it!" He kisses me again, harder this time, his hands pressed against my head, his tongue invading my mouth.

I give myself a few seconds to enjoy it before I pull away and slap him across the face.

His head snaps back. His eyes glow with anger. That vein in

his neck throbs wildly, an erratic pulse that matches the pounding of my heart.

In a harsh, barely controlled voice, he says, "I'd appreciate it if you could find another way to deal with how uncomfortable you are with how much you like kissing me."

"You smug son of a bitch."

"You coward."

I gasp, enraged. "You...you...philanderer!"

His chuckle is dark. "That's the pot calling the kettle black, baby."

Baby. I can't decide if him calling me that makes me want to sigh or scream.

We stare at each other. The moment stretches out. The tension rises until it becomes unbearable. Then, without a word, he gathers my wrists in his hands, presses them over my head against the books, and presses his chest against mine. He rests his hot cheek against my temple.

"You did so well yesterday, Victoria," he says into my ear. "All that truth-telling. Did the nasty little lies get worried they'd never come out to play again and force you to act like an asshole?"

I'm so angry, my entire body trembles. I want to kick myself for being stupid enough to tell him the truth about anything, even if it was part of a plan to disarm him. This man can't be trusted with even a single *grain* of truth.

I won't make the same mistake again.

"How dare you throw that back in my face?" I say through gritted teeth.

"Because I'm going to call you out on all your bullshit. Because I won't be one of your whipping boys. Because I'm not a man you can fool." He adds sourly, "*Belíssima.*"

"You're calling *me* out on my bullshit? Mr. 'every time I see you I get this funny feeling'? What a crock of shit!"

"I didn't say it was a funny feeling. I said it was a feeling.

And it's one I can't describe, because I've never felt it before, and that's the goddamn truth."

"Oh, really? All these indescribable feelings and not even twenty-four hours later, you show up to a party with Lolita on your arm? Who do you think you're dealing with here, Parker? Give me a little more credit!"

He pulls away slightly, eyes flashing, and stares into my eyes. Whatever he sees there makes him blink in surprise.

"Holy shit. You're jealous of her, aren't you?"

"Don't be ridiculous." I turn away, avoiding his gaze.

A tremor passes through his chest. After a moment, I realize it's laughter.

He's laughing at me.

I want to scratch out his eyes, only I can't because he's got my hands pinned over my head, and he's too strong for me to pull away.

Still laughing, he says, "You arrive with your stupid, pretty pet on a leash—who I'm sure was selected just to annoy me—and have the balls to be jealous of Marie-Thérèse?"

The possessive way he says her name makes my breath catch. But I'm not about to admit defeat, so I say flatly, "You're delusional."

Without another word, he marches over to the velvet sofa with me in tow, ignoring my howls of protest. He sits down on the sofa and hauls me facedown over his lap. Then he drags my dress up over my legs, exposing my bare bottom.

He smacks me smartly on the ass.

I jerk. My eyes fly wide open. A scream lodges inside my throat. I look over my shoulder and glare at him in outrage.

Seething, I say, "Do that again, and you won't wake up tomorrow."

He smiles at me. "You know, you *really* deserve this."

He rains down four more sharp, stinging smacks on my behind.

Livid, I squeal and buck, trying to squirm free, but he's got one hand flattened across my shoulders. He holds me in place with annoying ease. The other hand—the traitorous, hateful hand that just smacked me and that I'll be cutting off at the first opportunity—tightens around my hip.

He flips me onto my back.

Blood pounds in my head, in my face, in every limb in my body. Parker leans over, presses his weight into me, and takes my face in his hands. He slides a leg over both of mine so I'm pinned.

I hiss, "If you try to kiss me right now, I'll bite your damn tongue!"

He's breathing hard. I can't tell if he's furious, excited, or both.

Like me.

"You didn't like that?"

"No!"

"Good. You weren't meant to."

I close my eyes to escape the intensity of his gaze. My breath is ragged. I can hardly drag enough air into my lungs to. "No one has ever done that to me before. Not even my father."

He says in a husky voice, "I'm sorry."

I open my eyes and glare at him. Though I hate to admit it, he does look sorry.

Slowly, he moves one of his hands from my face. It drifts over my shoulder, down my bare arm, over my waist to the top of my thigh—exposed by the stupid, ginormous slit in my dress—then gently slides up and around. He cups my bottom. He strokes my stinging behind with the softest of touches as I bite the inside of my lip so I don't gasp.

"I'm sorry," he says again.

"No, you're not."

Why am I not pushing him away? I should be pushing him away. But the way that feels, oh Lord...

He's silent a moment, caressing my burning skin. "I'm mostly sorry."

We're both still breathing heavily. His growing erection presses into my thigh.

"Should I kiss it and make it better?"

I narrow my eyes. "No. I'm too busy hating you at the moment."

His gaze drops to my lips.

"Don't you dare kiss me."

"I really want to, though."

"No!"

"What if I let you insult me a little more? Maybe you can call me a few more names, make yourself feel better."

He's still staring at my mouth. He moistens his lips. In response, my nipples harden.

I say, "Let me try it out. Here goes. You're a smug, no-good, lying, egotistical, heartless, money-grubbing bastard with no redeeming qualities whatsoever."

"Money-grubbing? Now you're just being petty."

"I wasn't finished."

His cock, now rock-hard, twitches against my thigh. "Excuse me. Please proceed."

"You're overconfident. And bossy. And...mean."

Parker's eyes soften. His caresses on my ass are growing a little firmer, a little more sensual than soothing. "Are you feeling better yet?"

I swallow. My voice drops. "No."

We stare at each other, our faces inches apart. His erection is now insistently throbbing against my leg.

I wish I could ignore it. Instead—much to my chagrin—I'd like to take it out and have a play date.

All thoughts of Luciano and Marie-Thérèse are now toast.

I whisper, "And you're...scary."

Parker knows exactly what I mean by that. He breathes, "Oh, baby."

"Please stop calling me that."

"Why?"

"Because I like it too much."

He gazes at me, unblinking, his gorgeous hazel eyes both hot and soft. "So that feeling I was telling you about yesterday? The one I can't describe, that you called a crock of shit?"

"Yeah?"

He whispers, "It's back. And it's bigger than ever."

Because that really throws me for a loop, I decide to distract him. "Bigger than ever like the churro in your pants?"

My little plan works. Parker's smile is wicked. "The very same. I believe you said it was your favorite thing to eat?"

"Churros in general, not yours in particular."

He chuckles. "Ouch. You sure know how to make a man feel special, Cruella."

"And you sure know how to push all my buttons. Which I hate, by the way."

"No, you don't. You love it."

I roll my eyes. "Ugh. The ego has landed."

Parker growls, "Did you just roll your eyes at me?"

I freeze. "Um. No?"

"Yes, you did."

He pinches my behind. I gasp, both because I'm surprised and because it feels good. He says, "Do I need to give you another spanking?"

I wriggle beneath him, an involuntary little twitch of my traitorous hips. It brings my crotch into direct contact with the steel rod trying to escape from his trousers. His breath hisses through his teeth as he sharply inhales.

Seeing the look of lust on his face, I warn, "Remember what I said would happen if you tried to kiss me!"

Without missing a beat, he says, "I'll take my chances."

Then his lips are against mine. The kiss is hot and demanding, and because he tastes so delicious, I moan into his mouth.

That sound sets off a chain reaction.

He moans too and presses himself harder against me, sinking his fingers into my bare flesh. I arch against him, opening my thighs to allow his erection to rub against my heat as I flex my hips. He makes a noise deep in his throat and, just above my tailbone, slips his fingers beneath my thong. I sink my fingers into his hair and pull, using my nails, scratching him. He slides his hand over the crest of my hip, then puts his open palm between my legs. He rubs me through my damp panties.

I whimper, pushing against his hand.

He growls, slipping his fingers beneath the silk.

I mew like a kitten when his fingers find my wet center, again as he circles my clit with his thumb. When his fingers slip inside me, I break the kiss on a ragged gasp.

"Goddamn beautiful treacherous viper," he says, breathing heavily, and then takes my mouth again.

His mouth is devouring, but his fingers are gentle. He knows exactly what he's doing.

This isn't the sweet, fumbling teenager I knew, the boy who was more eager than experienced. The boy who cried in happiness after the first time we made love.

This is a Man with a capital *M*. Every cell in my body recognizes it, is screaming it so loud they can probably hear it downstairs.

Parker. Parker. Parker.

I'm dizzy. Breathless. Aching. Low in my belly, a coil of pleasure winds tighter and tighter. His fingers push deeper. My hand finds his hardness. When I wrap my fingers around his erection, he groans.

Parker.

Parker?

At the same moment I realize the voice in my head calling

Parker's name isn't a voice in my head, Parker breaks our kiss, panting. He cocks an ear toward the door.

"Parker, where are you? Someone find the guest of honor. He's gone MIA!"

Scattered laughter, a sharp squeal of feedback from a microphone, and we realize that from somewhere downstairs, the mayor is hailing Parker to come speak to the crowd.

Parker drops his forehead to my chest. "Jesus Christ. He's killing me."

Me too, but I'm thankful for the interruption. Another sixty seconds and the Mistress of All Evil would be getting shagged on a velvet sofa by her archenemy.

That's just unbecoming for a Bitch of my stature.

I push against Parker's chest. He withdraws. I sit up, straighten my dress, wipe my swollen lips with my fingertips. Parker runs a hand through his disheveled hair and looks at me.

"Stay here," he orders, pointing to the sofa.

I don't answer.

"Victoria."

I say coolly, "Your audience awaits, Mr. Maxwell."

His face darkens. He stands, pulling me to my feet with him. He winds an arm around my waist and lifts my chin, forcing me to meet his eyes. "Stay. Here."

"Okay."

He considers me in silence. "Was that a lie?"

"Probably."

He curses under his breath. Downstairs, the mayor makes a terrible joke about his wife's cooking.

"It sounds dire down there, Parker. You really ought to get a move on. We don't want to kill your political career before it's even begun."

"I can't believe you're smiling when you say that."

I push him away. "Believe it or don't. Not my problem."

He makes a sound of exasperation and turns to go. At the

door, he turns back and looks at me. "Will you be here when I get back?"

"I guess you'll have to wait and see, won't you?"

He stares at me long and hard, his eyes burning. In a husky voice, he says, "If you're not, you'll only spend the rest of the night thinking about what I was going to do to you next."

Then he lifts his hand to his mouth and sucks on the fingers that were just inside me.

He spins on his heel and leaves.

17

PARKER

"*A*h! Here he is! Call off the search party. The guest of honor has appeared!"

The mayor beams at me as I stride through the crowd, buttoning my jacket and trying to look like a sane, responsible adult with political aspirations and not the single-celled organism Victoria Price has reduced me to.

At this moment, I'm a giant walking cock. Nothing more. Everything I am is between my legs.

I have no idea how I'm going to get up in front of this crowd and string a coherent sentence together. I can still taste her. I can still feel her body beneath me. I can still hear those erotic, enticing moans working from her throat as I sank my greedy fingers into her slick heat.

Jesus. The way she responded to me. The way I responded to her.

Our chemistry is thermonuclear.

"Thank you, David," I say graciously. "I'm afraid I took a wrong turn on the way to the men's room."

The mayor looks relieved. I smile widely, accept the mic he's holding out to me, and turn to the crowd.

"I'll keep this brief so everyone can get back to their cocktails." *Cock. Oh, for the love of God.* "Most of you know me. Some of you don't, and I hope to remedy that this evening. New York has been my home for the last six years, and of all the places I've lived in the world, I can honestly say this is where I feel most connected. This is where I feel most..."

Victoria appears at the top of the stairs. She's looking right at me, wearing a Cheshire Cat grin. She licks her lips, tosses her hair over her shoulder, and begins to descend the staircase. Her gorgeous bare legs gleam in the light, courtesy of the most perfect hip-high slit ever created in the history of dressmaking.

"Alive."

The word is spoken before I have time to think. Looking amused, Victoria arches a brow and then shakes her head, her smile turned acerbic.

Is she mocking me?

I want to drop the mic, sprint across the room, grab her, throw her over my shoulder, carry her into the nearest room, and fuck her until we both come so hard, we pass out.

Only once before in my life have I felt this level of heat, of utter, soul-shaking *need*.

I screwed that up royally. I won't allow myself to make the same mistake twice.

"There are many things to love about my adopted home, but first and foremost, the people are what make it so special."

Almost to the bottom of the staircase, Victoria laughs. She shakes her head again as if amused by my audacity—because she knows I'm speaking directly to her—and flashes me a look that could be either hate or desire.

Fuck. I have to have her.

I have to have her *now*.

Abandoning the prepared speech that I can't remember anyway, I blurt, "It's my commitment to the amazing people of

New York that's led me to the decision to run for a seat in Congress."

The room erupts into applause and cheers. Now on the bottom step of the staircase, Victoria stifles a fake yawn.

I'm going to spank you so damn hard, you won't be able to sit for a week, you impossible, infuriating woman.

Two can play at this game.

I say loudly into the microphone, "Marie-Thérèse, will you please join me?"

Victoria stiffens. Her eyes gain a murderous light.

Marie-Thérèse makes her way through the crowd, smiling broadly, and I can tell Victoria wants to turn away but can't. She watches with glittering malice as Marie-Thérèse approaches and takes my outstretched hand.

And I feel a satisfaction so profound it's almost sexual.

I was right. Victoria *is* jealous.

It's her eyes that always give her away. Her expression might be bored, her indifference feigned, even her words smoothly lying. But those knife blade eyes always tell me the truth.

I imagine if she knew that, she'd put them out with acid.

I drape my arm around Marie-Thérèse's shoulders. She clasps me around the waist, gazing up at me adoringly.

Victoria curls her hand around the polished wood staircase railing as if she were wishing it were my throat.

"My mentor, the late Alain Gérard, once told me that the true meaning of life could be found only in service to others. He embodied the values of selflessness and service, and this legacy lives on his daughter, Marie-Thérèse, whom I've recently appointed head of The Hunger Project, my foundation that serves the underprivileged children of the rural South."

I look down at her with fondness. "She and I are siblings of sorts, though of course I'm much older and therefore, in her view, very uncool."

She smiles and gives me a sisterly poke in the ribs.

Across the room, Victoria looks confused.

This is starting to be a hell of a lot of fun.

"So tonight I'm very proud and grateful to stand before you and announce my candidacy for the House of Representatives of the United States Congress, so that I may continue to honor the memory of my mentor by serving others, giving a voice to the voiceless, and using my practical business experience and passion for this community to make it a better place for all."

As the crowd applauds and whistles, I plant a chaste kiss on Marie-Thérèse's forehead, then look at Victoria, making sure she sees that there's nothing whatsoever romantic about the gesture.

What does the Queen B do in return for this olive branch I'm extending?

She golf claps.

Three slow, sarcastic claps, her eyes narrowed and her lips twisted into a smirk.

My fingers tighten around Marie-Thérèse's shoulders. She glances in the direction I'm looking and shudders.

"That woman is scary," she whispers.

"She's all bark and no bite," I reply through one side of my mouth, nodding at the crowd. "A pussycat."

Marie-Thérèse snorts. "Cats have long claws and sharp teeth and kill billions of small mammals a year. They're basically cute serial killers."

As people move forward to shake my hand and offer congratulations, I watch from the corner of my eye as Victoria locates the still-wobbly Luciano Mancari, takes him by the arm, and leads him to the front door. Over her shoulder, she pauses to confirm I'm watching, then sends me a withering smile.

I should've spanked her harder.

18

VICTORIA

$\mathcal{T}$he first thing I do when I'm back inside Luciano's ridiculous limousine is call Tabby. The second thing I do is shush Luciano as he slumps against the door, moaning and holding his face.

His nose is a bloodied mess. Apparently, he used his schnoz to break his fall.

"Tabby!" I shout into my cell when she answers.

"Uh-oh. I can already tell things aren't going well in the evil empire. Should I send out the flying monkeys?"

"You can find out everything and anything about Marie-Thérèse something-or-other, daughter of the late French chef Alain Gérard, and do it before I get back."

She makes a noise of disbelief. "Back? You left like an hour ago!"

I ignore that. "And what have you found out about the other stuff?" I glance at Luciano, who now appears to be crying. I want to smack him upside the head.

"If by 'other stuff' you mean the dirty deets about Parker Maxwell, unfortunately nothing at all. The boy's clean as a whistle. Not even a traffic ticket."

"Are you sure? You dug deep? Deeper than deep?"

"I'm looking into some other avenues, but so far we've got nada."

I curse. "And his father?"

"Nope. His dad retired about ten years ago. The only thing he seems to do is play golf. His mother's the president of the Laredo opera, heads up all the charity events at their church. The Maxwells are practically the friggin' Cleavers, boss."

"Drat!"

"Woah. You didn't just say 'drat,' did you? Because if you did, I might have to hand in my resignation. 'Drat' is totally cliché, even for a super villain like you. *Especially* for a super villain like you. You'd never hear Darth Vader saying—"

"Can we please forgo the *Star Wars* references and get back to the fact that you have to find me something I can work with?"

Tabby makes a disgruntled noise. "Maybe there's nothing there. You ever think of that?"

"Don't be ridiculous. Everyone has something they're hiding. It's just a matter of finding out where they're hiding it."

"I know. I was just trying to be positive."

"Or negative, in this case."

"Well, if it were me and I had some dead bodies to hide, I'd bury them in my own backyard, if you get my meaning."

Beside me, Luciano withdraws a monogrammed handkerchief from his coat pocket and uses it to dab delicately at his swollen, bloody nose. When he whimpers, I shoot him an exasperated glare.

"Don't be obtuse, Tabby. I'm in no mood."

She sighs. "Look, if he's really smart, he'll have burned, shredded, or paid someone like me to scour the web clean of any incriminating evidence. So the best place to find something is going to be right in the dragon's lair, so to speak."

I sit bolt upright in the seat. "At his house!"

"He's got a safe. I'd bet my favorite Hello Kitty handbag on it."

"A safe? What am I, a bank robber now? How the hell am I going to get into a safe?"

"Why don't you try some of those feminine wiles I see you practicing in front of the mirror all the time?"

Deliberating, I chew my lip. "Or maybe you could get me some roofies. Or mollies, whatever they're called. Something to knock him out while I search for a key."

Luciano turns to me with wide eyes. I smile at him, pat his hand, and whisper, "Not you, darling."

His answering smile is grateful, if a little frightened. He goes back to being slumped against the door.

Tabby says haughtily, "I don't do drugs, Victoria."

"But you must *know* people. From like, the underground. Your Electric Daisy Carnival friends?"

"If you think the EDC is the underground, we've got way more serious problems than breaking into a safe."

"Fine, Burning Man. Whatever."

Tabby says, "I'm hanging up on you now."

"Wait!"

Once again she sighs. "What?"

I look at Luciano. "Do you know anything about stopping relentless blood flow?"

I can almost hear her eyes bug out of her head. "I'm going to pretend you didn't just say that. And do *not* bring a corpse back to this house, Victoria. I signed up to help you hide figurative skeletons, not literal ones. And by the way, dead bodies tend to stink after a few days. The scent of decomposing flesh will clash with your Chanel No. Five."

With that, she hangs up on me.

"Ingrate," I mutter, and shove the phone back in my clutch.

Luciano whimpers. "*Belissima*, I must go to the hospitals. I am having very much pain in my face. I think my nose is broken."

I certainly hope so.

"Driver?" I lean forward, raising my voice so the driver can hear me through the lowered glass partition. I direct him to take me home and then take Lucky to the hospital.

Lucky bristles. "I am needing the medical help before he drives you home, *belíssima*!"

I smile sweetly at him. "I think the hospital's on the way."

His watery-eyed glare is clearly disbelieving. I could care less but decide to try to smooth his feathers in case I ever need him again. I take his handkerchief, dunk it in the champagne's ice bucket, then carefully wipe away the blood from his chin and upper lip.

"Here, pinch your nostrils. It will help stop the bleeding."

Lucky takes the handkerchief, holds it to his nose, and applies pressure, wincing and moaning like the giant wuss he is. I fell off my horse and broke my nose when I was twelve and didn't whine half as much.

"And don't worry. I have an *excellent* attorney for you. She's a client of mine, a real bulldog."

Confused, he blinks.

"You're pressing charges, of course."

He blinks again. "Charges?"

I do my best impression of someone who's righteously indignant. "Against that beast, Parker Maxwell. What he did to you was clearly assault!"

It wasn't anywhere near assault. But at the very least, a lawsuit against Parker will raise some interesting questions from his soon-to-be constituents. The fact that he didn't lay a finger on Luciano is unimportant. The fact that he's had two public altercations in the past month is.

Far better men than he have had political careers derailed for less.

Lucky frowns and lowers the handkerchief. "But I am thinking I don't really want to have people knowing about this. It is an embarrassment to me, no? Everyone laughed." His face darkens. "I don't like it when people laugh at me."

Oh dear God, save us from a man's fragile ego.

I take his hand gently in my own and stare deeply into his eyes. "Lucky. Parker Maxwell thinks he can do whatever he wants to you. He thinks he was in a fight with you...and he thinks he won."

I watch that sink in, then pounce. "You can't let an *inferior* man get away with insulting the great Luciano Mancari like this. An inferior *American* man. He didn't just insult you—he insulted all your countrymen. He insulted *Italy!*"

Luciano's face grows even darker. He snarls, "And he insulted my mother!"

"Your mother?"

"*Si!* He said she was a goat!"

It's all I can do not to double over in laughter. I suck my cheeks between my teeth and stare at him, shaking my head as if I'm dumb with disbelief.

"You are right," Lucky says, sitting straighter in the seat. "I cannot let this stand." He thinks for a moment and then nods briskly. "I will have my people schedule it."

"Schedule what?"

He looks at me. "The duel."

An entire city block passes by outside before I'm able to speak again. "I'm sorry. That martini must have really gone to my head. I thought I just heard you say 'duel.'"

Lucky gently strokes the back of my hand. "I know the manly ways are frightening, Miss Victoria, but you must be strong. This is how we settle the things between the men in my country."

"Really? What century is it in Italy now? Because in America, I'm thinking it's the twenty-first."

He waves his hand dismissively. "The old ways never die. Also I am very good with the guns." He frowns. "Unless he chooses the swords. In this case, I am having a little more worry."

He's serious. He's actually friggin' serious.

I'm not exactly sure how to feel about this development. On the one hand, it's hilarious. The thought of Luciano calling Parker—or, more correctly, having his *people* call Parker—to schedule a duel is beyond entertaining. My God, the press would have a field day. I can just see the headlines now: *Celebrity Chef Showdown in Central Park!* If they televised it, the entire Northern Hemisphere would tune in.

On the other hand, it's disturbing.

What if Luciano hurt Parker? Or even…killed him?

Why is the thought of Luciano killing Parker disturbing? If anything, that should make you happy.

Well, because I'm going to kill him, of course! Figuratively, that is. I can't have someone else destroy him before I can!

But isn't the whole point that he's destroyed, no matter who actually does it?

No, the whole point is that I get my revenge! Me, not someone else!

You sure about that, Maleficent? You sure you don't have a teeny, tiny soft spot for ol' Mr. I've Got a Funny Feeling About You?

Oh, shut up.

Even in imaginary conversations in my head, Tabby's logic is annoying.

"You know, Lucky, I would never contradict you, because obviously you're so much smarter than I am, but may I make a suggestion?"

He inclines his head in a kingly nod. Clearly his nose feels better now that I'm stroking his ego.

"Well—and of course this is just my silly opinion—if you

don't want people to know about what happened tonight, a duel might not be the best way to go. It's very manly, and obviously you would kill him—he might even die from sheer terror—but it might be a tiny bit...public. Don't you think?"

He purses his lips. I can see he's not convinced.

"This attorney I know, she can keep it all very private. You can sue him for millions, ruin his political chances, and have your revenge, all without giving any more people the chance to laugh at you. You can destroy him, and no one outside of that room tonight will ever know what happened."

"But a lawsuit is public information, no?"

Shit. He chooses now to display a glimmer of intelligence?

"Far less public than a duel. If word gets out that the best chef in the world is going to shoot someone, the television networks will go wild. You know how silly we Americans are about our reality TV. Plus, people might even feel sorry for Parker. Seeing as how you're going to kill him, I mean. We don't want him becoming some kind of martyr."

I can tell that last part was the nail in the coffin, but just to make sure I haven't trod on his wafer-thin ego with all my inferior womanly opinions, I demurely add, "But of course you know best."

When I bat my lashes like there's a piece of lint in my eye, he melts.

"Ah, *belíssima*," he sighs. "You are making someone the very fine wife someday." He kisses my hand. Hovering above it, he murmurs, "Maybe even me, no?"

Um, no.

The universe takes pity on me, because at the precise moment I'm deciding how to deal with that fresh horror, my phone rings. I answer it so quickly, I don't even look to see who it is.

"Victoria Price speaking," I chirp, acting all businessy so Luciano takes the hint that he's supposed to allow me a moment to compose myself after his swoon-inducing declaration. Thankfully he does, releasing my hand and leaning back against the seat, secure in his opinion of the effect he must be having on me with all his powerful machismo.

"After you've dropped your injured puppy dog off at the veterinarian, I'm coming over. We need to talk."

It's Parker. Judging by the growl in his voice, he isn't happy. My heart starts to thump.

"Oh, hello, Mom! So good to hear from you. Now isn't a great time, though. I'm on a date with the most *amazing* man."

Luciano's smile is the absolute definition of smug.

"Victoria."

What is it about the way Parker says my name that makes all my girly bits tingle? I close my eyes, blocking out everything but the sound of his voice.

"Yes, Mom?"

"I'm. Coming. Over."

Oh, that tone. It promises everything. All my tingly bits collectively throb. But then, as I'm simultaneously enjoying the throbbing and wishing it would stop, inspiration hits.

"No. I'll come to your place."

The line crackles with electricity. Parker's voice drops low, low, low. "If you come to my house tonight, you're not leaving until tomorrow morning."

My throat turns dry. My hands tremble. And my heart starts to hammer so hard, I have to press a hand over my chest.

I say, "Give me the address."

He does, then demands, "When?"

"Ten o'clock."

"If you're not there—"

"I'll be there."

Something in my voice must set his mind at ease, because he says, "Don't be late," and hangs up.

After I tuck the phone back in my bag, Luciano asks, "You don't know your mother's address?"

I laugh breathlessly. "She just moved."

He doesn't question me. He simply nods, appeased, while I marvel at the adrenaline crashing through me in wave after glorious wave.

I can't remember the last time I felt this alive.

19

VICTORIA

*P*arker lives in an ultra-modern skyscraper on Park Avenue. The building itself looks like something out of a movie about New York in the year 2300, all sharp points, odd angles, and glittering glass. It's reminiscent of a giant icicle.

No wonder I like it.

It's two minutes to ten. I've been home, changed out of the pornographic slit dress and into a more comfortable skirt and blouse, and gotten an update from Tabby about Marie-Thérèse.

Apparently she's the child of the late Alain Gérard and his fourth wife, a model who was thirty years younger than he. When Parker lived with Gérard, Marie-Thérèse was all of ten years old. They stayed close when he returned to the States, so close that he'll be walking her down the aisle at her wedding in September.

Which means there's nothing between them. She like his little sister.

Which means I was needlessly, stupidly jealous, but even worse—Parker knew it.

And rubbed it in my face.

I admit I deserved it, but that's not the point. The point is that

I experienced the feeling in the first place, that my enemy correctly guessed I was experiencing that feeling, and that he proceeded not only to call me on it but also to twist the knife a little deeper when he brought her up on stage with him, knowing it would infuriate me.

In other words, the son of a bitch played me.

He didn't let me dangle for long. He gave her a brotherly forehead kiss and said they were like siblings. But I refuse to give him credit for *gently* playing me. I could tell by the look on his face he was having fun at my expense.

He enjoyed my jealousy.

The more I thought about that, the more furious I became.

I march into the lobby of the building and approach the smiling young man at the front desk. In my best sword-wielding Xena voice, I bark, "My name is Victoria Price, and I'm here to see—"

"Yes, Ms. Price. You can go right up. Mr. Maxwell is expecting you."

He gestures to the elevator bank. His smile never wavers, even when I narrow my eyes at him.

This guy is good.

I turn and walk stiffly to the elevators. The fortieth floor is already selected. The elevator doesn't go higher. On the ride up, I pace inside the car like a caged animal, imagining every nasty thing I'm going to say to Parker.

When the elevator doors open, he's standing right there, barefoot, in jeans and a black T-shirt, breathtakingly handsome... and smirking. He looks at his watch.

"Exactly ten o'clock. Your punctuality is a compliment, Ms. Price. Just couldn't keep away one moment longer?"

"Don't you dare smirk at me, you smug bastard. I have half a mind to—"

He steps inside the elevator, takes my face in his hands, and kisses me.

It catches me completely off guard. I freeze, caught between anger and pleasure. Then heat explodes inside me like a bomb.

I throw my arms around his neck and kiss him back.

He pushes me against the elevator wall and pins me there, devouring my mouth, his hands gripping my head.

I've never had a kiss like this in my life. We're both ravenous, insatiable, blind with lust. We don't break for air until an alarm rings—it's the elevator, buzzing for someone to select a floor.

Without a word, Parker swings me into his arms. I hang on to his broad shoulders as he strides from the elevator into the dark silence of his home. Floor-to-ceiling windows spectacularly display the cityscape glittering outside and give enough light to show the modern furnishings. We move into the living room, passing a grand piano, and continue past a large, open kitchen.

"Where are you taking me?" I whisper.

"Bedroom."

The need in his voice gives me chills.

I could object. I don't. I could tell myself it's because I know exactly what I came here to do, which is snoop and sneak until I find his ruinous secrets, but I'd be lying.

Right now, I don't give a shit about his secrets. I'll worry about them later.

Right now, I just want him to fuck me into next week.

Parker kicks open his bedroom door, crosses to his bed in a few long strides, tosses me down on the mattress, then swiftly crawls over me so he's hovering inches above me, his bent legs on either side of my hips, his arms braced beside my head.

Looking into my eyes, he says darkly, "No more bullshit. No more games. No more of this Luciano Mancari crap. I want you so fucking badly, I'll do almost anything to have you, and I think you want me the same way. But I won't beg. I won't be lied to. And I won't be led around by my balls. I want it only if it's real. So decide right now if you can give me real. Yes or no."

My breath is ragged. I feel as if I'm standing at the top of a high, windy cliff, looking down to waves crashing over rocks far below. "Parker—"

"*Yes* or *no.*"

His intensity scares me. So does the knowledge that he can't be manipulated. He sees right through me. If I'm going to do this thing, if I'm really going to move forward with my plan for revenge, I have to accept the possibility that it might cost me a hell of a lot more than I've bargained for.

It might cost me what's left of my cold, dead heart.

What the hell. I've lived through worse.

In the faintest of whispers, I say, "Yes."

Parker's reaction is instantaneous. He breathes, "Thank fuck," and crushes his mouth to mine once more.

I pull him down atop me. He gives me his weight. I wrap my legs around his waist. One of his hands slides up my thigh, pushing my skirt to my hips, and I flex my pelvis, wanting, wanting, *wanting.* A moan escapes my throat.

Parker rears back and rips open my blouse. I gasp in shock as buttons go flying.

"No bra," he growls and then cups both my bare breasts in his hands, latches on to one of my rigid nipples with his gorgeous, hot mouth, and sucks.

The sound I make is purely animal. I arch into his hands, my head thrown back, my eyes closed, lost.

He pinches the nipple he's not sucking on, rolling it between his fingers. I grind my pelvis against his, feeling the length of his hard cock, desperate to have it inside me.

"Please, Parker," I whimper. "Please."

Instead of giving me what I want, he breaks away from my breast, shoves my skirt all the way up to my waist, yanks aside my panties, and buries his face between my open thighs.

When his lips close over my swollen clit and he suckles it, I cry out. My body bows against the bed.

"Yes. Give it to me," he murmurs, then sinks two fingers inside me and goes right back to sucking.

I.

Am.

On.

Fire.

I moan brokenly. His name escapes my lips over and over as I writhe against the delicious heat of his mouth. I sink my fingers into his hair and pull, grinding my hips into his face, pleasure building, coiling, tightening, all my muscles clenched and my nipples throbbing.

"Oh God. Parker!" I gasp, stiffening.

In convulsions that shake the whole bed, I come.

He makes a noise deep in his throat, a humming that reverberates through my core. The orgasm lasts and lasts, ripping through me like a detonation. It's a high, brilliant peak, an intense blast of pure pleasure.

When it subsides and I'm left a limp mass of arms and legs, Parker turns his head and gently sinks his teeth into the flesh of my thigh.

"Fucking beautiful," he whispers. He pulls my panties down my legs, tosses them aside, then rips open the fly of his jeans. His stiff cock springs free. He pulls a condom from his back pocket, tears the foil open with his teeth, rolls it down his swollen length, and positions himself between my legs.

I groan in disappointment.

Parker tenses, breathing hard. "You weren't a foregone conclusion, if that's what you're thinking. I was only hoping, not expecting."

"It's not that."

"What, then?"

I sink my fingers into the hard muscles of his ass. "I wanted you bare."

With a moan, he shoves inside me.

He fits his mouth to mine. I taste myself on him. I pull my knees up and rock my hips, feeling him hot and hard deep inside, filling me. He fucks me slowly, kissing me and fondling my breasts, bringing me quickly back up to that bright peak again, so quickly I'm dizzy and gasping for breath.

"Come on my cock, baby," he commands, gazing down at me. "Give it to me again."

I'm flying. Flying and burning and suddenly there's water in my eyes and my throat is closing up and my chest feels like there's a thousand-pound weight on it—oh God, what's happening?

I turn my head, desperate to escape those eyes of his that always see right through me, but he won't allow it. He grasps my jaw in his hand and turns my head back so I'm forced to look at him.

"Don't hide. Let me in. Let me see you. Please."

It's that soft, pleading "please" that does it.

I come again, silently this time, though no less savagely. Throughout it, I look at him, feeling raw and bloodied as a scraped nerve, until finally I can't contain the feelings inside me anymore. Water slips from the corners of my eyes.

He whispers, "Yes. God, yes. That right there. I'd kill to keep you looking at me like that forever."

I say his name, and he starts to thrust faster.

Sweat breaks out on his forehead. His arms are tense and corded. His breaths come in harsh pants. When he moans, long and low, I know he's close.

I pull his head down and say into his ear, "Fuck me hard, lover. Come inside me."

Grunting in pleasure, he bites me on the long muscle above my clavicle. He slides one hand under my ass and uses it to lift me as he pumps into me, deeper, harder. My breasts are flattened against his chest, my fingernails bite into his flesh, my legs tremble as my thigh muscles tense.

Then he stiffens, throws his head back, and comes with a shout.

It's a beautiful thing to watch.

His eyes are closed. His lips are parted. Even in the low light I can see his face is flushed with color. I feel him throb and twitch deep inside me, and experience an emotion I'm unfamiliar with. It feels like I'm being stabbed over and over through the center of my chest.

A little sound escapes my throat. Parker opens his eyes and looks down at me. His eyes are shining. He leans down and kisses me softly on the lips, cheeks, eyelids, his warm breath washing over my face. Balancing himself on his elbows, he cradles my head in his hands. Against my chest, I feel his heart thrumming a crazy, irregular beat.

We're quiet for several minutes, our arms around each other, letting our breathing return to normal. Finally he says, "Okay, that was seriously fucking amazing."

"Or seriously amazing fucking."

He chuckles, nosing my hair away from my ear. "Both. Jesus."

"You don't have to call me that. Your Royal Highness will do."

He chuckles again and kisses a path from my ear all the way down my neck. Without withdrawing from me, he rolls to his back and settles me atop him so I'm straddling him, looking down, my hair falling into my face. He reaches up and brushes it back with both hands. To avoid the softness in his eyes that's almost killing me, I sigh.

"What?"

Acting coy, I shrug, then glance at my bare breasts. "You owe me a shirt."

His gaze drops to my breasts. He smiles. "I'll take you shopping."

"I doubt you could afford it."

His smile widens. His hands follow the direction of his gaze, and he cups my breasts, running his thumbs back and forth over my sensitive nipples. He watches as I bite my lip.

He says gruffly, "You like that?"

"Yes."

I can tell he's pleased by how quickly I answered. And that I didn't try to lie or hide. He gently pinches both my nipples. When my lips part in pleasure, he pinches a little harder. I moan, enjoying the feel of his big, rough hands.

"You like that too."

It isn't a question. He's talking to himself, watching me as he continues to fondle my breasts, alternating between stroking his thumbs over my nipples, pinching them, and squeezing the fullness of the globes. Inside me, he's still rock-hard. A tiny contraction in my core makes him pull in a quick breath.

He sits up and wraps his arms around me, which drives his stiff cock even deeper inside.

"And that," I whisper, slowly rocking my pelvis. He drops his head and sucks one of my nipples into his mouth. I close my eyes.

When he sucks harder, using his teeth, I arch and shudder. He pushes my torn blouse over my shoulders and off my arms, breaks away briefly to pull his own shirt over his head and toss it aside, then quickly goes back to lavishing my breasts with attention.

"And your skin," I breathe, running my open hands over the muscles in his back, shoulders and arms. His skin is like silk, smooth and hairless. I'm losing myself again, drowning in the pleasure of him. Of us, the way we fit together.

I change the motion of my hips from a rocking one to a slow up-and-down slide. Parker groans against my breast.

"Ride that cock, baby," he says roughly, his tongue flicking my nipple. "It's yours. Ride it."

It's mine. It's mine. Yes, yes, it's all mine.

I don't realize I've spoken aloud until he agrees via a grunt of approval.

I push him down so he's flat on his back. Then I run my hands all over his chest and stomach, admiring the sculpted muscles. I reach down behind us and circle his cock with my fingers, squeezing and stroking as I take him in and out, my own wetness slipping between my fingers.

With steady pressure, Parker strokes my clit with his thumb as I ride him. He wraps the other hand around my hip. He watches me all the while, his look intense and unwavering, his eyes taking in everything on my face.

And I'm giving him everything. I'm letting him see exactly what I'm feeling, how good he feels, how much I like it, everything. I'm past caring. Past caution.

I never want this to end.

Suddenly he grabs both my hips, rolls out from under me, flips me onto my stomach, hikes my ass in the air, braces one arm against the mattress, wraps the other around my waist, and plunges deep inside me from behind.

I cry out. He starts to fuck me hard, holding me in place with that arm around my waist, his breath hot and rough at my ear.

"Are you mine, Victoria?"

My face half buried in a pillow, I moan.

"Say it."

Thinking I know what he wants, I whisper, "My pussy's yours."

"Not your pussy, baby. *You.* Say it."

I don't. I won't. This is one line I will never, ever cross. If he wants dirty talk, he can have it. If he wants my body, obviously he can have that too.

But he can never have *me*. Not for real.

Not again.

I turn my face to the pillow. Parker slows, runs a hand up my back, fists that hand in my hair. He pulls my head back until I'm looking at him, my neck craned to the side.

"Say you're mine."

He whispers it, our gazes locked together. I shake my head.

He falls still. In the quiet of the room, our heavy breaths are loud as thunder.

"What are you afraid of?"

I swallow. I know I must tell him some shade of the truth or he'll know I'm lying, so I say, "You. This. Everything."

He releases my hair, leans back on his heels—taking me with him by holding me around the waist—then gathers me against his chest and buries his face in my neck. Against my skin, he vows, "You're safe with me. I promise you. You're safe."

I swallow a silent sob and close my eyes. "You can't know that. You don't know what lies ahead."

His arms around me are crushing. Against my back, his chest heaves. Slowly, enunciating every word, he repeats, "You are safe with me."

But you're not safe with me, my lying lover. You're holding your own destruction in your arms.

After a moment, when I don't respond, he softly kisses my neck. He takes us down to the mattress, lying on our sides with my back to his front, our bodies still joined. Across the room in the wall of windows, I see our ghostly reflection in the glass, two lovers entwined in an intimate embrace.

Gently, slowly, he starts to move again. His arms stay wrapped around me. His lips rest against the furious pulse in my neck. He drops a hand between my legs and strokes me as only he knows how, drawing moans from my throat, giving me pleasure and pain as only he can.

Just before I come, I close my eyes to block the vision of that ghostly woman in the glass, her face a mask of misery.

20

PARKER

$\mathcal{J}$ wake up alone.

The clock on the bedside table reads three a.m. I sit up in bed and call out, "Victoria?"

No answer.

Rising, I pull on the jeans I discarded on the floor last night and walk out of the bedroom. My bare feet are silent against the floor. I pass my office door, which is slightly ajar. I frown, pausing outside it.

I know I closed the door yesterday. I always keep the door closed when the housekeeper comes. No one is allowed in my office, not even her. I know I closed it.

Didn't I?

Silently, I push the door open and take a quick look around. Everything looks as it always does: perfectly ordered. I close the door and continue down the hallway toward the living room, which is where I find her.

Victoria stands nude at the window, staring out into the night. I stop, admiring the picture she makes, her body silhouetted against the wall of glass, lights softly playing over her skin. She senses me and turns.

"You're awake."

She murmurs, "Couldn't sleep."

I draw closer. On my way past the sofa, I grab the cashmere blanket folded over the arm. Victoria watches me as I approach, her eyes unreadable in the shadows. When I'm finally standing in front of her, she looks up at me with a small, sad smile.

"I didn't mean to wake you," she says.

I wind the blanket around her body and hug her, pressing a kiss to her temple. "You didn't."

"You're an insomniac too?"

I chuckle, enjoying the scent of her hair, the feel of her in my arms. "Just a light sleeper."

She allows me to nuzzle her for a moment, then turns her head and stares out into the night. She seems so melancholy.

I hope she doesn't regret what happened between us, because I sure as hell don't.

"Do you like the view?"

"Mine's better."

She says it with such casual disregard, I can't help but laugh. At least she's telling the truth. It's a start.

"I'll have you know this is the premier unit in this building, Ms. Price."

"This giant penis of a building, you mean? I've never seen anything so phallic. Let me guess: the architect was a man."

"And what if it was a woman? Would it be a tall, ovary-shaped building?"

"Now there's a frightening thought. Can you imagine a forty-story ovary?"

I turn her around, gather her in my arms, and pull her against my chest. She winds her arms around my waist and tilts her head back, gazing up at me with that faint melancholy smile.

"Why are you sad?"

She turns her head, depriving me of her eyes. "I'm not."

I cup her face. As I've had to do many times before—and

probably will many times again—I make her look at me. I'm determined not to let her hide. I want no walls between us. "Don't bother acting tough. I can see you're sad. Tell me why."

A long silence follows. Then, instead of answering me directly, she sidesteps. "Why is it that you see me so clearly when no one else does?"

A stray lock of hair is falling into her eyes. I brush it from her forehead. Keeping my voice low, I say, "Why is it that when I'm inside you, I feel like I'm finally home?"

She ducks her head and hides her face in my chest, but not before I see the pain that crosses it.

"Victoria—"

"Please. It's just a lot. Please, just this once, let it go."

Her voice is so hollow and hopeless, it makes me fall still. I tighten my arms around her, wanting to comfort her. But for what, I don't know. She obviously doesn't want to tell me. I debate a moment, knowing I could get it out of her if I push, but finally decide to do as she asks and let it go.

We'll have plenty of time to work through whatever issues she has. I'm not going anywhere and, if I have any say in this at all, neither is she.

I whisper, "Come back to bed, baby."

When she nods, I'm relieved. At least for now, she's not running away. I tuck her under my arm and lead her back into the bedroom, then crawl in bed beside her and gather her in my arms. She's still wrapped like a little burrito in the cashmere, but she seems to need it, like a security blanket. If it makes her feel safer, she can have it. She can have anything she wants.

Lying beside her in the dark, I listen to the sound of her breathing, feel the gentle rise and fall of her chest. At some point, feeling a contentment I haven't felt in years, I fall asleep.

When I wake in the morning with the sun streaming through the windows, Victoria is gone.

VICTORIA

*W*hen I arrive at my penthouse, Tabitha and Darcy are sitting together at my kitchen table, cackling over something on Tabby's cell phone. They look up and see me standing in the doorway.

"Well, well," says Darcy, eyeing me up and down. "Look what the cat dragged in."

"I *am* the cat."

Darcy snorts. "More like something the cat coughed up."

"Whose shirt is that?" asks Tabby.

"Whose do you think?" I mutter, pulling out a chair and flinging myself dramatically into it.

Wearing a Day-Glo pink tank top with the words "Stop staring at my tits" written across her boobs, paired with a leather miniskirt, an armful of silver bangles, and biker boots, Tabby smiles brightly at me and says, "What happened to the blouse you were wearing when you left last night?"

When I make a sour face, she grins at me.

Darcy says, "You know, it's not a walk of shame if you stop for brunch on the way home."

I prop my chin on my fists. "Good to know. Why are you people in my kitchen so early on a Sunday morning?"

"Because your assistant here called me and told me you didn't come home last night, so I had to come see for myself the state you were in when you finally showed up." She purses her lips. "And what a state it is."

I drop my head to the table, rest my forehead on my folded arms, and sigh.

"Uh-oh," says Tabby.

Darcy asks, "What?"

"I know that sigh. It's the precursor to some really vile plan. She's probably going to tell us now about the body she needs us to help her move."

Darcy says reasonably, "Girl, what are friends for if you can't count on them to help you move a body?"

"Thank you," I grumble to the table. "At least I know I can rely on someone around here."

Tabby rises. I hear her move to the counter, hear the sound of liquid being poured. She returns and sets a steaming mug of coffee in front of me.

"Don't be so quick to judge, Maleficent. You can rely on me. For important stuff too, like, for instance…finding out about the girl Parker was dating who killed herself."

I sit bolt upright and stare at her. "You found out? Tell me, tell me!"

Darcy says, "Whoa—what's this?"

"Parker told Victoria he was dating a girl who killed herself."

"Actually, what he said was, 'I once killed someone,' which is vastly different, but when I pressed he admitted she actually killed herself."

Tabby adds, "He just drove her to it."

Darcy makes a face like she just ate a piece of bad sushi. "Y'all are crazy."

"Get on with the story, Tabitha! What happened?"

Tabby sits, folds her hands on the tabletop, and looks at me. "What happened is your boy lied."

I hear a faint, faraway ringing in my ears. "What?"

Tabby shakes her head, holding my gaze. "No girl Parker ever dated killed herself. I searched everywhere, all the way back to when he was in high school, even cross-referenced morgue records in every place he lived in case I missed something. There's no one. He lied."

I lean back against the chair, stunned. "But...Europe. He went to school in England. He lived in France..."

"I searched everywhere, V. When people die, there are records. Medical records, obituaries, death certificates, articles in the newspaper. I mean, his entire dating history is public knowledge. He's been famous for ten years. You can connect the dots from one to the next, all the way back, but even before that, there's nothing. I'm certain of it. He lied."

Because I know how good Tabby is at what she does, I know what she's telling me is accurate. If there were any scrap of information that would corroborate his story, even a crumb, she'd have found it.

I say softly, "Mother. Fucker."

Darcy mutters, "Oh boy. I feel one mutha of a bitch slap comin' for Captain America."

"He fucking lied to me? That son of a bitch LIED to me?" I jump to my feet and start to pace. I can't believe it. I can't believe I fell for his bullshit *again.*

"Okay, now, let's keep calm," says Darcy, sounding worried.

I spin on my heel to stare at her. "Calm? You want calm? I'll show you calm! I'm so calm my hands won't even shake when I chop off his fucking head!"

Tabby says, "Victoria, please don't chop off *my* head for saying this, but what did you expect? You know him better than anyone. He's a liar. It's what he does."

And he does it so well. He actually had me believing he had feelings for me. It all felt so...real.

When really it was just a brilliantly calculated lie to get me to let down my guard so he could fuck me.

Sickened, I sink back into the chair.

Darcy looks back and forth between me and Tabby. "Okay, can someone please tell me what exactly the history is with this guy? All I know is you two have a past. How much of a past is it?"

At that moment, my cell phone rings. I left it on the counter by the sink when I left the night before. The three of us stare at it as it continues to ring.

"You gonna answer that?" asks Darcy.

"Tabby."

At my prompt, she leaps to the counter and picks up the phone. "It's him."

I make a throat-slicing motion with my hand across my neck. She hits a button and the ringing stops.

Silence reigns in the kitchen until Tabby asks, "So, was there a safe?"

I nod. "A wall safe. Hidden in his office, behind a copy of *The Lovers* by Magritte."

Her eyes widen. "You're kidding."

"Nope."

"Dude. Talk about symbolism."

Darcy sighs. "Translation please."

Tabby provides the insight for her. "It's a famous French painting of two lovers kissing, but both of their heads are wrapped in white veils. The fabric barrier prevents true intimacy between the lovers, transforming an act of passion into one of isolation. It's generally interpreted to be about frustrated desires, a depiction of the inability to unveil fully the true nature of even our most intimate companions."

Darcy looks at me. "I'll ask you later what it's like to spend your days with a walking encyclopedia, but for now, answer me this: what's in the safe?"

"I don't know. That's what I need to find out. It took me a while to find it, so I didn't want to risk spending more time searching for a key." My face hardens. "That will have to be next time."

Tabby glances at Darcy, then focuses her gaze on me.

"I'm sure the answer is no, but I still have to ask. When you were playing hide-the-sausage and going through his closet to find something to wear and whatnot, you didn't slip and tell him about the other thing, did you?"

Darcy perks up. "What other thing?"

Without thinking, I say, "The baby thing."

Darcy looks at me in utter confusion. "Baby? What *baby*?"

Shit. Great job, Victoria. I close my eyes and gather my thoughts. Then I say, "Tabby, cancel whatever I'm scheduled for through Tuesday. And call NetJets. Book me the first flight to Laredo."

"Why? What're you gonna do?"

I look at her, then at Darcy. I see the concern on their faces, but all I care about now is finishing what I've started. And there's only one person in the world who can help me with that.

"I'm going to see my daughter."

VICTORIA

*W*hen I giggle, Parker tries to shush me, but he's giggling too. He can't help it. He loves it when I laugh.

"Bel, we have to be quiet. My parents can't know you're here."

"It tickles!" I try to hold still, try to muffle the squeals of pleasure and happiness desperate to escape my throat.

"Tickles!" Parker pretends to be offended. "It's supposed to feel good!"

He slowly drags the tip of the feather between my bare breasts, down my rib cage, and across my belly. When he whorls it around my belly button, I have to cover my mouth and bite my lip so I don't shriek with laughter.

"It does feel good. But it tickles, too."

He grins. He's stretched out naked beside me, propped on an elbow, his golden hair mussed, his heavy leg thrown over both of mine. We're in his bed in his parents' house, the bed sheets tented around his head and shoulders, snug in our own lovely world. It's eleven o'clock on a rainy school night, and—as I often do— I've snuck out of my house to visit him on the other side of town.

My parents are deep sleepers, but I share a bedroom with my little brother. Parker, an only child, has a giant bedroom on the upper floor of his parents' mansion, far away from the cocktail party going on in the great parlor downstairs.

His parents like to throw cocktail parties. My parents like to eat frozen dinners in front of the TV.

"The book says this is supposed to be super sexy. You're supposed to be, like, all worked up right now." He purses his lips, trying to act stern. "You don't seem very worked up."

"If you count trying not to pee my pants because I'm laughing so hard, I'm very worked up."

Parker drags the feather lower down my belly, over my hipbone, across the slope of my upper thigh. When he flicks the feather between my legs and I shiver, he smiles.

"You're not wearing any pants," he whispers, and leans down to kiss me.

"Neither are you." I brush my hand across his stiffness, which twitches restlessly against my leg.

His grin, always at the ready, appears again. "How'd I get so lucky to be with the most observant girl in town?"

It's my turn to pretend to be offended. "Observant? So you're saying you love me for my mind?"

His grin fades. Into his eyes comes a look so warm, I feel bathed in heat. "Yes, I love you for your mind. And for your heart. And for your soul and your eyes and your hair and your smile and the way I feel like I'm ten feet tall when you look at me. I love you because I'm more me around you. Around you, I'm the best me I'll ever be."

Parker rests his hot cheek against my chest. My body hums with joy. I wind my arms around him and close my eyes. My heart is so full, it's bursting.

No one ever told me it could be like this. No one ever said it would be so easy to lose myself in a beautiful, brilliant boy. To lose myself and find myself, all at once.

Without warning, Parker's bedroom door flies open and hits the wall with a thunderous bang. Beneath the covers, we jump.

"Who you got there in your bed, boy?" booms Parker's father.

In a sudden move that leaves me gasping in shock, the covers are stripped away. Naked in each other's arms, Parker and I stare up in horror at his father's livid face. Parker jumps up, attempting to cover me with the sheet, but his father backhands him across the face and sends his son staggering. He stumbles into a chair, loses his balance, crashes against the dresser, then tumbles to the floor.

Bill Maxwell leers down at me as I cower on the bed, starting to cry.

"I find you in this house again, you little slut, you'll be spreadin' your legs for both the Maxwell men."

Parker shoots to his feet. In a red-faced fury, he lunges at his father, but it's too late. The older man, a former quarterback, broad in the shoulders and strong as a bull, throws a punch to Parker's solar plexus that knocks him right off his feet.

I scream as Parker collides with the wall. The windows shake with the force of the impact. He slides to the floor, clutching his stomach and gasping for breath.

Before his father leaves the room, he looks at me cowering on the bed, at his son gulping air on the floor. He adjusts his tie, smooths a hand over his hair. He's not even sweating.

"No son of mine is gonna fraternize with the help. You got a decision to make, boy. Keep your whore or keep your inheritance. You choose her, you're cut off without a cent, you hear?"

He looks at me, hatred shining in his eyes. "Don't throw your whole life away on a worthless piece of pussy."

When he leaves, I crawl from the bed and run to Parker's side. I curl into a ball beside him, sobbing, listening to Parker wheeze and gasp, wishing with all my might that I was a different girl, good enough for someone like him, good enough for his parents and his future and all the things he was destined to do.

But I'll never be that girl, and everybody knows it.

~

The private jet touches down on the runway, and I awaken with a jolt.

My heart pounds painfully fast. The back of my neck is drenched in sweat. I fumble in my handbag for my medicine, wash a pill down with a swig from the Evian bottle on the small table in front of me. Then I sit still for a moment, allowing my breathing to slow, letting the awful images and feelings from the dream begin to dissipate.

Nightmares and self-hatred and old, bitter memories. This is always how it is when I come home. Which is why I so rarely do.

I'm met on the tarmac by the private car Tabby arranged for me. I packed lightly—I'm not staying long—and soon the silent driver and I are on the way to my mother's house.

He keeps glancing at me in the rearview mirror. I'm glad I've got my sunglasses on and have wound a scarf over my hair. The last thing I want is to be recognized. *Here*, of all places.

Another reason I so rarely come home.

The drive to the ranch isn't long, but by the time I'm finally standing on my mother's porch with my Louis Vuitton overnight bag in hand, I feel smaller than I have in years.

I feel reduced.

I look around at the plain yard, the chicken coop my mother refused to take down long after she could afford to buy her own eggs, the expanse of cultivated fields on one side of the road beyond the white clapboard house, and the wild acres of scrub and mesquite on the other.

God, I hate this place.

I ring the bell. My mother opens the door. We look at each other for a moment without speaking. She's older. Thinner. There's far more gray threaded through her black hair.

"*Hola, Mama*," I say softly.

She looks at the duffel bag in my hand but doesn't ask how long I'll be staying. Her dark eyes flash up to mine. She examines my face for a moment, then says in Spanish, "I just made pozole. Come on in. It's still warm."

We go inside. The moment I cross the threshold, I'm assaulted with goblin memories, sour old ghosts that have long been waiting in cold graves for me to return.

I'd forgotten how small this house is.

Everything is exactly the same as it was the day I left for New York as a teenager, right down to the macramé hangers filled with dead ferns hanging from the corners of the popcorn ceiling, and the dusty stacks of *National Geographic* magazines crowding the two bookcases that flank the plain brick hearth.

Inhaling a breath, I drop my bag on the sofa in the living room. The last time I was here, it was fall, during the harvest, the air redolent with the rich scent of upturned soil. Now it's spring, cool and crisp, and the air reeks of fertilizer.

That smell always depresses me.

My mother sets a steaming bowl of pozole on the kitchen table. I step out of my heels, take off my glasses and scarf, pull out a chair at the round wooden table where I ate all my childhood meals, and sit.

She sits across from me and watches as I begin to eat. She glances at the diamond-studded timepiece on my left wrist, the black pearl necklace around my throat, the matching pair of pearls in my ears. Her gaze has a weight to it, a palpable warmth, like the touch of a hand.

"Five years. You look well, *mija*. Too thin, though."

I slurp the soup. It's delicious, the one dish she makes

perfectly. I've missed it, this hearty peasant soup. And, though I'm surprised to realize it, I've missed her too.

I care deeply for my mother, but being in her presence is like having a scab ripped off before the wound has had a chance to heal. Over and over again.

"There's not one decent Mexican restaurant in New York City."

"There's not one decent anything in New York City."

We both know whom we're talking about, but continue on as if we don't.

"The fields look good."

"Eh. The company you hired to work them is very good. Too good. I have nothing to do all day, just sit here and watch myself grow old. Hard to sit around and do nothing so much." Her gaze, still warm but, God, so penetrating, never wavers from my face. "You know."

Yes, I do know. Seven months I sat around and did nothing inside this house. Seven months of enforced solitude, pacing and staring at the walls and trying not to go insane while Parker's baby grew big inside me. My father wouldn't allow me out of the house until after the pregnancy was over. Said the shame was too great. Said it was the shame that made him drink and drink and drink.

Near the end, he couldn't even bear to look at me, stopped coming home at all most nights. That's when I first began writing, during those endless black nights when I could hear my mother crying softly in her room. When every second was an hour, every hour a lifetime, every tick of the clock pure torture to my ears.

I started writing to escape the terrifying feeling that I was going mad.

I take another swallow of my soup. "How's church?"

My mother shrugs and looks away. Lines radiate from the corners of her eyes, are etched in deep parentheses around her mouth. Her hair is gathered in a tight bun at the nape of her neck. A few rebel strands have escaped and curl around her face, glinting silver in the afternoon light.

"I still go. But me and God, we have our differences. I don't talk to Him so much anymore."

"I keep telling you we can move you, *Mama*. There's no reason to stay in this house. There hasn't been in years."

The hopeless shrug appears again. "And go where? And do what? Eh, I can't start over, *mija*."

There's a slight emphasis on "I." It gets my hackles up. "And what would you have had me do? Stay here with you, after…"

My mother reaches across the table and clasps my hand. "No. It was right that you left. At least one of us escaped this place."

We sit in silence as a dog barks far off in the distance. Then, because she's my mother, because she knows me so well, she knows without asking why I've come, and what it is I need to do.

"She's big. You won't recognize her."

I stare at the bottom of my soup bowl, watch as it begins to slowly waver, then blink rapidly to clear my eyes. "You still go by the school?"

"Only on really bad days." She pauses. "I went after I saw the picture of you and…*him*…in the newspaper."

She won't say Parker's name. She hasn't since the day I read the letter he mailed me and didn't stop screaming until the paramedics arrived and gave me a shot.

When I glance up, there's a new, harder edge to my mother's mouth. A steely glint in her eyes.

"So? What's happening?"

I don't have to ask what she means. I sit back in my chair and push the bowl away, ready to give my report. "I've got him where I want him. I found his safe. I'll get into it. Tabby's working her angles, looking into him and his family. It won't be long before we have something we can ruin him with."

With blistering vehemence, my mother says, "His father—look into that son of a whore! He's as dirty as they come!"

Startled, I stare at her. To the best of my knowledge, my mother's never met Parker's father. It was always made perfectly clear that my relationship with Parker was as much a shame to the elder Mr. Maxwell as my pregnancy was to my own father. We were the poor farmers with the wrong pedigree; they were the privileged elite. My biggest crime was not knowing my place. Her reaction makes no sense to me.

"Why do you say that? I mean, I agree with you, but…did you ever meet him?"

A fleeting look of hatred disfigures her face. It's gone almost as soon as it appears. She stands abruptly and goes to the sink. Over her shoulder, she says, "No. Of course not. But I hear things. The way he treats his workers, things like that. He has a reputation as a ruthless bastard."

She opens the cupboard, takes out a glass, fills it with water from the tap, and drinks the entire thing down without stopping for a breath.

I watch her, noting the stiffness in her shoulders, the slight tremble in her hand.

"Why are you so upset?"

She turns from the sink, eyes glittering. "He's the father of that *puto bendejo* who gave you a stroke, that's why!"

Suddenly exhausted, I blow out a hard breath. "It wasn't a stroke, *Mama*."

"Atrial fibrillation, heart disease, whatever! He's the one who caused it! You're healthy as a horse until he dumps you like a bad habit, then you have to take medicine every day because your heart fell apart? It's his fault!"

In all likelihood, I'd had the heart condition from birth, but it went undetected. It took a "mitigating event," as the doctor put it, to uncover the problem. But for my mother, the mitigating event was and will always be Parker Maxwell.

Just one more mark to add to his tally of doom.

"Either way, I'm looking into both of them. It's only a matter of time before I dig something up." I stand and go to her, wrapping my arms around her frail shoulders. "And then I'll even the score. Okay?"

It takes a few long moments before the tension begins to fade from her body. Finally, she sighs and pats my back. "I'm sorry, *mija*. I don't mean to shout. I'm tired today."

"It's okay," I whisper, staring over her head through the window and out into the yard. "I'm tired too."

She pats my back again, withdraws from my arms, goes over to the big pot on the stove, and starts to ladle the rest of the soup into the freezer-safe plastic containers stacked ready on the counter. Keeping her back to me, she says, "We'll go by the school tomorrow afternoon. Clean sheets and towels are in the hall closet. Truck's got a full tank if you need it."

There's more to be said—there's always more—but I simply nod and push away from the counter.

I wander through the living room and down the hall, pausing to look at the faded pictures of my brother and me, framed in cheap plastic frames and hung on tacks stuck through the wallpaper. In pictures, the progression of his disease is painfully clear: crutches, wheelchair, hospital bed with metal rails. I'd almost forgotten how angelic his smile was.

So many old ghosts. I wonder if they'll ever let me go.

With a painful tightness in my chest, I turn away from the pictures. I take my duffel bag into the room I used to call my own, change into jeans and a T-shirt, shrug on a jacket, wind a scarf around my hair and don my big black sunglasses, and grab the keys to my mother's truck.

Then I go for a drive in the chilly Texas afternoon to revisit all the places that still haunt me.

~

The next day at ten after three, my mother and I sit in a parking lot, watching the outpouring of students that bursts from the school doors after the end-of-day bell.

The school is a good one—a private one—a sprawl of red brick and majestic white columns set on a lush, landscaped green hill on the good side of town. It looks like something out of a movie set. Like a spy, I'm peering at it through a pair of binoculars.

"We're too late. We missed her."

In the passenger seat, my mother squints into the bright afternoon sun. "No, she hasn't come out—" Suddenly she clutches my arm and points. "There!"

I follow the direction she's pointing, and my heart stops dead in my chest.

Emerging from the shadows of the building into the warm afternoon sunlight is a girl. She's tall, honey-blonde, leggy, dressed in the school uniform of white shirt and navy plaid skirt, carrying a stack of books in one arm.

My daughter—my beautiful daughter, the beautiful stranger —lifts her hand to shade her eyes from the sun.

My voice choked, I say, "She's so tall. When did she get so tall?"

"Children grow like weeds. The last time you saw her she was, what? Ten? Now she's fifteen. A young woman."

Fifteen. The age I was when I met Parker.

Two years before my life imploded.

I lift the binoculars and stare through them again. Viewed closer, Eva is even prettier. She has her father's dimples, his easy, long-limbed grace. I watch breathlessly as she waves to a few friends, then skips down the steps, turns a corner, and disappears.

It's not until I take the binoculars from my eyes that I notice the wetness on my cheeks.

My mother and I sit in stifling silence until I can compose

myself. She politely keeps her gaze turned away. After most of the cars have left the parking lot and the doors to the school have been shut, she says quietly, "Robert died."

Stunned, I stare at her. "Eva's adoptive father? When?"

"Last year. He was hit by a drunk driver."

"Why didn't you tell me?"

My mother finally looks at me. Her eyes are full of sympathy, and it makes me furious.

"Why, *mija*? What could you have done?"

"I'm sure I could've done *something*."

"No." My mother's voice is firm. "You could not."

Even through my anger, I know she's right. What could I do? Eva doesn't know me, has never known me. I gave her up when she was only minutes old. I never even got to hold her. The doctor took her from my body and whisked her away, into the care of the agency my mother chose to handle the adoption. I've only ever been a part of her life like this, hovering out of sight, stealing glimpses of my own child like a thief.

Even this is more than I should have.

The adoption was private, the records sealed. But long before I had Tabby on my payroll, I had someone else who hid and unearthed information for me. A man named Dooney whom I met in a grief counseling group after I gave birth. He was an expert in information technology who'd been a bigwig in the military before a dishonorable discharge for manslaughter. Something to do with his wife and another man, although he never provided the details. He helped me forge a new identity from the ashes of my former life, helped me find out who had adopted my baby, and later hanged himself from the rafters of his garage.

Tabby I have to pay. Dooney did it because he was in love with me.

Birds of a feather flock together, and so do birds with broken wings.

My mother sighs. I know she wishes I'd never found out where Eva went, but she stopped telling me long ago that these clandestine visitations were an unhealthy thing to do. Besides, she's been unable to keep away either. Like addicts, we're still drawn to the thing that ruined us.

"I visited your father's grave the other day."

Rage rears its ugly head inside me. I mutter, "Why?"

My mother thinks for a moment. "Sometimes I need someone to talk to."

My breath huffs out between my gritted teeth. "And you decided the man who spent every last dime of yours gambling and drinking himself to death and every minute before that screaming at me about what shame I'd brought on the family because I got pregnant was the one you needed a friendly chat with?"

Her voice is soft when she answers. "I told him how much I still hate him. I told him his weakness is what killed your brother. If he hadn't wasted all our money, we could have gotten Eduardo better doctors, more help. His illness wouldn't have been cured, but he could have been in less pain. He didn't have to suffer so much, disfigured and helpless, shitting himself like an infant."

She's silent a moment, staring out the window. Then says with vehemence, "I hope your father is rotting in hell."

I tilt my head back against the headrest and close my eyes. "It wasn't Dad who killed Eduardo. It was Parker. Before I got pregnant and Parker deserted me, we were fine. Everything was fine. And then it wasn't. Because of him."

Silently, my mother nods. This is an old theme between us, a conversation so well-worn it's really no longer necessary to speak it aloud. The fact is undisputed. Parker Maxwell was the catalyst of my family's misery. He is the cross on which all our pain hangs.

And now the daughter he's never met is fatherless once again.

When I exhale a long breath, my mother guesses what I've been thinking. "You can't interfere, *mija*. Anything you do that puts you in the path of that girl, you risk being discovered. Think what would happen then."

I can see the headlines now. *The Queen Bitch Has a Hidden Love Child!* If I try to help Eva and I'm found out, her life will be miserable. The press will descend like vultures. Then she'll discover who her real father is, and he'll desert her just like he did fifteen years ago.

"You're right. Better to let sleeping dogs lie and concentrate instead on kicking the shit out of their useless master."

I start the truck and pull out of the parking lot, headed back home.

In my handbag, my phone begins to ring. At the exact same time, my mother and I both mutter, "Speak of the devil."

We look at each other. She says, "Jinx."

My depression lifting, I look back at the road.

She just gave me a brilliant idea.

PARKER

*T*uesdays in the restaurant business aren't typically the craziest nights of the week, but tonight is an exception. Kai is having another meltdown in the kitchen—this time over beets, of all things—we're so overbooked, two scuffles have already broken out in the bar over the availability of tables, and my shipment of wagyu beef never made it, which means I'll be serving filet mignon—at half the profit.

But none of those things are the reason my mood is so black.

"Still no call, huh?"

Bailey, trying her best not to smirk, peers around my shoulder. I shove my cell phone into my coat pocket and cross my arms over my chest. The only answer I give her is a glower.

"Okay, I don't mean to say I told you so, boss, but…I totally told you so."

"Not helpful, Bailey. And shouldn't you be working right now instead of giving me grief?"

She shrugs. "Shouldn't *you* be working instead of obsessing over your booty call?"

"It wasn't a booty call!"

Bailey chuckles. "Really? Because I thought when a woman

calls you for the express purpose of coming over for a quickie shag and then sneaks off in the middle of the night and doesn't return any of your gazillion phone calls, it's the textbook definition of a booty call."

I say through clenched teeth, "*I* called *her.*"

She grins. "Which is completely beside the point, because she's obviously pulled the infamous Maxwell Disappearing Act, and you'll never hear from her again."

I stare at her in stony silence. "You're enjoying this a little too much."

Her grin is so wide, I can see all her teeth. "It's just amusing to see the shoe on the other foot for a change. Honestly, Parker, if I had a dollar for every female you ghosted, I'd be filthy rich."

She turns and saunters away, leaving me fuming.

I won't allow it. I will NOT allow Victoria Price to give me everything I didn't know I needed, then disappear.

I drag in a deep breath, close my eyes, and count to three, marshaling every bit of self-control at my disposal to refrain from taking out my phone again and calling her. Again.

But when I open my eyes, a miracle has occurred, because there she is.

My heartbeat takes off like a rocket. She stands near the front door, looking around, wearing a lovely knee-length white dress that accentuates her curves. When she spots me by the kitchen, she freezes. Our eyes lock.

What I see in her gaze is something that catapults me across the room.

I'm at her side in four seconds. She says, "Can we talk?"

"Not here. Come into my office." I gently take hold of her arm and steer her away from the door, ignoring the curious gaze of the hostess, feeling a hundred pairs of eyes on me as we walk. Victoria seems tense—her head is held at a stiff angle, her back is ramrod straight—and I have the horrifying thought that she's come here to dump me in person.

Fuck that. She's not dumping me.

When we're in my office, I lock the door behind us and turn to her. "You ran away."

"I panicked."

She doesn't hesitate, there's no strange inflection in her voice, but something tells me there's more to the story. I step closer, closely watching her face.

"You've been avoiding my calls."

"I had an emergency."

"Did the emergency involve your cell phone dying? And your office phone dying? And every other phone within a hundred-mile radius?"

"No, it's... I had to fly out of state suddenly. To California. It was a family situation. My mother..."

She looks away, and my frustration with not being able to get in touch with her and fear that our affair is over before it's even had a chance to get going are instantly replaced with concern.

"Is everything all right? What happened?"

"She's not well. She's...declining."

Her face pinches. It does something to my heart. I reach out and take her in my arms. When she buries her face against my chest and wraps her arms around my waist, I'm so relieved, I almost groan.

She's not dumping me. She had a family emergency. Thank God.

Don't be such a selfish dick!

I murmur into her hair, "Are you okay? Is there anything I can do?"

She lifts her head and stares deep into my eyes. "Yes," she says, her voice husky. "You can kiss me."

It takes me all of a tenth of a second to obey this command. When our lips meet, she melts against me. My body tingles with need. My arms tighten around her. She makes a soft, feminine noise in her throat that sends a flash of heat straight to my groin.

"You have to stop running away from me," I whisper when we break apart. We're both breathing hard, and it's all I can do to keep my hands from drifting toward her breasts. Her perfect, delectable breasts.

"I'm sorry. I told you I'm shitty at relationships. I hate spending the night. All that awkward small talk and eye-avoidance in the morning…ugh."

She shudders, and I chuckle. "I know. I have a rule against spending the night too."

For the first time since she walked in tonight, she smiles. "You do?" When I nod, she turns playful. "Any other of your rules I should know about, Romeo?"

This new lightness in her makes me happy. I'm so relieved she's smiling instead of blowing me off that I'm giddy. "There are three. The first, which you already know, is no spending the night. The second is no expectations for the future."

"And the third?"

Because I'm not thinking straight, I answer. "No questions about my past."

The moment it's out, I regret it. In other circumstances, I'd never tell a woman about my rules. They only invite more questions and the inevitable pressure for me to reveal more of myself than I can or will.

But Victoria, my elusive, enigmatic Victoria, accepts what I've said as if it's the most commonsense thing in the world. She nods, holding my gaze.

"Very wise. I couldn't have said it better myself. But there's only one problem."

"Which is?"

"You've already told me about your past, Parker," she murmurs. "You've told me a secret you've never told anyone else."

"I have. And you've told me a secret or two of yours."

Our faces inches apart, we stare into each other's eyes. I have the oddest sensation of falling. A sensation of stepping off a tall building or jumping from a tree, my arms flung wide, my feet no longer on solid ground.

I'm not looking down.

Why do I feel like I know you? Why do I feel so damn good when you're near? How can you affect me like this, so soon?

I blurt, "Do you believe in soul mates?"

Her eyes, gorgeous dark eyes the color of fine chocolate, flare. "No."

"Me neither," I lie, and take her mouth in a deep, demanding kiss.

As she always does, she reacts instantly, arching into me, digging her fingers into my skin. The kiss lasts and lasts, getting hotter by the moment, until there's a sharp knock on my office door.

"Boss! Kai's got the sous chef by the throat! You need to come deal with this!"

Victoria and I break apart. I mutter, "Fuck."

"It's okay. I was on my way to have drinks with Darcy, anyway. I just stopped by to say hi." Her voice drops. "And that I'm sorry for leaving like I did."

I take her face in my hands. "Promise me you won't do it again. No matter how freaked out you get, promise me you'll at least wake me up to tell me you're running away." I gently kiss her. "And I promise I'll let you go and not stalk your phone if you do."

"That sounds suspiciously like an invitation to spend the night, Mr. Maxwell," she teases, batting her lashes.

Fuck, I love it when she flirts with me.

I grin. "Call me when you're finished with drinks, and I'll come get you, wherever you are."

"Such an eager beaver! I'll have you know I have a very important meeting first thing in the morning."

I kiss the corners of her mouth, the tip of her nose, her petal-soft cheek. "Then I'll have you up bright and early for work. And you probably shouldn't say the word *beaver* in my presence unless you'd like the bulge in my trousers to get even bigger than it already is."

She throws back her head and laughs.

"Boss!" shouts Bailey through the door. She bangs her fist against it again.

I'm really going to have to talk to her about her attitude.

"I'll let you get back to work. Call you later."

Victoria plants one final kiss on my lips. She slips out of my arms, and we walk to the door.

When I open it, Bailey stands there glaring at us like an ex-wife in divorce court. She says, "Finally!" shoots Victoria a lethal glare, then spins on her heel and stalks off.

Victoria smiles. "Oh dear. I see your sidekick doesn't approve."

I decide it's prudent not to answer. I lift her hand and kiss it. "Until later, baby."

At my endearment, her cheeks color. It makes me hard.

"Until later, Mr. Beaver." She winks and walks away.

I watch her go, grinning from ear to ear, until Bailey reappears around the corner.

"Hold your horses, Bailey. I'm coming."

She looks at the bulge in my crotch. "Or you would've been if I hadn't knocked!"

I say quietly, "Watch yourself."

She flushes and looks away. After a moment she mumbles, "Sorry."

Shaking my head, I brush past her on my way to the kitchen. She falls into step beside me.

"So—what was her excuse for blowing you off?"

It pleases me greatly to say, "Her mother was sick. She had to fly out of state on short notice to visit her."

In my peripheral vision, I see Bailey's face fall. "Oh. I guess that explains why she was in Texas."

I stop dead in my tracks. "Texas?"

Bailey nods, lifting a shoulder in a nonchalant shrug. "Yeah. I read it on the Drudge Report. She was spotted in Texas in some shitty border town. Must be weird to have people following you all the time."

She turns and continues on toward the kitchen, but I'm rooted to the floor because a wrecking ball has just blasted a hole straight through my chest.

Victoria said she'd been in California, but she'd actually been in Texas.

What the fuck is in Texas?

It takes me only another second to recall how deftly she'd sidestepped any more questions from me about her mother by asking me to kiss her. Had she known how that would distract me?

I stand there in the hallway for several more moments, grappling with the sudden, gut-deep instinct that something is terribly wrong.

VICTORIA

"*G*irl, have you lost what's left of your vodka-soaked *mind?*"

"Darcy, just hear me out—"

"No! The answer is no! This is a stupid plan, and I don't have nothin' to do with stupid plans!"

Darcy's in a snit. Why she's in said snit, I don't really understand because I know this would work. She's told me so herself. Not only that, but also she's already taken part in my scheming where Parker is concerned, so I can't see what her problem is.

"Look, you've told me—on more than one occasion, I might add—that in addition to being a first-rate, crystal-ball-gazing fortune-teller, your mother is a voodoo priestess of legendary stature in New Orleans. Am I right or am I not?"

Scowling, Darcy pops a cocktail onion between her fire-engine red lips and chomps on it. Obviously the answer to my question is yes.

"And did you or did you not once tell me that all it would take to put a hex on someone is a lock of his hair?"

Darcy downs the rest of her Gibson. I sense a chink in her armor, so I go for the jugular.

"And did you or did you not just a few days ago say, and I quote, 'What are friends for if they won't help you move a body?'"

"Yes, yes to all that shit! But girl, you do not want to mess with black magic. Seriously. You do. *Not.* My great, great, great, great-grandpaw-paw once asked the spirits for immortality, but the caster forgot to ask for health along with endless life. And do you know what happened?"

Eyes wide, I sit forward in my seat. "What?"

"The same thing that would happen to any hundred-and-thirty-year-old human body. It disintegrated. Only he stayed alive. You remember the Crypt Keeper from that old HBO show *Tales from the Crypt?*"

When I nod, she says, "That's Paw-Paw on a *good* day. The man's nothing more than a rattling bag of bones. My mother keeps him propped up in a rocking chair in the parlor. Her new clients think he's fake, one of them Halloween skeletons." She chuckles. "Until he gets up to pee. On their shoes."

I stare at her. "That's not true."

She stares back at me. "Or is it?"

"Oh, for God's sake! C'mon, Darse, you *have* to help me put a curse on Parker! I can easily get a lock of his hair, and we can just mail it to your mother." A new thought occurs to me. "Wait —do spells work if they're cast from far away? Because if not, I can fly her up here."

Darcy groans, rolls her eyes, and flips both hands in the air, as if giving up all hope of having an intelligent conversation.

We're at one of my favorite bars in the city, a rooftop deck on the fifty-fourth floor of the Hyatt in Times Square, enjoying a spectacular view of the city lights.

In my purse, my cell phone rings. It's Tabby. I ignore it and go back to harassing Darcy.

"I'm just trying to cover all my bases. I've got Tabby searching for serious dirt on Parker on the Internet, I'm going to break into his home safe, and you can do your part by getting your mother to jinx him."

Darcy mutters, "How's that for an unholy trinity?"

My cell phone chirps, indicating Tabby's left me a message. She'd left an earlier message saying she'd gotten food poisoning over the weekend while I was gone, but was feeling better, and she'd see me tomorrow morning at the house. I wonder why she'd be calling again but decide it can wait until after Darcy and I are finished. I turn the phone to silent.

When I look up, Darcy has folded her arms over her chest and is staring at me with a disappointed frown like she's the school principal and I've just been called into her office for throwing a firecracker into the girls' toilet.

"Was that your baby-daddy?"

Uh-oh. I know that tone. I'm about to get a verbal smackdown.

When I open my mouth, Darcy sits forward in her chair, points a manicured finger in my face, and says, "No."

"No, what?"

"No, you do *not* get to ask me for favors when—after knowing you for how many years?"

Knowing where this is going, I mumble sheepishly, "Eight."

"When after knowing you for eight looong years, and being your best friend for the entirety of that time, you choose to keep the fact that you have a child a secret."

I look down, fiddling with the stem of my martini glass. I say quietly, "Had a child."

"Excuse me?"

I glance up at Darcy. "I had a child. Past tense. I gave her up for adoption when she was born."

Darcy blinks. "You said you were going to see your daughter."

"And I did."

After a moment, Darcy prompts, "Are you going to elaborate on that, or am I going to have to kick your Armani-clad ass?"

So, because she really is my best friend, the cat's already out of the bag, I'm on my second martini, and I need her help to put a curse on Parker, I tell her the whole story, beginning to end, not leaving anything out. It takes another two rounds of drinks for me to get through it all.

At the end of it, she's staring at me in with her mouth hanging open, speechless.

Finally, sounding awed, disturbed, and unusually somber, she says, "Holy shit, girl. I don't think I've ever heard anything so depressing."

I take a long drink of my martini.

"So...basically you've lived your life since you were eighteen as a different person? Different name, made-up history, new face, everything? No one knows the real you?"

I shrug.

"Gawd. It's like you're in the witness protection program."

"Only with a lot more money."

Her laugh is shaky. "Damn. I can't even imagine how lonely you must be."

That stops me cold. "I'm not lonely."

Her big, dark eyes unblinking, Darcy looks at me long and hard. "Don't get so comfortable with your own lies that you start believing them."

The waiter comes and asks us if we want another round. We both decline. After he leaves, we sit in silence for a few minutes, listening to the sound of laughter and chatter around us. Sirens pierce the night, drifting up from the street far below like the wailing of mourners. Over and over, I push away the word that's scratching at the inside of my skull.

Lonely.

Darcy says, "I'm sorry about your little brother."

My throat gets tight. "Thanks."

"What was it—his illness? What did he die of?"

"Muscular dystrophy."

Because she can see that the turn in conversation is hitting me hard, Darcy takes pity on me. "All right. Look here. I'm only gonna say this one thing, and then we'll let it go."

She reaches across the table and takes my hand.

"I'm here anytime you need me. To talk, whatever. I've got your back. You know I won't say a word to anyone about this. But now that I know why you are the way you are, what happened to make you so closed off, I think you should seriously reconsider this plan of yours for revenge. Maybe Parker came back into your life for a reason, V. Maybe if you told him—"

I snatch my hand from hers. "If I told him, he'd screw me over just like he did the first time, Darcy!"

She sighs, downs the dregs of her Gibson, and then says, "Honey, if every man had to pay a fine for all the stupid shit he did in high school, not a single one of them would have a cent left."

"Really? What's your excuse for the lie he recently told me about his girlfriend who killed herself?"

She scoffs, "Oh, please, I hardly think you're in any position to get pissed off when someone else tells a whopper. The poor bastard was probably just trying to get laid!"

"By saying his girlfriend *killed herself?*"

She says reasonably, "You're a tough nut to crack. Maybe he thought pity was the way to get a bite of your cookie." She smiles. "Obviously he was right."

I glare at her. "I can't believe you. And by the way, you rated Xengu an A-friggin'-plus even after the funky truffles, and knowing Parker's my arch-nemesis? What the hell?"

In a highly uncharacteristic move, Darcy lowers her lashes demurely and starts to hem and haw. "Er, um, well, it *was* a lovely meal. And the ambiance was…amazing."

She peeks up at me, finds me staring at her with a frown, and looks back at the table again. "I mean, everything except the truffles was top-notch, V: the service, the chef, the décor, the food, the music, the chef—"

"Oh. My. God!"

Startled by my tone—and also probably by the way I've just slapped my open palm against the table—Darcy looks up at me with wide eyes. "What?"

"You've got a thing for Parker's crazy German chef, don't you?"

Her expression is classic puppy-dog-chewed-my-new-shoes guilty. "Um...no?"

I gasp, outraged. "Don't you dare lie to me!"

For a few silent seconds, we stare at each other. Then, at the same time, we burst into laughter.

I laugh so long and hard, tears stream down my cheeks. Darcy covers her face with her hands, her whole body shaking. She falls sideways against the glass wall separating us from fifty-four stories of air. We hoot and snort and guffaw until we're finally both worn out, clutching our sides, our faces aching.

Finally, dabbing her eyes with her napkin, she says, "That was priceless."

"Almost as priceless as you and Kai as a couple."

"He's too sane for me, isn't he?"

The two of us break out into laughter all over again.

The waiter, obviously worried that we're drunk and disorderly, deposits the check we haven't asked for on our table and then scurries away. We split the check and rise to go.

"Hey," says Darcy, "I have a fabulous idea!"

"What's that?"

"We can double date!"

"Say something like that again and I'll strangle you with your own wig."

"Oh, c'mon! It'll be fun! I can watch all the carnage up close!"

On our way out the door, I say, "I take it this means I'm not getting that curse."

Darcy chuckles and links her arm through mine. "I think you're cursing Parker Maxwell just fine on your own, Miss Thing."

That remains to be seen.

I take out my phone and send the accursed a text.

In less than ten minutes, Parker pulls up in front of the entrance to the Hyatt. I'm waiting impatiently by the bell desk, trying to fend off the advances of a drunk businessman in a plaid jacket who followed Darcy and me from the bar. He's made it clear that she was his first choice, but as she's already left, I'm an acceptable second.

Needless to say, I jump into Parker's car as if a fire's been lit under my ass.

"You okay?" he asks, glancing around me. When he sees Parker's look, the businessman turns and lurches back toward the revolving doors of the hotel.

"I'm fine. He was harmless."

As we pull away into traffic, I notice Parker's jaw is clenched almost as tightly as his hands are around the steering wheel. "Are *you* okay?"

He shoots a glance in my direction. "Sure. Why wouldn't I be?"

There's something in his tone that sounds an alarm bell in my head.

I've lived with this particular alarm bell for as long as I can remember. It was worse in the beginning, when I first moved to New York and was newly famous after my book became a bestseller. In those days, I was certain that I was just about to be discovered, that any minute some reporter would break the story that everything from my degree from Stanford to my name was a lie.

But after a few years, when no fingers were pointed, when no one called my bluff, I began to accept that the work Dooney had done to create Victoria Price was enough to protect me forever.

But even the most solid wall of stone has its cracks. Better to apply a little fresh mortar now than risk the whole thing crumbling later.

I rest my hand on Parker's arm. "What is it? Tell me."

He glances at me again, his sidelong gaze piercing. He drops his gaze to my hand, and then he looks straight ahead. Beneath my fingers, his arm muscles tense. "Sorry. I'm just tired. It was a bad night."

I know a lie when I hear one. My heart starts to thump. My mouth goes dry. In the pit of my stomach, a churning ball of acid forms.

What's he found out?

Parker drives fast and erratically. He narrowly misses several pedestrians, almost side-swipes a bus, blows through two yellow lights as they turn red. By the time we arrive at his building, I'm so tense my jaw aches. The valet takes the car. Parker silently guides me through the lobby and into the elevator.

As soon as the doors close behind us, he pulls me against his chest and kisses me. It's rough, edged with desperation, and takes my breath away.

"Parker—"

He growls, "Don't talk unless you're going to tell the truth."

Oh fuck. Oh fuck, fuck, fuck!

He definitely knows something. I think of that missed call from Tabby and feel the first stirrings of panic deep in my gut.

The panic deepens when I realize I left my handbag in his car. *Shit!* There's no way I can sneak to the bathroom for a quick call before this gets too far out of hand. I'm flying totally blind.

Parker kisses me again. I feel the tension in his kiss. Even as my body warms, feeling his heat and strength against me, my brain goes a million miles an hour.

If he's found out about me, he could ruin me before I get the chance to ruin him. He could expose me to the world as a liar, a figment of my own imagination, and I could lose it all!

But then he wouldn't be kissing me. It can't be the worst-case scenario.

He breaks away. His lashes lift, and he pins me in his knowing stare. "So. What do you have to say? What truths do you have for me tonight, Victoria?"

Oh God. He's not giving me anything! How can I find out what he knows before I answer?

Then it strikes me—the best way to catch a snake is in a snare.

I say, "Any truth you want. Ask me anything you want, and I'll tell you."

It catches him off guard. He was expecting evasion, not an invitation. But he's not so easy to trap. He turns the tables on me so fast I'm stunned.

"Okay. Tell me how you feel about me."

I gape at him. "How I...*feel* about you?"

He nods. His eyes blister me. A million emotions careen through my body. A million words flash through my mind. All my ready lies go up in smoke.

I whisper, "Anything but that."

"I know it's the last thing you want to do. Which is why I need you to do it."

When I close my eyes to escape him, he warns, "You said you could give me real. *Give it.*"

Real is how my body is so high just from having him close. Real is how my entire adult life was shaped by this man, by what he did and didn't do, by all the ways I can't let him go.

Real is the look of pity in Darcy's eyes when I told her my story.

"I can't even imagine how lonely you must be."

Without opening my eyes, I say, "You make me want to believe in happily-ever-afters."

It comes from the deepest part of me, the darkest part, a silent pit I thought I'd buried a long, long time ago. It's raw and whispered, and the worst thing of all?

It's the truth.

Parker says, "Look at me."

I open my eyes and stare at him. He looks first in one of my eyes and then the other, his gaze intent, deeply searching. After a moment he says, "You never fail to amaze me. When you let down your guard, Victoria, you're the most beautiful thing I've ever seen in my life."

There is a moment—a terrible, terrifying moment—when I almost break down and give it all up. I am *this close* to admitting everything, to purging myself in one epic, truth-telling spew. But then the elevator slides to a stop and the doors to his penthouse open, and the moment is gone.

Parker kisses me softly on the lips. He takes me by the hand. He leads me silently through his house, into the bedroom. He doesn't turn on the lights. Standing at the foot of the bed, his gaze never leaving mine, he slowly unbuttons his shirt and drops it to the floor.

He takes my hand and places it flat on his bare chest. "Do you feel that?"

Beneath my hand, his heart pounds wildly. Because I don't trust myself to speak, I nod.

He wraps his arm around me and pulls me close. "That's what you do to me. Every time I see you, every time I hear your voice. If you can't trust me, trust that. Hearts can't lie."

My eyes squeezed shut, I lower my head to his chest. When I don't answer him, Parker flattens his own hand over my chest and waits.

And my heart—my broken, withered heart—tells him the truth. With every throb and crazy beat, my own heart betrays me.

With a soft groan, he whispers, "Oh, baby."

He kisses me again, this time with breathless urgency. I kiss him back, my arms around his waist, my breasts pressed against his chest, and feel his heart surge.

His fingers find the zipper on the back of my dress. He pulls it down, exposing my skin to the cool air. I shiver, my nipples hardening, my body enflamed. He slides my dress down over my hips. It pools on the floor around my feet.

When Parker looks down with ravenous hunger at my body, I feel a rush of desire so strong, my cheeks go hot.

I push him down to the bed so he's sitting on the edge of the mattress. He looks up at me, his expression expectant, eyes burning, pulse pounding in his neck.

As he watches, I unhook my bra and let the straps fall slowly down my arms. I toss the bra aside. He reaches for my hips, slips his fingers beneath my panties, tugs them impatiently down my thighs. I step out of them so I'm standing nude before him wearing only my heels.

What I see in his eyes, on his face…it's intoxicating.

I've never felt this powerful.

I already know how this game will end. I know there are no happily-ever-afters to be had, no eleventh-hour reprieves to spare our fates. In hours or days or weeks, this house of cards I've built will come crashing down, and I'll have my sweet revenge.

That will come. But this moment isn't for revenge.

It's for remembering. It's for savoring. It's for saying a final goodbye to whatever hesitation I might have been holding onto.

Because this is the moment Parker fully surrenders himself to me.

Even though he has doubts, though I can tell he knows something about me he isn't disclosing, I see in his eyes that his desire for me has trumped his logic, and now he's lost.

A smile spreads over my face. *Hello, little fly. Welcome to my web.*

Parker whispers, "Why are you smiling?"

"Because I know something you don't know."

"What's that?"

Between his spread legs, I sink to my knees. Still smiling, I reach for his zipper. "You, my friend, are about to get royally screwed."

His laugh is husky but falters when I've got his zipper down and his hard cock in my hand. When I lean over and slip the engorged head into my mouth, he moans.

I flatten my hands over his abdomen and push. He falls back against the mattress. The motion makes his hips flex, driving him deeper into my mouth. I pull aside the fly of his trousers, open my throat, and take him all the way to the base.

Shuddering, he moans louder.

That's right, Parker. Moan for me. Let me hear you fall apart.

I begin a ruthless assault on his cock, sucking hard on the crown, my fist curled around the shaft, fingers sliding up and down as I take him in and out of my mouth. I'm relentless, setting a furious pace, egged on by Parker's helpless sounds of pleasure.

When my teeth graze his cock on an upward sweep of my mouth, Parker grabs my arms, drags me up his body, kisses me, flips me to my back, and pins me to the mattress.

Panting, he says roughly, "Why are you angry?"

Just like that, because he can see me so clearly and I absolutely hate it, my temper snaps.

"Fuck you, Parker!"

I struggle to get out from under him, but it's impossible. The man is too strong. He tightens his grip on my wrists, lowers his face to mine so we're nose to nose, and growls, "What. The. *Fuck.*"

His erection is pressed between my open legs. I feel the vein that runs along the underside throb, and resist arching my hips to allow him to slide inside me.

"Get off me!"

"If I thought you really wanted me to, I would. What the hell is wrong? Stop squirming!"

I fall still, breathing raggedly. I can't meet his eyes. Suddenly I feel claustrophobic. I have to get out of this room.

I close my eyes and turn my head, wishing my heart would slow down.

Parker nudges my earlobe with his nose. "Hey. What's going on with you? Talk to me."

With my lips pulled between my teeth, I shake my head.

"I like a challenge as much as the next guy, sweetheart, but this is getting ridiculous. Now *spill*."

"I'm...I..." I take a moment to catch my breath. I was just about to say something dangerously truthful. Finally, I go with, "You lied to me earlier."

His whole body stiffens. When I open my eyes, he's staring down at me, his expression wary.

"When?"

I find it interesting he has to ask.

"When I asked you what was wrong in the car. You said you were tired. That was a lie."

He releases my wrists and props himself up on his elbows, his hands resting on either side of my head. He doesn't move his pelvis, however.

His cock is obviously very impatient with this break in the action.

"It wasn't a lie. I was tired. I also said it had been a bad night. Both of those things are true." His voice drops. "Now ask me what made it a bad night."

My heart begins to flutter. "What made it a bad night?"

He caresses my face, trailing his fingers down my jaw. In a conversational tone, he says, "Well, this incredible woman I've been seeing—a woman who literally drives me insane in every way—left me alone in bed, didn't return my calls for days, then showed up out of the blue and told me an interesting story about how she had to go visit her sick mother in California."

His voice loses the conversational tone and becomes deadly soft. "When she was actually in Texas."

His gaze bores into mine. Ice water is injected into my veins. *Oh God oh God oh God.*

"Um…Texas?"

Parker nods. When I don't respond, he says sarcastically, "Go ahead. Lie to me. I promise I'll believe you."

I have several choices. I can follow my earlier impulse and tell him everything, then get out of his bed and never look back with the knowledge that at least I got him to fall for me and then dumped him. I know it will sting.

A sting doesn't seem very satisfying.

I could also cry—which I know horrifies men—gaining me a momentary reprieve, at least long enough to concoct a good cover story.

Unfortunately, at the moment the likelihood of me being able to summon fake tears is basically zero.

So I decide to go with option three: sling some bullshit and see what sticks.

"I did go to California to visit my mother. But on the way, I stopped in Texas."

Though I have no idea what he knows, if perhaps a story has already run that exposes all my lies—or, worse, he's been having me followed—I'm proud of how even my voice sounded.

Now I just have to figure out what to say next.

Parker studies my face. "Why?"

The image of my brother's smiling face crosses my mind. "To visit the grave of someone I once loved."

My voice is no longer steady. It wavers with emotion. True emotion. Because I did visit the grave of someone I once loved. Someone I once loved very much, and still do, and always will.

My little brother.

I don't tell Parker that, of course. When he asks who the person was, I fabricate a story about a college boyfriend who was originally from Texas, a boy I'd once planned to marry. When he died in the military, or so my story goes, his family had his body shipped back to his hometown so he could be buried like the hero he was.

I keep my fingers crossed that this story jibes with whatever Parker's found out about my trip.

With genuine sorrow in his voice, he says, "I'm sorry to hear that."

Awash in relief, I close my eyes. "Thanks. It was a bad weekend."

More honesty, more emotion in my voice, more softening in Parker's body.

Well. Except *there*.

He kisses my throat, his lips soft and warm. It feels exquisite. Against my skin, he murmurs, "I'm originally from Texas too. Did you know that?"

"No. Small world."

Please don't ask what city I visited. Please don't tell me what city you're from.

He doesn't. Seemingly satisfied by my story, Parker kisses a tender path down my throat, over my collarbone, to my chest. He rests his cheek against my breastbone. He holds still for a moment, listening. I know what he hears, because I feel it in every vein in my body:

Boom! Crash! Thud!

Stupid, traitorous, truth-telling heart.

Parker inhales deeply. He cups my breast in his hand. He whispers, "Maybe you're destined to fall in love only with men from Texas," and lowers his lips to my hard nipple.

When he sucks it into his mouth, I softly groan.

He flexes his hips, bringing the head of his rigid cock to my wet entrance. I slide my hands beneath the waist of his trousers, cup his ass, and pull.

As he slides inside me he says roughly, "We're both still wearing our shoes."

"Would you like to take a moment to remove them, Mr. Maxwell?"

He thrusts, burying himself to the hilt. "Not a fucking chance, Ms. Price."

He slides out and then thrusts in again. My breasts bounce against his chest. I gasp, arching against him. My fingers dig into the firm, succulent flesh of his ass.

He stills. When I whimper, writhing, jerking my hips, he chuckles. "Again?"

"Yes, again!"

He lowers his lips to my ear. "Say please, my beautiful little liar."

Ah. It's game time, is it?

I inhale, stretch my arms over my head, then sigh as if utterly bored. I gaze up at him, smiling, my eyes half-lidded. "Or what?"

A muscle in his jaw flexes.

My smile grows wider. *Oh my dear, darling bastard, how I love pissing you off.*

"Or I won't just make you say please. I'll make you beg."

He twists his hips in a small circle, wringing an involuntary cry from my lips, then lowers his mouth to my breast.

"And beg." He sucks hard on my nipple, using his teeth in the way he knows I like.

I gasp.

"And *beg.*"

He grips a hand in my hair, slides the other under my bottom, and grinds his pelvis into me, hard and fast, before falling still again.

My groan is broken. I exhale, and it's his name.

"I'm not your plaything, Victoria."

"I never said you were."

His unshaven cheek is sandpaper-rough against my skin, but his voice is even rougher. "Then stop trying to lead me around by my dick."

"You're the one playing games right now."

"Only to level the playing field. The only time we're on even footing is when you allow yourself to be vulnerable. And one of the only things I know makes you feel vulnerable is asking for what you want. You're so used to demanding or manipulating, you've forgotten how to ask."

He flexes his hips. His cock slides deeper inside me, sending shock waves of pleasure through my pelvis. I bite my lip to keep from moaning.

He whispers, "That's why I like you to say please, baby. I'll give you anything you ask for—God help me, I'd give you my own head on a platter—if only you say please."

Trembling, I say, "I-I'd like a Rolls-Royce. Please."

His chuckle is dark and satisfied. "What color?"

I exhale in a loud rush. "I'm thinking black on black. With the blacked-out rims."

Parker slides halfway out, then stops. I bite my lip harder.

"Done. Anything else?" He peppers sweet, reverent kisses over my cheeks, my jaw, my nose, my lips.

I tilt my hips up, but he won't let me gain the upper hand. He simply withdraws in the exact amount I advance, keeping just the tip of his cock inside me. Frustrated, I pound the sheets with my fists.

"I want my own island! In the Caribbean!"

"Mmm. I'm on it. What else?" He lowers his head again and

sucks even more aggressively on my nipple. His hot mouth draws hard. His hand is firm and possessive around my flesh.

I pant, straining to maintain control, but ultimately crumble. The words tumble from my lips in a wanton rush. "I want you to please make love to me Parker please oh please oh God *please*."

A tremor runs through him. He raises his head, looks at me, and whispers, "Hearts can't lie, baby."

"Shut up with that crap."

He laughs. "Don't worry. I won't tell anyone you just fell in love with me."

"I hate you."

Parker flexes his hips again, and his hard cock sinks all the way inside me. He says roughly, "Sweetheart, if this is hate, I don't want to feel anything else ever again."

Then he gives me everything I've asked for, everything I need, and drives a stake straight through my chest when he climaxes, calling out my name like a hallelujah.

Hours later, Parker sleeping like the dead beside me, I rise from his bed and creep through the dark rooms, until I'm standing in front of his closed office door.

25

PARKER

*O*nce again, I wake alone.

My disappointment quickly turns to pleasure, however, when I see the note on the pillow beside me.

Dear Parker,

I promise I'm not running away. But you, sexy beast, sleep like a coma patient, and I really did have to be at an early meeting this morning. There's a fresh pot of coffee in the kitchen, and I might have made you French toast.

Don't let it go to your head.

Last night was a game changer. One more thing not to let go to your head. I'll be thinking of you all day.

I can still taste you.

Victoria

She signed her name with little hearts for dots over the two *i*'s. I stare at them, grinning. The last time I felt anything close to this—the only time—I was a teenager, deep in the heady flush of first love.

I rise from bed, shower, and dress. In the kitchen, there is indeed a fresh pot of coffee. A plate in the oven holds three thick slices of French toast. I didn't even know I had the makings for French toast in my kitchen.

Didn't she say she couldn't cook?

I shrug that thought away. I doubt frying bread in a skillet qualifies as cooking.

I drizzle the buttered toast in syrup, wolf it down with a cup of coffee—which may be the best coffee I've tasted in my life, because she made it—and rinse my dishes in the sink, whistling the entire time. When the kitchen is clean, I head to my office to get my briefcase, but stop dead at the end of the hallway.

My office door is open.

It's not wide open, but it's not fully closed either. And this time I *know* I closed it when I left for the restaurant yesterday. I haven't been in there since.

The skin on the back of my neck crawls.

I move slowly down the hallway, then push open the door and look inside.

Nothing's out of place...except the faintest hint of Chanel No. Five lingering in the air.

Fuck. She's been in here.

Why?

I walk around my office, visually scanning it all: the book-cases, the coffee table and chairs, the credenza with the flat-screen TV, and my desk, which I pay special attention to. I toggle the mouse, and the computer screen lights up, asking for my password. The password is so long and convoluted, it would take an expert hacker with a codebreaker program to get in, so I'm satisfied there. All my desk drawers are locked, and nothing appears to be tampered with. Everything's perfect.

Relieved, I release the breath I've been holding.

Then I look at the Magritte.

To anyone else, it would be impossible to spot. The painting is only half an inch off kilter, an inch at most. But to me, it might as well have a sign hanging on it that screams, *I've been touched!*

Behind that painting is my safe.

I can't deny it, no matter how much I want to. Victoria was searching for something in my office.

Why? And what?

"Maybe she got lost on the way out," I say aloud to the empty room. "She thought it was a bathroom."

Right. Let's conveniently forget that the last time she was here, the office door was open, too. And why would she have touched the Magritte?

I stand still as a statue, thinking back over everything that's happened between us so far, including everything that happened last night. When I recall our words, a chill runs down my spine.

"Why are you smiling?"

"Because I know something you don't."

"Oh? What's that?"

"You, my friend, are about to get royally screwed."

I thought she'd meant that in the obvious way—in light of what we were about to do—but maybe she'd meant something else altogether.

Whatever I'd been feeling before when I awoke—the tenderness and happiness, that awful, blinding hope—turns to a sour knot in my stomach.

I pick up the phone on my desk and dial a number I know by heart. When it's answered on the other end—the same heavy silence as always, no greeting, only dead air—I say, "Connor. It's Parker."

The dead air comes alive with the rumble of a rich baritone. "Long time no talk, brother. What's up?"

Looking at the Magritte, I say darkly, "I need your help."

∾

The man who stands in my office an hour later with his bulging biceps folded over his massive chest is what one could politely call big.

At six-foot-four and two hundred forty pounds of solid, military-grade muscle, Connor "Hollywood" Hughes owns and operates Metrix, the private security firm I've employed for years. He's half Samoan and half Irish, and gets his nickname from his sparkling-white movie-star smile.

"Connor, sit. You're making the room look cramped."

Connor waves a giant paw in the air in a dismissive gesture. "I don't sit on the job, brother." He eyes the pair of white leather chairs opposite my desk. "Especially in something like that. The fuck is that, Barbie furniture?"

"Those are five-thousand-dollar Barcelona chairs." When he looks at me with his brows raised, I say, "They're designer."

"You paid five large for chairs that don't even have arms?"

"No. I paid ten large for chairs that don't have arms. And if you're not going to sit, we might as well go into the living room so I can make myself a drink."

"A drink? It's nine o'clock in the morning."

I blow out a hard breath. "I'm surprised I waited this long."

Connor's eyes, the color of obsidian, bore into mine. "That bad, huh?"

"Maybe. I don't know. That's why you're here."

I rise and leave the office. Connor follows. For such a huge guy, he's surprisingly light on his feet. I can't hear his footsteps behind me. When we reach the living room, he leans against the wall with his hands shoved in the pockets of his black cargo pants and watches as I pour myself a glass of scotch from the crystal decanter on the sideboard. I raise the glass to my lips, swallow its contents, and fill it again.

Connor drawls, "Haven't seen you this wound up since the night we met."

The night Connor and I met—at a seedy cowboy bar—was

the worst night of my life. I was twenty-two, piss drunk, and crying like a baby. I picked fights with all the biggest guys I could spot, including him. I wanted to kill everyone. I wanted them to kill me.

I wanted to die.

An hour earlier, I'd learned that the love of my life was dead.

Connor, five years older, fresh out of the Marines' Special Operations Command and already running Metrix, knocked me out cold with a single punch and then dragged me out to his pickup so I could sleep it off in the back.

When I woke up with a hangover and a black eye, he was leaning against the cab of the Chevy, calmly smoking. He looked at me and said, "You better do somethin' about that death wish, brother, before it comes true."

I stare out the wall of windows into the bright afternoon. A forest of skyscrapers stares back at me. Windows like blank eyes wink in the sun.

"There's a woman."

Connor laughs. "With you, there's always a woman."

I turn to look at him. I say quietly, "Not like this."

He examines my face for a long moment. "Go on."

I turn back to the glass. "There's a possibility I might be a mark."

Silence. A moment later, Connor stands beside me at the glass, gazing at the view. "Money?"

I shake my head. "Doubtful. She's got her own. Maybe more than I do."

He slides me a look. "Blackmail?"

I shrug and take another swallow of scotch.

"This skank got a name?"

"Victoria Price. And if you ever call her a skank again, I'll rip out your fucking throat."

Not even mildly intimidated by my threat as almost every

other man would be, Connor looks amused. "Wow. She must have a gold-lined pussy to get you so up in arms."

I mutter, "You have no idea."

Connor's dark brows pull together. "Wait. Victoria Price? How do I know that name?"

I chug the final few swallows of scotch. It burns all the way down. *"Bitches Do Better.* Sound familiar?"

After a beat, Connor says, "You're fuckin' kidding me, brother."

I run a hand through my hair. "No, brother, I am not."

He stares at my profile and then—in his deep, hearty baritone—starts to laugh.

I growl, "Shut up, asshole."

"You? The guy who goes through more tail in a week than he does underwear? You're in love with the woman who makes a velociraptor look like a family pet?"

"I never said I was in love with her!"

Connor stops laughing. "Uh-huh. And denial isn't just a river in Egypt."

I curse under my breath and pour myself another two fingers of scotch.

After watching me carefully for another few seconds, Connor turns back to the view. "All right. Tell me what you got."

I start at the beginning, from the moment Victoria walked into Xengu and sent me a death glare the likes of which I'd never seen, up to this morning and the crooked painting. Connor doesn't think it adds up to much and tells me so.

"Don't get your panties in a wad when I say this about your girlfriend, brother, but she's a professional bitch. Famous for it. Made a career out of it. Acting batshit crazy is like the golden rule for bitches."

"She also lies. About everything."

He shrugs. "She's a fuckin' broad. Show me a broad who

doesn't lie to a man and I'll show you another man. What else you got?"

I shake my head. "That's it."

"That's it? Seriously? You called me up here for that?"

I close my eyes, exhaling. "There is something else. But you'll think I'm crazy."

"I highly doubt it. Try me."

It takes me a moment to gather my thoughts. Then I open my eyes and look at my old friend. "I think I know her somehow. I think I might have met her somewhere before, but I have no idea where, or when. She just feels so...familiar."

He stares at me. "What, like in a past life?"

"Jesus. Forget it. Forget I said anything. Maybe you're right. Maybe I am in love with her and I'm trying to come up with any excuse to fuck it up, because that's what I always do with women. Fuck things up."

Connor clasps a hand on my shoulder. His voice drops. "Easy, brother. Don't start with that guilt shit again. What's past is just that: past."

I shrug off his hand. He always tells me not to feel guilt over what's in the past, but he doesn't know the whole story. I never told him what happened that night, the real reason I wanted to die.

If he knew the whole story, he wouldn't be telling me not to feel guilty.

Unable to stand still any longer, I turn away and walk to the opposite side of the room. Connor watches me with that stillness he has, not a muscle moving but his entire body giving off a sense of taut readiness, of violent action held in check. He's watched me like this so many times, I've lost count.

It took a long time after we met for him to trust that I wasn't going to do anything stupid to try to hurt myself.

He doesn't know this, but one day I just decided it would be much better punishment for me if I lived.

"So I'll look into her, then, yeah?" says Connor, still watching me from across the room. "See what I come up with. You need eyes and ears in her house?"

"No. Just see if there's anything strange in her background. Any connection between us…I don't know. I'm not sure what we're looking for." I think of my office door, cracked open a few inches. "And put a lock on my office door, same type you've got on the safe."

"All right. Lock'll be on by tonight. I'll get you some paper on her by Friday. Can do a quick scan today, call you if anything interesting pops up, but the other stuff'll take a few days."

"Thanks."

Connor crosses the room, stops in front of me, and holds out his hand. We shake.

Holding my gaze, he says, "It's probably nothing."

I nod.

His black eyes grow piercing. "But if not, you should decide now what you want to do about it. Get your head straight, yeah? Because if you got feelings for this girl and she's gunnin' for you—"

"I know." I cut him off, my voice curt. He doesn't have to say more, and frankly, I don't want to hear it. Because if Victoria Price *is* gunning for me, I'm going to have to make a choice between the two of us.

After last night, I'm not entirely sure I wouldn't let her win.

Connor says good-bye and lets himself out, while I go back to staring out the windows, nursing my scotch and brooding.

Victoria. Who the hell are you?

26

VICTORIA

$\mathcal{T}$he moment the elevator doors slide open to reveal the private entrance of my penthouse, I call out, "Where are you?"

Tabby's faint response comes from my office. "In here!"

I hustle in there so fast, I don't even stop to take my heels off, though my feet are killing me. My new Louboutin platforms are over six inches high, and my arches hate me right now. I burst through the door, see Tabitha sitting at my desk, peering intently at the computer screen, and yell, "What the hell happened?"

Without looking at me, she calmly replies, "I told you. I was in the emergency room with food poisoning."

I glare at her, huffing. "I just spent a hundred bucks bribing a valet guy to get my phone out of Parker's car, the last fifteen minutes in a cab hyperventilating because you didn't pick up your phone and only responded to my frantic texts with a VERY unhelpful 'Chill, dude, it's all good'—and now you're sitting at my desk like the Queen of England, surfing eBay for your next Hello Kitty handbag while I'm suffering a heart attack about what leaked online? Tabitha, this is *unacceptable!*"

She looks over at me, blows her bangs from her eyes, and smiles. "Did you just stomp your foot? That was cute."

When I holler in frustration, she says, "All right, calm down! Take a load off, and I'll give you the 411." She waves to one of the chairs in front of my desk—*my* desk—and turns back to the computer.

"You're so fired!"

She says nonchalantly, "I know. Sit."

I make a growly noise, stomp over to the chair, sit, and toss my handbag on the desk. "Start talking, girl genius. What happened?"

She leans back in my chair, turning her attention to me. "The Drudge Report is what happened."

All the blood drains from my face.

Tabby rushes to add, "But it was only a tiny mention. A few sentences, no pictures, only one eyewitness who claims he saw you at the Laredo airport exiting a private jet. It's a total nothing story. It wasn't even picked up by any of the other major entertainment outlets."

I'm incredulous. "Nothing story? It mentions *Laredo*."

She shrugs. "There's nothing that ties you to that city, so...so what?"

I stand and lean over the desk with my hands braced against the desktop. "Parker Maxwell is *so what*!" I collapse back into the chair, groaning. "Oh God. He's going to figure out the whole thing. I'll have zero credibility left. He's going to ruin me. Everything I've built, everything I've worked for..."

I can tell Tabby is resisting the urge to roll her eyes.

"Listen. Think about it. Even if he did think it was a strange coincidence you were in Laredo, *there's nothing to tie you to it.* Everything created by me and my predecessor, the late, great Mr. Dooney, says you're from California. School records. DMV records. Voting records. Everything. And everything tying you to Laredo has been wiped out. Anyone looking for traces of you in Texas will hit nothing but dead ends. You're a ghost there."

When I don't answer because my face is buried in my palms, she asks, "So how'd you explain it to him?"

"I had to make up a cover story on the fly about stopping to see my dearly departed old boyfriend's grave on my way to see my sick mother in California, because my number one henchman —hench*woman*—got sick and went AWOL."

Tabby leans back in the chair, puts her feet up on my desk, crosses them at the ankle, and says sarcastically, "Why, yes, I *am* feeling much better, Victoria. Thank you so much for asking."

I finally sigh and meet her gaze. "I'm sorry. I'm glad you're feeling better. What was it?"

"Sushi, I think."

"I keep telling you not to eat that disgusting sea urchin."

"If someone told you filthy Grey Goose martinis were disgusting, would you stop drinking them?"

I wrinkle my nose. "Martinis can't give me food poisoning."

"They can give you cirrhosis."

Tabby doesn't drink. Normally I consider that a character flaw in a person, but she has other redeeming qualities, so I let it go.

"Can we please get back to the subject at hand? Namely, what can you do to prevent something like this from happening in the future?"

She swings her legs off the desk. "Nothing's foolproof, Victoria. I told you that when I was hired. I'm one of the best, but I'm only human—and there's only one of me. I've got programs in place that alert me to any mention of your name, but if I'm out of commission, that intel is useless. And once a story's out there, trying to contain it is like trying to cut off a hydra's head."

She casually inspects her fingernails. "Maybe we should consider staffing up."

She's been at me for at least a year to hire her an assistant. I've always given her an unequivocal no. There are only so many people I want knowing my business.

As in, one. Her.

Watching her so nonchalantly inspect her manicure, I'm hit with a terrible thought. I gasp. "Tell me you didn't do this on purpose so I'd hire you an assistant!"

She scoffs. "You think I'd risk my job—my extremely *well-paying* job—to try to teach you a lesson? Besides, if you go down, I go down. I doubt the trustees of Stanford University, the Secretary of State of California, the IRS, or a dozen other public and private institutions will appreciate all my extracurricular activities associated with keeping the Queen Bitch on her throne."

Her logic, as always, is impeccable, but I'm still not convinced. "Why couldn't you just go in and crash Drudge's servers like you did with that story from TMZ?"

She explains slowly, with exaggerated patience, as if speaking to a child. "Number one: if I had to crash every server of every company that ran a story on you, half the servers in the United States would go down. Number two: there are people who track that stuff. People who work for government agencies with three initials, like FBI. CIA. Too much weird activity like that and it would eventually point a big red arrow at your head. At *my* head. Number three: I once met the guy who owns TMZ, and he told me I looked like the love child of Pippi Longstocking and Marilyn Manson. So any chance I get, I fuck with that dude. Number four: the story in Drudge had already been published, and it was a dud. It wasn't worth the risk of drawing attention to it by taking it down. That would've made it more conspicuous, not less."

"According to you!"

She looks at me from under her fringe of red bangs. "Yes. According to me. Who's the expert here. And by the way, the best way to keep this kind of thing from happening again is to stay the hell away from Laredo, Texas."

Game, set, and match: Tabby.

Defeated, I sag back into the chair and rub my fingers into my pounding temples.

Unlike me, Tabby isn't one to wallow in a victory. She moves right on to the next topic.

"Any luck with his safe this time?"

"His desk drawers were all locked. Locked! For a man who lives alone, he's definitely paranoid about someone getting into his stuff. So I took another look at his safe, and I realized why there wasn't a dial." I give Tabby a meaningful look. "The round silver thingy that I first thought was where you insert a key is actually where you insert your finger."

Now I've got her full attention. She looks at me with eager eyes.

"Biometrics? Sweet!"

"No—not sweet! Extremely *un*sweet! How the hell am I supposed to get past that? Chop off his thumb?"

She purses her lips as if she's considering it. When I groan in frustration, she relents.

"I'm kidding. No chopping. Now, listen, this is important. Since I didn't find anything incriminating about him in the usual places, I dug deeper, like you asked. I hit both his business and home computers."

Instantly I'm all ears. "And?"

One corner of her mouth curls up, as it always does when she finds something delicious. "And he's got defenses on both systems that are so sophisticated, it made my panties moist."

I blink, grimacing. "Honestly, Tabby. The things you find arousing."

"One thing's for sure. Whomever Parker Maxwell employed to secure his shit is *good*. Like, National Security Agency good.

Like, World of Warcraft level 100 good. Like, *Star Trek: Deep Space Nine* good—"

"Oh, for God's sake, I've got it, he's good! But that's bad for us, right?"

She tilts her head, smiling. "I've already mounted a brute-force attack with administrator obfuscation and a custom fifty-GPU cluster to get the encryption key."

I stare at her. "Any time you'd like to revert back to English, it would be appreciated. The natives here don't speak computer geek."

"Forget it. The bottom line is, I'll have access soon. And then we'll see what dirty little secrets Mr. Maxwell is hiding in cyber-space. They might be even better than what he's hiding in his safe."

For the first time since Parker asked me about Texas last night, the knots in my stomach start to loosen.

Tabby has relieved some of my concerns about the Drudge Report story and given me renewed hope about finding something compromising in Parker's background that I can use to screw him over. I take a deep breath, close my eyes, and rest my head on the back of the chair.

After several moments, Tabby's hesitant voice breaks the silence. "So...how was Laredo, anyway?"

I know what she's really asking: how was Eva?

Without opening my eyes, I admit, "About as fun as having all my skin peeled off with a potato peeler and being thrown into a saltwater bath."

Another span of silence follows. This time when Tabby speaks, her voice is deadly serious. "You know the real reason I do this job isn't for the money, Victoria. You know that, right?"

I tilt up my head and look at her.

Today her outfit of choice is a pair of black men's suspenders attached to black skinny jeans, a tiny white T-shirt with the Batman logo in electric blue stretched taut across her boobs so it's pulled all out of proportion, and Chucks with no laces that look as if she's owned since junior high school. The jewel in her belly-button ring matches the blue of the Batman logo, and so does her nail polish.

I ask, "Are you about to confess that you're in love with me?"

She doesn't even bat an eyelash. "I've had a major girl crush on you since before we even met, superstar, but that's not the reason either."

I lift my brows. This is getting interesting.

She says, "I work for you because I believe in what you're doing."

"Which is?"

"Empowering the powerless."

She says it with deep respect and reverence, as if it's Gandhi or Nelson Mandela she's speaking about. I'm a little taken aback by the quiet passion in her voice. I've never heard her talk like this before.

I joke, "Maybe we should make that the company slogan."

"Kid all you want, but it's true. You're the only one out there telling women that the source of our own power is within ourselves. That we don't have to rely on anyone else for our happiness. That what's in our best interest isn't having babies and playing house, but stretching ourselves and finding our true potential, because that's also in the best interest of the rest of humanity. We had the sexual revolution and the big feminist movement in the sixties and seventies, made all kinds of strides forward for women's equality and rights, and almost fifty years later, we're still only making seventy-seven cents on the dollar compared with what a man makes. And we're supposed to be content with that. Well, I'm not."

"Believe me, sweetheart, you're making a hell of a lot more than any other man in your position."

She says vehemently, "Yes, *I* am. Because I have a badass

boss who cares only about the quality of the job, not what's between my legs. And if every other employer in this country were like you, we'd have true equality. Women wouldn't be afraid to leave their shitty marriages, because they'd be able to support themselves and their children alone. Women wouldn't have to put up with all the crap they put up with from men, and compete against one another, and freak out about getting older, and deform themselves with Botox and fake tits and lip injections, because men have more money, and therefore more power, and ultimately more *worth* than women do. You're the only loud, proud, unapologetic voice left telling women to stop being so fucking passive and take control of their lives. And that's why I work for you. Because you're not afraid of anything, you don't take shit from anyone, and you've got a pair of balls on you bigger than any man's."

When I sit there staring at her in silence, she smiles.

"And also because I'm a little bit in love with you."

To my deep surprise, I'm moved by Tabby's words. Seeing the look on my face, she scoffs, "If you cry right now you'll nullify everything I just said, you big wuss."

I sniff. "I can still be a badass and get a little misty-eyed, can't I?"

She rises from the chair. "No. Don't be such a girl. God, I hope we crush Parker Maxwell soon, because your hormones are starting to get out of control."

Don't I know it.

Rule #5: Men make bitches messy.

Tabby stands behind me and starts to massage my shoulders, something she occasionally does when I'm really grouchy. For such a wisp of a thing, she's got hands like a rugby player. I groan in pleasure as she works the knot in my left shoulder that never completely goes away.

"All right." I sigh, ready to start kicking butt and taking names. "What's on deck for today?"

While Tabby recites a list of meetings, phone calls, and tasks to be completed, I allow myself one fleeting, beautiful memory of the way Parker looked at me when he put his hand over my heart last night, the way his eyes were so soft and so thrillingly wild.

"Hearts can't lie," he said.

Maybe not.

But that's only because they're so stupid.

27

PARKER

*T*he call comes as I'm headed to Xengu at five o'clock. I hit the Answer button on the steering wheel and say hello.

Without bothering with any preliminaries, Connor says, "I need you to come to the shop to take a look at something. Soon as you can."

I steer the Porsche through the heavy afternoon traffic but am no longer paying attention to the road. "Why? What's up?"

He pauses. "Somethin' you need to see. And Parker?"

"Yes?"

"Shut off your phone as soon as we hang up. Don't forget."

Connor disconnects the call.

I make a hard right turn, cutting off a taxi in the process and earning me a shouted curse from a guy stepping off the curb whom I nearly run over, but all I care about is getting over to Connor's to see what he's found out.

From the sound of it, it's not good.

~

Connor's "shop" is located in a converted warehouse in the Meatpacking District, a block from the Hudson River. There are no signs that advertise the name of his business, and it's not listed in any directory, online or otherwise.

Metrix is off the grid, in all the ways that count.

All its clients are referred by word of mouth and accepted only after ironclad contracts have been signed, exhaustive background checks have been conducted, and substantial amounts of money have changed hands.

There's nothing Metrix can't secure, but it'll cost you.

I pull up to the solid steel entry gate, roll down my window, look up at the small black bubble mounted high on the barbed-wire-topped brick wall that flanks the gate, and wait.

I know that behind the black bubble is a scanner reading both my license plate and the contours of my face, and behind the scanner is a computer analyzing the results, and at the computer is a man who can kill me with a single blow to my windpipe if he's in the mood.

I hate to think what would happen if I failed the scan, because I suspect the two panels inset in the brick wall on either side of the driveway would burst open to reveal a pair of computer-operated machine guns.

In seconds, the gate slowly swings open. I drive through.

The warehouse itself is your typical three-story, institutional-looking brick affair built at the turn of the previous century. You don't notice until you're walking up to the door at the front that all the windows are blacked out, and there appears to be only one entrance. As soon as I approach the door—hammered steel, ten feet tall and half as wide—it slides open on silent tracks.

There stands Connor, arms crossed over his broad chest, legs braced apart, wearing head-to-toe black, a Glock semiauto handgun strapped to his waist, and an expression that would do a serial killer proud.

I ask warily, "Why do you look like you're about to invade a small country?"

In answer, he jerks his head and turns, expecting me to follow.

If the outside of Metrix looks average and unassuming, the interior is anything but. It's like walking into a bank vault...if the bank were on a spaceship manned by anal-retentive aliens with genius IQs and itchy trigger fingers.

The ceilings are high, the lights are low, and the temperature's cool enough to make me shiver through my coat. The polished concrete floor gives off a subtle, expensive sheen. Black computer towers extend the length of the north wall in blinking, softly humming rows. The video and television screens that glow from dozens of cubicles on the east wall are stared at by hard-jawed men at keyboards wearing headphones. Locked, backlit cases of weaponry displayed in military precision along the south wall look eerily menacing.

They're also new. Last time I visited Metrix, they were absent.

"What's with the hardware?" I ask Connor's back as we walk toward his office.

He replies over his shoulder, "Gotten into extractions recently. Good money in it."

Extractions? I decide not to ask.

Then we're in Connor's office. The first thing he does when the door is closed is turn to me and hold out his hand.

"Phone."

I stare at him. "Okay, now you're starting to scare me."

He insists, "Gimme your damn phone, brother."

I withdraw my phone from my coat pocket and hand it over. Connor inspects it, then nods, satisfied.

"You turned it off. Good."

"Why is that good?"

He looks at me. "GPS is disabled when the phone's off. You can't be tracked."

That doesn't make me feel any better. "Now would be a great time to tell me what the hell is going on."

"What's goin' on," he says, moving to his desk, a slab of black granite at least six feet wide, "is the fuckin' sixty-four-thousand-dollar question, my friend."

He swivels his computer monitor so it faces me. It's dark, except for an odd animated character cheerfully waving as it slowly bounces from top to bottom, side to side. It's whiskered, white, and cartoonish, and vaguely resembles a cat.

A thought bubble over the cat's head reads, "Nice try, idiot!"

"Interesting screensaver. What is it?"

He says sarcastically, "Oh, that? Yeah, that's only the emblem of one of the most notorious hackers out there."

I frown. *Hacker?* "So what's it doing on your computer?"

"Aggravating the fuck outta me, is what it's doing!"

I raise my brows, lifting my gaze to his. If there's one thing Connor Hughes is known for, it's his nerves of steel. If something's aggravating him, it must be bad.

Really bad.

I say, "I can see that. Are you going to fill me in as to why?"

Connor folds his arms across his chest and glares at the computer as if he'd like to whip out a pair of six-shooters and start blasting. "*This* asshole," he snaps, jabbing his finger toward the screen, "has been a thorn in my side for *years*. He's arrogant, subversive, smart as fuck and, worst of fuckin' all, *untraceable*. Goes by the code name Polaroid because of his supposed photographic memory." He mutters, "Prick."

I'm starting to have a terrible feeling about this. "And Victoria Price is somehow related to this Mr. Polaroid?"

He grunts. "Not that I could easily prove it. The son of a bitch has developed mathematical obfuscation software that not only cloaks his identity but also erases all traces of the source code and location once the payload has been delivered, like those self-destruct messages in the *Mission Impossible* movies. The only thing he ever leaves behind is that"—Connor jerks his chin in disgust at the cartoon cat on the screen—"because he wants you to know he's the one who just bent you over and fucked you."

"I don't get it. If his code name is Polaroid, why a white cat and not a camera?"

Connor barks, "Because he's a dick, that's why!"

Then it hits me.

White: the only color I've ever seen Victoria wear is white. Her clothing, shoes, handbags...all white. Even all the furnishings in her apartment are white. It's her signature color.

Cat: I remember what I told Marie-Thérèse said about Victoria: *"She's all bark and no bite. A pussycat."*

To which Marie-Thérèse responded: *"Cats have long claws and sharp teeth, and kill billions of small mammals a year. They're basically cute serial killers."*

Photographic memory: Victoria is known for the rousing, intelligent speeches given at her sold-out seminars...all made without the assistance of a teleprompter. Every word is inside her head.

I sink slowly into the chair in front of Connor's desk. He stares at me, the questioning look on his face no doubt caused by what must be the expression of utter shock on my own face.

He prompts, "What?"

"How do you know Polaroid is a man?"

Connor answers without hesitation and with total conviction. "Of course he's a man. Chicks don't hack, and if they do, they're never this good. Don't have the brains for it."

I have a feeling Connor's going to eat those words one day.

Blowing out a hard breath, I rake a hand through my hair. "I think you should start at the beginning, when you left me this morning. Walk me through what happened. And then tell me what it all means."

Connor sets my phone on the desk and lowers his bulk to the large leather captain's chair. He leans back in his chair, crosses his arms over his chest, and begins.

"Started on your girlfriend with the usual background check. No felony or misdemeanor charges or convictions, clean DMV report, credit that would make Warren Buffett green with envy. No liens, civil judgments, or bankruptcies, pays her taxes on time, has more cash in one of her many checking accounts than I make in a year. And you were right, she has more money than you." He pauses. "Wanna know how much more?"

I say emphatically, "Absolutely not."

Connor chuckles. "Good. 'Cause it'd be a serious blow to your manhood, brother."

I clench my teeth together so hard, I'm surprised they don't crack. "Moving on."

"Right. Moving on. Other than a single prescription required for a minor heart condition, she's drug-free. No history of mental instability, no major surgeries, gets annual checkups with her gynecol—"

"Enough." I hold up a hand to stop him. "Don't tell me about her gynecologist. I feel bad enough prying this much as it is."

Connor drawls, "—and no history of STDs. Gets tested regularly. Latest one was last month, and it was clear." He smirks. "So you're cleared to go ungloved."

I stare at him so long and hard, he finally relents, putting his hands in the air in surrender.

"Moving on."

"Exactly," I growl. I don't care how big he is and how long we've been friends. If he makes a rude comment about Victoria's reputation or sex drive, I'll leap across his desk and put him in a chokehold until he apologizes.

I'll probably get my ass kicked in the process, but I don't care.

"Education checks out, Social Security number checks out, everything right down to her birth certificate is legit. Didn't see any obvious past connection between you two, though I'll have to search other channels to confirm that. Cross-reference travel dates, business and social memberships, whatnot. Since private communications are always the best place to start to dig real dirt, I tried getting into her email."

He glances at the computer screen with a glower. "Which is when I run into the problem."

I'm relieved that Victoria doesn't have any red flags in her past, and also relieved there doesn't seem to be a connection between us. Also, she doesn't have money problems, which means there are only two reasons she would've been trying to get into my safe.

One: she was simply snooping. She knows my reputation as well as I know hers. Maybe she was just curious. Maybe she *did* take a wrong turn on the way out and decided a quick look around my office couldn't hurt.

Two: she's digging for dirt on me too. But why?

And we're back to square one.

"So this Polaroid character." I gesture at the bouncing cat on the screen. "Is he security for hire, like you?"

Connor looks insulted. "He's not security, brother. He's a fuckin' anarchist! Likes to play games, blow shit up, cause problems! He hacked into Citibank's computers about six years ago just to prove he could, left a message that said, 'Your security is shit.' And guess who was Citibank's security firm at the time?"

"Oh no."

"That's right," says Connor sourly. "Yours fuckin' truly."

I'm flabbergasted. Connor's reputation in the security industry is unrivaled. If someone got past him, it means that someone is scary smart.

And possibly a little unhinged. You don't want a man like Connor Hughes as an enemy.

I say, "I didn't hear anything about that breach."

"That's because no money was stolen. Though he had access to hundreds of millions of dollars in credit card and bank accounts, Polaroid didn't take anything. He didn't steal any customer data at all. He just hacked in for the fuck of it and cost me one of my biggest clients. But I'm not the only one. Every major security company has had to deal with this fuckwit at one time or another. He goes after all the big boys. Military, business, religion, you name it. Once took down the Church of Scientology's computers for a full month." He adds in a disgruntled caveat, "That one wasn't so bad."

"So if he's not security for hire, what the hell is he doing protecting Victoria Price's email accounts?"

"Like I said, brother—that's the sixty-four-thousand-dollar question."

We gaze at each other in silence for a moment while my tangled thoughts drift.

"You like to play games, don't you?"

"Only games I can win."

Finally, Connor says, "Maybe he's one of her exes. Still got a flame burnin', thinks he's being a gentleman by looking out for her. Or maybe she doesn't even know him or have any idea this kind of protection is in place, she's just the lucky recipient of an obsessed fan's particular skill set." His voice grows serious. "Or maybe—and I'm just sayin' maybe—Victoria Price has all kinds of secrets she's hiding, and keeps some very interesting people on payroll to make sure those secrets don't ever come out."

Or maybe she's actually Polaroid herself.

Aloud I ask, "How can we find out?"

Connor smiles his getting-down-to-business cutthroat smile. I knew he'd already have a plan.

Unfortunately, it's one I immediately dislike.

"We need to get inside her house."

"I'm not authorizing you to break into her house."

He makes an irritated noise. "Man, get your dick outta your brain for a second. This broad you're bangin' is somehow connected to a serious fuckin' cybercriminal who's on *all* the most wanted lists."

"Most wanted? You said he didn't steal anything!"

He snorts. "You think the government cares that Polaroid didn't sell national security secrets to our enemies, that he just wandered into our military computer systems and took a look around because he was amusing himself? This guy is considered highly dangerous. And if the authorities found out that Miss *Bitches Do Better* had any connection whatsoever to him, she'd already be in an interrogation room."

His look turns penetrating. "And so would you."

He's right. Jesus Christ, he's right.

Am I cavorting with an international criminal? Is the woman I can't get out of my head the mastermind behind a series of ingenious cyberattacks? Could I be arrested for complicity?

More importantly, do I care?

Connor settles back into his chair and laces his fingers over his chest. His voice comes out deceptively calm, but I sense what's brimming beneath.

War.

"So here are my thoughts on the matter. I conduct a search of her premises, real quiet and real thorough. I get hands-on access to any and all documents, safes, computers. Hardware's easier to crack than code, especially considering the software her hacker friend's got lined up as a defense. I can get a block-level clone of her entire hard drive in under ten minutes if I'm at her desktop. I can also seed her computer with keylogging software so we'll be able to see everything she's typing, but she won't know. You'll have all the answers you want, I'll maybe find out who this douche bag Polaroid is, and all it'll take is making sure Victoria is out of the house for a few hours."

He watches me for several moments as I try to wrap my head around the hugeness of the betrayal I'd be guilty of. When I remain silent, he slides my phone across the desk toward me and says drily, "Or you can sit there with your limp dick in your hand as she makes a fool out of you."

"We don't know that she's tracking me with my phone. Or targeting me in any way, for that matter. This is all total conjecture at this point."

Connor's answer is immediate. "We don't know that she's not. Or, if she's not—*who is*."

The way Connor looks at me makes my skin crawl. "I know you have some deeply ingrained trust issues, Connor, but please tell me you're not suggesting I'm the target of espionage at the hands of a genius, criminal computer hacker."

Please tell me we're not thinking the exact same thing.

"To be honest with you, Parker, I don't know what to think. All I know is that your lady friend looks squeaky clean on paper but has someone on her side who once intercepted the source code of the International Space Station, which caused NASA to shut down their computers for two weeks. If that doesn't concern you, I want what you've been smoking."

Inhaling deeply, I rise. "I need to think about this."

Connor says with chilling softness, "Roger that. But you should know, brother, whatever you decide, I've got a score to settle with this motherfucker Polaroid. You don't want to look further into Victoria Price, that's your call. But her friend has cost me millions in contracts and just fried all thirty-three drives on this Origin system I spent a year perfecting because I got a little too close."

He jerks his chin at the mocking cartoon cat bouncing around on his computer screen. "If I hadn't secured the network with my own custom anti-intrusion software that cuts off an infected machine, my whole shop would be compromised right now. In other words, my entire business would be toast."

His gaze burns into mine. "Nobody fucks with my business, brother."

We stare at each other while the clock on the wall ticks and ticks and ticks.

I say, "Give me a few days."

He nods. I pick up the phone from his desk, slip it into my pocket, and turn to leave. When I'm at the door, Connor's voice stops me.

"Parker."

I turn and look at him. He glances at his computer screen and then back at me. "Be careful."

Though I'm not anything close to happy, I smile. "Roger that."

Feeling as if my feet are sunk in quicksand and it's only a matter of time before I drown, I head to Xengu.

VICTORIA

J'm up to my neck in bubbles when my phone, perched on the ledge of the bathtub, begins to ring. I stare at it with trepidation, as if it's the gynecologist calling with the lab report on a suspicious-looking vaginal sore.

Today has been one nightmare after another.

My editor called to inform me that due to high demand for my next book, the publication date was bumped up, which means I need to complete copyedits within the next week, and I haven't even started on them yet. Then my long-time trainer, Duke, asked for a loan to open his own gym, which of course I shot down because Duke has the business acumen of a jock strap, which I told him, which is when he threatened to sell a highly unflattering story about me to *People* magazine, which is when I reminded him of the confidentiality clause in his contract and informed him I wouldn't hesitate to crush him if he breached it, which caused him to call me a few choice names, ending with a four-letter word that ends in *unt*.

That word was not *aunt*.

To top it off, the hotel Tabby booked for my seminar on Friday called in a panic to say their ballrooms had all been flooded from a malfunctioning fire sprinkler system. I have to find a new venue with seating capacity for over two thousand people, and notify all those people...within the next two days.

I'm tempted to throw the phone across the room and watch it shatter against the vanity mirror. Naturally I don't—I love the Swarovski crystal-studded cover—but answer it instead.

"Victoria Price speaking."

"Why do you sound like your cat just died?"

My lips tug upward. It's Parker. "I don't own a cat."

His answering chuckle is deeply arousing. "I happen to know for a fact, Ms. Price, you own a *beautiful* pussycat."

My smile grows wider. "Oh? Do tell."

"Well, let's just say she's pretty high-maintenance and demanding, but if you stroke her exactly right, she'll purr so loud, the neighbors will hear. She's the sweetest little pussy in the world."

I break into a big, stupid grin. "I can be as high-maintenance as I want. I'm the one paying the bills."

"We were talking about your cat, remember?"

"Ah yes. My mistake." I decide to torture him a bit, just for fun. In a playful tone, I ask, "Would it interest you to know what my kitty cat *really* enjoys?"

I hear his slow inhalation before he replies, "Yes. That would very much interest me."

I lift my leg from the water and admire the way the bubbles slide down my wet skin in a glossy meander. "She loves to be kissed."

When he answers, his voice has dropped an octave. "I recall that."

"In particular, she loves to be kissed and stroked at the same time. It drives her mad."

He clears his throat. I imagine him loosening his tie.

"And after that?"

In a husky whisper, I reply, "She likes to be fed."

Electricity crackles through the phone. "I hope she likes churros, because I've got a big one fresh from the oven that's ready to go. I can be there in ten minutes."

High from the need I hear in his voice, I laugh. "Why, Mr. Maxwell, how generous of you! My kitty does indeed like churros!"

"Churros in general, or mine in particular?"

The smile flees my face. I lower my leg to the water and sit up, my heart beginning to beat a little faster. "Yours in particular," I say softly, letting him hear the truth in my voice.

There's a long silence in which I can hear him breathing. Then: "I need to see you."

The rawness of that, the way he puts everything he feels into those five simple words, takes my breath away. "I...I have to work early in the morning. My schedule over the next few days is crazy. I'm not free until the weekend."

"All weekend?"

There's a sudden shift in his mood, from sexy to sharp. I hear it in his voice. It's almost as if something has occurred to him.

"Why? What did you have in mind?"

After a short pause, he says, "A surprise. I know how you love those. When should I pick you up?"

"After five on Friday. I have a seminar."

"Text me the location. We'll leave from there. Pack an overnight bag."

Taken aback by both his sudden intensity and what he's just said about the overnight bag, I frown. "Where are we going?"

This time the pause before he speaks feels intensely fraught. Or maybe I'm just imagining it because all my nerves are squealing at the thought of seeing him again.

"To a place of no secrets," he says quietly. Without another word, he hangs up.

I stare at the phone in my hand for a long time, wondering what those cryptic words could mean.

29

PARKER

*a*fter I hang up with Victoria, I turn my gaze back to the computer screen I've been staring at for the past thirty minutes.

I'm in my office at Xengu. It's hours until closing. I should be on the floor overseeing business, but tonight, for the first time ever, I'm incapable of conducting business.

I'm in too much shock.

Because after leaving Connor's, I decided to look up that story about Victoria on the Drudge Report website that Bailey had told me about. It was short, only a few sentences long. But one word stood out to me like a glaring neon sign, the afterglow seared into my retinas:

Laredo.

I stare at that name—the name of the city where I grew up, the city where I lost my soul and buried my heart, the city where once upon a time, I fell violently, irrevocably, fatally in love— and feel the first, faint tremors of anger stir in my gut.

It's not a coincidence. I'm sure of that. Especially considering Victoria's initial story about California omitted any mention of Laredo. It wasn't until I brought it up that she said she'd been to Texas…and now her tale about visiting the grave of her ex-boyfriend is in question too. So is what she said about her mother being sick.

I don't need to ask myself if she could be that good a liar, because I already know the answer.

But why? What's her end game?

I don't know, but whatever it is, if that woman thinks she's going to blackmail me with the ghosts of my past, she's got another thing coming.

I'm not above getting my hands dirty if it means getting what I want. And what I want is her.

No matter what it might cost me.

30

VICTORIA

*T*he sound of thunderous applause jerks me back into the present. I smile, nodding and waving to the crowd, relieved the seminar is finally over.

It's been a hellish few days, but Tabby pulled off a miracle by not only securing a new venue but also communicating the location to all the ticket holders. Once again, it's a standing-room-only crowd.

Too bad I'm too distracted to enjoy it.

I haven't heard from Parker in days. I can't get our conversation from Wednesday night out of my mind, and I'm not talking about the cat innuendos.

I'm talking about the mysterious "place of no secrets."

The more I thought about that, the more ominous it sounded. At this point, I've almost convinced myself he's going to take me to a basement somewhere, tie me to a chair, and inject truth serum into my arm.

Wouldn't that be inconvenient.

"Okay, before we wrap up, I have time for a few quick questions from the audience."

Hands shoot up. I point to a woman in the fourth row

wearing a Mickey Mouse sweatshirt. She has an unfortunate haircut that looks like someone plopped a soup bowl on her head and hacked around the edges.

"Yes—the lovely lady in the Disneyworld sweatshirt. Please hand her the mic."

An assistant trots over to the woman and hands her a wireless microphone. She holds it tightly in both hands as if it might try to escape.

"Hi, um, I'm Barbara. Um, Victoria, you said earlier that confidence is the sexiest thing a woman can wear. But what about, um, the women who don't have any confidence? How do we get it?"

Flushed, she hands the mic back to the waiting assistant and sits down. Many heads are nodding in the crowd. She's asked a popular question.

"I'll let you in on a little secret, ladies. You don't actually have to *have* confidence for other people to *think* you do. That might sound nonsensical, but in the same way studies have shown that forcing a smile will actually make you feel better when you're unhappy, pretending you have confidence and rock-solid self-esteem will cause others to treat you better, which then makes you feel more confident, which then starts a feedback loop wherein you end up gaining confidence simply because you acted like you already had it. So the next time you're in a situation where you're feeling insecure, just ask yourself, 'What would Victoria Price do?' Then pretend you're me, and do it."

I pause, smiling at the crowd. "Unless it's chopping off your husband's pecker. Please don't blame that on me."

Laughter. I point to another woman standing on the far side of the ballroom, jumping up and down and waving her arms enthusiastically in the air.

"Yes, the woman in the red polka-dot dress."

Another assistant holds out a wireless microphone to her. She doesn't take it from him but leans over his outstretched hands to speak into it.

"Victoria, I'm Claire from Kearney, and before I get to my question, I just wanted to say you are such an inspiration to so many women. I saw you on *Good Morning America* last year, and you said something that stuck with me. You said, 'I'm fighting for all the girls who never thought they could win.' And I just thought that was so amazing. So thank you for being such a champion for women."

Massive applause erupts from the audience. Touched, I put my hand over my heart.

"Thank you, Claire. That's so wonderful to hear."

Claire beams. Then she says, "Okay, so my question is about men."

The audience hoots, and Claire laughs along with them. "Whenever I ask my husband to do something around the house, taking out the trash just as an example, he says he will but then doesn't. Or he says he'll do it later. There's always some excuse. The shelf in my laundry room has been broken for six months, and my husband has promised about ten times he's going to fix it. How can I get him to do it without acting like a nag, which doesn't work anyway?"

The sound of two thousand women nodding as a collective is depressing. For about the forty-millionth time in my life, I wonder why men are such stubborn mules.

"Okay, here's the answer. Are you ready?"

I wait for their shouts and clapping to die down and then say, "Sometimes you have to play the role of a fool to fool the fool who thinks he's fooling you."

Crickets. Obviously an explanation is in order.

"Men hate being told what to do. When a wife gives her husband a command, to him it feels like he's being scolded by his mommy. Even if it's something as innocuous as telling him to take out the trash, he'll feel emasculated if you ask in the wrong tone or word it the wrong way. The best way to get a man to do anything is by *motivating him to do it himself.*

"So don't mention that shelf to your husband ever again. What you should do the first chance you get is go ask the most attractive man in the neighborhood if he would be so kind as to assist you with fixing your shelf, because, and I'm quoting what you should actually say here, 'You're so much better at these things than I am.' Then, when the neighborhood stud shows up to fix your shelf, watch how fast your husband moves. He'll have built you a new shelf and probably an entire new laundry room in thirty minutes. Nothing motivates a man more than competition."

When Claire says, "Oh my God, I know exactly who I'm going to ask," the room erupts into laughter.

"Good for you, Claire! Okay, next question."

I point to a mousy woman sitting quietly in the front row. Unlike the other women in the audience, she hasn't smiled, laughed, or clapped once during the entire seminar. I'm surprised she's participating now. She's looked as if she's been in pain all day.

"Yes, lady in the front."

She stands. The assistant hands her the mic. She holds it for a moment, looking at the floor, and then raises her eyes and drills me with them. "When I told my boyfriend I was coming to this seminar, he tried to kill me."

The entire room falls silent. Goose bumps march like fire ants down my spine.

"He said that you've done more to ruin relations between men and women than anyone else since Eve took the apple from the serpent."

Everyone waits nervously to hear what the woman is going to say next. Wondering if I'm in danger, I look nervously stage left, trying to catch the eye of the burly security guard standing in the wings, but am stunned to see Parker there instead.

He's unsmiling, standing with his arms crossed over his chest, watching me. When our eyes meet, a strange tingle of premonition zips through me.

How long has he been standing there? And what is that look in his eyes?

The woman continues. "But I remembered what you'd written in the afterword of your first book, *Bitches Do Better.* You wrote, 'The beautiful thing about life is, you always have the power to say, This is not how my story is going to end.' I remembered that when he had his hands around my throat. I decided that wasn't how my story was going to end. So I fought back. And I got away. And now he's in jail and won't be able to hurt me again. So I guess I don't really have a question. I guess I just wanted to say…you saved my life, Victoria. You literally saved my life."

My throat is closing up. An invisible fist squeezes my windpipe. After a long moment, I manage, "What's your name, sweetheart?"

The woman answers, "Jennifer."

I look to the audience. With a little hitch in my voice, I say, "Can we all please give Jennifer a round of applause for being so fucking awesome?"

The roar that explodes from the crowd is like nothing I've heard before. It sounds like a rock concert. Jennifer blushes and looks down. Before she can sit, I jump off the stage and engulf her in a bear hug.

The crowd goes wilder. Suddenly there are ten women around us, then twenty, then who knows how many more, all of them hugging and clapping and hollering, patting me on the back, the shoulders, my hair.

Jennifer and I break apart, grinning at each other. She tells me I'm her hero, I tell her she's mine, and then I have to run away because there's water pooling in my eyes and I'd rather have a colonoscopy with no anesthesia than be seen crying in public.

I throw a final wave to the crowd before disappearing off the stage, where I bump right into a solid, unmoving bulk that turns out to be Parker.

He grasps me by the upper arms. Blinking, I look up at him. When he sees my expression, his face softens.

"You're just a big marshmallow under all that titanium armor, aren't you?" He pulls me against his chest, and I bury my face in his coat.

"Don't make me tell you to go fuck yourself."

That makes him laugh. He winds his arms around me and nuzzles his nose against my ear. "I wouldn't care if you did. There's nothing like a woman with a brilliant mind and a filthy mouth."

"Don't forget the high-maintenance pussycat."

He presses his lips against the pulse in my temple. I can feel by the curve of his lips that he's smiling. "How could I possibly forget? She's all I've been able to think about for the past forty-eight hours."

Relieved that we're joking, I peek up at him with an eyebrow cocked and pretend to frown. "A one-track mind, I see."

"It's my finest trait. That and being smart enough to take out the trash before Fabio shows up to beat me to it."

I can't help the way my lips twitch because I'm trying not to smile. "This is why men aren't allowed in my seminars—now you know all our secrets!"

A flicker of emotion crosses his face, there, then instantly gone. "Not all of them."

With that, I'm right back into high-anxiety mode about this mysterious land of no secrets he mentioned before.

Parker sees the change in my face and puts a finger over my lips. "I said it was a surprise, didn't I?"

I nod. Satisfied, he nods too. "And so it is. Did you pack a bag?"

I nod again. He drops his hand to my shoulder and squeezes it.

"Good. Are you ready for your first surprise?"

Narrowing my eyes, I ask, "Exactly how many will there be?"

His smile is maddeningly smug. "It's a surprise."

I'm about to dig in my heels and insist on an explanation, but just then someone hollers my name. When I turn toward the voice, I see Tabby striding toward me with a scowl, a sheaf of papers clenched in her fist. She sees Parker and her step falters, but then she smiles brightly and keeps walking toward us as if nothing is wrong.

I know her too well, though. That smile she's dangling in front of Parker is about as real as my boobs.

Something's happened.

Tabby fixes Parker in her piercing green gaze and says curtly, "Hey."

I make the introductions. "Parker, this is my assistant, Tabitha. Tabby, Parker."

Parker looks with bemusement at Tabby's outfit du jour, a mash-up of heroin chic and Elizabethan Goth that features a ruffled black mini, black stockings ripped at the knees, six-inch black stiletto booties, a man's sleeveless white undershirt, and a huge, chunky black cross on a rosary around her neck, which I know she's wearing ironically because she's an atheist.

"Nice to meet you."

Tabby's fake smile grows brittle. "You too. Can I borrow her for a minute?"

"Of course." Parker graciously inclines his head. "I'll wait for you in the lobby." He kisses me on the cheek, then turns and walks away.

There's a certain swagger in his walk, a satisfaction, as if he's a big game hunter who's just bagged an elephant.

Tabby notices it, too. Watching him go, she mutters, "I don't like this, Victoria. This weekend getaway to a place of no secrets thing?" She shakes her head. "I think you should cancel and call this whole revenge thing off. Especially after *this*."

She smacks me on the arm with the sheaf of papers. I take it from her, unroll the pages, and peer at it in confusion. The pages are covered in gibberish, rows of random numbers and symbols that are as indecipherable as hieroglyphs.

"This looks like your computer threw up. What is it?"

She pins me with a look of such apprehension, it makes my blood run cold. "Evidence that someone's been creeping a little too close to home."

"Meaning?"

"Meaning there's a fox trying to get into the henhouse." She jerks her chin at the printout in my hand. "This is proof that someone's trying to hack into our system."

My heart does a somersault. Dreading the answer, I ask, "Did they get in?"

She looks at me with deep insult, as if I've just taken a poop inside one of her Hello Kitty handbags.

"Of course not! But this is some high-level shit, Victoria. It's a kernel rootkit worm that can subvert intrusion detection software and basically hijack the entire system and enslave it."

When I slow blink, she sighs.

"Your computer would be at someone else's control. They could spy on you, see everything you're doing, and you'd never know they were there."

I gasp.

She says, "Exactly. It's bad. Also there's the fun fact that I haven't yet been able to get past whatever software is protecting Parker's systems, because now there's someone on the other end who keeps changing the passwords." Her voice turns sour. "Every *two minutes*."

"Wait, what are you saying? What does this all mean?"

She takes the papers from my hands and crushes them into a ball. "My best guess? Your boyfriend has someone like me on his side who knows what we're up to and is trying to do to us what we're trying to do to him."

My mouth drops open. "*What?*"

"The pooch has been screwed, is what. The fat lady has sung. All the backdoors I could've exploited have been slammed shut on Parker's system, and his admin has put traps in place that will lead him right back to me if I try to enter. It's tighter than any military system I've ever seen. I'd have a better chance at getting in the Pope's asshole undetected."

She adds grudgingly, "Honestly, it's pretty impressive. If I didn't hate this prick so much, whoever he is, I'd want to pick his beautiful, bastardy brain."

"Rewind a second—*military* system? When did you work on military systems?"

Tabby looks at me silently for a moment. "Remember before, when I was telling you about President Underwood's minion who insisted on keeping certain nefarious details confidential so the president could plead ignorance if questioned?"

I say carefully, "Tabitha. Please tell me you're not involved with anything to do with *hacking* the *government*."

She shrugs. "Not anymore."

Oh God. My head is spinning. I think I need to sit down, but I panic at the thought of Parker waiting for me in the lobby. Then something horrible occurs to me.

"Does Parker know it's *us* who've been trying to gain access to his system?"

"There's no proof where the attacks originated. So far, I'm invisible. But it can't be coincidence that we targeted him, and then this happens." She waves the crumpled wad of papers in my face. "And if I keep trying to get in, I'll lead him right to us."

"So there's nothing more we can do? We're screwed?"

"Six ways to Sunday, boss. The SS *Cyber Revenge* has sailed."

"Shit. Shit, shit, *shit!*"

I dig my hands into my hair and stand for a moment with my eyes closed, breathing deeply, trying to determine what my next move should be, when Tabby says with utter nonchalance, "Unless I break into his house."

I drop my hands to my sides and stare at her. "You're joking."

"I only joke about politics, religion, and the size of men's dicks, never about something important like work."

I look around, worried that anyone standing nearby might overhear this outrageous conversation. Except for a few banquet guys conferring about setting up for another event tomorrow, we're alone. In a lowered voice, I hiss, "Are you crazy? If you're caught, you'll be arrested!"

She smiles a vague Mona Lisa smile. "So you're not against the idea per se. Your only objection is that I might get caught?"

I open my mouth to deny it but catch myself. "Well...yes."

When I see her smile turn smug, I insist, "But Tabby, there's no way you can guarantee you won't get caught! If he's got major defenses on his computer—not to mention the biometric security on his office safe—there's no telling what kind of security system he has installed on his home!"

"Sure there is—"

"No! I'm not letting you do that, Tabitha. It's too dangerous for you. The answer is no."

She stares at me with her lips pursed, a lock of red hair falling into her eyes. "So you're cool with me breaking and entering electronically, but physically it's a problem... I assume you're aware of the definition of the word *hypocrite*? Because

I'm thinking if we looked it up in the dictionary, your picture would be right next to it, Maleficent."

I want to wring her neck for arguing with me but exhale in exasperation instead. "Last time I checked, there weren't policemen with guns pointed at your head in cyberspace. If you trip an alarm at Parker's house, it will be swarming with armed cops before you can say '*Guardians of the Galaxy* rocks!'"

Tabby's nostrils flare. "Do *not* mock *Guardians of the Galaxy*, Victoria. Chris Pratt was super hot in that! And don't even get me started on the special effects—or the soundtrack! And remind me again how you're going to ruin Parker's life if we can't get into his safe, *or* his computers, to find his dirty laundry?"

She's being sarcastic, the little smartass, but she has an excellent point. If I'm cock-blocked by Parker's smarty-pants security firm and can't get any more information on him, and the intel Tabby's come up with so far is *bubkes*, what's my next move?

My brain waves a big red flag that reads: *a place of no secrets.*

It could be my last shot.

I square my shoulders, toss my head, and decide to go for broke. "I'm finishing this, Tabby. I'm too far down the rabbit hole to give up now. Whatever happens this weekend, Parker Maxwell will end up regretting he ever fed this kitty his churro."

Tabby looks disgusted. "You named his dick after a donut?"

"It's a pastry."

She snorts. "Well, like I always say, all a girl really needs is fifty million dollars and a pastry."

"Meet me in five with my bags in the lobby. I've got to go to the ladies' room before my bladder explodes."

I turn to head to the bathroom, but Tabby grabs my arm. "Victoria, wait."

Worried by the new tone in her voice, I stop and stare at her. She looks back at me silently for a moment, then sighs.

"Just be careful, okay? I've got a bad feeling about this."

I study her face, noting the worry in her eyes. "Worse than the feeling you had after the last *Avengers* movie?"

"Way worse." She pauses for a moment and then adds softly, "You remember how to access the bug-out bag, right?"

All the hairs on my arms stand on end. "We're not even going there. Everything will be fine. You know I can handle myself."

"It's not you I'm worried about, boss. It's him. Don't forget what's at stake here. If this situation with Parker goes sideways, you could lose everything. *Everything.* And we both could wind up in prison."

She releases my arm, turns, and walks away, leaving me to stare after her with those terrifying words echoing in my ears.

VICTORIA

*A*s promised, Parker is waiting for me in the lobby, leaning casually against the concierge's counter with his arms folded across his chest and a secret smile on his face. When he sees me, he straightens. His smile grows wider.

Walking beside me, Tabby mutters, "Would you look at that shit-eating grin? This is so fucked up."

"Shhh!" I manufacture a smile that probably looks more like a grimace. Tabby is really starting to freak me out.

"Ladies," says Parker when we stop in front of him. He looks at me. "All set?"

"Ready to go!" I answer brightly. "Wherever it is we're going!"

If I thought Parker's smile was secretive before, now it's positively covert. I've never seen anyone's mouth take on such a sly, mysterious slant.

Tabby nudges me with her elbow. I resist the urge to kick her in the shin.

Parker snaps his fingers, and a porter hustles over from across the lobby. "Put these in the black Rolls in front," says Parker, gesturing to my bags.

The porter immediately obeys. I've seen speeding trains move slower. I'm not sure which one of us the porter recognized, but I'm sure he's hoping for a nice fat tip.

I glance at Parker. *Here's a tip, darling: I put the hot in psychotic.*

I don't care if I have to set him on fire to do it. I *will* have my revenge.

"Well," says Tabby, "have a great weekend." Her gaze on me grows sharper. Her voice drops. "Call me if you need anything, whatever time it is. You know I'm always available for you."

Parker settles his arm around my shoulders. "Victoria's lucky to have such a dedicated assistant."

Tabby laughs mirthlessly. "You have no idea." She gives a little wave using only the tips of her fingers and then abruptly turns and leaves without saying goodbye.

Watching her go, I have the sudden premonition that it will be the last time I'll ever see her. My entire body goes cold.

"Are you all right? Your face is white."

Parker stares down at me with concern. I realize I'm standing there frozen and have stopped breathing. I put a hand over my throbbing heart and weakly laugh.

"Oh...yes, I'm...sorry, I just realized I haven't eaten in hours! I'm famished!"

I turn to him with a bright smile and fake words, swallowing the silly lump in my throat. I'm being overly dramatic. Imagining things. I need to put my game face on and concentrate.

"I can fix that," says Parker with that strange, sly confidence.

My feeling of doom intensifies.

He gently takes me by the arm and steers me through the lobby to the valet area outside. The porter who took our bags bounds up like an overexcited Labrador.

"Your car is ready, sir!" He gestures to a black sedan parked right in front. It's sleek, long, and beautiful. A driver in a dark suit stands next to the passenger door, waiting.

And my brain executes a sprint so quick, it could win an Olympic gold medal.

It can't be, he couldn't have, holy Mother Mary what could this possibly mean, Tabby was right this is fucked!

I ask indifferently, "New car?"

"Yes, as a matter of fact, it is." Parker leans closer to my ear. When he speaks again, his voice is incredibly sexy. "You did say you wanted one."

I did. I remember it perfectly, primarily because it's not often I demand a black-on-black Rolls-Royce with blacked-out rims during sex.

Not often as in *never.* I should've tried it years ago.

"A Phantom, no less. How did you guess I wouldn't be satisfied with a Ghost?"

Parker's lips quirk into another of his secretive smirks. "My personal motto is, 'Be all in or get all out, there's no halfway.' The Phantom is definitely all in. Plus, a Ghost just didn't seem like your style. Not when a much more expensive model was available."

I wonder if, in addition to my heart problem, I've developed a nasty case of asthma, because every breath I take is like trying to drag air through a straw full of sand. My game face is firmly in place, however, so I manage a smile as enigmatic as Parker's.

"So you're all in, are you? I should expect that Caribbean island next?"

"Of course," he says, like it's the most obvious thing in the world. I have no quick response because my brain gives up on this conversation and decides it's time for a nap.

I'll never win with logic, anyway. The only thing that's going to carry me through this weekend is sheer animal cunning, which is something different altogether.

Looking at Parker—at his perfect hair, chiseled jaw, cocky grin—I smile again, only this time it's real. "I should warn you, Parker, bitches aren't kept. They do the keeping."

Rule #6, and one of my personal favorites.

His grin turns wolfish. "I can hardly wait."

We approach the car. The driver opens the rear passenger door for me, murmuring, "Ms. Price." I settle myself into butter-soft leather and try not to cackle hysterically when I see a picnic basket between the seats that looks right out of a Grimm Brothers' fairy tale.

Which one of us is Little Red Riding Hood and which is the Big Bad Wolf?

Judging by Parker's smile alone, I'd say I'm the one in the red cape.

Parker enters from the other side, the driver shuts my door and gets in the front, then we're off.

We don't speak as Parker opens the wicker basket, removes two crystal champagne flutes and a bottle of Dom, and pours a measure in each glass. He hands me one. I decide I'd rather not be the little girl in the cape who's about to be devoured, so I raise my glass and make a toast thick with threat.

"Here's to those who wish me well, and those who don't can go to hell." Without waiting for Parker's response, I tip my head back and swallow the contents of my glass.

Parker chuckles. "My sentiments exactly." He downs his champagne, sets the glass back in the basket, and removes a plastic-wrapped cheese board. "Gouda?" he inquires, so innocently I know I'm in real trouble.

You want me to eat your cheese? I'll eat your cheese, you sneaky prick. I'll eat your cheese, and then I'll eat your heart, and for dessert I think I'll eat your black, selfish soul.

I purr, "I'd love some Gouda."

We trade a pair of sinister grins and settle in for the ride.

∽

After a ride to JFK in the Rolls, a flight on a private jet, and a winding drive from a colorful port town through a dense, tropical jungle in a Jeep with no windows and a canvas roof, we've finally arrived at the mysterious place of no secrets.

Casa de la Verdad, reads the wooden sign nailed to the lintel above the front door.

Literal translation: *House of Truth*.

Carrying my bags, Parker steps past me with a sideways glance, smiling. "Told you."

"Oh, you're good."

I shake my head in disbelief, taking in the place. It's a classic Caribbean-style home—saffron-hued, open air where walls should be, white linen curtains blowing in the gentle trade winds—perched atop a hill surrounded by lush vegetation. The moon is high and the crickets are singing. Palmetto palms rustle in the breeze. Down a small path beside the circular driveway, wooden stairs lead to a private beach. Hidden lamps spread pools of golden light over the scarlet bougainvillea that cascades in waves over the walls surrounding the high side of the property. The other side looks straight out to the sea. I close my eyes and inhale the sweet, heady scent of orchids and night-blooming jasmine.

It's heaven.

Except it's named House of Truth, so it's my own personal hell.

Parker unlocks the front door and heads inside. He calls over his shoulder, "Are you just gonna stand there with your mouth hanging open, Cruella, or are you coming in?"

My lips pinch in displeasure at the way he pronounces his pet name for me. His voice is light and playful, *familiar*, as if we've been going on vacation with each other for years. Even more disturbing is how chipper he seems. There's such bounce in his step, the man is practically floating.

He's obviously got a major trick stashed up his sleeve.

Maybe Tabby was right. Maybe this is fucked up, and the weekend will end in a fiery blaze and enough regret that I'll be eating it for breakfast for the rest of my life—along with my ration of prison gruel—but I'll be damned if I'll let on that he's getting under my skin. I might have little candor, less compassion, and a total lack of moral turpitude, but one thing I do have in spades is backbone.

If life has taught me anything, it's that the whole idea of the meek inheriting the earth is bullshit. The only thing the meek will inherit is whatever the strong deign to throw their way.

Devour or be devoured. There's no greater law.

Staring at Parker's receding back, I mutter, "Let's get this party started," then follow him inside.

The interior of the house is even more beautiful than the outside. Travertine floors, soaring ceilings, and muted tropical-print furniture all scream expensive, understated elegance. Though I don't want to admit it, I'm impressed.

"Your decorator is very good."

I accept the glass of Chablis Parker offers me as I walk into the large, open kitchen. A picture window above the sink displays a moonlit view of the ocean so gorgeous it looks fake.

Though the temperature is at least eighty degrees, a cluster of fat gray clouds lurks on the horizon, promising rain.

"Thank you. But I don't have a decorator. I did all this myself."

I rest my hip against the counter opposite him and don't bother keeping the disbelief from my voice. "Really? In all your spare time between chasing women, running your restaurant empire, and planning your new career as congressman? Impressive."

"What can I say? I'm multitalented."

His smile is devastating. There should be a law against this kind of beauty, the kind that stuns and disarms a woman in one fell swoop. Because I feel as if I might spontaneously combust, I look away and take a big swallow of the wine.

"I'm going to start on dinner. Grilled steaks and a green salad good for you?"

I wonder what kind of miracle worker he employs who runs fresh steaks and vegetables out to a remote seaside hideaway on a moment's notice. I should hire this person.

"Steaks sound wonderful."

"Good. We'll eat on the lanai." He peers out the window. "Looks like we have a while before the storm hits."

I follow his gaze. Those clouds on the horizon now look a lot more sinister. "Storm? I thought summer was hurricane season?"

The devastating smile makes an encore. Parker moves closer to me, reaching out to brush his fingers along my cheekbone. "Don't tell me the Queen B is afraid of a little thunder and lightning."

I look up at him. Noting the mischief in his eyes, along with a deep, surprising tenderness, my heartbeat kicks up a notch. The tenderness in his caress is surprising, too. There's an unexpected protectiveness in the way he strokes my skin. It's almost paternal, as if he's both proud of and worried about me.

All things considered, it's highly suspicious.

"No more than the next girl standing on the highest spot on land during an electrical storm."

I hold still as he moves closer, takes my wine and sets it on the counter, snakes an arm around my waist, and pulls me against him. He cups the back of my neck and lowers his head so our foreheads are touching.

"I'll never let anything hurt you, Victoria, no matter how bad the weather gets."

There's something unequivocal in his voice, like a promise. Like a vow.

"Parker—"

He doesn't let me finish. He takes my mouth in a kiss that sends a flame roaring along my nerve endings, head to toe. I inhale, arching against him, taking his scent into my lungs, feeling the strength and heat of him against my body, feeling my resistance crumble.

Why? Why with him? Of all the men in all the world, why does my body burn for this one, ache for this one, want this one with a ravenous desire that borders on greed?

Well, dumbass, it could be the fact that he's the only man you've ever loved.

The thought sends a bolt of pure terror through me. I jerk out of Parker's arms.

"Whoa," he says softly, watching my face as I settle a few feet away, trembling and pale. "Easy, tiger. What just happened?"

I close my eyes and moisten my lips, determined my heart will *not* fail me now and explode like it's threatening to. "I... sometimes you...we..."

I can't find the words. I drop my face into my hands and groan.

Then his hands are on me. He gathers me into his arms, tucks my head into his shoulder, rocks me gently, and whispers, "I know. It's overwhelming for me, too."

Inside my head, a bell rings. It's the opening bell for the final round of the heavyweight title fight between my mind—a ruthless savage—and my broken, senseless, longing heart. A heart I was convinced was dead and buried until Parker Maxwell walked back into my life and resurrected the ragged shreds of it.

I've been without hope for so long, without love for so long, shunning all but the most casual of encounters for so long —insert tab A into slot B, run like hell, repeat—that this banquet of emotion Parker is feeding me has set every circuit to overload. One minute I'm cool, calm, in control...and the next I'm exploding like the fireworks finale on the Fourth of July.

Into his chest, I whisper, "I hate that you make me so weak."

"There's strength in surrender."

"There's *destruction* in surrender."

His voice comes out rough with emotion. "It's not a zero-sum game. If we both surrender, it's a win-win."

I pull away from him again and stand near the big stainless steel refrigerator with my fists balled, my chest heaving. I say bitterly, "There's no such thing as win-win. Someone wins and someone loses. Anyone who thinks differently is a child."

"Or in love," he replies, his voice soft.

I inhale sharply, then whisper, "Don't."

He stands motionless. His beautiful mouth takes on a hard slant. "Remember where we are, sweetheart: Casa de la Verdad. This is a no-bullshit zone."

His eyes dare me to contradict him, but we both know I can't. Even if my lips aren't speaking the words, my body tells him exactly how I feel about him every time he touches me. So I do the only thing I can: turn my back to him, wrap my arms around myself, and change the subject.

"I think I'll freshen up while you cook, if you don't mind."

My voice is surprisingly steady, probably because I'm not looking at him. *Note to self, avoid all eye contact for the next forty-eight hours.*

"Sure." His tone is soft again. Caressing. "Dinner will be ready in about thirty minutes. The master's upstairs at the end of the hallway." I hear him open a cabinet, remove something, close it. He adds quietly, "Can't wait to wake up in bed tomorrow morning and find you still there."

Oh, dagger to the heart.

This is why I avoid the truth at all costs. It hurts like a motherfucker. Honesty is just one big cesspool of need and weakness with the power to strip you bare and leave you whimpering.

If I ever build myself a Caribbean vacation home, I'm naming it House of Death to Honesty and painting the whole thing black.

I walk stiffly to where Parker left my bags in the entry, pick them up, and go upstairs.

VICTORIA

*I*n the elegant master bathroom, I run myself a bath in the huge tub. While it's filling, I hoist my overnight bag onto the king-size bed and unzip it so I can unpack.

Atop my clothes sits a smiling white stuffed animal with a pink bow perched between its pricked ears. A pink ruffled dress decorates its chubby body.

Touched, I pick it up and squeeze it. "Aww, Tabby."

This isn't the first time she's done this. She's deathly afraid of flying—her parents died in a plane crash when she was little —and has developed all kinds of superstitions around air travel. I suppose a Hello Kitty plush doll is as good as a rabbit's foot for good luck.

God knows I'll need it.

I prop the stuffed cat against the lamp on the nightstand beside the bed, hang my clothes in Parker's cavernous walk-in closet, and head to the bathroom, where I strip, leaving my clothes in a careless pile on the floor. I step into the steaming heat and release a soft groan when my aching feet hit the hot water. I lower myself into the bathtub, stretch out my legs, and close my eyes.

Okay, so this hideous House of Truth might have *one* redeeming virtue.

Rattled from what just happened downstairs, I mentally review my game plan. Unfortunately, it primarily consists of waiting to see what Parker's got up his sleeve. In the meantime, I'll continue my nocturnal snoop fests. I've got tonight and tomorrow night to see what I can find in this tropical getaway of his.

Though I already checked behind all the paintings in the master bedroom for a safe. No luck.

"I thought I'd bring you your wine."

My eyes fly open.

Parker stands in the open bathroom door, holding my glass of Chablis. His gaze shifts from my face to my breasts peeking above the water line, then travels slowly down the length of my body to my feet propped on the ledge. His eyes cut to mine.

The heat in his gaze puts the temperature of the water to shame.

"Thank you."

I want to sit up and cover myself, but don't. The urge is ridiculous—I've had the man's cock in my mouth, for goodness' sake—but I feel so vulnerable just lying here, allowing his eyes to drink me in and pierce me through like knives.

He demands, "Tell me what you're thinking right now."

My heart flutters. I swear if I survive this weekend, I'll need a transplant.

"It's more like what I'm feeling."

"Which is?" He takes a step inside the room.

A flush of warmth spreads up my chest, and I know it's not from the water. Real, honest-to-God, genuine emotion is coursing through me, which is a disaster in the making. Especially if I admit it.

Distract him. Distract yourself. Get on safer ground—sex!

I lower my voice and say, "Hungry."

There's a direct, invisible line from his tongue—which travels slowly between his lips—to my pussy. I press my thighs together and hot water sloshes over my nipples, sending another pulse of pleasure down between my legs.

Parker takes another slow step toward me, then another. He kneels beside the tub and holds out the wineglass.

"Me too."

I lean forward and tilt up my chin. He presses the glass against my lips and lifts it. I allow him to pour a sip of cool, crisp wine into my mouth. I swallow, lick my lips, and smile.

"Well, it's been a while since you've eaten."

Hazel eyes flash, then his mouth is against mine.

I hear the clink as he sets the wineglass on the tile floor, feel one of his hands slide into my hair, pulling. The other slips beneath the surface of the water and grips my thigh. His hand slides down my flesh, and his fingers stroke over the entrance to my sex. I moan into his mouth.

"You're right. It's been way too long," he rasps against my lips.

He hauls me out of the water until my butt is balanced on a four-inch ledge of porcelain. He pushes my legs open, grips my hips in his big hands, and buries his face between my wet thighs.

I moan and rock my hips against his mouth. I sink my fingers into the plush thickness of his hair and keep rocking, helpless to resist the waves of pleasure pulsing through me. When he slides two fingers inside me, I suck in a breath.

"God. Yes. Yes, Parker."

Suckling me, he makes a noise like a growl in his throat. He slides his fingers in and out, in and out, moving in slow, tortuous circles, until I'm breathing in short gasps, my back arched and my eyes closed, my nipples aching for his tongue.

When he slows for a moment, I look down at him.

He's looking up at me with eyes that burn.

"Does kitty need to be fed?"

He flicks his tongue over the sensitive head of my clit. When I do nothing but softly groan, he does it again, slower, this time in a swirling circular motion that makes me whimper.

"Kitty likes her French kisses," I pant. "Please don't stop."

Parker's lips curve to a satisfied, seductive smile. "Ah, she said please." He closes his eyes, presses his mouth against my core, and sucks so strongly, my back bows and the cry that rips from me echoes off the bathroom walls.

I come, screaming his name.

It isn't part of my plan, my wanton cries of pleasure that form the shape of his name, but it's so damn good, I can't help myself. His name falls from my lips over and over, a delirious chant as I writhe against his face, my fingers clenching his hair.

Just as I'm about to collapse into the tub, Parker lifts me up under my arms.

In a rough voice, he demands, "Wrap your legs around my waist."

When I do, he takes several short strides over to the wall, pins me against it, holds me up using only one arm, and tears down his fly. His erection presses against my wetness, and the head of his cock catches in the right spot and slips inside me. I make a noise that's part impressed laugh and part groan.

He's fucking me against the wall.

Standing with his legs braced apart, fully clothed, bearing all my weight, Parker is fucking me against the wall of his bathroom.

He thrusts, sinking deep, his fingers digging into the flesh of my bottom. When I drop my head back against the wall and close my eyes, I feel his mouth on my throat. His teeth press against my skin with just enough pressure to make me shiver. He thrusts again and grunts as my inner muscles contract around him.

"I claim this beautiful pussy," he says harshly at my ear.

"You understand, woman? I know you'll never give me your heart, but this—"

He thrusts again.

"—is—"

Again, harder, deeper.

"—*mine*."

Something inside my chest unravels and breaks free.

He's the best sex I've ever had, the father of my illegitimate child, the object of over a decade of hatred, and the catalyst for my success. He ruined me, and I've sworn to ruin him—*and what will I do when this is over?*

When I have my revenge, what will be left? When I break his heart, or his soul, or destroy his career or reputation, who will I be without the bitterness that's driven me? What will I see when I look in the mirror?

What if hating him has been the only thing that's kept me going?

I kiss him ravenously, my tongue invading his mouth, my teeth clashing with his. I tighten my arms around his shoulders, press my heels against his spine, and buck, my hips relentlessly flexing back and forth, meeting his thrusts, shoving his cock deep, claiming him as he's claiming me, marking him as he's marked me.

He shudders. His groan is long and low. His final thrust into me is violent. He puts his hand around my throat, lifts his head and stares into my eyes, and comes inside me.

Warmth, throbbing, a spreading shock of pleasure—my orgasm hits just after his.

He holds my neck while I come, his grip tight. Dominating. The look in his eyes is dominating too, a look of *gotcha* that should frighten me but thrills me instead.

I don't want to know why. I don't want to examine my emotions. I just want to relish this last bit of paradise before I burn it to the ground.

When I collapse bonelessly against him, he carries me into the bedroom with me still impaled on his cock. When he stops abruptly a few feet from the bed, I lift my head and look at him.

Wide-eyed, he's staring at the nightstand.

"Oh, that." I chuckle. "My good luck charm. Cute, isn't it?"

Slowly, oh, so slowly, Parker turns his head and shifts his gaze to me. "Someone recently told me cats are basically cute serial killers."

I smile drowsily. "No wonder I like them."

A muscle in his jaw flexes. "You love to play with fire, don't you?"

I trail my fingers over the jumping muscle in his face. "Darling, I don't play with fire. I *am* the fire."

"Yes," he murmurs, "you definitely are."

He plants a rough kiss on my neck, closes the distance to the bed, takes us down to it, and proceeds to demonstrate to me once again what exactly I'll be missing when this house of mirrors comes crashing down.

A few orgasms later, we sit outside on the candlelit lanai at a table filled with the remnants of our meal, watching thunderclouds billow in from the sea.

The steaks were perfectly grilled. He prepared a simple green salad to accompany the meat. We've enjoyed an exceptional bottle of Syrah, a dessert of pineapple marmalade with soft cheese, honey, and figs, and easy conversation filled with infrequent but comfortable silences. We've talked mainly about our businesses, travel, hobbies, safe topics that flow easily from one to the next without requiring anything in the way of real self-disclosure.

Which makes his question all the more stunning when it comes.

"Do you want children?"

"Children?" I repeat it as if it's a word from a foreign language.

Parker glances over at me. His face reveals nothing.

I look away, my mouth dry. The breeze riffles through my hair, swirling it around my shoulders. I stare at the dark horizon, at the stars being slowly obliterated by clouds, and long for them to obliterate me.

"I wouldn't be a good mother."

"Why do you say that?"

I can tell he isn't being sarcastic. He actually seems surprised by my statement. As if it isn't obvious.

"In case you haven't noticed, Mr. Maxwell, I'm not exactly the nurturing type."

"Most men aren't either, but no one considers it a negative for them."

"That's because they typically have a partner who is."

"So if you had a partner who was nurturing, the problem would be solved?"

This conversation has taken a turn I don't like. I shrug and gaze into the distance. "I've never really thought about it."

"You should."

I look at him. He's serious. It's terrifying. "Let's change the subject."

His voice softens, as do his eyes. "No."

My stomach is in ropes. Beads of sweat break out along my forehead. I manage, barely, to swallow. "What if I said please?"

"You haven't said it yet."

I open my mouth, but Parker beats me to the punch.

"I've always wanted kids," he says, looking right into my eyes.

I feel as if my dinner is about to make a violent reappearance. Cold flashes over me, then scalding heat, then an anguish so complete it floods every cell, every atom of my being, straight down into the marrow of my bones.

For a blind, bottomless moment, I'm no longer Victoria Price. I'm no longer a woman looking at a man, or even a human being at all.

I am Pain.

Then I'm out of my seat, stumbling over wooden floorboards to the railing that surrounds the lanai. I grip it like a life vest, my knees and elbows locked so I don't slide down to the floor.

He comes up behind me and surrounds me with his arms. I close my eyes and lower my head, fighting the swell of sobs rising in my throat. Parker puts his face into my hair.

"I want to know all the dark places in you," he whispers vehemently, his arms like a vise. "I want to be the one who has the key that unlocks all your bolted doors and chases away all the monsters you keep hidden behind them. I want to be the light inside your darkness. I want to be your rock and your safety net, the soft place you can fall."

When I don't reply, he turns me around, holds me by the waist, and lifts my chin.

"I meant what I told you before, about you being safe with me, Victoria. Whatever happened to you in the past, with me you'll always be safe. I promise."

My breath catches in my throat. "Why?"

Eyes shining, he says simply, "You move me."

I drop my head to his chest. My voice comes out hollow, an ugly rasp against the muffled boom of the distant surf. "You don't know me. You said it yourself."

"I know enough."

A gull cries, soaring somewhere overhead. The breeze grows more restless, snapping the curtains by the sliding doors, pulling my dress into billowing folds around my knees. The pungent sting of ozone hangs in the air, and I know that rain is imminent.

I whisper, "Why are you saying these things to me? Why did you bring me here? What is it you want?"

Parker strokes his hand over my head and combs his fingers through my hair, his silence contemplative. Then, finally, with a soft sigh, he says, "I need to show you something."

He takes my hand and leads me away from the railing, inside through the kitchen, and up the stairs. We pad silently down the hallway toward the master bedroom, but turn instead to a door to the right. It's closed. Parker grasps the handle and looks at me.

"Have you ever heard of something called spousal privilege?"

What an odd question. My brow wrinkles. "I don't think so."

"It's a legal term. It means that a husband can't be forced to testify in court against his wife."

I dread the answer, but know I must ask. "What does that have to do with anything?"

Parker stares down at me, his eyes as focused as lasers on mine. Light burns behind them, catching fire to the flecks of gold in his irises. A tingle of animal recognition courses through me.

Whatever he's brought me here for is behind this door.

He turns the knob, pushes it open, and lets his hand fall to his side. "Just keep it in mind."

Filled with trepidation, I look inside the room.

The first thing my gaze falls on is a picture displayed prominently on the opposite wall, a framed eight-by-ten surrounded by dozens of other pictures, similarly framed.

My heart stops.

It's a picture of two teenagers laughing in each other's arms, blue sky and tall pine trees making a magnificent backdrop behind them. The summer sun shines bright on their faces. They are young, carefree, and blissfully in love.

It's me and Parker.

My mother took the picture three weeks to the day before he left.

33

VICTORIA

 $\mathscr{M}$ y shock is so total, I feel frozen. Everything inside me hardens, crystallizes, chills to crackling ice. I stand there stupidly gaping, silent and unmoving as Parker walks past me into the room. He stops in the middle of it, examining the framed pictures. They cover most of one wall.

Other than all the pictures, the room is empty. Only a single plain bench is set opposite, so a person could relax and contemplate the display. It's like a museum.

Or a shrine.

"I come here when I need a reminder," Parker says sadly.

Why does he have that picture of us? Why isn't he accusing me of anything? Why doesn't he seem angry? What the hell is going on here?

I find my voice, a whisper of breath in the quiet room. "Of?"

When he turns his head and looks at me, his eyes are full of ancient sorrow. "Who I used to be. And everything I've lost."

My gaze flashes back to the pictures. Some of them depict his parents at various parties and social events, his mother in silk and pearls, his father's florid face grinning, always grinning that hateful, entitled grin. There are photos of the mansion where he grew up, family gathered on the green expanse of lawn, photos of football games, of Parker in his letterman jacket from senior year, photos of him from childhood, of the city of Laredo, of his favorite polo pony, and on and on.

And there isn't just the one shot of the two of us, there are many more. In formal wear for a school dance, at a pumpkin patch close to Halloween, at my brother's hospital bedside on his thirteenth birthday. I'm holding balloons, Parker's holding my hand, and my mother's got her arms around both of us. Everyone is smiling.

Inside, I'm sick. I'm a volcano with a vomit core, about to blow. But I don't show it. I give him nothing. I've come too far. I have too much invested.

If this is the goal line, I'll be damned if I'll fumble the ball now.

I draw myself to my full height. I look straight at his face. In a voice devoid of emotion, I say, "Why don't you explain what you mean."

He takes a seat on the bench slowly, as if it pains him to bend his legs. He props his elbows on his knees and drags his hands through his hair. When he speaks, it's to the floor.

"I've spent the last fifteen years of my life on hold. I've opened over twenty restaurants, founded a nonprofit organization, traveled the world, met celebrities, politicians, and even a king. I've become wealthy beyond all my expectations, given away millions to charity, built myself an empire."

His voice drops. "And none of it makes up for one mistake I made at eighteen."

All the air is sucked from the room. The clocks stop ticking. The earth stops spinning under my feet. I'm no longer ice, I'm granite.

I couldn't move if I wanted to.

Parker raises his head and stares at the wall of photos. "My father was a terrible man. *Is* a terrible man. The textbook definition of a bigot. Why my mother married him, I'll never know. The woman is a saint." He shakes his head. "I'm grateful she doesn't know what I did. The shame would cripple me."

The silence in the room is deafening. Into it, Parker sighs.

"The girl I told you about, you remember? The one who killed herself?"

He looks at me. I must nod or make some other kind of acknowledgment that I don't realize I've made, because he continues.

"That's her."

He turns again to the pictures. His expression hovers somewhere between searing agony and crushing defeat. "Isabel was her name. She was my best friend. My first love. I would've done anything for her. So when my father made me choose between destroying my own life or hers, I chose mine."

His laugh is bitter, the laugh of a man who's lived too long with guilt, whose soul has been corroded by it. "What a fool I was."

I can't speak. I stare at the photos of myself, the girl I used to be, thick glasses and a too-big nose, crooked teeth and a weak chin, cheap clothes and deeply bronzed skin from spending so much time outdoors. That awful haircut my mother gave me. A smile like the sun.

I'm unrecognizable. That trusting, happy girl is just another of my ghosts.

Parker exhales a heavy breath. "Her family was very poor. Mine was filthy rich. In the beginning, my father tolerated our relationship because he thought I was like him. He thought I was just sowing my wild oats. Getting experience." His voice gains an edge of disgust. "'You're not a man until you've fucked the help,' he once said to me, clapping me on the shoulder. Like making love to the girl of my dreams was just a rite of passage. Like she was a thing to be used. That's when I began to hate him.

That's when I began to hide my feelings for Isabel from him. To pretend."

Parker's voice grows rougher. "It lasted for two years, until he found out. I think he had me followed after he discovered us together one night. But he didn't confront me right away. He waited. He planned. And then, when he had what he needed, he forced me to make a choice."

My hands shake. My palms sweat. My heartbeat increases to a nearly impossible rate, pounding with such frantic beats, I feel faint.

But my mind is clear and cold. I have the most bizarre feeling of hovering above myself, outside my body, watching this horror unfold with detachment as if it's happening to someone else.

Parker stands. He contemplates the photos with his hands on his hips, his shoulders rounded, the normally proud line of his back bent.

"Isabel's father had a gambling problem. I have no idea how my father discovered that, but he organized a private poker game, one with a low enough buy-in so that her father could play. And then my dad did what he does best. He cheated. He let her father gain confidence with a few substantial wins, let him get a taste of real money, then pulled the rug out from under his feet. The man got so desperate, he ended up betting the deed to his farm. And, of course, he lost.

"When my father had the means to destroy Isabel's entire family completely, he came to me and said I could stay with her —and her family would lose their livelihood and be out on the streets, and I'd be disinherited so I couldn't help them—or I could leave that very night and go to school in England, never to return. He'd already arranged everything. Plane ticket, apartment, tuition, everything. All to get me away from a girl he hated because of the color of her skin."

When Parker turns to look at me, his eyes glitter with self-hatred.

"So I agreed. Though it broke my fucking heart, I thought that I was being strong for her. That it was the right thing to do, saving the farm, saving her family. I knew my father would follow through on his threats. And, stupidly, I thought she would eventually move on, have a beautiful life, forget all about me."

His voice cracks. "Instead she killed herself. Because I didn't have the courage to stand up to my father, she died."

I don't understand. I don't understand what you're saying.

My words must have been spoken aloud, because Parker replies, "He made me write her a goodbye letter, then I left. For a few years, I was in school in England, then I lived in France for a year with Alain. I was miserable the entire time. Heartbroken. When I couldn't stand it anymore, when it got to be so bad that I knew I had to go back or go insane, I booked a flight to Laredo and went straight to her house as soon as I got off the plane. I was going to confess everything, beg her for her forgiveness. But I was too late. She was already gone. Her mother told me the whole story."

One by one, the cells in my body begin to shrivel up and die.

Horrified, I whisper, "Her mother?"

As if he can no longer bear to meet my eyes, he looks away and hangs his head.

"She loved me like a son. She was always good to me. But when I saw her that night, I knew her love had turned into the kind of hate that eats you alive. She said things to me, screamed things...things I'll never forget. She told me that after I left, Isabel killed herself. That she'd taken her father's gun and put it to her head. And that she'd been cremated, so there wasn't even a grave I could visit. She was gone."

His voice cracks. "I had her blood all over my hands. I still do. It can never be washed away, no matter how hard I try, how much I give to charity, how long I try to make amends."

My knees give out. Slowly, inch by agonizing inch, I sink silently to the floor where I sit ashen, shell-shocked and shaking, red pulsing in the corners of my vision like flames.

Lost in his painful memories, Parker doesn't notice my distress.

"I went a little crazy after that. Got into a lot of fights, did a lot of stupid shit, got myself into a lot of trouble, because I wanted to die, too. I couldn't shake the guilt. I drank. Wandered. Spent a few months in jail for a minor drug possession charge. I probably could've gotten out of it if I'd contacted my father, but by then he was dead to me. I didn't want his help or his dirty money. I met a guy inside who was a cook. We got to be friends. We were released at the same time, and he offered me a job in his family's restaurant, cash under the table.

"I took it because I had nothing else to do. Started as a busboy, moved up to cook. Turns out I was pretty good at it. I guess I picked up a lot living with Alain that year in France. The restaurant got a good write-up in the local paper, started making more money. I started trying different dishes. Reservations started selling out. One day some bigwig comes in with a boatload of money, says he wants to make me the head chef at his fancy new restaurant. I said sure, on one condition: we name it Bel Époch. The investor said that was a stupid name for a gourmet Mexican restaurant, especially since it was spelled wrong, but I said no name, no deal."

Gazing at my picture, Parker pauses for a moment. His voice turns reverent.

"I wanted to name it after Isabel, you see. That was my nickname for her. Bel. It was an homage to her, and to the time we had together. Bel Époch, beautiful era. The best time in my life. So the investor eventually relented. And that was my first restaurant."

Almost as an afterthought, he adds, "I started The Hunger Project in memory of her, too. I thought she would've liked the idea of giving food to the underprivileged kids in the South. Kids like her, who never had money for school lunches. And the donations I make to the Muscular Dystrophy Association, those are in memory of her little brother who died of the disease."

He heaves a heavy sigh. "I guess…I guess I've been trying all these years to somehow make it right."

Tears slide down my cheeks. I make no move to brush them away. I don't have to ask Parker about my letters, because I know now he never received them. Whether my mother or his father made sure of that, I doubt I'll ever find out. But I know by the honesty in his voice, the deep emotion and unfathomable regret in every word, that what Parker has just told me is the truth.

He doesn't know I'm Isabel.

He doesn't know I was pregnant when he left.

He believes I'm dead, and that he's the cause.

He's done all these wonderful things—naming restaurants and giving to charity and starting a nonprofit to help poor kids —for me.

Me, the perfect, dead love he told me about on our first date.

Reality folds in around me like a complicated origami form, angles and layers I can't see through, sharp edges that cut. The out-of-body detachment from before vanishes, replaced by a distinctly painful *in*-body experience.

I feel each and every screaming nerve, each and every agonizing intake of breath.

I'm underwater. I'm going to drown.

Everything I am, everything I believed, all the rage and vengeance that has driven me for the past fifteen years was built on a sandcastle of untruths and misinformation, of pettiness and folly, of the hardness of two people's hearts.

Parker's father and his intractable bigotry.

My mother and that one, terrible lie.

A lie she's kept like a secret lover, all these years.

I remember all the times she railed against Parker, cursed his name, wished him dead, and I'm sick all over again.

I understand why she did what she did. It's simple, really: revenge. She wanted to make Parker pay for the agony he put me through when he left. But she didn't know that he was just trying to do the right thing. She didn't know he'd already paid, and paid, and paid. And would be paying for years to come. Would pay forever.

So this is the poisoned fruit that bigotry and revenge have borne. Here we sit, two broken hearts, two ruined souls, two loveless people staring at the ghosts of their former selves hanging on the walls.

I put my face into my hands and sob.

Parker rushes over to me. He kneels in front of me and grips my upper arms.

"Please, don't be upset! I didn't tell you this to try to make you feel sorry for me, or jealous of her, or for any other reason than that I wanted you to know everything about me, what makes me tick! I want you to know all my secrets so that you'll trust me when I say I can keep *your* secrets. I want us to be on even footing going forward, equals. You understand?"

I have no idea what he's talking about. I cry harder.

He gathers me into his arms. His voice comes out in a rush, the words spilling over one another in his hurry to get them out.

"Listen to me. After I opened Bel Époch, I got obsessed with trying to get my father back for being such a prick. Through a friend I'd made—a guy with a military background who owned a security company—I found out my father wasn't running a legit import/export business, he was a drug dealer. We'd lived in Laredo because Mexico was right across the goddamn river. What he really was importing was mountains of cocaine."

I lift my head and stare at him. Tears stream down my cheeks.

What I wouldn't have given for this information even one hour ago.

Parker nods. "That's how he made all his money. The only reason I didn't turn him in to the police was my mother. I knew she didn't know anything about the drugs, and she probably would have been implicated in an investigation. Even if she wasn't, the scandal would've killed her. So I made him a deal. Retire, become a fucking pillar of the community, give away most of your money, and you get to stay out of prison. One little slip and you're taking it up the ass by a guy named Big Daddy for the rest of your life.

"My friend Connor covered up the nasty fact of my family business, erased any connections my father had to the cartel, but nothing is foolproof. I'm sure if you wanted to leak that to the press, someone would come forward to corroborate it. Some criminal would use it in a plea bargain, and my company would kick me off the board. And forget about my run for Congress. Who knows? I might even get thrown in jail for collusion. For all intents and purposes, my life would be over.

"So there's another of my secrets, okay? My father's a former drug lord. I'm basically a murderer. And I've already told you I spent time in jail. That was for possession of pot, by the way. I've got enough dirt in my background that you could bury me with it."

His voice gentles. "I'm telling you all this so that you feel safe with me knowing what I know about you. So that you know I'll never tell anyone who you really are, because I trust you, and you trust me, and together our secrets are safe from the world."

I don't know if it's the emotion that's making me unable to comprehend what precisely it is that Parker's telling me, or if I'm just in the middle of a mental breakdown.

"W-who I really am?"

Parker smooths the hair off my face, wipes my wet cheeks

with his thumbs, and smiles a smile of such tenderness it almost sends me into a fresh onslaught of tears.

"Yes," he says softly. "I know who you are, and you don't have to hide from me, Victoria. You never have to hide again."

A terrible feeling of doom settles in the pit of my stomach.

I whisper, "Who am I, exactly?"

He shakes his head and smiles wider, as if I'm playing a game. "Polaroid."

When he sees the furrow form between my brows, he adds, "The Hello Kitty hacker. The woman who breaks into government computer systems for fun, writes sophisticated software programs that can't be traced, is on law enforcement's most wanted lists. I suspected it before, but when I saw your little good luck charm on the nightstand, the calling card you always leave behind when you hack a system—like when you tried to hack into mine—well..."

It hits me with such force I lose my breath.

Tabby. Oh my God, Tabby.

He thinks I'm her.

Outside, the clouds open and release their burden of rain. It falls in a torrent, pounding hard against the roof.

He nods in satisfaction when he sees the horrified recognition on my face, taking it for an admission of my guilt. Then, when I put together what he's just said about us being on equal footing, about keeping my secrets—*"Have you ever heard of something called spousal privilege?"*—I realize what this whole exercise in disclosure is really all about. Why he really brought me to the House of Truth.

Blackmail.

34

VICTORIA

*B*ecause all my muscles are frozen under the crushing weight of my spirit, which has collapsed upon itself like a black hole formed from a dying star, I can't walk. So Parker lifts me up and carries me into the master bedroom.

The inside of my head is Armageddon.

In contrast, Parker seems better for telling his story. His step is sure and easy. His expression is calm. Apparently unburdening yourself of all your past transgressions, accusing the woman you're sleeping with of being a criminal computer genius, and making a passive-aggressive suggestion that you won't testify against her in court if she becomes your wife have psychological benefits.

Catharsis, if you will.

Parker lays me on the bed. He gently arranges my frozen limbs—legs together, arms by my sides—then climbs into bed beside me. He slides his arm under my neck, wraps his other arm around my waist, and nuzzles his face into my hair. His sigh is deeply content.

He says, "So."

That's it. One syllable. Two letters. That's all it takes to seal your fate.

I stare at the ceiling, listening to the relentless drum of the rain on the roof, and think about the seminar today. I think about all those women who came to hear me speak about being strong, standing up for themselves, not taking any shit from their men.

I think about the woman in the front row who said I was her hero.

I'm nobody's hero. Especially not my own.

What would those women think of me now if they could see me lying here, as limp as a rag doll beside the man who was my greatest enemy until moments ago? What would they think if they knew that instead of standing up and fighting, I was mutely weighing all my options, calculating every possible outcome, parsing every way I might get myself out of this situation without blowing it all to hell?

Because hell is exactly where I suspect this is leading.

Though I'm not sure, I've got a strong suspicion that if I don't continue with Parker's assumption that I'm Polaroid, if I admit my true identity as the formerly deceased and suddenly resurrected Isabel Diaz and say, *Gee, sorry, this has all been one huge misunderstanding!* Tabby and I will soon be wearing matching orange jumpsuits.

I've deceived him in every conceivable way. My own mother told him just about the worst lie I can think of, which he's spent years crucifying himself over. I can't possibly turn around now and cheerfully declare, *Hey, great news, I'm not really dead!* and expect him to treat me with any level of civility.

I suppose I could try it. Roll the dice and see if they come up lucky. But I'm not gambling with only *my* life. There's Tabby to think of. He mentioned most wanted lists. Definitely not good. He put that out there for a reason. And God—he'd probably confront my mother. I can see it now, the two of them screaming at each other on her porch.

And what if my mother slipped? What if, in her rage, she told him about Eva? About the daughter kept hidden from him for so many years?

What would Parker do then?

What would happen to Eva?

If a child is given up for adoption and the biological father didn't agree to it, what kind of legal nightmare would ensue if he tried to contest the adoption? He'd said at dinner he'd always wanted children. What if the child he wanted turned out to be the one he never knew he had?

Too many questions crowd my mind. I can't think. I close my eyes, swallowing the sound of despair trying to crawl from my throat.

Parker says, "There's something I have to know."

My eyes fly open.

"I don't believe in belaboring a point, so I'll only ask this once, but I need you to be honest."

I break out in a cold sweat. The rain on the roof sounds like gunfire.

His voice low but intense, he says, "You were in my office. You found my safe. You tried to get into my computers. Why?"

I shudder. It's involuntary, a little seizure, one of those twitching nerve things dead tissue can sometimes do. We had chickens on our farm. When you cut off their heads, they would stagger around for minutes afterward, the body still able to perform motor functions without a brain.

I am one of those chickens.

Finally, I breathe, "I just…wanted to be sure…I could trust you."

What's one more lie when your entire life is built upon a mountain of them?

"And now you know," he says tenderly, stroking my face.

I swallow, inhale a slow breath, and test the waters to see how shark-infested they are.

"You're not worried I'll leak all this information to the press if we break up?"

He tenses. I hold my breath as I wait for his answer.

"Neither one of us is going to the press. We both have too much to lose."

Contained in that sentence I hear a clear but unspoken threat. If I out him, he outs me.

So there you have it:

Checkmate.

He adds with cold finality, "And we're not breaking up. We belong together. We're so much alike, it's scary." He pauses, then says more gently, "When we get back to New York, we'll pick out a ring."

He's trapped me into marriage. It's over.

He won.

I don't say anything, because there's nothing more to say.

Parker turns my head and kisses me on the lips. The kiss begins tenderly but quickly turns ardent. Soon we're both naked, doing what we do best.

Even though I'm empty, though inside I feel as if I've been hollowed out by knives, my body responds to him the same way it always does, with desire and desperation. He is, and will always be, the center of my universe, the axis on which everything else turns.

Afterward, lying sweaty and sated in his arms in the dark, I think of all those women again. My fans. I see them staring at me, their faces accusing, their eyes so disappointed. The image of the woman in the front row quoting my own words haunts me.

"You always have the power to say, 'This is not how my story is going to end.'"

I'm their idol, the person they wish they could be, confident and successful, unyielding, strong…and here I lie, letting someone else write the ending to my story. I'm cornered. Giving in. A kitten thrown to the wolves.

The funny thing about me is, if you throw me to the wolves, I'll return leading the pack.

Rule #7: Bitches never surrender.

For the first time since I arrived at Casa de la Verdad, my lips curve into a genuine smile.

My mother was right, in a way. I did commit suicide. I killed Isabel Diaz with my own two hands. Then, like a phoenix, I rose from her ashes and created something new, something better.

Victoria Price.

I listen to the rain pounding the rooftop and wonder if it's time for Victoria Price to be laid to rest as well. Time for me— the real me, whoever she is—to finally have a chance to live.

Later on, I'll realize I was in shock. My emotions were chaotic. My brain had shut down, and I wasn't thinking clearly. But at the moment—coerced, cornered, optionless—it seemed the most perfect solution in the world.

I waited until Parker was sleeping deeply, then I crept from the bed, quietly dressed, dashed off two notes on the pad by the kitchen phone, and made my way through the dark house and out into the storm.

Then I went down the wooden stairs to the sea.

35

Author and Entrepreneur Victoria Price Missing, Presumed Dead

Early Saturday morning, police were called to the vacation home of Parker Maxwell, CEO of Maxwell Restaurant Group, to investigate a report of a missing woman. Mr. Maxwell and Victoria Price, bestselling author of the *Bitches Do Better* series of women's self-help books and life coach to many A-list celebrities, had arrived at his home on St. Thomas in the US Virgin Islands the evening prior. They planned on spending the weekend at his residence. Mr. Maxwell told police he awoke to find Ms. Price gone and an apparent suicide note on his kitchen counter.

Local police confirmed that several items of clothing belonging to Ms. Price washed up on the beach south of Mr. Maxwell's residence, indicating she might have drowned herself.

A body has not been recovered, and the investigation is ongoing.

Mr. Maxwell was not available for comment.

36

PARKER

*E*ight days after the second-worst night of my life, I exit
the Rolls-Royce I bought for Victoria and am instantly
beset by a jostling crowd of reporters screaming questions into
my face.

I shoulder through the crowd, head down, teeth gritted, unresponsive to their shouts of "What did the suicide note say?" and
"Were you fighting?" and "Did you have anything to do with her
disappearance, Mr. Maxwell?"

Connor, walking beside me, has to grab me and physically
restrain me from lunging at the leering fat guy who asked that
last one.

"Keep your shit together, brother," he mutters, easily pushing
men with cameras out of our way with wide sweeps of his
muscle-bound arm.

I am, in fact, having a hard fucking time keeping my shit
together.

Over the course of the past week, I've been interrogated by
about two dozen different detectives and investigators from both
the St. Thomas and New York City police departments. I've been
vilified in the press, slept a total of maybe twelve hours, and

developed an extremely unhealthy relationship with Johnny Walker Blue Label scotch, which is quickly turning into a full-blown addiction. If it hasn't already.

And I'm obsessed with finding Victoria. *Obsessed.* To the point of insanity.

Because I know she isn't dead.

Unfortunately, locating her is proving extremely difficult.

So today I'm meeting with the only two people who might be able to give me a clue as to her whereabouts.

Connor and I barge through the elegant glass doors of the lobby of Victoria's condo building. As soon as we're inside, the clamor falls silent. The press can't follow us onto private property. I resist the urge to turn and flip them off and instead introduce myself to the young man at the front desk, who shows Connor and me to the bank of elevators.

"I'm sorry for your loss," he says in a muted voice, eyes lowered.

I want to strangle him.

Connor drags me into the elevator, jabs his finger on the penthouse button and, when the doors slide shut, drawls, "Maybe you should let me do the talking. You don't seem like you're in the right mood."

"You want mood? I'll give you fucking *mood*," I growl, raking a hand through my hair. "I'll give you so much mood, you'll think I'm a lava lamp."

Connor sighs, rolls his eyes, and crosses his arms over his chest. "Man, a word of advice? Chill the fuck out or these broads aren't gonna tell you anything."

He's right. I know he's right. But there's no way I can *chill out.*

Not when Victoria has slipped through my fingers. Not when my goddamn heart is dying, just when it was learning how to live again.

When the doors open, I burst from the elevator as if I've

been coughed out. I'm pounding on Victoria's closed front door before Connor has a chance to catch up to me.

"Tabby!" I shout, alternating pounding on the door with stabbing my finger on the doorbell. "Open the goddamn door!"

"Yeah, a lava lamp you're not," Connor mutters.

Victoria's assistant, Tabby, yanks open the door. She stands there red-faced with clenched fists and crazy eyes, in an outfit I can only describe as call-girl-meets-cartoon-character, and snarls, "You mother*fucker*!"

She takes a step forward and punches me in the face.

"Whoa!" shouts Connor.

He gets in front of me and pushes Tabby back into the condo by her shoulders. As she stumbles back, she keeps her furious gaze glued to mine.

I work my jaw, rubbing it where she hit me. I thought Victoria had a pretty good swing, but her assistant has her beat by a mile. For such a small thing, she's got an arm like Babe Ruth.

"It's nice to see you too, Tabby." I step inside the condo and slam the door behind me.

"Get your hands off me, you ape!" Tabby snaps at Connor, slapping at his hands.

He releases her, his expression hard, but I see the amusement shining in the depths of his obsidian eyes. He thinks it's funny that the little badger just clocked me.

From around the corner of the living room, Darcy LaFontaine appears, clutching a bag of Doritos and looking distraught.

"You better start talking before I stress-eat this entire bag of chips." She stuffs a handful into her mouth and says through it, "I already plowed through half the fridge, and I haven't even been here ten minutes."

At least she doesn't seem inclined to beat me. It's a step in the right direction.

I say what I didn't want to say over the phone when I arranged this meeting, and declare, "Victoria isn't dead!"

Tabby's rolled eyes and sarcastic "No shit, Sherlock" aren't quite what I was expecting.

Nobody knows about the second note Victoria left but me and Connor. And I know for a fact that she hasn't accessed any of her bank accounts, used her credit cards, or made phone contact with either Tabby or Darcy, because Connor has been on top of everything. Victoria left her cell at my house—along with her handbag, wallet, everything—but all the calls coming in to her home landline and Tabby and Darcy's phones since Victoria disappeared have been traceable. No mysterious numbers from the Caribbean, no random pay phones, no nothing.

So unless Victoria sent a letter or a carrier pigeon, they should be in the dark.

"You mind telling me how you know that?"

The look Tabby gives me is meant to disembowel. In a voice dripping acid, she says, "You first, dickhead."

Connor snorts.

Tabby cuts her eyes to him and narrows them. "And who the fuck is this? G.I. Joe on steroids?"

Connor flexes an enormous bicep. "Ain't no steroids in these guns, baby. That's one hundred percent pure American male."

Tabby says, "Call me 'baby' one more time, jarhead, and you and John Bobbitt will have something in common."

Apparently Connor has no problem being threatened with penile amputation, because a slow grin spreads over his face. "Feisty, aren't you?"

"Tabby, this is Connor. He's a friend."

"I'm not talking about Victoria in front of your boyfriend, so come back when you don't need him for moral support, you big pussy."

I scowl. Connor just smiles wider.

He asks her, "You kiss your mother with that mouth?"

"Fuck you."

He chuckles. "Gladly, sweet thing. Any time you want the ride of your life, just hop on."

Nostrils flared, Tabby looks at me. "Get this Neanderthal out of my face before I rip off his balls."

I want to break something. This situation is already out of hand, we're getting nowhere, and all I want to do is find out where the hell Victoria could have gone and go after her. "Connor works for me, all right? He's familiar with the situation, and he can help us find her."

He adds, "I'm in security."

Tabby looks Connor up and down, her gaze scrutinizing, calculating, and highly disbelieving. "You?" she says, a brow arched. "*You're* his security guy?"

The way she says it is so condescending, I feel insulted on Connor's behalf. "We've worked together for years. You can trust him. He's the best in the business."

Tabby turns her disdainful gaze to me. "If you think this knuckle dragger is the best, you're as stupid as you look."

Connor laughs while I bristle in indignation. "What's your problem with me, Tabby? I walk in here, tell you your boss isn't dead, and you don't even bother to find out how I know or what happened the night she disappeared. You just start breaking my balls. What the hell?"

Tabby's fierce eyes fill with tears. Her voice comes out choked. "She wasn't just my *boss*. She was my idol and my friend and the only fucking family I have, and *you're* the asshole who ruined her life!"

Astonished, I blink. "How did I ruin her life? By falling in love with her?"

Darcy drops the bag of chips. It lands on the floor, spraying Doritos at her feet. "You're in love with her?"

Tabby says bitterly, "He's a fucking liar, is what he is.

Always has been, always will be." She turns and walks away, shoulders hunched, arms wrapped around her body, shaking.

As I watch her retreating back, I ask Darcy, "What am I missing?"

Darcy purses her lips. She looks down at the bag of chips on the floor, then back up at me. "I think we should probably go into the kitchen for this. I'm gonna need something stronger than Doritos. And *you*, Captain America, are probably gonna need a strong-ass drink."

She turns and follows Tabby.

Connor and I look at each other, he shrugs, and I exhale through clenched teeth. If we want to find out what's going on, we have no choice but to follow, and so we do.

Darcy sits at the kitchen table, cradling a pint of chocolate ice cream to her chest. She's spooning it right out of the container into her mouth. Connor sits opposite her, his big frame dwarfing the chair. His gaze is on Tabby, who's pacing back and forth in front of the sink, chewing her thumbnail. I stand in the doorway with my arms crossed, watching everyone, waiting for someone to speak.

Finally, Connor cuts through the tension, addressing Tabby directly.

"She left a note."

Tabby spins on her heel and glares at him. "The police told me about that bullshit note, and there's no fucking way she wrote it!"

When her eyes flash to me, I realize she's accusing me of forging Victoria's suicide note.

"Hold the fuck on," I say, irate, but Connor cuts me off.

"No, sweet cheeks, *another* note. She left two. One for the police, one for Parker. And for the record, she wrote both. I evaluated the handwriting. It's hers."

Tabby's green eyes widen. She sucks in a hopeful breath. "Where's the other note? What did it say? Give it to me!"

She thrusts her hand into Connor's face.

He grins. "I'll give it to you…if you promise to be nice."

Slowly Tabby lowers her arm. Her breathing is erratic, her spine is straight, and her eyes are steely and full of venom.

If I were Connor, I'd honestly be in fear for the future health of my testicles.

Glaring at him, Tabby says quietly, "I'm good, jarhead, but I will never, ever, be *nice*. I'm *real*, and I don't give one single fuck about conforming to your misogynist ideas about how women should act, so you fucking hand over that motherfucking note *right now*, or I swear to the Goddess I will rain down a shit storm of such epic proportions on you, you'll think your name is Noah."

Connor looks over at me. "It is inappropriate for me to have a boner right now? 'Cause my dick is so hard, it might actually explode."

"Just give her the damn note, Connor."

Tabby says, "Thank you!" and snaps her fingers in front of his face.

Smirking at her, he removes a folded piece of white paper from the inside pocket of his leather jacket. He flicks it out between two fingers like a magician with a card trick, and she snatches it from his hand.

She reads it once, her eyes darting from line to line. She frowns, glances up at me, then reads it again. She sinks into the nearest chair, staring at me with big, disbelieving eyes.

"You asked her to marry you?"

Darcy chokes on a mouthful of ice cream. Connor leans over and pounds her on the back.

"Yes. Well, no, not exactly. I sort of…implied that we'd get married. Whatever. The point is that we agreed we'd go ring shopping when we came back to New York, and then we went to sleep, and the next thing I know, she's gone."

Tabby digests that in fraught silence for a moment.

Darcy says, "Gimme that," and rips the note from Tabby's hands. She proceeds to read it silently, her lips moving, but I've already memorized every word.

Dear Parker,

Forgive me for leaving like this again, but you've left me no choice. I'm not interested in marriage...or any other institution.

Thank you for everything you shared with me tonight. You have no idea what it means to me. I'll never tell another soul, so please don't waste one minute worrying about that.

The other note is for the police, so you won't be a suspect in my disappearance. And no, I don't have cancer. That's just for the media. I plan on living a long and productive life, out of the spotlight. Please don't try to find me. It will only make things worse.

There are so many things I wish I could tell you, but there's just too much at stake. Maybe in another life.

I wish you happiness, Parker. You deserve it.

Yours always,

Victoria

When she finishes reading, Darcy glances at Tabby. A look passes between them that prompts me to ask, "I assume you both knew all along who she really is?"

Tabby—the fierce, indomitable Tabby—blanches to the color of a bedsheet.

"She told you who she really is?"

"Not in so many words. But she admitted it when I

confronted her." I think for a moment and then correct myself. "Actually she didn't admit it, but she didn't deny it either."

When Tabby and Darcy both give me the same bug-eyed look, I say impatiently, "Look, the bottom line is that I figured out she was Polaroid, I confronted her about it after showing her a bunch of my own skeletons so she'd feel secure that she could trust me, we agreed on marriage, and then this."

I point to the note in Darcy's hands. "And I need to know where she might have gone, so I can go after her and fix this. Which is why I'm here—because I assume you two are my best chance at figuring out where she went. I would've come sooner, but the St. Thomas police held me up. I had to cooperate with the investigation there. I got back to New York only yesterday, and I spent most of the day with the NYPD."

There follows a silence so cavernous, I can hear my own heart beating.

Then Tabby says hollowly, "Polaroid."

"Yeah," interrupts Connor with a wry shake of his head. "Blew my fuckin' mind, too. Never woulda thought a skirt could pull off the shit she pulled off. Un-fuckin'-believable."

Tabby's face goes from white to red. The look she gives Connor should melt him into a puddle, but he remains unscathed, just shaking his head at the impossibility of it all.

An obviously confused Darcy asks, "Who's Polaroid?"

I can tell Tabby knows, but maybe Victoria didn't disclose quite as much to Darcy as she did to her assistant. It makes sense, I suppose. Tabby was with Victoria every day, all day, running her schedule, basically running her entire life. She'd mentioned once that Tabby was her right hand, the support she couldn't live without.

Tabby must know where all the bodies are buried.

In a casual tone at direct odds with the sharp look in his eyes, Connor asks Darcy, "You've never heard that name before?"

Darcy opens her mouth, but Tabby cuts her off before she can utter a word.

"Victoria didn't tell her about Polaroid, or about her past. She doesn't know anything." She cuts Darcy a warning look. "Isn't that right, Darcy?"

Darcy carefully sets the ice cream carton on the table. Staring right at it, she nods. "Yep. I mean, nope. I don't know anything. We weren't even really that close."

Connor looks at Tabby, then at Darcy, then chuckles. "Ladies, that's just about the shittiest lie-telling I've ever seen."

"Agreed," I snap. "Somebody better start telling me what the hell is going on, or I'll get the police in here to get the story for me."

Tabby says coldly, "We've both already been interviewed by the police. And no, in case you're wondering, I didn't tell them about Polaroid. Did you?"

"Of course not! I want to protect her, not put her in jail!"

Her lips twist. "That's clearly not what she thought, evidenced by that line in her letter, 'any other institution.' She was obviously talking about prison." Her look darkens. "Or a hospital."

She's glaring at me with such disgust and hostility, I'm taken aback. "I didn't hurt her or threaten to hurt her. I only wanted to make her happy!"

Tabby leaps to her feet. "Make her happy? You drove her to the edge and pushed her off, you moron! Whatever you said to her that night forced her to do this. And now we'll never see her again—thanks to you!"

That hurts, all of it, mainly because I've been thinking the same thing. I never would have disclosed Victoria's real identity to the police or anyone else, but the way I worded it...thinking back, I realize my attempt at trying to convince Victoria to marry me was an absolute fucking disaster. Never in a million years did I think she'd do something like this. Worst case scenario, I thought she'd refuse me and call my bluff, and I'd run home with my tail between my legs.

I'm such a dick. And Tabby sees right through me.

I try to deny it anyway. "We don't know that we'll never see her again. She could just be spooked, lying low—"

"She's not coming back," Tabby interrupts bitterly. "She'd never have accessed the bug-out bag if she planned on coming back. I checked. It's gone. And so is she. For good."

Now I'm confused. "What's a bug-out bag?"

Connor says, "A portable kit with supplies, typically used for short-term survival situations when you have to leave an unsafe area due to disasters. Earthquakes, terrorist attacks, the outbreak of war, that kind of thing."

He and Tabby lock eyes. He adds softly, "In this particular bag, I'd guess we're looking at new identity papers, passport under a different name, and lots and lots of cash. Right, sweet cheeks?"

Darcy groans. "Oh Lord, *another* fake name? That poor thing!"

The three of us look at her, Connor and I with eagle-eyed interest, Tabby with a death glare.

When Darcy realizes her mistake, she winces. "Oops."

I say, "Her real name isn't Victoria Price?"

"That's impossible," says Connor, his body still, his ruthless gaze on Tabby. "Everything checked out, right down to her birth certificate. Her entire background checked out. It was spotless."

Tabby lifts her chin, gazes down her nose at Connor, and sniffs. "I said you weren't the best in the business, didn't I?"

My heart is doing something unusual. It might be trying to rip itself out of my chest. "What's her real name?"

Tabby looks at me with hatred in her eyes. "Fuck you, Parker Maxwell. Fuck you and your pretty face and your prettier lies. I'm not telling you anything."

My mind is going a million miles an hour. My hands shake. I feel a bit dizzy, so I pull out a chair and sit.

"Darcy," I say hoarsely, looking at her. "What's Victoria's real name? And why does Tabby keep calling me a liar?"

"If you tell him, I'll push you into traffic," snaps Tabby.

"Pipe down, woman," says Connor, rising to his feet. He puts his hands on his hips, towering over Tabby. Unintimidated, she rolls her eyes and turns her back on all of us.

I reach out and touch Darcy's arm. "Darcy. Please. I have to know. I have to find her. I need to make this right."

She looks at my face for a long, silent moment, her large dark eyes sizing me up. Finally, she exhales and shakes her head. "Sorry, Parker, but after everything you've put that girl through—"

"Darcy, if you don't shut up, I will personally ensure that you'll never walk again!" yells Tabby.

My fingers tighten around Darcy's arm. "What did I do? Tell me, please! Help me understand!"

Tabby glares at us. Connor folds his arms over his chest and steps in front of her like a barrier. Darcy simply shakes her head again, mute.

I set my elbows on the table, drop my face into my hands, and groan loudly.

They're not going to tell me anything. I've hit a brick wall. There's something else at play here that I can't understand and probably never will, because Tabby and Darcy are too busy protecting Victoria...from me.

Why are they protecting her from *me*?

What did Victoria tell them about me?

I think of the trip she took to Laredo—which I stupidly neglected to ask her about during our stint in St. Thomas—and wonder for the hundredth time what that was about.

But there's no way I'll ever find out now. Unless they're

willing to give me something, some detail of the underlying plot that I'm missing, I'll never...

Hold on. What if I give them something first?

It comes to me as if I've been slapped upside the head. I've got to tell them what happened that night. I've got to tell them the truth, the whole truth, dangerous as that might be to my reputation, my career, and everything else. It's the only card I've got left to play.

It's the only way I'll get them to trust me.

I've got to put my future into the hands of Psychotic Redhooded Goth Barbie and her sidekick, the Stress-Eating Bloggess.

I'm fucked.

I lift my head and stare first at Darcy and then at Tabby, who's still glaring at me from around Connor's shoulder. Because Tabby seems the more furious and emotional of the two, and I suspect she knows more than Darcy does, I address her first.

"My father was a drug lord."

Connor swings around and barks, "Fucking shit, Parker! You high?"

I don't even bother answering him. The look of shock on Tabby's face tells me I'm headed in the right direction. "He imported cocaine from Mexico by the truckload during the eighties and nineties—"

"Jesus Christ," Connor groans, lifting his hands to his head.

"—and when I found out about it, I blackmailed him into stopping by telling him I'd turn him in to the police."

Darcy says, "Huh. And I thought my family was interesting."

"I also spent six months in prison on a drug charge unrelated to my dad's thing. I was just really fucked up at that point in my life. Connor helped me make all that information disappear, by the way."

"That's it. We're outta here." Connor strides over to me and waves me up. "Not another fucking word, brother."

I keep right on ignoring him, encouraged by Tabby's expression, which hovers somewhere between wary interest and full-blown surprise. I can tell I've got her hooked.

"I also caused my girlfriend to commit suicide. I left her without even saying goodbye, because my father blackmailed me into it because he hated her guts, which is why I later blackmailed him about the drug thing, because by then I hated *his* guts. But to make a long story short, by the time I realized what a stupid thing I'd done by agreeing to leave her, she was already dead. Because of me."

This is when Tabby's face takes on an expression I can't accurately describe, because I've never seen it on another human being. It's outrage, hate, pity, disgust, and more hate. A lot more. With a side order of serial killer.

She shakes her head and begins to laugh softly, a sound utterly lacking in humor.

"It's uncanny how good you are at that," she says. "Seriously, you should become an actor. Oh, right—you already are! You get an Oscar for that performance. Wow. Just wow. You really had me going. Congratulations: you're the fucking bullshit artist of the century."

Blood rushes to my head. I shoot to my feet. Connor grabs my arm, probably thinking I'm following his directions and getting ready to leave, but I'm not leaving.

I'm fucking losing my fucking mind.

"I'm not lying!" I roar.

Tabby hollers back, "I already know there's no dead girlfriend, you piece of shit! I checked! You *are* lying!"

"What the fuck are you talking about? You think I'd make up something like that?"

"I know you did, assface! There's no goddamn death certificate for any goddamn former girlfriend of yours anywhere in the world, so don't you dare stand in this goddamn kitchen and try to tell me there is!"

"What? Wait—*what?*"

Connor, who'd been about to remove me bodily from the room, stops and says impatiently, "Okay, what's this bullshit about a dead girlfriend?"

Tabby points at me. "This douche nozzle told Victoria one of his girlfriends offed herself so Victoria would feel sorry for him. Can you believe that?"

It's clear from Connor's expression when he looks at me that he's put two and two together. He says softly, "So that's what you were so messed up about the night we met."

Tabby's eyes widen. "Oh my God, he told you the same story?" She cuts her vicious gaze to mine. "You're pathological!"

"I'm not a liar!"

Sneering, Tabby crosses her arms over her chest. "Oh, really, fuckwad? Then what was this dead girl's name?"

My head feels as if it's a pressure cooker, and my brain is an artichoke being turned into mush. I lose the last remaining shred of my self-composure and shout so loudly my voice breaks, "Her name was Isabel Diaz, and she was the goddamn love of my life!"

The air in the room turns to ice.

Every drop of color drains from Tabby's complexion. After a long, silent moment, she whispers, "Who told you she killed herself?"

Confused by Tabby's reaction and her question, I glance at Darcy. She's frozen in her chair, staring at me wide-eyed, her open mouth in the shape of a perfect O.

"Her mother did. Why?"

The squeak of horror that emits from Tabby is so high-pitched, I imagine every dog in a five-mile radius just leapt to its feet and started barking.

The hair on the back of my neck stands on end. Whatever's happening here, I have to keep talking.

"I showed up on her mother's doorstep after I'd been living in Europe for a few years. I couldn't stay away anymore and was going to confess the truth: that my father had finagled the deed to her family's farm through a fixed poker game and made me choose between staying with Isabel and destroying her family, or going away to school and never seeing her again. But I never got the chance to explain myself. As soon as her mother saw my face, she started screaming. She told me Isabel was dead. That she'd shot herself with her father's gun when I left, and had been cremated. Then she slammed the door in my face. I haven't spoken to her since."

Tabby crumples into the nearest chair as if her legs have given out and raises shaking hands to cover her mouth.

Darcy exhales hard, shaking. "Sweet baby Jesus. The tangled webs we weave."

Frowning, Connor looks back and forth between the two stunned women. "What?"

After a long, excruciating pause, Darcy stands slowly, as if it pains her to move, walks to the counter, and grabs a crystal decanter of scotch. She turns back and looks at me.

What I see in her eyes gives me the willies.

"I think it's time for you to get that strong-ass drink, Parker. You're gonna need it."

37

VICTORIA

*M*exico.

I visited once when I was little on a trip with my father to his hometown. I loved the color and the noise and the people, the happy, chattering people, who all looked just like me.

I've never forgotten the feeling I had as a child, stuffing my face with *antojitos* from a street vendor as I walked by my father's side on our way to the church where the grandfather I'd never met was displayed in a coffin draped with a Mexican flag, surrounded by bouquets of white roses and wailing women in black lace veils.

I felt as if I'd finally come home.

I belonged in that beautiful land of life and splendor with its pungent smells, tangled streets, gridlock and pollution. Mexico City should have been overwhelming for a small child, but somehow it felt freer to me than all the wide-open spaces of Texas. Somehow I felt less a stranger in a country I'd never set foot in than in the town where I grew up.

So it seemed like a good place to open the third act in the tragicomedy play of my life.

It took three days to get to Miami from St. Thomas. Three hellish days of sailing rough Atlantic waters with a grizzled old captain from Barbados who looked as if he'd been born at sea. He had a ragged white beard and skin the color of midnight, and only smiled once, when I bribed him for a ride with my Rolex. He started drinking rum at six a.m. with his coffee and didn't stop until he passed out when the sun went down.

The first night, I'd been terrified, convinced the boat would capsize or run aground while the captain slept, but apparently its navigational system was sound because we never ran into trouble. After that, I felt more comfortable about the trip but was plagued by thoughts of discovery. I'd been careful to take only half the cash in my wallet, careful to fling the extra shirt and skirt I'd worn over my jeans into the sea, careful to stay out of sight on the winding, rain-swept road that led from Casa de la Verdad to the port. I'd arrived soaked and shivering at five in the morning and went straight to the big catamaran I'd noticed on the trip in, the one that had a sign on its jib that read, "Charter Me."

Luckily, the Captain woke up as early as he passed out. He was on deck when I approached, eyeing me warily. I told him my name was June and my husband had tried to kill me so I needed safe passage off the islands, but all he cared about was the timepiece on my wrist, a chunk of rose gold glittering with diamonds.

I figured it was a small price to pay to avoid jail.

I gave it to him after making sure he understood that if he pawned it, he'd say he found it washed up on the shore. He said he didn't care if I wanted him to say it arrived from outer space, and he knew how to keep his mouth shut anyway.

I got the feeling I wasn't the first person to pay for a charter with unusual means.

From Miami I took a Greyhound to the main bus terminal in Newark, New Jersey, where I then hired a cab—with the last of the money from my wallet—to take me to the storage locker I'd rented nearby. I had a change of clothing along with other necessities in the large duffel bag I'd stashed there years before in case of an emergency like this one. Thankfully, I hadn't gained any weight. The clothes smelled a bit musty, but they still fit.

I should've sealed them in vacuum-packed plastic like I did the cash.

I'd already hacked off all my hair on the boat, but then bleached it with peroxide in a grungy gas station bathroom before I rented a car and got on I-40, headed west. My fake driver's license and passport photos showed me in glasses, wearing a short blonde wig, so I picked up a pair of cheap readers at a convenience store. I arrived at the US/Mexico border in Brownsville, Texas, after another three days of driving.

Then I paid a small toll to a sweating immigration agent and walked across a bridge into my new life.

Well, the toll was small. The wad of cash I pressed into his hand so he wouldn't search my lumpy duffel bag was not.

Now, a week after I left the Caribbean, I'm sitting on a rented sofa in a rented room in Mexico in the wee hours of the morning, watching my rented black-and-white television. It's tuned to an American news station, which features a story about the tragic death of one Victoria Price, author and celebrity hand-holder—and celebrity in her own right—who, according to her suicide note, decided to take her own life after being diagnosed with terminal pancreatic cancer.

The perky news anchor is trying desperately to appear solemn, but her mouth keeps breaking into a toothy smile.

A celebrity's death is always good business for the news industry.

"After an exhaustive search, the body still hasn't been found," says the anchor, blue eyes twinkling. "Officials have stated it's possible that it will never be recovered. The storm that hit St. Thomas the evening of Ms. Price's disappearance was strong, and her remains may have washed far out to sea. For now, the case remains officially open as that of a missing person, but inside sources say the authorities have found no evidence of foul play. They are convinced it is indeed a suicide, in spite of the lack of identifiable remains.

"Parker Maxwell, owner of the home Ms. Price was staying in, and her rumored lover, has refused to speak with the press, but Luciano Mancari, star of the popular television cooking show *Mangia with Mancari*, and another rumored lover of Ms. Price's, has given several passionate interviews wherein he has challenged Mr. Maxwell to a *duel*, of all things, for what Mr. Mancari insists is his alleged rival's part in Ms. Price's disappearance. No word yet from the Maxwell camp if they'll accept the challenge or file a lawsuit for slander. We'll return after this."

The station breaks for a commercial. When they return, the blonde anchor moves on to a story about global warming.

So there you have it.

I'm dead.

It's funny how easy dying is.

Compared to living, it's an absolute breeze.

38

PARKER

*W*hen faced with the inconceivable, the human brain does one of two things.

A: release copious amounts of the stress hormone cortisol into the bloodstream, kick-starting the fight-or-flight response so important decisions can quickly be made.

Or B: go blank.

After hearing the impossible, incredible, and outright horrifying story told to me by Tabby and Darcy, my brain opts for option B. I stand staring at them, frozen, my body as numb as all the gray matter in my head.

Then blankness turns to denial. I say, "No. *No.*"

"I'm sorry, Parker, but it's true."

Tabby is subdued now. I suppose admitting my employer had conspired to ruin her lover's life in history's most tragic case of mistaken identity, love-obstructing parents, selective obliviousness, and revenge romance would put a damper on my spirits, too.

It's Shakespearean in scope. My mind can't wrap itself around the truth.

I protest, "Victoria doesn't look anything like Isabel!"

Tabby sighs. "Fifty thousand bucks of plastic surgery can make anyone unrecognizable. Add to that a new name, an entirely new history, fifteen years of time passing, a few inches of growth in height, and—sorry—the fact that you'd been told she was *dead*. You couldn't have recognized her. No one could. That was the whole point."

I remember the feeling of familiarity I always had around Victoria. The way she'd tuck her hair behind her ear, the way she felt when I held her, the constant sense of déjà vu.

This is crazy. This can't be happening. I'm having a bad dream.

I shake my head in denial. "Isabel's mother would never have told me she killed herself just because I broke up with her. That makes no sense. It's too cruel! Why would she do that?"

Tabby and Darcy exchange another of their loaded glances, and I know whatever I'm about to hear will be worse than what I've heard so far.

Still, when it comes, I'm totally unprepared for it.

"Because Isabel was pregnant when you left."

My knees buckle. The room narrows and starts to fade to black. Connor grabs me and shoves me into a chair before I can fall.

Pregnant. Oh my fucking God.

Connor goes to the sink, pours a glass of water from the tap, and thrusts it into my shaking hand.

"Drink," he orders.

I choke down a few gulps before I finally pull myself together enough to rasp, "She...she had an abortion?"

Tabby makes a face. "Not exactly."

And the horrible day I'd been having proceeds to get worse.

∿

"Parker. Say something. What's going on inside your head?"

Connor's tone indicates he's not entirely convinced I'm hanging on to my sanity.

Which makes two of us.

It's been about half an hour since Tabby finally revealed all the sordid details. In that time, I've charged through three of the five stages of grief. Denial, anger, bargaining—those all came and went with lightning speed. At the moment, I'm mired in depression. I doubt I'll ever arrive at the final stage, acceptance.

Acceptance requires forgiveness.

And I will never, ever forgive myself for what I've done.

I should have stood up to my father. I should have refused to leave her. I should've told Isabel…Victoria—*Christ, I can't keep it straight in my head*—the truth from the beginning.

We could've worked it out together. And the way I spoke to Victoria in St. Thomas, the way I worded everything… Tabby was right. I *did* drive her away. First I abandoned her when she was pregnant with my child. Then, fifteen years later, I forced her to abandon the life she'd built for herself, out of fear I'd turn her into the police for her extracurricular cyberspace career.

On the bright side, at least I finally found out what Victoria was doing in Laredo.

I have a daughter.

God, what a bloody mess.

"Parker?"

I lift my head from my hands and stare up at Connor. He's standing over me, concern written all over his face. Darcy and Tabby are sitting at the kitchen table with me, one on either side. They look almost as wrecked as I feel.

"It's gonna be okay, brother. We'll find her," he insists.

I drain the dregs of the glass of scotch Darcy poured me, swallow the burn, and set the glass on the table.

"We haven't been able to find any trace of her in St. Thomas, except the washed-up clothes she obviously wanted to be found. No one spotted her in Newark, though we know she went there to get the bug-out bag, which means she wasn't spotted anywhere on the way from the Virgin Islands to New Jersey. She's traveling in disguise. She has a new identity and, according to Tabitha, a million bucks in one-hundred-dollar bills, and another five million in unregistered bearer bonds. She has the means to live more than comfortably for the rest of her life.

"And if she thinks she's being followed or thinks the police are getting close, she can simply create any new identity she wants, along with an entirely new history to match. She knows how to become someone else. Even you couldn't find a hint of her, Connor, and you've been looking for a week. And if you can't find her, no one can."

I exhale, hard, and close my eyes. "It's over. She's gone."

Tabby says, "Well…"

When I look at her, she's twirling a lock of her red hair between her fingers and looking suspiciously guilty.

"Jesus Christ. Please tell me there isn't *more*."

She glances back and forth between me and Connor. "First I need you to promise me that what I'm about to tell you doesn't leave this room."

At the same time, I insist, "Absolutely!" Connor snaps, "Spit it out, woman!"

Tabby drops the lock of hair from between her fingers. She gazes up at Connor with fire in her eyes. "*You* have to promise too, jarhead," she says, and smiles. Her grin looks a little like something an alligator would be proud of, dangerous and toothy.

"He promises. He signed a contract with me, right now he's on the job, and anything that's said in the course of his work for a client is completely confidential."

Tabby's smile grows wider. She appraises Connor with a challenging look. "Is that right, jarhead? No matter what I say, you can't tell anyone? Not even the police? And you can't use it against me?"

A carnal smile overtakes his mouth. He lets his gaze drift down to her chest, then he says gruffly, "Oh, I'll use something against you."

Darcy snorts. "You men are seriously obsessed with your dicks, you know that? How you walk around with those things, I'll never know."

I pound my fist on the table. "For fuck's sake—nothing is leaving this room!"

Tabby's smile grows satisfied. "Good. Because Victoria isn't Polaroid." She turns her gaze to me. "I am."

Connor does a double take that looks as if it might cause him a serious case of whiplash.

"*You?* Edward Scissorhands Pixie Dust Fairy?"

Oozing sarcasm, Tabby drawls, "The very same. How d'you like me now, bitch?"

Nodding, Darcy says, "I can totally see it. And now I'm getting more ice cream." She rises from the table and heads to the fridge.

Incredulous, Connor says, "The Citibank hack? The Scientology job? The International Space Station?" His voice rises. "My fucking Origin system?"

Tabby giggles. "Sucks to be you right now, doesn't it, Mr. Machismo? I bet all five of your poor little brain cells are really scrambled! Outdone by a girl...the tragedy!"

He curls his hands into fists and makes a sound like a bear awakened from hibernation. Tabby laughs in delight.

"But the Hello Kitty doll in Victoria's luggage," I protest, my already overloaded mind struggling with this new piece of information.

"That was mine," answers Tabby. "I packed it for her as a good luck charm."

"Then why would Victoria say she was Polaroid? Why wouldn't she have corrected me?"

All the laughter fades from Tabby's eyes. "Because she was protecting me, Parker. That's what you do for the people you love."

That skewers me straight through the heart.

Connor says, "You mean for the person who was paying you to fuck with other people's livelihoods."

Tabby snaps, "That's just because you tried to fuck with ours."

"I only tried getting into her email account. You fried my entire system!"

"It's not my fault that you left your back door wide open, jarhead."

"If you think you're insulting me by calling me a jarhead, woman, think again. I'm proud to be a Marine. I was in goddamn Special Ops!"

Tabby retorts with a snotty, "Not smart enough for the Navy SEALs, hmm? Or does that apelike body of yours not float?"

My mind is going too fast for me to pay much attention to Tabby and Connor and the bizarre hate-fuck vibe zinging back and forth between them. Because if Tabby is Polaroid, that means *she's* the one with the incredible computer skills, not Victoria.

Which means she knows her boss's new identity.

I jump to my feet. My chair skids back with a screech. Darcy, Tabby and Connor all stop what they're doing and look at me.

"You created the new passport and new papers for Victoria, didn't you?"

Tabby nods. "Yes."

Relief floods me, quickly followed by a potent dose of adrenaline that makes my hands shake. "*So you know her new name.*"

Connor and Darcy connect the dots at once. Darcy whoops, Connor abandons his sexually charged glare-off with Tabby for a second to glance at me and mutter, "That's great," but Tabby shakes her head.

"I already checked for any activity with the new identity. Victoria used the new driver's license to rent a car in Newark. That's the first and last time she used it."

"What about the passport?"

"No hits on any train, airline or cruise ship manifests. Or anywhere else."

My heart pounds like a jackhammer. A wave of hope surges inside me. "So she's still in the States."

"Not necessarily. She's got more than enough cash to bribe a border crossing agent."

"Which leaves us with Canada and Mexico," says Darcy excitedly.

"Tabby, did Victoria return the rental car yet?"

"Not since I last checked."

My heartbeat rockets into the stratosphere. "Let's check again. Right now."

Tabby stands. "Computer's in the office."

She doesn't have to ask us to follow her. As soon as she takes a step, Connor, Darcy and I fall in line behind her like ducklings. She leads us to Victoria's spacious office, and we crowd in behind her as she sits down behind the desk and fires up the computer.

Tabby types in concentrated silence for a moment while we watch behind her shoulder as she hacks into Hertz's mainframe.

Connor mutters, "Those bozos need to hire me." Beneath the irritation, there's a grudging respect in his voice.

Tabby points to the screen. "Here! She turned the car in yesterday in Texas!"

I lean over the desk and stare at the computer screen. "What city?"

"Brownsville."

I know it well. It's a town about two hundred miles south of Laredo.

And, like Laredo, it's situated right on the US border with Mexico.

"Mexico," I whisper, my blood rising.

"It's a big fuckin' country, brother," says Connor, folding his arms over his chest.

A smile spreads over my face. "Yeah. But it's a start."

39

VICTORIA

Six months later

"*C*arlos!" I holler at the ceiling, mopping at my forehead
with a handkerchief that's already soaked with my
sweat. "*¿Dónde está ese pinche ventilador?*"

You'd think he'd answer me after the first two blistering
screams I sent his way, but my friend and coworker Carlos is
what one could kindly call a flake.

At present, he could be enjoying a siesta facedown on his
desk, having sex in his office with one of the boozy barmaids
from the cantina across the street, or composing another terrible
ballad on his guitar to woo said barmaids. There's only about a
five percent chance he's actually doing the work he's been hired
to do, which is help people with very little money and even less
English apply for work visas in the States.

Which means that in this dumpy law firm of three people—
me, Carlos, and the proprietor, one very shady Ignacio Maximil-
iano Colón, who only shows up on Mondays for two hours

before lunch to sign paperwork—I'm the only one doing any work.

I drop my armload of manila file folders on my desk and heave a sigh, gazing around the office. I suppose I'm looking for a stray fan to pop out from behind the dented file cabinets, or maybe hoping for a random breeze to filter through the sweltering room from the open windows near the front door, but no luck. It's just as stifling as it was in here before I went into the other room to pull these case files.

Late summer in Mexico City. I might as well be standing on the surface of the sun.

I lift my chin and glare at the ceiling. "*Carlooos!*"

A voice behind me says in Spanish, "Calm down, Anacita, I'm standing right here."

I whirl around.

He *is* standing right there, leaning casually against the doorway smoking a cigarette, as if he's been there all along. He's tall, young, and good-looking in a shaggy, unkempt sort of way. Rumpled clothes, a three-day beard, and black hair desperately in need of a trim do nothing to distract from his long-lashed eyes, the color of topaz, or the muscles rippling beneath his T-shirt, or his easy, suggestive smile.

You get the picture: Carlos is hot.

But he's also ten years younger than me and a certified man-whore, and I happen to be pining hard for someone else whose name I don't permit myself to say. Or think.

Or moan in the middle of the night when I've got my hand between my legs.

Carlos flashes his smile and says in his slow, sexy way, "Though I do love hearing you scream my name."

I press my lips together so I don't smile. Though I refuse to give him one iota of encouragement, I have to admit it's nice being flirted with. Especially considering this god-awful bleached hair of mine, which makes me look ridiculous. I had hoped it would give me a Marilyn Monroe vibe, but all it did was make me look cheap.

Which, I suppose, is still better than looking like the late Victoria Price.

Not that anyone's looking for her anymore, in Mexico City or anywhere else. I followed the news avidly for months. Apparently Tabby paid someone to write a fake medical report and pose as my doctor, because the police said they'd corroborated my cancer diagnosis with my personal physician, and the case had been officially closed.

God bless Tabby. I really miss that girl.

I left her everything in my will, so it makes me feel a little better that she'll be a rich woman soon. With an official case determination by the police, the court can declare me dead in absentia, and Tabby will inherit my assets. She's been instructed what to distribute to my mother and anonymously to Eva, but a substantial chunk of cash and my home will be hers.

If I somehow find out she installs Hello Kitty wallpaper in my gorgeous penthouse, I'll kill her.

"Carlos, please tell me you brought me that fan I asked you for three hours ago," I say, hands on hips.

Carlos looks around, down at his feet, behind him, then back at me. He says innocently, "Do you see a fan in my hands, Anacita?"

I cross my arms over my chest. "Carlos."

The way I say his name makes his smile widen. He pushes away from the wall and strolls toward me. "Don't be angry. I brought you something better than a fan. Me."

It might sound cheesy, but he pulls it off. If I wasn't still hung up on a certain unmentionable someone, I'd be tempted to take the hot young Carlos for a spin.

"Keep it in your pants, Rico Suave. It's too hot to do anything but sweat." When I see the gleam in his eye, I scold,

"Not that I'm saying things will be different when the weather cools down!"

He *tsks*, shaking his head. "Oh, my silly Anacita. You know what's between us is too powerful to resist forever. Why not just give in and let it happen?"

I roll my eyes. Carlos may be hot, but he's definitely not original. I overheard him using exactly that line on a girl in the cantina just last week.

I don't hold it against him, though. If anyone knows how much bullshit people sling in their quest for connection, it's me.

Another wave of heat hits me. A bead of sweat rolls down my neck. "You know what, Carlos? It's too hot in here to work. It's almost noon anyway. Let's go get some lunch."

He pouts, pretending to be hurt. "Ah, but if I cannot have you, my love, then I cannot eat. I cannot live!" He heaves a dramatic sigh and presses a hand over his heart. "In fact, this might be my last moment on earth."

"I'm buying."

He takes a final drag on his cigarette, stubs it out in an over-flowing ashtray on the nearest desk, blows out a big plume of smoke, and grins. "In that case, I think I'll survive at least until this afternoon."

I knew that would distract him. The only thing Carlos likes better than an easy lay is a free meal.

We lock the office door and cross the street to the small, dark cantina, which smells like piss and cigarettes but is blissfully cold. So is the beer, which I never imagined myself drinking in my former life but have come to appreciate. We grab two seats at the long wooden bar and order *cervezas* and ceviche from a waiter with a droopy moustache and a lisp.

If Darcy could see me now—drinking beer, going out in public with no makeup on, wearing flip-flops and a cheap floral print sundress bought from a vendor on the street—she'd probably faint.

Strike that. She *would* faint. Promptly.

The thought brings a smile to my face, then sends a pang of loneliness through my heart.

I miss her, too.

But this is my life now. I rent a cute casita in the country. I go to work five days a week. I spend weekends reading and gardening and living in the moment, because it's too painful to allow myself to think of the past.

Overall, I'm content.

It's not exactly the same thing as being happy, but, as my mother used to say, beggars can't be choosers. I've trained myself to look on the bright side. I'm young and healthy, I have enough money that I never have to worry about going broke, and, in a smaller but more perhaps profound way, I'm still empowering the powerless.

I even own a cat, of all things.

He's a fat, lazy orange tabby with the bearing of an emperor and the attitude of a spoiled child. I adore him. I named him Perdón, the Spanish word for *forgiveness*, because after all these years I've finally realized that the only thing more damaging to your soul than hanging on to a grudge is...nothing.

Hate will devour you. Anger, no matter how righteous it feels, is a straight, short path to hell. Only forgiveness will set you free. Only forgiveness can heal your scars. Forgiveness not only for those who've wronged you but also for yourself.

Life is hard enough without making lovers of our demons.

The waiter brings our beers and ceviche with a plastic basket of tortilla chips still warm from the oven. Carlos orders the daily lunch special for two—*camarones* with rice—and we dig into the cold, delicious ceviche.

We eat in companionable silence until, through a mouthful, Carlos quietly remarks, "Don't look now, but that guy at the corner table in the cowboy hat is staring at you."

I snort. "He's probably never seen a woman inhale a pound

of chopped fish in under thirty seconds. Which reminds me, we need more chips. Where's that waiter?"

Carlos wipes his mouth with a paper napkin, takes a long swig of his beer, then politely belches. "I'm serious, Ana. He hasn't stopped staring at you since we walked in. Look." He sends a surreptitious glance to my right, then motions for the waiter.

Trying to be casual, I glance in the direction Carlos indicated.

There *is* a guy in a cowboy hat sitting at the table in the corner, but he's definitely not looking at me. In fact, he appears to be asleep. He's got his boots propped up on a chair, his long legs crossed at the ankle. His hands are folded across his stomach. His big white cowboy hat is tipped low over his face, obscuring his eyes and nose. His moustache is even droopier than our waiter's.

I turn my attention back to the bowl of ceviche. "The guy's taking a nap, Carlos, not checking me out. Are you this jealous with your girlfriends?"

"I know when a man is looking at a woman, Ana, and he's looking at you, no matter how hard he's trying to seem like he's not."

Well, if he is, he's probably just wondering who dropped a bucket of bleach on my head.

Leaving that thought unspoken, I finish off my beer. Then I match Carlos's belch with one of my own.

He lifts a brow. "Now you're just trying to seduce me."

"If I were trying to seduce you, darling, you'd already be naked."

Carlos laughs and slings an arm around my shoulders. "Ah, you see, Ana—this is why I adore you!"

I laugh along with him. "You have very low standards, my friend."

He shrugs. "Life is too short to look for perfection."

Truer words were never spoken. I squeeze his hand and then

toss his arm off my shoulders so he doesn't try to reach down farther and cop a feel.

By the time we finish lunch, I'm ready for a nap. Drinking in the daytime always makes me sleepy. Between the alcohol and the heat, I'm having a hard time keeping my eyes open. Since it's Friday, I know Mr. Colón won't be coming into the office, and the thought of dealing with the oppressive heat in there has me depressed.

"Carlos, if I bug out early, would you cover for me if anyone drops in?"

He sends me a sideways smirk. "Of course. Because then you'd owe me one."

"Yes. But 'one' as in a general favor, not sex."

"Sex can be a favor," he says reasonably. "I once had sex with a girl who was repaying me for fixing a flat tire on her car."

"Wow. That's a steep price to fix a flat."

Carlos smiles. "I think she flattened the tire herself."

"Of course you do." I dig a few bills from my purse and toss them on the counter. "And now I'm leaving."

I blow Carlos a kiss and walk away. He calls out behind me, "One day, Anacita, you will have sex with me, and then you'll see the true face of God!"

I've already seen the true face of God during sex, Carlos. And honey, it ain't yours.

I wave over my shoulder without looking back, then step through the door of the cantina into the searing heat of the street.

Six hours later, I'm finally driving up the long dirt road to my house.

I'd forgotten about my appointment with Mr. Hernandez, who was waiting outside the office with his wife when I emerged from the cantina. Then another client showed up, that one unscheduled. By the time I finished with the meetings and all the paperwork, the sun hung low over the distant mountains and the heat had loosened its chokehold on the city.

I stopped to pick up some vegetables and a piece of tilapia for dinner from my favorite local market and made the drive out of the clogged city to the rural borough I live in. It's a sleepy town with fewer than five thousand residents, no theater, hotels or shopping malls, and the lowest crime rate of all the sixteen districts in the greater Mexico City area.

There's also no Internet access, so I don't own a computer.

In the beginning, that drove me crazy, but I quickly realized it was one less way I could be tracked. Even though I rent the house with cash, paid cash for my car, am paid cash under the table by Mr. Colón, don't own a single credit card, and for all intents and purposes am dead under the laws of the United States, a part of me is still expecting the police to show up unannounced at my door with extradition papers.

Paranoia and I have gotten to be pretty close friends.

My car jumps and rattles over the bumpy road. Summer is the rainy season in this part of Mexico, and the rains take their toll on the roads. The city fixes the main streets, but my private driveway is in a state of disrepair. My landlord keeps promising to get someone in to fill the holes, but he works at the same speed Carlos does. I'll probably end up doing it myself. I've gotten quite handy with home improvement projects.

I park in front of the house, gather my groceries and handbag from the passenger seat, and head up the paved brick path to the front door. Perdón is stretched out across the welcome mat in all his plump orange glory. When he sees me approach, he rolls to his back and stretches, meowing a lazy hello.

The house is a pink adobe Spanish Colonial with an arched colonnade in front. It's shaded by a towering stand of palms on the west side of the property. Scarlet and orange dahlia bushes add a riot of color to the east. In the backyard, I have an herb garden—protected from the blistering sun by netting I hung myself—and a stone fountain carved in the shape of a mermaid that burbles happily day and night.

Sometimes late at night I turn it off, because all that cheerful burbling makes me wish I had someone to share it with. But the only male who's shared my bed in the past six months is of another species.

"Hey, big boy," I call lovingly to the cat. "Mommy's home. Are you ready for dinner?"

He leaps to his feet. Actually, *leap* is too generous a word. It's more like he flops to one side, struggles to get his paws beneath him, and pushes up. Then he yawns, shakes out his fur, sits back on his haunches, looks up at me, and issues a loud, demanding yowl.

"Okay, you little tyrant. In we go."

I unlock the front door. Perdón struts in between my feet, his tail swishing. I push the door shut with my hip, turn, then cry out in shock. I drop the groceries and my purse on the floor.

The living room overflows with bouquets of white roses.

They're everywhere. On the coffee table, on the side table between two chairs, on the mantel above the fireplace, on the floor. There are dozens of them, full and lush in crystal vases, perfuming the air.

I freeze, listening to the tick of the clock on the mantel, feeling the blood pound through my veins.

My brain is frozen, too. I should grab my purse and run, but instead I call out a tentative "H-hello?"

After a few eons during which I don't hear an answer or any unusual sound, I creep forward through the shadowed entry hallway on tiptoe. Wide-eyed, I peek into the dining room.

More roses.

I break out in a cold sweat. My hands start to shake. Terror, disbelief, and something I'm not allowing myself to recognize as hope churn in my stomach, wreaking havoc in my mind.

It can't be. It can't be. It can't.

I shuffle like a zombie through the house, finding bouquets of snowy roses stuffed into every room. It's a dream or a nightmare, I can't decide which. When I get to my bedroom and see what's plastered all over the big mirror above the dresser across from the bed, my frozen disbelief finally cracks.

I cover my mouth with both hands and sob.

It's a montage of Parker and me. Young and happy, smiling madly in every picture taped to the glass.

"Buenas tardes, Ana."

I spin around so quickly, I almost lose my balance and fall.

There in my bedroom doorway—wearing jeans, cowboy boots, a flannel shirt rolled up at the sleeves, a white cowboy hat, and a ridiculous moustache—stands Parker.

40

VICTORIA

*H*e's thinner than I remember, and his hair is longer, but he's no less beautiful, in spite of that caterpillar nesting on his top lip.

"Or should I call you Anacita?" he asks quietly, his piercing gaze never leaving my face.

"That was you in the bar today," I whisper hoarsely.

It's Parker. He's here. *Here.*

Dear God, please don't let me have a heart attack.

"I'd ask if that was your boyfriend you were with, but I know cradle-robbing isn't your style. Though he obviously wishes it were."

Parker makes no move to come closer. He just keeps staring at me with this devouring look as if he's memorizing every feature and curve of my face, burning the details into his mind.

For a long while, neither of us speaks. Then, because I can no longer bear the silence, I say shakily, "God. That moustache."

He strokes it thoughtfully. "I look like a porn star, don't I?"

"Not even a star. Like an unpaid extra. It's hideous."

He nods. "Your hair is nice, too. Did you lose a bet?"

My throat is getting dangerously tight. Not sure if I'm going to laugh, sob, or scream, I swallow.

Parker removes his hat, rakes a hand through his hair, and takes a step into my bedroom. The space seems to shrink.

"Do you have any idea how many Ana Garcias there are in this country?" His voice is gentle, but his eyes burn right through me. They sear me straight down to my soul.

I shake my head.

He says, "A *lot*," and takes another step closer. He drops the cowboy hat to the floor.

I would move, but I can't. I'm shaking almost to the point of vibrating. "Yes," I say, swallowing. "That was the point."

He nods again. So very serious. So very calm. In contrast, I'm about to tear out my hair in fistfuls and start screaming.

"How did you find me?"

"Tabby."

I stagger backward a step, my shock deepening. "She'd *never*—"

"She told me everything," he interrupts softly, "after I told her everything."

Everything. That word crashes around inside my skull, smashing and banging into things.

"She told me about your plan to ruin me. She told me that she was Polaroid, not you." His voice drops an octave. His eyes are ablaze. "And she told me about Eva."

A small noise escapes my lips. My heart thuds inside my chest. My eyes fill with tears.

Parker comes closer. When he's standing so near I can count the long golden lashes around his lids, he says gruffly, "Can you ever forgive me?"

My knees decide they've had enough of knocking and buckle.

He catches me before I fall. He swings me into his arms, strides over to the bed, and lowers us to it. He kisses me on the cheeks, murmuring passionately, "Forgive me, baby, please, please, forgive me."

I break down and start crying. "You asshole! There's nothing to forgive except that moustache!"

"I left you without saying goodbye." He tenderly kisses me on the lips. "I abandoned you when you needed me most." He kisses me again, deeper, leaving me breathless and gasping for air. "And then, years later, I made you run away from me with the absolute worst fucking proposal of marriage in the history of mankind."

This time when he kisses me, I *feel* his remorse. I feel all his anguish and sorrow and desperation, every ragged inch of his despair. And all the emotions I'd bottled up so tightly over the long, lonely years since he first left me burst free.

I break the kiss, bury my head in his neck, and bawl like a baby.

He lets me. He rolls to his back and takes me with him, pinning me against his body with his strong arms around me, keeping me together when I would otherwise shatter into a million little pieces and die. I cry on his chest until the sun sets and a big glowing moon rises over the mountains, then I cry some more, until eventually my eyes are swollen, my voice is hoarse, and I'm completely spent.

"For the Queen Bitch, you're surprisingly weepy," muses Parker, lovingly stroking my back.

I sniffle. "I'm not the Queen Bitch anymore. I'm just a lowly office clerk with a crappy hairdo and a bad-tempered cat."

"Oh, I don't know. Your cat seemed pretty nice to me. He didn't even bat an eye when I broke in through the patio door."

"You bribed him with food, didn't you?"

Against my temple, I feel Parker's smile. "I might have given him a treat or two to keep him quiet."

We lie in silence for a few minutes, just breathing. The

shadows on the wall are long and soft. Outside, a cricket starts to sing.

I say quietly, "I can't believe you're here."

Parker's arms tighten around me. He kisses the top of my head.

"I'm so sorry, Parker. For all of it."

"So am I."

Tentatively, I ask, "How's Tabby? And Darcy? Are they angry with me?"

"Darcy's fine. She misses you like hell, but she's been distracted lately with a new project." His voice warms. "She and a certain insane German chef are collaborating on a cookbook. Among other things."

"Other things? Is that your roundabout way of saying she and Kai are dating?"

"'Dating' is one way to put it. Another is 'screwing like rabbits every chance they get.' I accidentally walked in on the two of them in the stock room at Xengu." He chuckles. "I had to throw out four crates of artichokes, two dozen boxes of strawberries, and an entire pallet of escarole that had been crushed in their enthusiasm."

I smile, missing Darcy so hard, it's a physical lump in my stomach. "And Tabby?"

Caressing my hair, Parker sighs, a sound layered with emotion. "She's a tough nut, that one. Her loyalty to you is remarkable. Connor's convinced she's a lesbian."

"She's not. And who's Connor?"

"My friend and security guy. He's the one who tried to hack into your email. He's got a huge haterection for Tabby, but she won't give him the time of day. He's been trying to get her to come to work for him, but he won't admit she's smarter than he is, which is her one condition for accepting the job. Last I heard, he'd offered her seven figures a year in salary, but she still turned him down. Apparently she told him that unless he said the words, 'You are superior to me in intellect, class, and fashion sense,' he could find another world-class hacker.

"So far he's refused, but I think he's getting desperate. He's got a big client who was recently infiltrated by some radical Russian group, and the client is threatening to sue Connor unless he tracks the source and assists police with prosecution. Which, apparently, he can't do without Tabby's help. So she's got him by the balls."

We share another silence as I digest what he's told me.

Until he murmurs, "I visited your mother."

I haven't spoken to my mother at all in the months I've been gone. There's a distinct difference between forgiving and forgetting, and though I've let go of my anger at her for her part in the tragedy of Parker and Isabel, I haven't yet wanted to try to reach out.

Truth be told, I don't want to talk to her about what happened. I don't want to know if she'd discovered what Bill Maxwell did with his rigged card came, if the hatred she displayed toward him that day in her kitchen went beyond what she'd said.

Knowing wouldn't change anything, anyway. The past is fixed in stone. We can't carve new endings to old stories, no matter how desperately we might want to.

When I don't respond, Parker exhales heavily.

"She told me about all the letters you sent after I left. I never received any of them, of course."

I whisper, "Your father."

Parker's voice turns bitter. "He didn't even bother to deny it. The day I called him, he was drunk at two o'clock in the afternoon. I won't be speaking to him again."

He's quiet for a moment, and then the bitterness is gone from his voice. "She misses you too."

I close my eyes. "I can't see her, not yet. It's too fresh. And besides, if I go to Laredo, I'll want to go…I'll want to see…"

I don't finish my thought, but he knows who I'm talking about. With a new, infinitely soft tone in his voice, he whispers, "She's so beautiful. Like her mother."

My chest tightens. Fresh tears threaten to fall. "You went to the school?"

"Yes. Sat in the parking lot like a creeper, staring through binoculars. Thank goodness your mother was with me, or I'd really have felt like a perv."

Parker and my mother, staring at Eva through binoculars. Though I've done it myself countless times, the thought makes me unbearably sad.

"In a few years, she'll be eighteen, a legal adult," says Parker softly.

I nod.

"Which means she can make her own decisions...about things like meeting her birth parents."

My head snaps up. I stare at him, my pulse a freight train speeding out of control.

He says, "It's worth a shot."

"What if she doesn't know she's adopted?" I ask breathlessly.

"She talked about it on her Facebook page. She knows. She thinks it's cool, like she was chosen, not something to be ashamed of. She sounds remarkably well-adjusted. I think her parents did an amazing job raising her."

"B-but if I meet her, I'll be exposed... No one can know who I am."

"You're Isabel Diaz of Laredo, Texas, daughter of Tómas and Guadalupe," he says gently. "That's all anyone ever needs to know. No one in Laredo or anywhere else knows about your connection to Victoria Price or to Ana Garcia. And besides, it's the truth. You *are* Isabel. I think we can both agree that the truth is a much better alternative to lying."

Possibilities spin inside my head. The future is suddenly so much brighter, so much more full, than it was merely a few minutes ago.

"But your political career, your run for Congress. The tabloids will go crazy."

Parker laughs. "That was over before it even began. I aban doned everything else when I started to search for you. I've been living in Mexico full-time for the past few months so I could concentrate on finding you."

When he sees my look of distress, he's quick to add, "Because I finally got my priorities straight. Opening two new restaurants a year, dating a different girl every week, aspiring to political office... That was all driven by emptiness. I was trying to distract myself from loneliness and self-loathing, I know that now. I didn't give up anything that really mattered, and you didn't ruin my life by leaving, okay?"

His words ring with truth. I'm relieved, until something else occurs to me. "She'll want to know why we gave her up for adoption."

There's a shrug in his voice. "Because we were teenagers. We wanted her to have a better life than we could give her."

"But—"

Parker silences me with a kiss. "We'll figure it out as we go. Nothing's set in stone. We have a few years to figure out logistics, if that's even what Eva ultimately decides she wants to do. When the time comes, we can reach out to her through the adoption agency to arrange a meeting and see how she responds. Okay?"

Shaking, I lower my head to his chest. "Okay."

We're quiet for a long time, listening to the sounds of the night, until finally I take a deep breath and whisper, "So what happens now?"

Parker lifts my head. He sweeps his thumbs over my cheeks. He looks at me in silence until a smile begins to curve his lips.

"Now I think I should produce that ring I promised you."

I should probably go get my medicine from the bathroom. What's happening to my heart doesn't seem normal.

I say, "Threatened me with, I think you mean."

"Yes. Excuse me. And before you say no, I need to tell you that it's a ten-carat flawless stone, round brilliant cut, with tapered baguette side stones in a platinum setting. It's quite impressive, even by your standards. It cost more than your Rolls-Royce."

My laugh is feeble. "Only ten carats? How miniscule. Tiffany?"

"Cartier."

"Ah. Well. In any case, this might be a good time to mention that I've already told you I'm not ready for an institution."

Parker's smile is not one of a man who thinks his proposal has just been refused.

"Fair enough. I'll ask again in the morning. Things always seem better in the morning."

"Oh, really? Does this mean you're inviting yourself to spend the night? Whatever will we do with ourselves?"

His lids drop, and his voice comes out husky. "Well, I could try to make you see the true face of God."

My heartbeat, which had settled down to more reasonable levels, immediately skyrockets into the stratosphere again. "Now you're talking, Mr. Maxwell."

"I'm glad you agree, my beautiful Bel."

Before I can start to cry again, Parker kisses me hard, swallowing the sob of joy rising from my throat.

Our clothes come off with such speed, it's almost magic. We fall on each other in desperation, clutching and moaning, stroking and sighing, our mouths as greedy as our hands. Months of separation are erased in an instant.

Just as Parker is about to thrust inside me, a loud, screeching howl brings us both to a stop.

Sitting in the bedroom doorway, Perdón glares at us in disgust.

"Shut up or I'll make a rug out of you," Parker says, craning his head over his shoulder.

I take his face in my hands and turn it back to mine. I kiss him, putting every atom of my heart and soul into it, then murmur, "I think you can focus for a few minutes, love."

Hearing that word on my lips makes Parker's eyes come alive. He gazes at me in adoration. A smile tugs at one corner of his mouth.

I add, "I mean, if I have to ignore that flaccid cowlick under your nose every time you kiss me, you can certainly ignore my cat."

"Flaccid? Oh, you're gonna pay for that," he breathes, flexing his hips.

I feel him between my legs, hot and hard, and my laugh is throaty. "Promises, promises." I pull his head down and kiss him once more.

Which I plan on doing every day from now until forever.

Rule #8 and the most important one of all: Life is short, bitch. Do what makes you happy.

EPILOGUE

A few years later

"*I*t's going to be fine, baby."

I stare out the window, watching houses and trees and cars flash by in the bright spring day, seeing nothing. "I know."

Parker reaches over and squeezes my hand. "You don't look like you know."

I inhale a few deep breaths, trying to slow my heartbeat. I squeeze Parker's hand so hard, he chuckles.

"Sweetheart."

I look over at him in the driver's seat. He's smiling. His eyes are wonderfully soft. "I promise you, it's going to be fine. Okay?"

In a tiny voice, I say, "But what if it isn't?"

He says firmly, "It will be."

"Think of everything that could go wrong!"

He shakes his head. "Think of everything that could go *right.*"

I drop my gaze to our joined hands, to the diamond glittering on my ring finger, and say a silent prayer that he knows what he's talking about. Because at the moment, I'm about as stable as a lit stick of dynamite with a short fuse. A slight change in the wind could set me off.

In what I know is an effort to distract me, Parker switches on the radio. Ranchero music fills the cab of the truck. It's a big, macho black Chevy that Parker bought after moving permanently to Mexico with me. His beloved Porsches couldn't handle the country roads, so he made up for losing speed and performance by gaining burly engine noise, terrible MPG, and tires so big they look like they belong on earth-moving equipment.

Perdón takes every available opportunity to pee on them. I don't think he's quite yet adjusted to having another male around.

To cover my anxiety, I ask Parker how Tabby's doing. He spoke to her last night on the phone after I was in bed. As he does every time her name is mentioned, he laughs.

"Did you know that Hello Kitty's real name is Kitty White, she's a Scorpio, and that she loves apple pie?"

"Dear God."

"And she has a twin sister named Mimmy. Apparently she also lives outside London. All of which I know because Tabby attended the Hello Kitty retrospective at the Museum of Contemporary Art in LA."

I stare at him. "You're making that up."

Grinning, he lifts a hand in the air. "Hand to God, I'm telling the truth. It seems our beloved Tabitha isn't the only person with an unhealthy obsession with this particular cartoon character. She said the opening was mobbed."

I try to picture thousands of Tabby look-alikes swarming

through a museum filled with Hello Kitty memorabilia. "I wish I could've seen that."

Parker pulls his phone from his shirt pocket and hands it to me. "Check out her Instagram account. Though I warn you, prolonged viewing might make your eyes bleed."

I take his phone, open the app, and navigate to Tabby's page. Within moments, I'm laughing out loud. "How did she convince Darcy and Kai to go with her?"

"Well, apparently Ms. LaFontaine couldn't pass up the opportunity to blog about the food at the event—which included such culinary delights as petit fours with Hello Kitty's face on them and ten-dollar donuts with a frosted pink bow. And as Darcy's fiancé refuses to go anywhere without her, Kai tagged along."

Thinking of Darcy and Kai, I can't help but smile. "That wedding is going to be outrageous."

Judging by the invitation alone, whose first line read, "*Shit just got real.*"

Of course I won't be attending, but they're honeymooning in Acapulco, and we've made plans to see each other then.

We've been careful in our communications, relying on Tabby's genius with technology to ensure nothing can be traced. Not that we think anyone's looking, but the cryptophones we're using ensure there wouldn't be anything to find if they were. She's going to meet us into Acapulco, too, and I can't wait to see all of them. I can't wait to tell them about today.

If I get through it. I haven't been this terrified in years. Maybe ever.

The truck slows, then pulls to a stop. When Parker says quietly, "We're here," my heart jumps into my throat. I set the phone on the seat and look outside.

We're parked at a curb on a lovely, tree-lined street. The lawns are green and the lots are large. This is the good part of Laredo. The house I'm staring in terror at is a pretty two-story flanked by a pair of big weeping willows. Yellow rosebushes in full bloom line the brick path that leads to the front door.

"Baby."

Wide-eyed and trembling, I look at Parker. He reaches out and caresses my cheek.

"She's gonna love you."

My hands shake. My stomach churns. I'm having trouble catching my breath. "What if she doesn't?"

His smile warms me straight through. "How could she not?"

He leans over, gives me a quick kiss, then exits the truck. He comes over to my side and opens my door, holding out a hand. He steadies me as I wobble getting out.

"Easy, tiger," he murmurs, pulling me against his side. "Take a few deep breaths."

Breathing is something that has suddenly become quite challenging. As is staying upright. Thank God for Parker's calming strength, because without his support, I'm not entirely sure I could remain standing.

"We're breathing," he gently reminds me when I remain frozen and breathless.

"Right. Deep breaths. Here we go."

My exaggerated inhalation and exhalation make Parker chuckle. "Okay. It's a start. Let me know when you're ready."

I close my eyes, take a few more breaths, then nod. "Let's do this."

He presses a kiss to my temple. "That's my girl," he whispers. He closes the door, turns, and leads me up the brick path with his arm firmly around my shoulders.

He rings the doorbell.

When I hear a faint female voice from inside excitedly call, "I'll get it, Mom!" I nearly faint.

"Breathing," Parker murmurs.

The door flies open. In it stands a stunning young woman.

She has long, honey-blonde hair, hazel eyes, and dimples that are on full display because she's grinning.

She looks so much like her father, I'm breathless all over again.

"Hi!" She sticks out her hand. "I'm Eva. And you must be Isabel."

Feeling as if I'm in a dream, I take my daughter's warm hand in mine and shake it.

"Yes," I hear myself say. "I'm Isabel. And it's so nice to finally meet you."

Eva's grin grows even wider. She turns to Parker. "And you're Parker."

They shake hands, grinning at each other with identical smiles, and I suddenly know, with bone-deep conviction, that Parker was wrong.

Everything isn't going to be fine.

It's going to be flat-out amazing.

ACKNOWLEDGMENTS

Thank you to my best friend, Jay, for always having my back. Everything I do is for you.

Big thanks to my beta readers, Donna, Kimber, Zita, Louise, and Yida for their help on the early version of the manuscript.

Thanks to my brilliant cover designer, Letitia Hasser, for working so hard on my covers and creating such beautiful work.

Thank you to Geissinger's Gang, my Facebook reader group, for supporting my books so enthusiastically, and for being a fun, safe group I can bounce my crazy ideas off.

Thanks to Linda Ingmanson for your help with all the edits. Allll the edits. You're amazing.

And finally, thank you to my parents for instilling in me a love of books and reading and for everything else. I love you.

ABOUT THE AUTHOR

J.T. Geissinger is a #1 international and Amazon Charts best-selling author of thirty novels. Ranging from funny, feisty romcoms to intense erotic thrillers, her books have sold over ten million copies and been translated into more than twenty languages.

She is the recipient of the Prism Award for Best First Book, the Golden Quill Award for Best Paranormal/Urban Fantasy, and the HOLT Medallion for best Erotic Romance.

Find her online at www.jtgeissinger.com

ALSO BY J.T. GEISSINGER

Standalone Novels

Pen Pal

Perfect Strangers

Rules of Engagement

Midnight Valentine

Queens & Monsters Series

Ruthless Creatures

Carnal Urges

Savage Hearts

Brutal Vows

Beautifully Cruel Duet

Beautifully Cruel

Cruel Paradise

Dangerous Beauty Series

Dangerous Beauty

Dangerous Desires

Dangerous Games

Slow Burn Series

Burn For You

Melt For You

Ache For You

Printed in Great Britain
by Amazon

24646660R00199